On the Edge

Patrick Dueck

Published by

MELROSE BOOKS

An Imprint of Melrose Press Limited
St Thomas Place, Ely
Cambridgeshire
CB7 4GG, UK
www.melrosebooks.com

FIRST EDITION

Cover designed by Jeremy Kay

ISBN 978 1 907732 10 2

Printed and bound in Great Britain by:
CLE Digital Solutions. St Ives, Cambridgeshire

FSC
www.fsc.org
MIX
From responsible
sources
FSC® C019549

Thank you to Fiona Armstrong (Broadcaster) and Alistair Moffat (Historian) for their wonderful television series, *The Reivers*, which was influential in the writing of this book.

To Kathy Kimbrough, for her support and assistance.

Many thanks to Steph, my website manager.

And to Margaret, without whose patience and encouragement this book could not have been written.

Contents

Chapter 1	**A New Dawn**	1
Chapter 2	**A Monastic Introduction**	10
Chapter 3	**A New Name**	27
Chapter 4	**The Written Word**	33
Chapter 5	**The Roman Tongue**	44
Chapter 6	**What Manner of Man is This?**	50
Chapter 7	**A Family Again**	61
Chapter 8	**A Cloud Descends**	87
Chapter 9	**My New Friends**	102
Chapter 10	**A Virgin Raid**	110
Chapter 11	**Revenge Raid**	130
Chapter 12	**The Quiet Time**	149
Chapter 13	**Is This the Truth**	163
Chapter 14	**Love and Heartache**	176
Chapter 15	**Let the Riding Resume**	197
Chapter 16	**My New Mentor**	214
Chapter 17	**A Flame in my Life**	234
Chapter 18	**A Flower of Scotland**	242
Chapter 19	**A Friendship Rekindled**	265
Chapter 20	**The Mist Rises**	290
Chapter 21	**Family Loyalties**	316
Chapter 22	**The Promise**	352
Epilogue		365

Chapter 1

A New Dawn

I start my story on an early November night in the year 1555, in a shallow valley in the Northumbrian hills between the village of Gilsland to the west and the north Tyne River to the east. I lived there with my father and mother, Thomas and Marie, and my sister, Sarah. My father was a strong hard man of the land and my mother, who was of the Charlton family, was a very beautiful woman who had a great dignity and bearing and was very much the opposite of my father, and that is why it worked so well, because they admired the best traits of each other and the very things that made each other so different. I knew I was growing up in a loving environment.

My sister, who was twelve and my elder by five years, was very much the image of my mother, and it was plain to see, even at my early age, that when she grew up she would marry a gentleman and live in a fine house, and have servants. I looked up to her so much, and sometimes I saw her working around the house or outside and I would think she was the most wonderful creature on God's Earth, but I would never tell her such a thing.

Our house was a Bastle, which was a strongly built farmstead, with very thick walls and of two floors. The ground floor was for the horses and the best cattle, to keep them safe through the night, in case those Scotties come raiding. If we lost the horses we would die, or that is what my father said, because without them we could not

1

work the land or take anything to market or Hot Trod the Scotties if they come calling. To 'Hot Trod' is to take off after raiders with your kinsmen, and my father said we could put seventy Milburns in the saddle, between Carlisle and Hexham, for a Hot Trod and along with our close kinsmen, the Charltons, who could put over one hundred in the saddle, it was a brave Scottie who would take us on. I have heard it said that the Milburns and the Charltons are some of the hardest and fiercest people of the English borders, and I always felt so proud whenever it had been said. The upper floor of our house was where we all lived, and we climbed a wooden ladder to it, which when we were in the house we lifted up so that, if we were raided, no one could get to us. There was a walled cattle pen to the side of the Bastle which afforded further shelter for other animals, and to the rear of the farmstead was a wooden hut, which housed the hens. It was my responsibility to do everything for the hens; I had to keep the hut clean, make sure there was fresh hay in their nesting boxes, and keep the hens safe from the foxes, which meant taking them in at night and letting them out each morning, and I always kept them well fed, with the corn that was gleaned from the ground at threshing time and any other cereal that I could get which was not used for milling.

There was a wonderful feeling of calm and tranquillity about our house that night; it had been a good summer and we had all worked in the hay fields and gathered in a good harvest of winter fodder for the cattle, and later had gathered the best harvest ever of corn, and the threshold was full of grain, waiting to be milled for bread making.

My mother sat by the fire, sewing some material she had got from Hexham Market the week before; I think it was for a new dress for Sarah, as the one she wore was now starting to get a little small for her. My father sat at the opposite side of the fire, sharpening his long knife, which he always wore about his belt. Sarah was sat on her bed, playing with a doll, made by my father, with a head made of wood and a body

made of sacking cloth filled with wool from the early summer sheep shearing. I sat on my bed with the wooden sword my father had also made, copying him, as he sharpened his knife. I could feel tiredness descending on me as my eyes started to feel heavy, when my father said, "Rob, your hens seem restless out there, I can hear them, that old fox must be about. Nip down and chase it off before it gets in and has a killing spree, and we lose all our chickens."

Along with my trusty wooden sword I climbed down the ladder to where the cattle were tethered, and, using my sword, gave one of the bullocks a hefty swipe, to get it out of the way, so that I could get out of the door. Having got outside and feeling the late autumn chill, I waited a short while for my eyes to get accustomed to the dark. All appeared still in the night. I walked to the rear of the house to where the hens were kept, and as I did so I could see a brilliant glow across the field. It was the field barn, it was on fire. I ran back around the front of the house, to tell everyone, but then there were horses, horses and riders, it seemed, all over the fields.

"Fadder, Fadder," I shouted, "Fadder, come quick, there's Scotties, Fadder, there's Scotties iverywhere." I could see, from the light of the barn blaze, riders galloping along, gathering up the cattle that had been left out in the fields. As I watched in terror at the scene that befell me, a rider came by me, passing very close. I raised my trusty sword to ward him off, his horse shied slightly, but he drove it on. The next thing I knew was that I was running, running, running faster than I had ever run before, everything seemed a blur; I did not know what was happening. Faster and faster I seemed to go, I looked to the left, and there by my side was a horse's head, I could tell by the way it was moving that it was at full gallop, and I was keeping up with it; how could this be? Onward I ran, my legs had never moved as quickly, I looked down, and my feet were not touching the ground, but my legs were still going like never before, faster and faster. I must not let this

3

horse get past me or I will be trodden underfoot. What was going on, was this a bad dream? Did I fall asleep, and only dream of my father telling me to check the hens, or was this witchcraft? I had heard stories of witches when visiting my uncles, at the house where my mother was born. Suddenly I stopped, then swung around as if to go back from where I came. This time I seemed to go much slower; was this because my legs were tiring? I looked down and my feet were still not on the ground but were still running. What madness was this? Slowly I was approaching the Bastle, and there was my father, with a sword in each hand, a rider coming at him with a lance pointed at him. My heart stopped. The rider was now bearing down on my father, the lance not an arm's length from my father's chest. In an instant he lifted his left hand, bringing his sword across the lance, slicing it in two and parrying it away from himself. Then, bringing up his right sword, he brought it across the rider's belly, cutting deep into his flesh, causing him to yell in agony before falling from his horse to the ground. As he made contact with the ground, I saw that he had landed across another body, already brought down.

At this very moment another rider came in, and before my father could turn to challenge him, brought down an axe into the side of my father's face. I could see that the blade seemed to cut deep into the bone; his legs just buckled as he fell to the ground. I had never seen such horrors in my short life and this rendered me speechless.

As this took place I turned to my left; the horse's head was still there. I looked over my shoulder and it was only then that I realised that I was being held up at arm's length by one of the riders. He held me in the middle of my back by my outer garment. I heard him say, "Ya should'na a seen that wee'an," at which point he put me face down over the front of his saddle and we galloped away.

In the cold of the night, I could feel the warmth of my tears as they ran from my eyes, yet not a sound of weeping did I make.

We rode on and on through the night for what seemed an eternity, then the details of the ground started to become more visible, the dawn was breaking; what was my fate to be? As the full light started to fill the land we stopped and I was lifted from my uncomfortable position by my captor, and placed on the ground with a severe warning that to try and run would result in instant death. I felt so drained, both mentally and physically, that I feared running was far beyond me. I just sat down on the ground feeling somewhat disoriented, having spent most of the night slung across a horse with my head facing the ground. Around me were many riders, herding in the cattle, many of which I recognised as being our cattle, which these Scotties had rustled. My mind flashed back to that axe slashing into the side of my father's face and my stomach started to retch. I became violently sick, my captor came over to me saying, "Have ye na stomach for the life of a reiver, wee'an?"

"Aye, Sir," I replied, "But not with a Scottie."

"My, my, we have a fiery wee man here ma boys, and tell me good Sir, whom might we be addressing?" he said mockingly, while bowing. I stood up to my full height of the seven year old I was, and said, "I'm a Milburn."

"Well, Mr Milburn, I am indeed honoured te mack yer acquaintance, though I fear ye'll nay mack se much ransom being a Milburn."

"Maybe not, but we will make two of any Scottie," I retorted.

"Awa wi' ye, wee'an, and get yer heed doon, for we have a lang night aheed," my captor said, and I thought his advice was the best course of action. I lay myself down, finding a soft tuft of grass in front of a stone as a comfortable pillow. I lay my weary head down, but sleep did not come quickly. Far too much had taken place through the night for me to sleep; my father dead, my mother and sister all alone without a man of the house. What would become of them, indeed would I ever see them again? I doubted I would. I put my arm over my face as I felt the tears starting to well up again. I thought I had cried myself out, through the night, but out they gushed again.

I felt a gentle hand patting my back, and I heard my captor's voice, far softer than before, saying, "Awa' te sleep, my wee man, awa' te sleep," as he continued to pat my back. Although this man had been the one who had taken me from my parents, my sister and my home, there was something reassuring in his manner. Sleep at last came to me.

I woke much later. The sun was already starting to dip in the sky. I woke with a start, and jumped up, not recognising where I was. I looked around; there was a group of men sat around a fire, eating, I could see others on horseback guarding the cattle. Although of tender years, and with little knowledge of the ways of the Reiver, I instinctively knew that we must be over the Scottish border, or these men would not have started a fire, giving a signal from a long way off to any who would be following.

It was the way in those days that, after a raid, the aggrieved parties would set forth in an attempt to catch the raiders and bring them to justice, that justice often being administered swiftly, and all goods redeemed to those who had been robbed. It was my hope that such a party was at this present time chasing after us, so that I would be returned to my family, and thus know the fate of my father.

After being given a meal of hot oats and milk, which warmed me both inside and out, the rest of the raiders started to mount up. My captor stood by my side as another of the raiders came over and said, "Well, Will, what fate awaits your wee trophy?"

"We'll decide when we get home I think, Andrew," Will replied. He then mounted his horse, leaned over with a hand out and said, "Come on, up yer get." I put out my hand and was whisked on to the back of the horse, behind him.

"Yer better hing on wee'an, we'll be riding hard tonight." I clenched the sides of Will's coat and we galloped off to round up the cattle and sheep and started to drive them on. I thought it quite exciting, riding on the back of Will's horse and driving the cattle, and wishing I had a horse of my own so that I could take some part in the cattle drive, then I felt terribly guilty for my thoughts, as some of these cattle were my father's, which had been stolen and were now being driven away. Also, I constantly had on my mind what fate awaited me at the end of our journey, though I kept silent as we rode along.

At around midnight, if the moon was anything to go by on this mid-autumn night, where the sky was clear apart from the odd light fluffy cloud, we stopped. Three of the riders rode forward of the herd and off into the hills we were approaching. I asked Will why we had stopped, and why the three riders had gone on ahead. Will told me that they were checking the way ahead in case of ambush. I had never heard of this but Will was patient with me and explained how sometimes the English would not only follow, but would circle around in order to get in front, and then attack. There was also a possibility that other Scots families would try and steal the cattle from them before they got them home.

As we now appeared to be talking easily, I asked Will, with great trepidation, what he intended to do with me, once we were at his home.

"You'll be ar'reet, dinnae worry your wee heed, a'll tak care a'ye. You'll come te nay harm." I thought it best not to pursue the issue, although I was far from reassured by what I was told.

We rode on at a steady pace, watching intently ahead, for whatever fate may befall us. I was in a strange position, where I didn't want our drive to be attacked, for what might happen, and on the other hand I hoped that a 'Hot Trod' was underway, in order that I might be rescued and returned to my family.

By the time the moon had circled around to our backs, which would make it a short while off dawn, we arrived at a ridge, and, looking down into the valley below, I could see the dark outline of a settlement, with various sized smaller shapes scattered around, surrounding the largest structure I had ever laid my eyes on. I asked Will where we were, to which he replied, "Melrose, and that's the auld abbey that stands oot from the rest o' the toon."

I was to find out later that this had been ruined by the forces of the King of England, and most of those from within either killed or banished from its grounds. We secured the herd of cattle and the sheep, and leaving the horses with four of the riders who were to stand guard over the animals, we walked into the town. All was in darkness. I thought it to be in the early hours of the morning; it seemed to be at its darkest point of the night, which my father had always told me was not long before the dawn. As we walked through the narrow streets I could see that one of the buildings ahead of us had a dim light coming from the gap around the door. Approaching this building, silently I thought, though there would be nearly twenty in our party, the door slowly opened and we all slipped through it to be welcomed by a roaring turf and wood fire in an ingle large enough for a grown man to walk into. Stood in front of the fire was a large man with the largest and reddest of beards, and an enormous round belly. As he spoke his voice boomed across the room.

"Well, ma boys, does the night go well for ye all?"

One of our riders replied, "Aye no bad, no bad."

"And what have we here?" boomed Red Beard, looking directly at me.

My captor, Will, answered, "A wee trophy fra across the border, a Milburn no less."

"And what sort of a ransom are ye likely te get for a Milburn, Will?" enquired Red Beard.

"Nay very much am afraid," replied Will.

"Will," came a voice from the corner of the room, "You'll have to despatch him before the day breaks, ye cannae be lumbered wi' a wee'an all the time." I looked and saw that it was the same rider that had enquired of my fate when on the drive from England. I could feel the fear arising in my body at the tone of the conversation.

"Aye, we'll wait a while a think," said Will.

"You'll no wait a while, Will, you'll do it now," came the voice from the corner.

"Aye, we'll away then, come on," as he took me by the scruff of the neck and drawing his sword as he did so, I felt my insides come away, and as we went back through the door Will turned and said, "What have ye done, ye stink, oh my, you're vile."

The discomfort I felt was overcome by the absolute terror and trepidation I felt at my likely fate, at the hands of this Scottie who I had, in a short time, grown to like and trust, although he had taken me from my home and family.

I walked unsteadily along the street, in the grip of my captor and soon to be my executioner. The outline of the buildings on either side now started to stand out bolder from the night sky as the dawn started to take over. I had already resigned myself to the fact that I would never see my father again, but now there was the realisation that I would never see my mother and sister again.

"What is your name, boy?" said Will.

"Rob, Sir," I replied.

"Then Rab it is."

Chapter 2

A Monastic Introduction

W e approached a large three-storey building, at the very edge of the town, that being unusual as most other buildings in the town, apart from the ruined abbey, were only single-storey. Although there was still very little light, I could make out that on all three floors there were very small windows, two on each wall, with the same layout on each floor. We came to a small wooden door, on the front of the building, which had large iron hinges, ornately forged and attached with heavy metal studs, but in front of this was a heavy metal gate that was locked from the inside. Will drew his sword aloft. I gasped; this was where my life would end. The terror had now left me, I was resigned to my fate; the moment I was lifted from the ground outside my home I had been a dead person. I think in my heart of hearts I had known what fate awaited me, but had always hoped that a 'Hot Trod' would have rescued me. Alas, this was not to be.

Will raised his sword and drew it back. I closed my eyes and cringed, waiting for the blow. I heard a loud banging just in front of me. I opened one eye, as if this was safer than opening two. Will was knocking at the wooden door with the hilt of his sword. After a short while I could hear bolts being drawn back behind the door, then very slowly the door started to open, but only a little way. There was no light inside the door and I was not able to see who was there. A voice came from behind the door.

"Aye, what is it?"

"It's Will Armstrong. I've a willing pair of hands for you, Father, to ease your labours."

"Wait while I open the yett," came the reply. I could vaguely make out the shape of a body, dressed in a long grey gown, as he stepped forward and drew back the bolts of the iron gate that was in front of the door.

As the gate was pushed open, a hand came forward, grabbing me by the hair, and I was pulled through the door with some force and hurled to the ground. "What is this stench that comes within these walls?" the voice bellowed. With the fear of my likely death, I had forgotten my accident, when first I had been taken from the first house by Will. The reminder of this brought back the discomfort and the smell.

The shadowy silhouette reached forward, taking me roughly by the arm, and I was dragged along a passage into a room I was unable to make out the details of, as there was no light of any sort within this building.

For a second time I was hurled to the ground, the dark figure growling, "Stay there and don't you dare move, you vile creature of Satan."

I lay there shaking, with fear or cold or both, and for how long I know not, but as the early morning light started to break through the small window at the far end of the room, I heard footsteps approaching along the passage I had been dragged down earlier. I looked up and before me stood a man with his hair cut in a strange way; it was straight across his forehead and around the back of his head. He was dressed in a long grey gown, tied in the middle by a length of rope, and on his feet was the strangest footwear I had ever seen, with a sole to the footwear and leather straps across his bare feet, holding them on. What manner of man was this?

The strangely dressed man then said in a loud voice, "Get up, seed of Satan, and get you out of here," as he pointed to a door at the far side of the room. Going through this door I was confronted by an iron gate, or yett. The man said, "Draw back the bolts," which I did, opened the gate outwards, and stepped out into a small high walled courtyard.

The gowned man came behind me and brought his hand with such force at the back of my head that I was sent spread-eagled across the floor.

"Get out of your filth!" he screamed. I wondered if this strangely gowned being was capable of speaking in anything other than a shout.

The morning was bitterly cold as I started to take off my clothes. When I was fully naked, my new captor pointed to a wooden barrel by the side of the building wall, which was full of water. "Get in there and wash your filth." I tiptoed over the stone flagged courtyard towards the barrel, and, as instructed, tried, but in vain, to pull myself up into the barrel.

"Get in!" I heard him bellow. I felt my hair being pulled, as I was lifted into the freezing cold vat. Never before had I felt the cold as I did now, it went right to the centre of my body, and I shook as never before. I thought I would surely die, being subjected to such torture.

I remained in the vat for some time, rubbing my body vigorously to try and get some warmth, when I was passed a piece of what looked like tallow, and was told to rub this over my body. I did as instructed and soon a strange white foam started to appear on my skin. Oh my! What was this that was coming from my body?

"You wonder what that is, vermin?" asked the man in the robe.

"Yes, Sir," I replied.

"It is the filth and badness coming out of you." Until that time, I had not really taken much notice of this man, but now, stood in that freezing cold barrel, and looking out, I could see that apart from the strange haircut and the strange clothes, there was a man with pure hate in his eyes, which were deeply set and in the centre of which was a thin hooked nose; he had shallow lips and sunken cheeks and a somewhat grey pallor to his skin. I had never seen this person until the early hours of this morning, and here he stood before me with nothing else but contempt for this poor seven year old boy.

Suddenly he turned and went back inside the building, shortly after which, another similarly dressed individual came out into the yard. This person had a much more pleasing face, and smiled as he came towards me. "Oh you poor wee lamb, out you get, and we'll get you dry." I took hold of the sides of the barrel and tried to lift myself from the freezing water, but the cold had taken its toll on me and I did not have the strength to pull myself free. The man stepped forward and took me under both arms and lifted me free, and, placing me on the ground, wrapped me in a cloth, and told me to dry myself. After I had rubbed myself dry, I was handed a robe, and told to put it on. It was a similar robe to those being worn by my new captors, but had been cut down from an adult one. It had a jagged bottom where it had been roughly cut, and it was split from the bottom of the garment to the right arm hole, so that when I placed it about myself, it was then wrapped around my body. The man who brought the garment then handed me what appeared to be the piece of cloth that had been cut off. "Wrap this around you, boy, it will keep the garment about you, and keep you warm."

This new garment was made of very rough cloth and it rubbed harshly against my skin. Nonetheless, I was grateful for the warmth of it, as soon my body started to tingle and the shivering started to ease.

"What of my clothes, Sir?" I enquired.

"They will be burnt, you will wear these while you are with us, but you may collect your boots, and wear those. I am Brother Matthias, and whenever you speak to me you will always use my name first, as with any of the Brothers in this manse, unless it is the person you have already met, and he is Father Francis. When speaking to Father Francis, you will always lower your head in his presence and only speak when he asks you to. Is that clear to you, boy?"

"Yes, Sir, but how long am I to be kept here?"

Without warning, Brother Matthias struck me across the face with his hand. "What have I just said to you, boy? Whenever you speak to me you will always use my name first. Failure to do this in future will result in a thorough beating, do you understand?"

"Yes, Sir," I replied, through tear filled eyes. Slap! On the other side of my face.

"Brother Matthias!" he yelled, "Not Sir."

"Brother Matthias, how long am I to spend here?" I asked.

"We never know our destiny, boy, only God will tell," he replied. "Come now, boy, there is much to learn and your duties will start right away, learn quickly and work diligently, be respectful to all you meet and most importantly, be pious at all times."

"What is pious?" I asked. This time Brother Matthias' hand caught me on the left ear with such force that I could hear whistling inside my head.

"Again, boy."

"Sorry. Brother Matthias…"

"Yes."

"Brother Matthias, what is pious?"

"It is to do all things as God would have us do."

"Brother Matthias, how do I know what God would have me do?"

"By watching and learning, boy," he replied.

We walked from the yard back into the building, locking the yett behind us, then closing the door. I was taken along a dark passage, where I was shown a small room, in which were three low wooden platforms with straw on them and a rough cloth spread over the straw. Apart from the three platforms the room was bare. Brother Matthias told me that this was where I would sleep, that there were two other Lay-Brothers, of which I was now one, and that our duties would be to do all the manual work for the Brothers, within the manse and the grounds that surrounded the manse.

I was also told that during every day I would have to stop whatever I was doing, whenever I heard the bell, and go down on my knees and say the prayer that Our Lord has taught us.

"You do know the prayer that Our Lord has taught us, boy?" said Brother Matthias.

"No, I don't, Brother Matthias," I replied.

"You really are the seed of Satan," said Brother Matthias. "You must learn it before the day is out or Father Francis will have you flogged until there is not a scrap of flesh on your back. I will teach you it now, I will say it twice and on the third time we will say it together, do you understand, boy?" said Brother Matthias. "Get upon your knees, boy," he said, and as we knelt he started to recite what I now know to be The Lord's Prayer.

From the dormitory, we then went further down the dimly lit passage to the kitchen, where an old grey haired man was stood at a heavy wooden table, cutting up vegetables.

"This is Daniel, he is our senior Lay Brother, and just like all the Monks in the manse you will take instruction from Daniel, and you will always do what he tells you, do you understand, boy?" said Brother Matthias.

"Yes, Brother Matthias," I said.

"Daniel, this is our new young Lay-Brother, who will do your bidding," said Brother Matthias.

"And what is yer name, boy?" said Daniel.

15

I replied, "Rob, Sir, er... Robert Milburn."

"No it is not!" roared Brother Matthias. "You will forget the name given to you by thieves and murderers; we will give you a Christian name without the mark of Satan."

"Now then, boy, said Brother Matthias, "we must continue. Daniel, I will return the boy for your instruction soon. Come, boy."

We returned along the passage to a very small room under a stone staircase. "This will be your first duty, boy, you will see Daniel and get some water and a brush, return here and wash this floor thoroughly, to remove the stench of where you lay on your arrival."

We then ascended the stairs and at the top was a large door as you turned on to the landing. "You will never ever enter this door, for any reason, and if you learn nothing else this day, make sure this stays in your head, do you hear me, boy?" said Brother Matthias.

"It is the Chapel, where the Brothers are called to prayer, but at Vespers, in the evening, the Lay-Brothers must attend, but you will enter through the small door at the far end of the landing. Come, boy," said Brother Matthias, as he took me along to the smaller door, where we entered. Inside was a tiny space that was partitioned off from the rest of the Chapel, thus blocking out any view. I was told that Daniel would bring me up when the time was right, and that I must never come up the stairs on my own, that it must be either with Daniel or one of the Brothers.

From there we continued on up another flight of stairs to the third floor, where there was no door, just the wooden boards on the floor, and eight wooden cots, with straw mattresses. This was where the Brothers slept, and I would only come here with Daniel, to empty the vessels used by the Brothers for their bodily wastes, and I was informed that should a drop be spilt, when carrying out this duty, I would be flogged.

Returning down the stairs, Brother Matthias told me to go to the kitchen and see Daniel, and get a bucket of water, some soap, a brush and return to where I had been brought, in the early hours, and to remove the stench I had left. I went along the dimly lit passage to the kitchen and stood in the doorway, waiting for Daniel to notice me. After a short while Daniel raised his head from what he was doing and said, "Come in, boy, what do you require?"

"Brother Daniel, Brother Matthias has sent me for some water, a brush and some s-s-s-sup."

"Oh-oh-oh," laughed Daniel, "You don't call me Brother, only the monks, and what was it you want apart from the water and a brush?"

"S-s-sup," I replied.

"Oh my wee boy, it is soap you want, do you not know what soap is?" said Daniel.

"I don't think so," I said.

"Come, come, boy and I will show you," he said, as he went over to a shelf and took off a block of the tallow I had used earlier, when in the barrel of cold water.

"Yes, Daniel, I used some this morning when I had to clean myself. I don't like it, it goes all white and slimy on the skin, and afterwards my body tingled for a long time. I don't think it can be good for you, I won't use it again."

"Oh my boy, you are a funny wee thing, it keeps the body clean and you will be expected to wash yourself fully as you have done today, each week, because we the Lay-Brothers do all the heavy work and through toil the body becomes dirty and smells and this is offensive to the Brothers," said Daniel.

He got me the water, brush and the soap and I set off on my first duty as a Lay-Brother. I got down on my knees and started to scrub the floor with the wet brush, when I heard a voice behind me.

"Rub the brush over the soap occasionally; that will help to clean the floor."

I looked around and it was Daniel watching me work. He had brought with him a piece of cloth, which he handed to me.

"Don't use a lot of water, and after scrubbing, wipe the floor dry with the cloth. I will come and check what you have done, when you finish."

"Thank you, Daniel," I said as I went back to my chore.

When I had finished, I went after Daniel in the kitchen and told him I was finished. Together we walked back to the scene of my labours and Daniel rested his hand on my shoulder and said, "Well, my boy, you may be from heathens, but you are a good wee worker, isn't he, Brother Matthias?"

I looked around and saw Brother Matthias standing just behind Daniel. "Yes indeed, he does not appear to be a complete wastrel, maybe we can make something of him yet!" exclaimed Brother Matthias. I felt so proud that my endeavours had pleased everyone.

"Come now, boy, Father Francis wishes to see you," explained Brother Matthias. My joy was short lived as I was taken to the one room on the ground floor I had not yet seen. Brother Matthias knocked on the door and the voice of Father Francis could be heard; "Enter," in a much quieter voice than I had heard earlier in the day. Before we entered, Brother Matthias leaned over me and told me that when in the presence of Father Francis I must keep my head bowed forward and my hands crossed in front of me, and not say anything unless asked to speak. We entered the room and I kept my head bowed and my hands clasped in front of me, so I never really saw what the room was like.

"Now, boy," the voice had increased in volume again. "We cannot have you within the confines of a holy building, despoiling it with the name given you by thieves and murderers; therefore after much consideration I have decided that henceforth you will be known as Isaac. It is a good biblical name and on Sunday, the Sabbath day, you will be taken into the Abbey, and Christened into the only church of God, in the hope that we may be able to wipe the mark of the Devil from you before it is too late. Now you may return to your duties."

"Say thank you, Father Francis," said Brother Matthias.

"Thank you, Father Francis," I said meekly, still with my head bowed.

"Father Francis, young Isaac has set about his first task for us, and has shown a will to do our bidding with diligence," said Brother Matthias.

"Take him away, Brother Matthias, he is still the seed of the Devil and I do not want to set eyes on him until he is brought to me to be welcomed into the true Church. Now take him out," said Father Francis, his voice increasing in volume and annoyance the longer we stayed in the room.

Brother Matthias returned me to the kitchen where Daniel was still at his labours. He left me there and returned along the passage out of sight without saying a word.

I turned to Daniel and told him that I was to get a new name, Isaac, but I did not like it, I liked Rob much better, but Daniel explained that while I was with the Brothers it would be better that I had another name. I told him what had been said about the Abbey on Sunday and that I did not know what Father Francis meant, but was too frightened to say anything. Daniel said that what was happening was a good thing and for me not to worry. I asked Daniel why did the Brothers seem to dislike me so much, when I had not done anything wrong? Daniel explained that it was understandable that the Brothers would not like me as it was the English who had raided the Abbey, and had cast it into ruins, and had killed many people when they raided, some of whom had been Monks from the Abbey. Some years ago, Daniel went on, there had been over a hundred Brothers at the Abbey, and as the years passed, and with raids by both Scots and English, the numbers had dwindled to only about twenty at the time of the big raid by the English King's men, of which some could have been my own kinsmen. After the raid and the ruining of the Abbey, where four Brothers were killed, nine left and retired from the Brotherhood. Seven had remained within the town, where the townsfolk who wished to stay with the old religion, housed the Brothers in this large house near the Abbey, but away from the gaze of anyone from outside, and in return the Brothers administered the Mass and Christenings and burials, and administered the people's spiritual needs, which I did not fully understand, but said nothing.

"Enough of all this now, young man, there is much to do; we will go about our chores, and I will instruct you as we go," said Daniel.

We went from the kitchen outside into the yard, and at the far end of the yard was a doorway in the high wall. Daniel opened the door, which opened out on to a large walled garden, with plants still growing this late into the year. I did not know what any of the plants were, and Daniel could see my bewilderment and said, "Don't worry my, boy, you will learn all about the garden under my guidance; we grow vegetables to eat all year round and we also have some buried underground and covered in bracken which we cut and bring down from the hill tops. The bracken keeps the vegetables dry and warm so that the winter frosts don't spoil them."

We walked over to a far wall of the garden and along the bottom of the wall were all manner of green leafy plants growing.

"We plant these by the wall to protect them from the weather; they are all herbs, which are used for cooking and for medicines," said Daniel.

"What are medicines?" I enquired.

"Medicines are potions that are used to treat all manner of illnesses," replied Daniel.

"But how do you know which plants to use, Daniel?" I further enquired.

"That, my boy, is a secret that the Brothers keep, and they and only they know what each plant can do, but I have learned much in my time serving the Brothers, as you will if you have a will to learn."

As the day progressed I was given small chores to do by Daniel, such as cleaning vegetables, sweeping the floor, or taking waste out to the midden in the walled garden, with the instruction that whenever I went out of the manse, that both the door and the yett were to be closed after me, and that even the gate from the yard to the garden had to be closed. This of course was second nature to me, as, from my earliest recollections, I had always been told by both my mother and father to close the door of the Bastle and secure the yett.

That first day I stayed close to Daniel, who proved to be a kindly old gentleman. I did not know how old he was, but to a frightened seven year old, he seemed very old. What hair he had was very sparse and white in colour and his posture was stooped over and his face was heavily lined with age. When he walked he had a shuffling gait, and tended to hold on to anything that was nearby, like tables or chairs, in order to steady himself. He spoke with a much softer Scottie accent than the ones I had heard from my earlier captors, and I mentioned this to Daniel. He told me that he came from a village to the north of Scotland, beyond Edinburgh, and had come to the Borders as a soldier many years ago, to fight against the English, for the Scottish King. He had been wounded in the battle and had been brought to Melrose and the Abbey, where the Brothers had nursed him back to health. He had found the Brothers to be much kindlier people than he had ever met, and had wished to stay with them and repay their kindness by his labours. He had toiled at many tasks over the years, but now that he was less able to get around, he limited his endeavours to the area of the kitchen and light garden duties.

Many times through the day the bell would ring, and each time both Daniel and I would go to our knees and say the Lord's Prayer, and as the day went on I noticed that Daniel found it increasingly difficult to get up and down, a matter I would try and address at a later date.

Towards the end of the daylight hours, a young man, possibly in his early twenties, came into the kitchen, and as I looked up from my chores, Daniel said, "Ah, Donald, this is our new Lay-Brother, meet Donald, boy."

"Now then, ma lad, and wits yer name?" said Donald.

Daniel interceded at this point, "He's an English reiver, so has had his reiver's name taken from him and will receive a new Christian name on Sunday, given by the Brothers."

"An English reiver, eh! Well they mak 'em a wee bit smaller than a thought, we've na need to worry in our beds tonight if this is what they're like." As he laughed Donald explained, as he washed his hands in a bucket of water, that his duties were to tend the sheep that belonged to the Brothers and other duties on the land around the manse and the Abbey. He went on to explain that he had spent many days helping to clear up around the Abbey over the last few years, and that the Brothers were now able to conduct services in the ruins, for the people of Melrose. He told me that on Sunday I would be able to see all the people come together in the ruins, and how it was all kept secret from the rest of the land.

Donald seemed to like me, so that along with Daniel's kindness, I was starting to feel a little less alone. It soon came time when we were called to the evening meal, which we took with the Brothers. Donald took me along to where we ate and sat me by his side at a table facing the wall. As I sat down I looked around at the rest of the room, which had a large table in the centre with long benches at either side for the

Brothers to sit on, and at the head of the table was a large high backed chair. The table had three wooden bowls placed on one side, two on the other side and one in front of the large chair. There were wooden bowls on the table where we sat, with wooden spoons by their side. Daniel came in to the dining room with a large steaming vessel with the food he had been preparing for most of the day. He placed the vessel on the table to be used by the Brothers, then came and sat down next to Donald.

The Brothers came into the room; there were four Brothers whom I had not seen before. They all sat down at the table, but Father Francis remained standing, and at the top of his voice yelled, "What is that seed of Satan doing at the table? Get you on the floor, you are not worthy to eat with men, you will eat like an animal until you are brought into God's house."

I slipped down off the bench on to the floor, cowering as I did so, and trembling with absolute fear. I was totally certain that if Father Francis got the opportunity he would surely slay me; such was this man's hate for this poor seven year old boy.

I ate my meal on the floor, and as Daniel got up from the table and started to clear away the wooden bowls and spoons he gently beckoned to me with his head, and I scurried out of the refectory and down the passage to the kitchen.

"Daniel," I asked, "Why does Father Francis hate me so? I know you said that it was English Kingsmen that ruined the Abbey and that some of the Brothers were killed, but I didn't do it."

"Don't worry yourself, my boy, said Daniel, "I am sure that once Father Francis gets used to you being around he will not be so harsh to you; now you away to your bed, it has been a long day for you and we will see what tomorrow brings."

I went to my bed and curled up into a little ball and sobbed myself to sleep, wishing maybe it would have been better if Will had taken his sword to me.

The following morning I was woken very early by Daniel and told to get up as there was much to do. Not long after rising, Daniel went off to the Chapel for Vigils. I was not allowed until my name had been changed. He arrived back sometime later and continued to make the boiled oats for the early morning meal. It seemed no time at all until the bell rang out for prayers, after which the oatmeal was taken to the refectory, and I was yet again forced to take up my station on the floor.

After morning meal, again I slipped out of the refectory, unnoticed, and hurried back to the kitchen. When Daniel arrived I asked about the other Brothers, whom I had seen for the first time last night. He told me that they spent much of their days working in the ruins of the Abbey, carrying away the large stones that had been brought down by the English. Sometimes it could take many days to move just one stone, they were that large.

Daniel then informed me that I must now go to the Brothers' dormitory and empty the vessels from the floor by taking up a bucket, which he handed me. He gave me a small piece of rough cloth and told me to wipe the floor, should there be any spillage, but to take every care not to spill, because Father Francis would be very annoyed.

I went to the dormitory up all the stairs with the bucket, which in itself was a struggle, and entered warily. There was no one around so I carefully took the first vessel and gently poured the contents into the bucket, and to my delight did so without spilling a single drop. Onwards I went, with renewed confidence to the next vessel, this time just the least drop on the wooden floor, which was easily wiped without a mark. I successfully completed the task and then set off for the stairs, having left no sign of me being there. I struggled down the stairs with the weight of the bucket and the unsteadiness of the contents, arriving eventually at the bottom without having spilt a single drop. Only the long dim passage now to negotiate, then out into the yard and this major task would be successfully completed. I then saw Father Francis appear from the kitchen, and bustle along the passage towards me. I stepped aside to allow him past me, but he reached out with his left hand and caught me on the side of the head, shouting, "Get out of my way, boy."

With the force of the blow and the fact that I was already unsteady with the weight of my load I stumbled over, sending the contents of the bucket cascading down the passage. Father Francis was incensed by the scene and started wielding blows down on me, screaming incoherently, and acting like a man possessed. I could not feel any of the blows making contact with me, as I was in a state of shock, by the ferocity of the onslaught by this so-called man of God. It was only the intervention of Daniel, who had been summoned by the noise of the incident, that possibly saved me from permanent harm or even worse. He came between the two of us, sustaining several hefty blows from the Monk, and wrapped his arms around Father Francis, talking in hushed tones for him to be calm and go to the Chapel to seek guidance from the Lord.

Father Francis turned and went off up the stairs, mumbling to himself as he went. Daniel then turned his attention to me and gathered me up from my now crumpled posture, still holding my arms over my head, in defence from the attack. It was not until we reached the kitchen that the enormity of what had taken place overcame me, and I started to cry uncontrollably. Daniel held me in his arms, comforting me as best he could, when after a while Brother Matthias entered the room. He asked Daniel why I was in such a state, and Daniel explained what had happened, and how viciously Father Francis had attacked me. Brother Matthias came over to where we were sat and took me from

Daniel, and gathered me tightly in his arms, patting my back, in an effort to console me. I was surprised at the effect that this had on me, as I seemed to quieten quite quickly. He then sat down with me on his lap and stroked the back of my head. For the first time since arriving at the manse I felt safe and secure; even though Daniel had showed me nothing but kindness, Brother Matthias seemed to have that ability to give out a feeling of security and love.

After I had settled down and stopped sobbing, with these two kind people on either side of me, I slipped off Brother Matthias' knee and said I would clear up the mess in the passage.

"No, no, don't you bother with such things today," said Brother Matthias.

"No, Brother Matthias, I will carry on and do my chores, and thank you both for your kindness."

I went and gathered up the upturned bucket and trudged out towards the well. As I did so I heard Brother Matthias say, "What a brave little man, I might have misjudged him; I think he has courage beyond his years. We will see how he goes from now; I might be able to help him ready himself for adulthood, through educating him, if he has the ability to learn."

Chapter 3

A New Name

The following morning we were roused from our slumbers, as ever, in the middle of the night, when the Brothers went into the chapel for Vigils, Daniel and Donald having to go and stand behind the partition during the service. I would go to the kitchen and watch over the oatmeal, which was being warmed over the fire, occasionally stirring it with a large wooden spoon to stop it from sticking to the pan. I as yet was banned from the chapel.

After a while both Daniel and Donald came into the kitchen, and we all started to prepare for the morning meal. This morning Donald took the food to the refectory and Daniel and I followed on behind. When the food was placed on the main table, I took up my position on the floor. The Brothers all came in and sat down, and after Grace had been said, Father Francis turned to Daniel and Donald and told them that this morning they were responsible for me and that they were to take me to the Abbey at the appropriate time. I did not know what this all meant, but I knew that Daniel would look after me.

When the morning meal was over we returned to the kitchen where everything was got ready for the afternoon meal. Daniel then told me to go to the yard, where the large barrel of water was kept, and to rub my hands in the water and to splash some water about my face, in order to clean myself, before going to the Abbey. The morning was very cold, but the water seemed colder still as I placed my hands in, then bracing myself, splashed water on my face. This has got to be the cruellest thing ever, but once I returned to the kitchen and dried off, I felt quite good.

A bell sounded in the manse, and I immediately went to my knees, but Daniel and Donald both laughed, Daniel saying, "No need for that now, that is the bell to tell us to go to the Chapel." We left together, through the kitchen door out into the yard, securing the gate and the iron yett, then on through the yard gate, into the walled garden, again securing the gate as we went. From the walled garden we then went on to the walled fields beyond, which were on an incline and rose up from the manse, giving a good view of the town, with the Abbey towering above the rest of the buildings. Donald pointed to the hills surrounding the town, and said, "If yer look out towards the hills, yu'll see there is a person stood on top of the rise, and as you look around there are others spaced along the tops. There are wooden posts knocked into the ground at all the best viewing points, and a person is sent out to stand at each post every Sunday, to keep watch while the monks carry out the Mass, and if anyone approaches the town they will signal and everyone will go back to their homes." Donald then pointed to the ruined Abbey and I could see that it was full of people.

"Look at that," he said. "They are all here to see you, ma wee man," as he laughed.

"Why must the people watch out for people coming?" I enquired.

"Well you see, ma wee man," said Donald, "Yur English Queen wants her own religion, and doesn't want the old religion, and doesn't want anybody else having anything to do with the old religion, and if she found out, we are feared that she might send her men to slaughter the whole town."

"But aren't we in Scotland?" I asked.

"Aye, we are, but that has never stopped you English from sticking your noses in where they're not wanted," retorted Donald. "Away now, ma boys, we better be on our way," said Donald, as the three of us walked down into the town and on into the grounds of the ruined Abbey.

I was taken to the front of the assembly, where I stood between Daniel and Donald. Father Francis was stood at the front of everyone facing us; there were also the four other Brothers, whom I didn't know very well, stood behind him, on a higher step, and to the side stood Brother Matthias, and when I looked over towards him, he smiled back at me. Although I was very nervous, as I did not know what was happening, that smile did much to settle my nerves.

After a short while, Father Francis started to talk, but in a strange language, and sometimes the people would also talk in this strange language. Maybe the Scotties talk like this on Sundays, when they are all together, I thought. I seemed to be stood there for a very long time when Daniel took me by the shoulder and walked me over to where Brother Matthias was stood. He then rested his hand on my other shoulder and smiled again. I felt comforted between the two people who had shown warmth towards me since my abduction.

Father Francis then came over to where the three of us stood; he then said something in this strange language, after which Brother Matthias replied in the same strange language. Father Francis then stepped forward and reached for my shoulder. I shied away, but Brother Matthias patted me on the back and nodded and smiled reassuringly. I went with Father Francis, just a few steps, to a small stone column on which was placed a flat stone dish, which had water in it. Father Francis, still with his hand on my shoulder, with his other hand reached into the stone dish, and while speaking in the strange language, took a hand full of water and ran it over my head. After this had been done he gently pushed me away, in the direction of Brother Matthias. I went over and stood by him until the people started to leave the ruined Abbey.

The four of us stood side by side, as Father Francis walked back to where he had been before; the other Brothers came down and stood either side of him. After everyone had left the Abbey, Brother Matthias led the way, still holding my shoulder, as we all went back to the manse.

On arriving back, Brother Matthias told me to go to the kitchen with Daniel and Donald and he would see me later. We all busied ourselves making the afternoon meal, and when it was ready, Daniel and Donald carried it up to the refectory, where all the Brothers were already assembled.

I took up my usual place on the floor, but Brother Matthias came over and placed both his hands either side of my shoulders and lifted me up from the floor and walked me over to where Daniel and Donald ate and sat me down at the table. "I think that is where he should now sit," he said, as he looked in the direction of Father Francis. Father Francis grunted in reply, and waved the back of his hand dismissively.

I sat with my two friends and ate my meal with renewed confidence, knowing that now, apart from Daniel and Donald, I had one of the Brothers who was now willing to look after me. The food tasted better today than any other day since my arrival.

After we had all eaten and the Brothers started to rise from the table, I also got up from where I sat, with my renewed confidence and walked over to the Brothers' table and started to clear away their dishes, without being asked. One of the Brothers, Brother James, laid his hand on the top of my head and said, "Bless you, my son."

I turned to the smiling monk and said, "Thank you, Brother James." His smile broadened and he playfully roughed my hair, as he walked away.

There had been bad times since my arrival at the manse, and there had been good, but I hadn't felt as good as I did now. I think people, maybe not all, were starting to like me, and it gave me such a warm feeling inside. That night I went to sleep, looking forward to the next day.

The day started as always, in the middle of the night, or so it seemed as it was very dark when the bell woke everyone. I staggered wearily from my bed and went to the kitchen, rubbing the night away from my eyes. Shortly after rising, the bell for Vigils was sounded, where we all had to go to the chapel. This morning, I had to attend, as I now had a new name. We entered the chapel and stood behind a wooden screen, where we could not see anything, and had to stay silent, but we could hear the Brothers chanting in that strange language I had heard the day before in the ruined Abbey. This went on for what seemed a very long time, but eventually it was over, and we went back to the kitchen. It hadn't seemed as long when I had waited in the kitchen on the other mornings for Daniel to return.

We prepared the morning meal and then took it along to the refectory, and the Brothers filed in shortly after. I still nearly sat on the floor, but Daniel beckoned me to the table, where I sat, hardly wanting to look around in case I caught the eye of Father Francis. This was to be the way for a long time to come, that whenever I was anywhere near Father Francis, I would look away in order not to catch his eye. I thought that this might stop him from attacking me.

After the meal was over and the Brothers were leaving the refectory, Brother Matthias came over to where I stood and told me to sit down.

"Now then, Isaac," he said. "After the mass which we celebrated yesterday, and you were brought into the house of God, and were given a Christian name, it has now fallen to me to take on responsibility for you. It is Father Francis' wish that I undertake your education. Do you understand what that will mean, my boy?"

"No, I don't, Brother Matthias," I said.

"Well, don't you worry about anything; you go about your chores with Daniel, and the rest will take care of itself." He then left the room and Daniel and I cleared away all the dishes and returned to the kitchen.

I asked Daniel what Brother Matthias had meant, and Daniel told me that it was a great honour for me to be taught by one of the Brothers, and that usually only boys of rich and powerful families were taught by the monks.

From that moment on I would go about my daily chores, rising in the middle of the night, going to Vigils in the Chapel, readying for the morning meal, then going to the Brothers' dormitory and emptying the vessels of bodily wastes, always ensuring that not a drop was spilt, although not always successfully, but I became very adept at covering over all traces of any mishap that might have occurred. On many occasions I came across Father Francis when in the midst of this odious duty, but I always placed the bucket on the floor, out of the way, as I saw him approach, and stood in front of it, with head bowed. This seemed to work, without incurring unprovoked onslaught. Was Father Francis warming to me? Of course not, he continued to treat me with complete contempt, though the other Brothers did seem to warm as time went on, but they never really took any interest in me, and dutifully went about their works, apparently oblivious to all around.

Chapter 4

The Written Word

In the middle of the afternoon of that first day after the service in the Abbey, Brother Matthias came to the kitchen at around the time the Brothers took a rest on their beds. He told me to go and sit at the table with him. He placed down on the table a piece of slate, and in his hand he had a piece of white stone that he called chalk.

"Now Isaac, today you will have your first lesson in reading and writing. I will show you first how to read and write in English, and if you show you are able to learn quickly enough we may be able to teach you Latin."

"What is Latin, Brother Matthias?" I asked.

"Latin is the language of the Bible, and if you are able to read and write Latin, you will be a very well educated young man."

"Is that the strange language that was used at the Mass yesterday, Brother Matthias?" I asked.

"Yes, that is right, Isaac," he replied laughingly. "Yes, I suppose to a young fellow like yourself, it is a strange language, but I hope that you are able to learn, and become a wise man for your future life."

Brother Matthias then wrote a letter on the slate using the chalk. It looked like the top of the bastle I had been taken from, only a couple of weeks before. The tears started to stream down my face, and Brother Matthias put his arm around my shoulder.

"What is it, boy?" he said.

"It looks like the top of the bastle where I lived before I was brought here," I said.

"Oh my poor boy, do not fret about such things; here you are safe from raiders and disease, you will be fed well, probably better than you have been and we, both Daniel and I, and Donald, and the other Brothers, are all here to look after you."

"But I miss my mother and father and my sister," I said.

"Come, come, young Isaac, look at the letter on your slate; it is the first letter of the alphabet, and the alphabet is a list of all the letters that go to make the English language. Now then, the letter you see is the letter 'A', what is it?"

"The letter A, Brother Matthias," I said. He then told me to copy the letter using the chalk. It seemed an easy enough task; however, the first attempt was less than a success, but continued efforts saw an improvement, and from there other letters were tackled, with varying degrees of success, or failure as the case may be, but Brother Matthias showed wonderful patience at my less than perfect first step with the written word.

As the following days, weeks and months went by, my studies continued and my initial unease with the written word lessened, and I started to enjoy, indeed, look forward to, my lessons. I also continued with my duties within the manse, including the daily task of emptying the monks' vessels, where I used every care to ensure that my endeavours were not traceable.

I also spent many hours in conversation with Daniel, and discovered that at one time, before the Abbey was ruined, there had been over one hundred monks serving the Abbey, which over the years had dropped to just twenty, before the destruction. Thirteen of the monks had retired from the order after the raid and seven had remained, at the request of the local people, in order to continue the old religion, and since then one of the brothers had died; he had been Father Emanuel, who had been the Abbot and had been buried inside the walls of the Abbey. Father Francis had then taken over from him.

I also learnt from Daniel that Donald was of the Nixon family, one of the riding families of the Borders, his father being the Heedsman of that family, the Heedsman being the head of the family. Daniel told me that where he came from in Scotland, the families were called Clans.

Donald had been struck with a malady which, when it attacked him, rendered him senseless, where he fell to the ground in convulsions. Daniel explained that his family thought that he was possessed by the Devil and had therefore brought him to the Abbey for the monks to look after him.

The malady had first struck him down at the age of seven, my age, and people who suffered such a malady did not live very long, but life within the Abbey and manse had agreed with Donald, and he now rarely had an attack. I asked Daniel if it was the Devil that attacked Donald, but Daniel laughed and said it was nonsense to think such a thing.

Over the next weeks and months, whenever the opportunity arose, I always ran out from the manse to be with Donald, whose company I enjoyed; he being younger than anyone else in the manse, I found it easier to relate to him. I spoke to him about his malady and he explained that when it happened he was aware just before, but during the attack and after, he knew nothing, sometimes going into a deep sleep afterwards, then waking, remembering nothing. He was aware that usually people with this malady did not live very long and that he was lucky to still be alive. He also said, which I shall never forget, that he hoped that when he died, it was not as a result of the malady.

I was getting close to Daniel, who was very much my new father figure and Donald, my new big brother, which I had never had; this now was my family, and although I often thought of my real family and what had become of them, since my abduction, and still often weeping in that time just before sleep takes over, I started to settle in to my new life, albeit ever watchful of Father Francis, for I knew that should the opportunity arise for him to strike me or worse, I felt sure that he would do so.

Brother Matthias came in to the manse from the town one day, a few weeks after my name had been changed, and under his arm he had a bundle of clothes.

"Isaac, come here, see what I have got for you," he said and handed me the bundle. "Clothes for you, try them on and see if they will fit." With glee, I took off the cut down habit I had been given, on the day of my arrival at the manse, which had been the most uncomfortable garment imaginable, and tried the new clothes on. They were wonderful; breeches, blouse and jack, even new boots. All were slightly big on me but I was a growing lad and these were perfect. Brother Matthias clapped his hands together and with a broad smile said, "Wonderful, you look a very smart young man."

Daniel said, "For the first time since you entered the manse we can see what a handsome fellow you are," as both he and Brother Matthias laughed.

I felt so proud of my new outfit, and later that day was walking through the manse, going about my duties when Father Francis spied me and came up to me with that ever familiar scowl. "Where did you get those clothes from, boy? Get out of them immediately and back into the clothes you were given."

From behind me I heard Brother Matthias' voice say, in quite an assertive manner, "I got them for him, Father Francis, is there a problem?"

Father Francis turned on his heels and went off down the passage, muttering to himself as he went. I was about to laugh at the way he had walked off, but Brother Matthias saw this and put his finger to his lips, but I could see in his eyes that he was laughing also.

"It is now my responsibility to see to your needs, Isaac, and part of that is to see you are clothed, and when you grow out of those we shall have to get more."

"Oh no, Brother Matthias, I shall never change these; they are the finest clothes I have ever had, and I shall wear them forever." I don't know what was so funny but Brother Matthias laughed as I had never heard before.

When Donald came in at the end of the day I made sure I was stood at the door, so that he could see me in my finery. As he approached I stood out from the kitchen with my head up proudly. "My, my, a new boy. Ah well you'll be company for wee Isaac, and what's your name?" said Donald.

"It's me, Donald, I have new clothes, Brother Matthias got them for me," I said.

"I know, ye wee scamp; my, yer look braw in yer new clothes, I'll think maybe too fine to mingle with the likes of us, ah Daniel?" he said, laughingly.

That night at meal time in the refectory, all the Brothers remarked at how fine I looked in my new attire, which did little to improve the demeanour of Father Francis, who scowled and grunted his way through the meal.

I knew yet again that although I had continued to stay out of the way of Father Francis, I would now have to be even more alert than before.

The following day my suspicions were found to be correct. It was early in the morning, and I was at my usual task of emptying the vessels from the Brothers' dormitory. I had just emptied the final vessel into the bucket, without a drop spilled, and turned to go back down the stairs, when there on the top of the stairs was Father Francis. He must have been stood there, watching me as I emptied all the vessels, and luckily this morning I had completed the task perfectly. He stepped from the top step towards me with his arm raised, about to bring it down on me, but without saying a word. I laid the bucket down and moved away from it, raising my own arm to protect myself and cowered down, awaiting the blows.

It seemed from nowhere came a voice saying, "I don't think you should do that, Father Francis." It was Brother Matthias, stood at the top of the stairs, and stood behind him on a lower stair, so that I could only see his head, was Daniel.

"Stay out of this, it has nothing to do with you," said Father Francis, in low hushed, guttural, menacing tones.

"Are you threatening me, Father Francis?" enquired Brother Matthias.

"I am the Abbot here, how dare you question me?" bellowed Father Francis.

"I question any man who would use such violence on a boy of his age; when we are surrounded by violence, and live in fear of violence, we must be the voice of reason, now come away and leave the boy alone," said Brother Matthias. Father Francis turned around and bustled past Brother Matthias and Daniel, pushing them aside as he went; the look of anger on his face as he turned towards everyone, having got past them, before descending the stairs was frightening.

"I had an idea something like this was about to happen after yesterday and Father Francis' reaction to your new clothes; that is why I asked Daniel to accompany me. You are safe now, Isaac, so don't worry; now give me the bucket and I will take it down for you," said Brother Matthias.

"No, it is all right, Brother Matthias, I can manage, thank you," I said as I picked up the bucket and struggled down the stairs as I did every morning.

"He's a tough little character, Brother Matthias; one day, if Father Francis does not kill him beforehand, he will make a formidable person," I heard Daniel say.

"Yes, and that is why we must ensure that he is never left alone where Father Francis is. I blame the events of the past years for the way he is, nothing else, and we must show compassion for him," I heard Brother Matthias say, as I went along the ground floor passage towards the kitchen.

"Indeed you are a very compassionate man, Brother Matthias," I could hear Daniel say, as I went out of the kitchen door and into the yard, with the bucket of waste, ensuring that I did not spill, lest I spoil my new attire.

When I returned to the kitchen Brother Matthias had gone, so I just continued my chores without saying anything.

The next time I saw Brother Matthias was later that day when he returned to the kitchen to give me my tuition. Again I was given yet more new letters to write down or copy from the writing of Brother Matthias. It was never going to be my favourite part of the day, but Brother Matthias was always kind, and patient, with this less than able of students. The incentive for me to concentrate and apply myself was that after my period of tuition Daniel usually allowed me to go out into the field and spend time with Donald. When Brother Matthias would say, "That's all for today, Isaac," I would run from the kitchen into the yard and beyond as if my tail were on fire, and I'm sure Brother Matthias just used to say, "That's all for today," to watch me scramble away, because I often heard him laugh as I ran off.

It was on such a day, some months later, when I had just finished my tuition, and hurried to be with Donald, that as I caught up with him, and he gave me his normal cheery greeting, I saw his eyes seem to roll up into the top of his head. His body went rigid, and he fell to the ground, like a tree being chopped down. I started to run away, but something stopped me; I turned and went back. Donald was writhing around on the ground; he was foaming from the mouth, as if someone had put that horrible tallow that they make you wash in, in his mouth. He was throwing his head back on to the ground, which I was sure would kill him. I got down on to the ground, frightened though I was, and gathered his head in my arms and held him tight to my body. This went on for some short time. Donald then settled, but I still kept tight hold of him, while he slipped off into a deep sleep. Though at first I thought he was dead, occasionally his body would twitch, which assured me that he still lived. The incident had greatly tired me.

As I sat there holding on to Donald I was pleased that Daniel had told me of this dreadful malady, but nothing could prepare me for what was taking place.

It seemed a long time later Donald awoke, with me still holding on to his head, tightly held on my lap, with my legs outstretched in front of me.

"Have you been there all the time, ma wee lad?" said Donald.

"Yes, if that is all right, Donald," I replied.

"And were you not frightened?" he asked.

"Yes, very," I said.

"I think yer can let me go now before yer squeeze the life oot of me," said Donald.

As I let go, Donald staggered to his feet, rather unsteadily, so I got up and put his arm over my shoulder, and we walked together towards the manse.

"Isaac, ma wee lad, yer a brave wee man and yu'll be ma friend for life, as small as yer are," said Donald, as he tightened his grip on my shoulder, affectionately. The feeling that here was a true friend who could look after me and me after him was very pleasing as we stumbled back towards the manse.

As we entered the manse, Daniel was there and said, "Take him to his bed, Isaac. Donald, you are excused Vespers tonight, I will tell Father Francis."

I went along with Donald, and waited with him until he had got into bed.

"Is there anything you want, Donald?" I asked.

"No, thank ya' ma boy, you've done far enough already, and I'll always be grateful to ye; now you run along te Daniel," he replied.

I did as Donald had bid me, and on arrival in the kitchen, I immediately asked Daniel how he knew that Donald had had an attack.

"I have seen it many times, as no doubt you will over the next years, that is if the good Lord does not take him from us before too long," said Daniel.

"Will the good Lord take him, Daniel?" I asked.

"He will take us all one day, Isaac," he said.

"But soon?" I asked.

"We will hope not, Isaac, we will certainly hope not!" he said. "Now, my boy, tell me all about what took place, and were you frightened when you saw Donald?"

"Yes, I was very frightened when I saw him; I started to run away at first, but then went back and held him until it had passed," I said.

"Good boy, that is what you should do, and hopefully we can all keep Donald alive if we do what is right when he is attacked," said Daniel.

"Daniel," I said enquiringly, "Donald said to me once that the malady would possibly kill him one day, but he hoped that he would die some other way. Should he have said that?"

"We none of us know how or when we will die, and it would be a sin to take your own life, but in the case of Donald, his malady is such a dreadful thing that you can understand that he would not want to die as a result of it, but he will not take his own life, if that is what bothers you," said Daniel.

The following day, Donald was up in the middle of the night with the rest of us, as if nothing had happened. He looked tired, more tired than when he normally gets up from his bed, but he appeared to be well again. I asked him if he was better again, and he replied that he felt well apart from a sore head. I replied that I was not surprised, after the way he was banging it on the ground. He laughed, and said, "What I like about you, Isaac, is that you don't care what you say. Others try to carry on as if nothing has happened, but you don't, and that is how it should be, and it is good that you learn of my malady, and not try to hide away from it."

We went to the kitchen and yet another day began, with cooking, cleaning, praying and keeping out of the way of Father Francis, and of course my tuition, which was becoming slightly easier. I did struggle at times, but Brother Matthias said he was pleased with me and that once I had mastered the written English word we would start to learn Latin, which he had warned of before.

I was grateful to Brother Matthias for taking the time to teach me to read and write, but all I wanted to do was to be in the fields with Donald, tending the sheep, and where I felt as free as the wind.

Many an afternoon when sat out with Donald, I would look towards the direction of the sun, knowing that in that direction was England, and my home and my mother and sister, and felt sad that my father was dead, and I was not going to see him again.

On many evenings during the long summer nights, after Vespers, instead of going straight to bed, as we did in winter, all the Brothers, Donald, Daniel and myself, would walk out into the fields and enjoy the warmth of the evening sun. It was the one time in the day when I could be in the same place as Father Francis without feeling under threat from him. As a matter of fact, Father Francis was at his best out there, and could sometimes be seen to be smiling, as he enjoyed being out. I still disliked him, even with a smile on his face. I once stood there watching him, and imagined him attacking me with that smile, and it sent a shudder down my back.

There were the days when it was not possible to go out, due to the weather, and on such days Brother Matthias would sit in the kitchen and talk of the days when he was a boy, in a place called Helmsley, near York, where his father was a weaver, and of the monastery that overlooked Helmsley where he went each day and was taught by the monks. He said that, from a very early age, all he had wanted to do was to join the Brotherhood and become a Cistercian monk, and teach young people as he had been taught. He said that all the Brothers at Melrose Abbey had come from the Helmsley monastery, where they had first taken their Holy Orders. After each Brother was ordained into the Brotherhood, they would be sent out to abbeys across the land, to do God's work, and to teach people about the church.

I asked Brother Matthias if he ever saw his father and mother again, but he said that the Brotherhood was now his family, and that, God willing, he would spend the rest of his life at Melrose, even if the Abbey had been ruined, if it was God's and the people's wish.

"What if it isn't?" I asked.

"Then I will go to wherever I am sent or wherever God wishes me to go," he replied.

"How do you know where God wants you to go?" I enquired.

"Look, Isaac, it has stopped raining, away you go and see Donald," said Brother Matthias, as I scurried from the kitchen.

Chapter 5

The Roman Tongue

Over a year had now passed since Donald was taken ill in the field where I had stayed with him until the dreadful malady had run its course. My studies had continued to the point where I was able to read and write English at a fairly proficient level, which, according to Brother Matthias, was little less than a miracle, considering that I was, in Father Francis' words, of thieves and murderers.

I listened to the many comments about my parentage, but kept my counsel, knowing that I was fiercely proud of my family, and that one day I would make the name of Milburn echo throughout the land. How that would be achieved was yet to be decided, but I knew that the learning I was receiving from Brother Matthias would help me in whatever endeavours I undertook throughout my life.

I would like to say that relations between Father Francis and myself had mellowed over this period, but alas, it cannot be so stated. He continued his indifference towards me, and had on numerous occasions struck out at me, when the opportunity presented itself. What I am pleased to report is, that as time elapsed, I gained an agility of foot, which rendered Father Francis' attempts fruitless. It may sound ridiculous, given my early encounters with my adversary, but I had come to almost enjoy the cat and mouse nature of our relationship, albeit while I was able to evade his evil intents.

Brother Matthias came to the kitchen one day for my tuition period, holding a most magnificent book under his arm. "Today, my boy, your education takes on an entirely different direction, for today is the day you will start to learn the language of the Bible, Latin," he said.

"Where is Latin?" I naively asked.

"Isaac, I sometimes wonder if I have ever been able to enter your head at all. Latin is a language, you silly boy," Brother Matthias retorted.

"But Brother Matthias, Latin must come from somewhere?" I asked.

"Indeed you are right, my boy, it is the language of the Romans, who lived in what we now know as Italy, and they came to this land many hundreds of years ago, and built many buildings and roads, which we can still see today," he replied.

"I have seen a large wall, stretching across the land near where my home is; my father would use the stones from the wall to build new parts to our bastle. He said it was the best stone he could use and would spend many days with the horse and sledge, bringing back the stone, he called it Roman stone," I said.

"Yes, that is all very well, now let us begin," said Brother Matthias.

He showed me the book he was carrying when he had entered the kitchen. It was a copy of the Bible, with the most wonderful writing, with large letters at the start of each page, with bright colours, and real gold, to make the letter stand out. At the edge of each page were pictures, which depicted what was written in the text, also very colourfully done. Brother Matthias told me that it had been written at Melrose, by the monks, and it had taken many years to complete. Father Francis had rescued it when the Abbey had been ruined, and that he had fled from the Abbey, clutching the Bible under his habit, and had been taken in by one of the families of the town and had been hidden high in the house, within the roof space, for many weeks, until all the soldiers of King Henry had departed. All of the monks had had to flee from the Abbey when the King's people had come to cast it into ruins, and had all been sheltered by the people of the town. Had any of the people been caught hiding the monks, they would have been killed.

Some of the monks had cast off their habits and had gone away from the town, never to serve within the church again, as they did not want to put the people in danger, from the soldiers, for hiding them.

When people in other towns had been caught hiding monks, they had been killed very slowly, undergoing the most horrible torture, before eventually dying. Fortunately, no one had been caught at Melrose. It was because the people of the town had been so kind to the monks, that they in turn had stayed, and had continued to teach and administer their services at the Abbey, with Masses, Requiems, Baptisms and all other services that the people wished.

Brother Matthias read from the Bible, in Latin, but it did not make any sense to me and I asked why the Bible was not written in English, so then everyone could understand it, but he said that only priests were to read the Bible, and that very few people could read.

I said, "But I can, Brother Matthias."

"Yes, and who made that possible, my boy?"

"You did, Brother Matthias, thank you," I said.

"Isaac, my boy, it gives me so much pleasure to hear you say thank you, for being able to read and write, it makes all my efforts worthwhile. Now I have read from the Bible in Latin, and you have heard what the language sounds like, I will give you some basic words to learn, and what their meaning is in English. Lux Lucet in Tenebris, which means, light shining in the dark…"

He said that as little as that was, he did not wish to take it any farther forward on the first day, but would continue to add three or four words each day, with the meaning, and in that way he hoped I would learn much more quickly, and it surely seemed to work that way, as I picked it up somewhat faster than I had English, which I had always spoken.

After just over a year of Brother Matthias' endeavours, I was able, albeit with much hesitation, to converse in Latin, and to some degree, read the classic language.

It was after one such particularly successful period of tuition in Latin, that Brother Matthias said that I could very well, if I applied myself, eventually take Holy Orders, and become a monk. I had no wish to insult this wonderful and patient man, but never had I thought of doing such a thing, and that he was indeed a wonderful person, but there was he who was Father Francis, and heaven forbid that I might end up in a monastery with the ilk of that man. Should I ever be unfortunate enough to meet such a person as I go through life I hope that it is in a place without walls, so that I can put as much distance as possible between the two of us in the shortest possible time without hindrance.

My duties within the manse had increased considerably over the ensuing years, as did my tuition, and I found myself with less and less free time than I had been allowed in my early years. I was finding myself working in the walled garden more and more, as Donald was having to take life at a more leisurely pace. It appeared that over exertion brought about the manifestation of his malady, and there instances were certainly becoming more frequent.

Daniel was now becoming more feeble, in mind as well as body, and was starting to become quite forgetful; therefore it was incumbent on me to ensure that the running of the kitchen remained smooth, and that Donald was not left on his own for overly long periods of time.

For a twelve year old boy, although I termed myself as a young man, this was quite a hefty responsibility. I still, whenever the time allowed, and I was not required to watch over, but just to be with Donald, would take off to the fields, and be with the flocks of sheep.

This seemed to be where I felt more at home than in the enclosed walls of the manse.

Then came the day when I was walking along the ground floor passage, and I was quoting some passage of Latin quietly under my breath, not noticing Father Francis bustling along the passage in the opposite direction. This was the opportunity he had waited for, for a very long time.

"What are you saying, demon? How dare you speak Latin in front of me, where did you learn that?" he spat out. He then raised his hand to strike me. I was shaken by the way I reacted; the anger I felt was as if I was possessed, unable to control my actions, I was feeling my body burning with rage. Before he could bring his arm down on me, I quickly raised my forearm and pushed it forward, at the same time stepping forward, and pushing Father Francis into the wall, my forearm taking position across the front of his throat, and pressing hard.

The shock on the face of Father Francis encouraged me as I yelled into his face, "Enough, enough of this, you will never raise your hand to me again, do you hear me?" I then made a statement which at the time I did not even understand, so why I made it I do not know. I said, "Remember this, that the last thing you will ever see in this life will be my face." I then released Father Francis, quite roughly, and walked away.

The incident was never ever spoken of again, but I was certainly aware of a change in the atmosphere between the two of us, in that I never, after that day, felt intimidated by the Father again.

After the incident, I went to my bed and lay down for a moment. My body was shaking and I felt quite sick. I did not know whether this was due to the intended attack by Father Francis, or whether it was because of my own actions. Whichever it was that had that effect on me, there nevertheless was an underlying feeling of satisfaction that at last, after nearly five years, I had overcome the one thing that had made my life so unhappy. I had been taken from my family, taken to a strange land, set with strange people, at the tender age of seven, and to add to all that, I had had Father Francis, who had been intent on making my life as difficult as possible.

I really felt that I had turned the corner from childhood to manhood that day. I had come a long way over the past five years; I had learnt to read and write, in both English and Latin, a remarkable achievement, according to Brother Matthias; I had learnt to lead a disciplined life; I had learnt how to look after my fellow man, and learn from them, no matter who they may be; and I had learnt to stand on my own two feet. How I wish that my father were alive to see me now, how I had matured and become a man. Would my mother and sister ever see how I had matured? I did not know.

Chapter 6

What Manner of Man is This?

I t was now late summer, that time of the year when the evenings are warm and sultry, when it is just nice to go out after Vespers and enjoy the warmth of the evening, and watch the setting of the sun over the western hills.

It had been a very pleasant day, but one of hard work as usual. My first task of the day had been the same for the past five years, emptying the vessels in the monks' dormitory, as ever, ensuring that there was no sign of me carrying out the task. I would then go to the kitchen to prepare the morning meal of oats, which by this stage was very much down to me. Daniel had seen a marked deterioration in his general health, and Donald's attacks were now a matter of great concern.

The bells had sounded seven times so far today as every day, for prayers; just once more, before everyone would go to bed, and then it would all start again.

Everyone, that is all the Brothers, Daniel and Donald, and of course myself, had, as on many such evenings, gathered out in the fields this evening, and were enjoying the last embers of the sun. It was going to be a truly lovely day on the morrow, if the glorious setting sun was anything to go by. The Brothers were gathered together, by the wall. Father Francis had set himself somewhat apart from them. Daniel was stood at the lower gate to the field. I stood not far away from him, as I liked to be near him due to his now increasing unsteadiness, and

Donald was stood in the centre of the field amid his flock of sheep, his shepherd's staff in his hand, stood proud, the lord of all he surveyed.

Suddenly, and from nowhere, a horse and rider came over the wall, the rider wearing a steel helmet on his head, waving a sword in his hand. Another horse and rider came over the wall, then a third, and a fourth rider was at the top gate, pulling at it, and dragging it open.

Donald ran forward, towards the first rider, his staff held high, challenging the rider. The rider turned his horse to face Donald, bringing his sword down and across the chest of the poor young shepherd. The blood poured from his chest, as he fell backwards to the ground. I could see his body give a twitch, then stillness; my friend was dead. I looked to the rider; I wanted to see what manner of man was this, who had slain my friend. There was no face in the steel helmet, I looked hard, but no, there was no face. Was this some demon sent to wreak revenge for all our sins; how could there be no face?

The horseman heeled his horse around to face the opposite way, and started to herd the flock of sheep out of the field. Oh no, this cannot be, this is surely not right, my eyes are deceiving me, I thought. But it was.

"Faither, Faither, it is me, Isaac, Faither, it is me, Isaac. Fadder, Fadder, it's Rob, your son, Fadder." The rider pulled the horse up hard, its back legs digging hard into the ground, and looked around. It was my father.

"Rob, oh Rob, my boy, hurry take my arm," as he swapped his sword to his other hand, he held out his right arm, which I grabbed, and was whisked upon the horse, and behind my father, whom I held on tight to, still not believing what was taking place.

As I took up my position behind my father, I could see Father Francis coming across the field towards my father, his fist held high. He reached the side of the horse, and brought his fist down upon my father's thigh. My father brought his sword back into his right hand

and brought it down with great force on to Father Francis' shoulder, just at the side of his neck. The old monk went down on to his knees, the blood spurting from his neck. He looked up, and his eyes made contact with mine. He knew this was his time, the look was that of knowing, and I think, at that moment, we both recalled the words spoken some time before: "The last face you will ever see is mine…" He then slumped forward, and fell face down on the ground.

Brother Matthias came running over, and my father brought up his sword again.

"No, Fadder, please no, not this one," I said as I placed my hand under his elbow to prevent his sword coming down. Brother Matthias reached Father Francis, and gathered him up in his arms. He looked up at me, sat behind my father. "Thank you for everything, Brother Matthias, I will never forget you," I said, as our horse was spurred on and we started to gallop away.

As we went I raised my arm, waving as I went, not daring to look around, to see the scene I had left. My one regret as we rode away was that I had never said farewell to my dear old friend, Daniel, who for this past five years had been my father, and had done so much to make my stay as pleasant as possible. I knew that I would never see the poor old man again.

I held on tighter than ever. This was my father, there was something familiar about the smell of his clothes. Yes, this was my father, he had not been killed after all, but I wanted to see him, which I could not sat behind him, but oh the joy of holding him so tightly.

As I sat on the back of that horse, I went over in my mind the events of this evening; the horse coming over the wall, my poor friend, Donald, killed by my father, Father Francis, killed by my father, and that look from Father Francis, that knowing look. I wondered, when my time came, would Father Francis' face be the last thing I would see? Time would tell!

And how had I not seen my father, when first I set eyes on him? There appeared to be no face in his helmet; was this just a trick of the twilight?

I so wanted to see him and talk to him, but sat behind him I just had to hang on and allow my thoughts to occupy my mind.

We rode on through the night, herding the sheep we had taken from the manse fields, but there were cattle along with the sheep; I did not know where they came from. Although there was a lot of livestock to be herded, we were making good progress, away from my home of the last five years, and I was far too excited at what was to come to have any regrets.

We had been riding for quite a long time when, as the initial excitement started to wane, I thought of my mother and Sarah. Oh my goodness, I was going to see my mother and Sarah! The excitement grew even more intense, so that I hung on even harder, I thought my arms would break.

The first words I heard my father say, since leaving the manse, were, "Ease up there, Rob, you're squeezing the life out of me, don't worry, you won't fall."

It was so lovely to hear his voice again, though now I thought his speech to be slightly slurred, which I had not detected earlier. Maybe it was the wind, distorting his voice. Mother and Sarah once again occupied my thoughts; how I wanted the night to pass quickly, so that I could see them again.

My thoughts as the night passed on returned to the journey that had brought me this way, many years before, behind Will, and the loneliness and fear and sorrow I felt that fateful night; that night that would have such an impact upon my life, and that of my family.

As the hills became more desolate than earlier, the dawn started to break over the hill tops. I heard my father say, "We'll have to take cover soon, until the night comes."

The animals were then herded round into a small but deep gorge between the rolling hills. My father turned and put his arm out for me to get down. I took hold and was lifted from the horse and placed on the ground. My father slipped from the saddle and put his arms around me, holding me tighter than anyone had ever done before. "Rob, oh my Rob, I thought I had lost you, oh my boy how grand it is to have you back, we thought you were dead. I never thought I would ever see you again, oh my dear Rob."

Although I had been only seven when I was taken from my home I could never remember my father showing such emotion as this. I was not able to speak, due to excitement, elation and relief, at once more being with my father again.

We sat down on the ground, and my father took off his helmet, and I gasped.

"Sorry, Rob, you weren't to know," he said. The left side of his face had almost disappeared; there was a large indentation where the axe had sunk into his skull, his eye was missing, his jaw was sunk in and his mouth did not open properly, but nonetheless, this was my father.

"It's all right, Fadder, I saw the axe hitting you, I thought you were dead. I saw you fall to the ground; Will said I should not have seen it but I did."

"Who is Will then?" my father asked.

"He was the one who took me away," I replied.

"Well, if we see him again I'll have his head," said my father.

"Oh, Will was not a bad man, and he looked after me, against the other riders, who wanted to kill me. He left me with the monks instead of killing me, so I suppose I owe him my life," I said.

"If he's a Scottie, you owe him nowt," said my father. "Anyway, my lad, you are bound to be worn out, get your head down, for tonight we head home," he continued.

"What of Mother and Sarah?" I asked.

"They are all well, now to sleep; we will talk all through the night tonight, and rest easy, my Rob, for nothing will harm you this night or any other from this day onward."

I awoke about mid-afternoon; the sun was still riding high and there was still plenty of warmth left in the day. Slowly looking around the scene that befell me, I could see three other people lying on the ground asleep. Indeed, one was in such a deep sleep, his snoring no doubt could be heard back at the manse, a day's ride away. I stood up and took in the whole vista; there were four men stationed in various positions around the livestock, that made seven in total, but I was sure there had been around ten or more when I had bedded down this morning, though I could have been mistaken. From the far side of the livestock came a rider, with steel helmet and lance set in front of the horse's saddle, held in by a stiff leather strap. As he neared I could make out that it was my father.

"You sleep well, Rob?" he said.

"Aye, Faither, it was a good wee nap," I replied.

"I'll tell ye what, Rob, you'll have te rid your sell o' that Scottie talk," said Father.

I had not realised that I had changed the way I spoke, but with spending so much time with Daniel and Donald, I suppose it was bound to happen.

Suddenly, from out of the north, over the ridge into the valley where we were, came five riders, yelling and screaming at the top of their voices. Father yelled out, "Hot Trod, Hot Trod!" The Scotties were riding in at full gallop, with lances down; they meant business. Father told me to get down behind the large rock that was to our left, while he mounted up, taking his lance from its holster and levelling it in readiness. The three men who had been asleep were running towards their horses, which, when on a raid, were never taken out of their tack, so that they were always ready. They were in their saddles and lining up beside father, and charged forward, to meet the Scotties. Two more riders who had been watching the herd came in behind the first four, giving a second wave attack, then from out of the southern horizon, the others of our party came into view. They had been scouting forward along our intended trail, and were coming back, and as they had come into view must have seen the Hot Trodders charging in, so had drawn their lances and were bringing in a third wave of attack. The Scotties, seeing this, pulled hard on their reins. The horses, digging in deep with their back legs, turned hard on the bit and fled back over the ridge as fast as they had come. My father's group continued giving chase, to make sure they left, and did not try another attack later.

After a while our party of four riders came back over the ridge, at a slow canter, and approached the rock that I was still sheltering behind. As they neared they all dismounted, and there was much chatter and laughter.

"You alright there, Rob?" came my father's voice.

"Aye, fine, Fadder," I replied.

"Good lad, come and meet everyone, you never got time last night," said Father.

I emerged from my rock and was greeted by nine men, all dressed in various sorts of armoury, all with steel helmets of differing design, some with peaks, some with peaks and cheek plates, like Father's, and some that had a brim going all the way around, culminating in a point at the back and front. Some of the riders wore steel breast plates, others had heavy leather jacks, some with small metal plates sewn on all over the jack, which protected them against sword and lance, and there were those whose jack were of heavy leather, with strips of even heavier leather sewn over the jack, to afford some protection, which was the preferred attire of my father.

Father pointed to the first of the riders; the tallest of the party, slim, bronzed skin, and light brown to blond hair, he reminded me very much of the way I remembered my mother.

"This is your Uncle James, and next to him is your Uncle Thomas. They are both your mother's brothers. The next one along is your Uncle Arthur, and next to him your Uncle John; they are my brothers, and bigger villains you'll not meet in the same place anywhere," he said as they all laughed loudly. "Behind these rogues, we have Michael Dodds, and next to him his son, Raymond, both fine gentlemen, and last of all we have our dear friend, Richard Robson. His father and two brothers are over with the livestock. And there, my lad, we have as fine a band of riders as these Borders have ever seen."

"What of the Scotties?" I enquired.

Thomas Charlton, my uncle, laughed. "I'll tell ye what, young Rob, they'll be back in Melrose as we speak. I'll be bound, when they saw how many of us there were, and who we were, I'll wager they filled their pants."

This was accompanied by loud and raucous laughter, by all there. I felt much assured among such strong individuals as these, my family, again, for yes, I was again a Milburn, Rob Milburn and proud.

Although we would have waited until dusk before setting off, due to the 'Hot Trod', it was felt that no danger was liable from them, because as my father said, they had badly miscalculated our numbers, that although we were but a small party, only three or four had been seen actually raiding. The Scotties in their haste to catch us up had thought five riders would suffice to overcome our party, so we rounded the stock up and set forth for England and home.

As we rode through the night, unlike the previous night, up behind my father, happy to be in a position where I could hold him, we talked all through the night. He asked me to tell him all that had happened, from the night of the raid, right up to his raid of the manse.

I had already mentioned Will, how he had lifted me from the ground outside the bastle, how I had seen him, Father that is, being cut down. How I had been carried across the horse into Scotland, of the threat to my life and how Will had left me with the monks.

I told him of my life with the monks, of my duties as a Lay-Brother, of having to get up in the middle of the night, every night, and of the bell sounding eight times a day, and having to stop and say prayers, of collecting and emptying the vessels in the dormitory, and of the consequences of any spillages, of working in the kitchen with Daniel, and of how good he had been to me, acting as a father figure over the five years I was there. There of course was Brother Matthias; how he had taken responsibility, for me and my tuition, of learning to read and write in both English and Latin. I told him of being renamed Isaac, and of Father Francis, and of the way he hated me and took every opportunity to strike out at me, and of how, not long before the raid to take me home, I had fought back against Father Francis.

The night went quickly, because I was still relating my story. I could see the dawn starting to break over the fell tops, and this was enhanced by the fact that I recognised the valley we were entering, it was my valley; after all this time I still recognised my valley. We were almost home! The first bastle we came to was that of my Charlton uncles; some of the stock was herded off to stay there, then we would be next. The Dodds and the Robsons lived farther down, at the other end of the valley. I was amazed at how much I could recall, from the time I was such a small boy.

We trotted on, along with my father's brothers, who lived over the hill in the next valley, and it wasn't long before they peeled off, taking their claimed stock with them.

"It's there, that's ours, Father, it is, isn't it, our home?" I cried out.

"Aye it's ours, Rob, you're home at last," Father said. We rode up to the bastle and Father lowered me to the ground, on the side of the horse away from the house. I heard Father say, "I've got you a present, my lass."

I ran around the horse. My mother was stood there; there was no light, I could just see her outline in the doorway. She pushed open the yett, and I ran to her. "Mother, Mother, I'm home."

Mother screamed, "Rob, Rob, it isn't you, it can't be, Rob!" Surely all the valley heard her cry out. I wrapped my arms around her and I held her so very tightly. I could feel the tears welling up, but I must not let them come, I was now grown up, I had to be strong and show how mature I now was. Mother sobbed and sobbed, and continued to cry out through her sobs, "Rob, oh Rob, my baby, my baby's back, thank you God, oh thank you for answering my prayers."

We were still in our embrace when Father came to the door, having had time to unsaddle his horse, wipe her down, and stable her.

"Come along, you two, you would think you hadn't seen each other for five years." Mother managed to laugh through her tears of joy. We entered the bastle together, Mother pushing me forward, up the ladder, beyond the cattle. As I got to the living area, I turned and waited for Mother to reach the top of the ladder, then I asked, "Where is Sarah?" to which Mother replied, "She is now with her husband, and she is having a baby, you are to be an uncle very soon". I was so shocked at the news that I was not able to ask more of my sister at this time.

The subject changed as Mother turned to me and said how much I had grown, and that she would hardly recognise me; not only was I big for my age but how strong I had become. We all settled by the fire, and it was not until then that I saw my mother properly for the first time, and I was quite taken aback by how she had aged. Yes, I had been away for a long time, but she had aged much beyond the five years we had been apart. Her once light brown to blonde hair was now streaked with grey, and that once silken sheen that came off her hair was now dry and wispy. Her face was now quite heavily lined, where I remember her having the softest skin, as I had sat on her lap and nestled into her cheeks before I had left. I tried and hopefully succeeded in subduing my alarm at the changes I saw. Mother then asked me to tell her all that had taken place over the years, so I set off again relating the saga that had taken all night to tell my father as we had returned home.

Chapter 7

A Family Again

I awoke in my old bed. The last thing I could remember was starting on my story, sat at the fire with both my parents sat with me. I raised my weary head and propped myself up on my elbow, rubbing my eyes with my other hand.

"You poor lad, you fell asleep mid-sentence, by the fire; Father had to pick you up and carry you to bed. My, you must have been so very tired, you have slept nearly all day," my mother greeted me. "Now get yourself up and I'll get you some food."

I dragged my weary body from my bed and staggered over to the table, but before sitting down, went over to my mother and gave her a hug.

"Oh Rob, my darling boy, I have sat here all day and have done nothing but watch you sleep, and it has been the most wonderful sight a mother could ever behold. I have missed you so very much."

I broke loose my embrace and looked at my mother, as she smiled, and I now saw that radiance that I remembered. I sat myself down and Mother placed a bowl of pottage in front of me, and I started to eat, then broke off.

"Mother?" I enquired. "Sarah, you say she is married, but who to?"

"Ruben Bell, I don't know if you remember seeing him," she replied.

"A Bell!" I exclaimed. "But Bells were poor, were they not? I think I can remember their bastle, it was a horrible dirty place. Father said once as we passed by to Hexham that he wouldn't let cattle live like they do."

"Now, now, Rob, we must abide by Sarah's choice; people said when I married your father that I had married below myself, which of course as you know was complete nonsense, and we have been very happy, apart from losing you for all this time, and I would not have wanted to be with any other man," Mother said.

This did allay my initial reaction; however, I still felt a great unease at the thought of Sarah, my sister, with a Bell.

"When can I go and see her, Mother?" I asked. But she said that I must wait a while, as we must not go uninvited. I was somewhat upset that I could not see my sister, and that she would not be aware of my return to our home.

Father came up the ladder, and said, "Come along, Rob, when you have finished eating and we will check the stock in the fields."

I quickly gulped down my bowl of pottage, and said, "Must go, Mother," as I scrambled down the ladder. I could see my mother stood by the fire with her arms folded across her chest, with a broad smile on her face.

As I went out to the field, I could see Father stood among the sheep we had brought down from Scotland.

"Come over here, Rob," called my father. I walked to where he was standing. "I will say this, your friends at the monastery, Rob, they certainly know how to look after sheep. I've never seen such a well-kept flock, their fleeces are in really good shape, and I've checked some of their feet, and nearly all have been recently cut back and cleaned in the clove. Your shepherd friend knew what he was about."

"Yes," I replied. "That was Donald."

"Was that the poor lad that I had to take my sword to, Rob?" said Father.

"Aye, I'm afraid it was," I said.

"I'm sorry about that, Rob, but he came at me, I could not take a chance."

"It is all right, Father," I replied, "It is what he wanted."

"He wanted to die?" Father said with great surprise in his voice. I explained about the malady which beset Donald, and of how he had once told me that he did not want to die as a result of his illness; also of how his malady had recently become much worse, so although I was sad that he was dead, I was also pleased that he had died the way I hoped he wanted.

Father explained to me that when he and his kinsmen go raiding, whether it be in Scotland or England, they never want to kill anyone, and will only do so if there is no other way, and they only raid for what they can take, because that is the way we live our lives here. He also explained that although we may raid mostly over the Border, we still have respect for the Scotties, and that we do not dislike them, but if we have to kill them, then that is as it must be, but there are many Englishmen who would be better put to the sword, than any Scottie.

We spent the rest of the morning walking around the stock, and re-familiarising myself with my home. I was surprised at the amount I could remember of the old place, but there had been some changes. There was now a stone stairway on the outside of the bastle, which my uncles had built, using stone from the old Roman wall. They had put it in when Father was poorly, many months after the attack, when he was just starting to walk around, but was not able to use the indoor ladder, because he was too unsteady on his feet. There were also extra walls around the bastle, and Father explained that it gave better protection for the stock.

There was one thing that I had not asked, and that was how he had found out where I was. Father told me that he didn't know where I was, and that it had been pure chance that he had found me.

At midday we went inside and Mother laid out our afternoon meal. During the meal she asked what sort of food I was used to getting from the monks. I was able to explain that I had helped prepare many of the meals, along with Daniel, and how over the years, as Daniel became less able to do so much, it fell upon me to do more in the kitchen. With great delight, Mother turned to Father and said, "Oh my, Tom, I will be able to hand over my chores to Rob, whenever I want to take a day off." They both laughed. I thought it a most awful idea, but kept my silence.

During the meal I once again asked about Sarah, and when could I go to see her, but again Mother was somewhat dismissive, saying that I would have to wait until we were invited, or that we may see her if we were to go to Hexham, as it was on the way, but that we must not intrude. This was not what I wanted to hear, and I was starting to feel increasingly frustrated at being kept away from my sister, but there was little I could do, so I resigned myself to having to wait.

After being back for five days, I found the frustration had risen to the point where I could no longer go without seeing Sarah, and though not wishing to disobey the wishes of my parents, I resolved that on the morrow, as I was still waking very early, as was the way at the manse, I would take myself to see my sister.

Before the dawn had broken I was awake, and slowly slipped from my bed. As I crawled around on the floor on my hands and knees, searching for my boots, I felt something under Sarah's old bed. It was the slate she used to draw on, using the white stone. Could I find the stone? I continued to quietly search, but it was fruitless; nonetheless, I took the slate with me as I descended the ladder, hoping that I might find something to write with. I did not know if Father could read, but was sure that Mother, being a Charlton, would have had some learning. I was only able to find a piece of granite, from outside, but was pleased to find that it marked the slate, and wrote, 'Gone to see Sarah, Rob.' I then carefully went back up the ladder and laid the slate at the top, on the wooden floor.

Excitedly, I set forth, not entirely knowing where I was bound, but sure of the general direction. I was fairly sure that at a steady pace, from what Father had said, it would take me until late morning to early afternoon to reach where my sister would be. I therefore hoped that the sun would remain in the sky, and not cloud over, thus allowing me to use it as a guide to the time I would be close to my destination.

By mid-morning I reached a stage in my journey when I passed by a bastle. The lady of the house was outside, stood by a heavy wooden table, that had a wooden tub, filled with water, and she was washing some clothes. By her side was a young girl, pretty and very fair of hair, and around the same age as myself, if I was any judge.

I approached cautiously, and asked as politely as I was able, "Excuse me, Ma'am, but I am looking for the home of Ruben Bell and his wife, Sarah."

"Good day, young Sir," she replied, "And may I enquire what reason you wish to know?" she replied as politely.

"Sarah is my sister, and I wish to visit her," I continued.

"Then, young Sir, you must be Rob Milburn," she said.

"Yes, I am, Ma'am, but how would you know that?" I replied, with some astonishment.

"Because, young Rob, I am Mary Dodds and this is my daughter, Annie." I looked towards Annie, who smiled broadly, and she was even prettier than I had first observed. "And my husband, Michael, and son, Raymond, were with your father when he got you back from the Scotties," she said.

"Indeed, Ma'am, I met them on the journey back, and was glad of their company," I said.

"My, you are a polite young man, those Scotties may be rogues but they have brought you up well, or should not your lovely mother also take some of the credit?" she said smilingly.

"She surely must," I replied.

After our cordial conversation, Mary Dodds directed me to where Sarah lived, which was now quite close. I bid farewell to Annie and Mistress Dodds, thanking them both for their help, and went hurriedly on my way.

It was not long before I came upon a sheil. This is a single-storey house, which is usually used in the summer, when the flocks are at their summertime grazing. I stood for a while, observing the sheil, to see who might be about. There was no movement to behold, but for some rather unkempt sheep about the place, and the odd head of cattle. I approached the building, the area around which was heavily trodden by the stock, and was greatly mudded. There was also a goodly amount of animal muck about the place, through which I now saw a woman with a wooden yoke about her shoulders and a bucket at each end of the yoke, filled with water, trudging through the squalor, unsteadily. Her clothes were soiled and her hair untidy, and she walked with her head down, but was this my Sarah, my sister, in this awful state? I neared her as she approached, unaware of my presence.

"Sarah?" I called, hesitantly. She raised her head in a startled manner, gasping with fright. I repeated, "Sarah?"

"Yes, Sir, who enquires?" she asked.

"Sarah, it's me, Rob," I said.

"Rob... Rob who?" she replied.

"Sarah, it's your brother, Rob, I am back home, it's me," I said excitedly. Sarah let go of the ropes that held the buckets to the yoke and clasped both her hands to her mouth in total disbelief, the tears welling up in her eyes.

"No it cannot be, my Rob is dead, he is surely dead," she said through tear filled eyes.

"No, it is me, Sarah, it really is," I said.

We flung our arms around each other, and where I had been the big brave man with Mother, I was not able to do so with Sarah, for we both sobbed on to each other's shoulders until we were both quite wet. This was a time which I had longed for over the years I was in Scotland, for I had always adored my sister, but we had never actually showed each other affection, though there was never the need; we knew what each other felt. But to hold her was truly wonderful.

After what seemed like forever, we let go of each other and Sarah took me in to the sheil. It was of stone structure, with a roof of turf and the floors were of mud. There were a crude wooden table and two chairs by the wall opposite the fire, and at the far end of the single roomed dwelling was a filthy bed. I could not believe that my sister was living in such squalor as this, and asked her why she had married this Ruben Bell, but she gently put her hand across my mouth to silence me and said that he was a good man and that I must not judge him unfairly.

We sat and talked for an age, when I was able to tell her much of what had happened to me over the past five years, and of how Father had chanced on the Abbey grounds on a raid, and of how we came together. I was also able to tell her of Mother's surprise and delight at my return. Sarah said that she knew exactly how Mother felt, as she had experienced the same, when seeing me.

Suddenly I heard this gruff voice bellow out, from the doorway, "Who is this in my house?"

Sarah stood and almost apologetically said, "It's Rob, my brother, come to see me."

"I thought he was dead, killed by the Scotties," he replied tersely. I stood up to greet him, but he just stepped into the sheil, took a step to one side of the door, then said, "Well you've seen her now, so you can be on your way."

I turned to Sarah and smiled and said my farewells and that I would see her again soon. I then turned and walked out of the sheil, Bell following behind me. He put his grubby hand on my shoulder heavily and leaned forward menacingly and said in a hushed hoarse voice, "Don't bother hurrying back and keeping my wife from her chores. Now be off with you." I did not turn around and show him that he had worried me, but worry me he did; I just kept on walking.

I passed by the Dodds' bastle after a while, where Annie was stood outside. I waved as I went by, and she waved back, accompanied with that broad smile, which helped to cheer my heavy heart. I would have liked to have stopped at the Dodds', but I was in no state to be cordial and engage in conversation with anyone at the moment.

As I continued my journey home my thoughts were solely with my dear sister, and her plight, at having to endure life with that vermin. I resolved to say none of this to my parents on my return. I would apologise for the deceitful way I had left to visit Sarah, although, in my heart I knew that I was not sorry, but indeed glad that I was now aware of the life Sarah was having to endure. I also resolved that I would return to see my sister, as soon as it was prudent to do so, and that again I would keep it from my parents. I was not happy, that having just returned after five years away from my family, I commenced my return by being deceitful in my actions, and not wholly truthful in what I was saying, but I knew of no other way of continuing my chosen path.

Sarah had told me that Ruben visited his parents on the same day each week, and that I had been lucky to choose this day to visit. I would make sure that my return visit would be on this same day, be it next week or the week after, and I would not stay as long as today, in order that I may avoid that Bell.

I returned home just as the sun was starting to dip in the sky, for I had been fortunate that the sky had remained clear throughout the day, thus helping me to time my journey. Mother was waiting at the bastle door, with arms folded and a stern look on her face.

"How dare you do this to me; you have only just arrived back and you put me through a full day of worry, how ungrateful you are," she snorted.

"Mother, I am so very sorry to have been so thoughtless, but I could not wait a moment longer to see Sarah," I pleaded. "Did you get the message I wrote?" I added.

"Yes, how clever of you, my darling," she said glowingly, then added, "But that does not excuse your behaviour."

"I know it doesn't excuse me, Mother, for there is no excuse, but I had to see Sarah, for which you may beat me to within an inch of my life, but I honestly must say, I cannot be sorry to have seen her after so long." Mother then just put her arms out and gathered me in, and hugged me, running her hand through my hair, adding, "You really are a lovely boy," then added, "but that does not mean you are forgiven."

"No, Mother," I replied, as I kissed her on the cheek.

We went inside and she placed a bowl of pottage in front of me. Today, fresh mutton had been added, giving it a richness and flavour that made me savour every mouthful, or was it that I had not eaten since yesterday and the events of the day had taken over any thought of food? I am sure Sarah would have offered me food, but we were so taken up with each other and the filling in of the lost years, that we never gave a thought to nourishment.

As soon as I had finished eating, which I had done greedily, which Mother did not fail to mention, she asked me of Sarah. As I had already decided, I told her that she was well, and of how I had first confronted her, and of her obvious surprise, and delight. I spoke of how we talked and talked, and how eventually I set off home. Mother asked about the health of Ruben, but I said that he was visiting his parents, and that I had come away before his return. I could see by her reaction that she was pleased at that piece of information, by the look of almost relief.

It was evident even to a twelve year old young man, as I regarded myself, that she was not at ease with the situation of Sarah's marriage to the creature, but I tried to make light of the day, and I was of the opinion that Mother was quite pleased with my actions, but still displeased at me. I asked of Father's whereabouts, and Mother told me he had gone to see her brother, Thomas, about some of the stock they had brought back from Scotland, and would be back shortly.

No sooner had she got the words out of her mouth when we heard the yett being closed and locked and Father coming up the ladder. I ran and embraced him as he put both feet on the floor, from leaving the ladder.

"Well, I hope your mother has scolded you for your stupidity," he said.

"Yes, Father, she has scolded me severely," I replied, looking over to Mother and smiling.

"Get away with you, you rascal," he said, as he roughed my hair and pushed me away playfully. "Well, how is your sister then?" he enquired. I told him the same story I had told my mother, and at the end of my tale he asked about Ruben Bell, as Mother had done. Again I told the same story and they seemed satisfied with the news they received, but I was aware, more than ever, of an underlying tension from both my parents that all was not well.

That night I slept the sleep of the dead, and for the first time since I arrived back from my term at the manse I did not wake in the middle of the night, but slept through until I was awoken by Mother stoking the fire in readiness for the morning meal.

After eating I went out with Father. Our first chore of the day was to muck out the cattle area in the base of the bastle. While we did this, Mother took the opportunity to sweep out the upper floor, sending all the dust and straw falling down on our heads as we worked, our protests being greeted with loud laughter from above. Father turned to me. His one eye, I swear, was filled with a tear, and he said, "I have never known her laugh, since the day you were taken, what a lovely sound she makes." I felt a warmth fill within me; I was home and I was surrounded by love.

The next week passed by uneventfully, where I started to get into a routine, and Father started to give me regular chores around the homestead, which although greatly occupying my time did little to occupy my mind and the ever present thought of Sarah.

I did over the next few days mention Sarah to my parents, but just within normal conversation. I also mentioned my visit to the Dodds on the way to see Sarah, the news of which I could see greatly pleased both my parents. I told Mother of the way Mary Dodds had spoken of her, to which I could see Mother was quite proud, but received the news with the comment that Mary Dodds was a delightful woman, and that she much enjoyed spending time with her.

It was one day short of two weeks that had passed since my visit to Sarah and I felt it was well time I returned. This time I forewarned my parents of my intent, the news being greeted rather coolly, but there was a certain reservation that it was bound to happen.

The morning came and I arose early, as before, readied myself quietly, then before I departed upon my journey, crept over to where Mother lay in bed, and bent over and gently kissed her cheek. Her hand came out from under her bed cover and patted my cheek. "Be careful, my pet," she whispered.

I smiled and tiptoed away to the top of the ladder, then descended to the cattle hold, quietly opening the wooden door, then the yett, securing both before leaving.

The morning was lightly overcast, and though there had been some rain the past few days, it did not look likely today. I set off with a light heart, in the thought of seeing my sister again, and the likelihood that on the way there or back, I might see Annie Dodds. My pace had been similar to the last time, and though the sun was not there to time my progress, I was sure it was mid-morning as I passed the bastle of the Dodds' family. All was still, so I therefore concluded that they had gone to Hexham Market for the day.

Having passed the Dodds' bastle I then veered off the track and climbed steadily over the ridge, to see the sheil where my sister was. As before, I waited and took in the scene, ensuring that the Bell was well away, and not posing a threat. After a short while I saw Sarah emerge from the sheil, going to one of the outbuildings, where there were young calves. She was carrying a bucket, I presumed with milk, to feed the calves. I continued to watch until she had finished, then descended the other side of the ridge toward the sheil. She looked up as I neared the farmstead, and saw me coming, and waved. Even from the distance I was from her I could see the smile that adorned her face, and through the filth of her clothes she was forced to wear, her beauty shone through.

I ran to greet her and we embraced as we reached each other. "Come, Rob, the last time you came I was dreadful, for I never offered you any nourishment nor drink for your thirst, what must you think of your sister?" she said, apologetically.

"I think I am fortunate to have a lovely sister," I replied. She leaned over as we entered the sheil, placed her hand on my shoulder, and kissed me on the cheek.

"You're a good lad, Rob, now come, let us eat."

I sat down with Sarah at the table, and said that water to drink was all I required. The conversation flowed easily, Sarah asking of Mother and Father, and of how I was settling in back at home. The question that was on my lips, and had been on my mind since first seeing her after my return, was about her present situation, and now was the time to broach the subject.

I felt my toes curling in my boots, and beads of sweat start to rise upon my brow, then hesitantly I blurted out, "Why Sarah, why did you marry Ruben Bell? You were made for better things than to spend your life like this."

I now felt that I had said too much, but it had been said and there it was, and I felt my body start to shake a little. I do not know whether this was with fear of my sister's reaction or my embarrassment.

Sarah looked almost lost as she answered, "But he is a good man, Rob."

"Sarah, he is not a good man, he is dirty, uncouth and of low breeding. How could you give yourself to such a person? I just do not know how you could first lie with such an animal, how, Sarah?"

I had gone too far, I should not have been so forthright, but should have had more thought to my sister's feelings, for I now saw the tears starting to build in her eyes. Then, in convulsions of tears she, in tones from her lower gut, screamed out, "He took me, Rob, he took me!"

Her crying was now uncontrollable. I knelt in front of her, holding both her forearms, as she cupped her face in her hands, the tears so profuse that they were seeping through her fingers, and down her arms, and on to my hands.

"Oh Sarah, I am so sorry, but why did you not tell Father when it happened, he would have been able to do something?" I said.

"I could not do that, Rob. You know that relations between the Milburns and Bells have always been strained; we have not been at feud, but it would take little to cause a feud between our families, and that would have resulted in a blood bath, and with Father having not been in the best of health since you were taken, and Mother was heartbroken when you were taken and has never got over the events of that night, I could not cause a war between our families," Sarah replied, through her sobs.

I asked if the coming baby was as a result of Bell taking her, and she said yes, because she had said nothing of what had happened, but when her stomach started to swell, both Mother and Father had noticed, and had forced her to say who it had been, but she had kept the full facts to herself. We continued to talk. All the while I was trying to comfort her, and though it took some time, she did eventually regain her composure.

When Sarah had calmed and I had reassured her that I would say nothing, though I knew that to keep such a secret would be the most difficult thing I would ever be asked to do, I told her that I would keep visiting, but that I should go, and not cause her any trouble. The words were hardly out of my mouth when at the door was Ruben Bell. This was what I had wanted to avoid, but he had returned early.

"What are you doing here, Milburn?" he scowled. "I thought I told you to stay away; now be on your way, and keep away."

I got up from my seat and walked past Bell. His upper lip curled, showing his brown teeth. I looked away, as I brushed past him. He followed me outside, and I felt his presence behind me, then I felt him push the middle of my back, at the same time saying, "If I see you here again, I will beat the life out of you, you little squirt, do you hear me, Milburn? This is Bell land, and I don't want your breed about my place."

I could feel the rage growing within me, my skin started to tingle and burn, my body was shaking. I kept my head down and saw in front of me a large stone. I looked around and Bell had turned and was returning to the sheil. I bent down and took up the stone. It barely fit in my hand. I turned and threw that stone with every ounce of strength that my body possessed. I had no idea of what I hoped to achieve, but the stone careered through the air and caught Bell on the side of the head, just above his right ear. His body went rigid, and he fell forward, like a tree being felled. I swear that as he hit the ground, his body bounced. He landed in the thick mud and manure that surrounded the sheil. Without a thought, I rushed forward, to where he lay. Slithering to a halt, I flung myself down and sat firmly upon his head, pressing it firmly into the mud.

"Sarah, Sarah, come quick, hurry!" I yelled. Sarah appeared from the corner of the sheil, just as his legs started to kick and thrash around. "Sarah, hurry, sit on his legs," I begged.

"Oh Rob, what have you done?" she said.

"Do it!" I screamed. Bell was starting to regain consciousness, and his strength was growing. I did not know if I could hold him, but Sarah dropped down on to his legs, and this greatly hampered his resistance. After a while of struggle, he gave out a mighty effort to break free, which caused me to lose my footing. My legs slipped forward, thus causing my weight to shift on his head, and this in turn caused greater weight to be thrust down on his head. I felt his body go limp, but I did not ease up, for fear that he might not be finished. I lay there, pushing down for all I was worth, not knowing what struggles Sarah may be enduring at the other end of the Bell.

After I had laid there for some while, and was fairly sure the Bell had expired, I slowly got to my feet, still keeping my eye fixed upon the Bell, in case of any likely movement. I then saw Sarah. Laying the length of his legs, I went to her, took hold of her arms and said, "It's over, come."

"Oh Rob, what have we done? We have killed a man," said Sarah, visibly shaking.

"We have killed no man, we have rid the land of nothing other than vermin, vermin I say." The anger had not yet subsided.

"What will we do now? We will be hanged, oh my God, we are to be hanged," Sarah sobbed.

"We will not hang, Sarah; now give me time to think what next to do," I said. My body now shaking, my head spinning, almost unable to think, I staggered over to the side of the sheil to where the wood pile lay and I set myself down to gather my thoughts.

Sarah came over, now somewhat composed. "Rob, we cannot leave him there, what are we to do?" she said.

"Wait, I think I may have the solution to our problem, Sarah. The burn that runs behind your sheil, does it run down the valley, towards the Bells' bastle?" I enquired.

"Yes, why?" she asked.

"Are there any parts of the burn where the banks are steeper, so that it cannot be seen from the path?" I further asked.

"Yes, well down the valley, why?" she replied. I ignored all Sarah's questions, being so deep in thought.

"Sarah, do you think we could carry the Bell along the burn, to where the banks are high? If we can, we will leave him there, clean off the mud from his clothes, then walk back up the burn to the sheil. There will be no sign that anyone has been there, and it will look as if he slipped, fell into the burn, and either banged his head or drowned, what do you think?" I ventured.

"Dare we do such a thing?" she said. I replied that we had little option, and that we must hurry, and do the deed.

We ventured over to where the Bell lay, I never having taken my eyes from him, the entire time we had been talking. Nonetheless, it was with some trepidation that I bent forward and took hold of the body from under the arms, Sarah taking station at his feet, and we started to transport the Bell to his watery resting place. The first few steps were quite easy for us both, but every step thereafter increased in difficulty, and as we reached the burn, we had to lay him down. Not a word passed either of our lips as we struggled with our burden, and after a short while we continued. The progress now even harder, as we had stepped down into the burn, the idea being that no footsteps would be seen in the soft ground, either side of the burn, when the body was found. Again, after a short while we lay our burden down. Through my ignorance at the time, I never gave thought to Sarah being heavy with child, and the strain this may be having on her. Nonetheless, we carried on, until eventually we reached a section of the burn that was far enough from the sheil, and with banks of sufficient height, that the body could not be seen from the path.

"This will do," I said, as we lay the body down. "No, it will not do," I corrected, "He is facing the wrong way, it must look as if he came from the direction of the Bell bastle." We then picked the body up and turned him around, then lay him down. I lay his head in such a fashion that the bump he had on his head, just above the right ear, was resting on a stone, in the bed of the burn. We then started to clean off some of the mud that was on his face and clothes, to remove any trace of him lying in the filth that was around the sheil. Sarah was having difficulty touching him, so I told her to keep watch, while I finished off.

"Not too clean," I said, finishing the task. "It would not do to get him too clean, for if a clean Bell were found anywhere, it would be out of place," I jested.

"How can you jest so at a time like this?" my sister asked. I thought it best not to answer, but said for us to make our way back to the sheil, the way we had come, along the bed of the burn.

"What do we do now, Rob? My mind is in such turmoil," Sarah asked.

"I have been giving the matter some thought as we trudged along the burn," I said, "and what I think is that I leave for home soon, and you will have to stay at the sheil tonight. Will you be able to do that, Sarah?" I queried.

"Yes, if I must," she said.

"Good, then on the morrow, you must go to the Bells' bastle and enquire why Ruben did not return last night. Of course they will say he did, and you will insist that he did not return, and of course, you will be upset, do you understand, Sarah?" I asked.

"Yes, but what will they do?" she asked.

"They will send out some of their filthy kinfolk to search the way for him, and no doubt, after some time he will be found, and you will be terribly shaken by the whole affair and so very deeply upset," I ventured.

"How did you think up such a dreadful scheme?" my sister put to me.

"Because I spent many nights while away, scheming the demise of another individual, in many different ways, so this has posed little in the way of imagination," I quipped.

I went on to tell Sarah that I would ask Father later in the week to take me to Hexham Market, as I had not been far since my return. Hopefully he would agree, and I would also say that Sarah had shown a desire to see him and Mother, and we could call when passing, then we could pick her up and take her home.

Sarah reluctantly agreed to the scheme, and at that point I embraced her, then went on my way. I decided to take a small detour on my way, avoiding the Dodds' bastle, in order no one would see me, then there would be no link between me and the dead Bell. Of course it would be most unlikely that someone of Sarah's size and condition could possibly have killed a person of the build of the Bell.

As I was about to begin my return journey, I had the good fortune for it to start raining, which wet my already wet clothes, so when I arrived home, somewhat earlier than my previous visit, firstly Mother wanted to know if everything was all right, then to get me out of my wet clothes.

I was able to tell her that Sarah was well, and that we had had a pleasant afternoon together, and had talked and talked, and that I had passed Mother's and Father's love to her. Then I explained that I had come away soon, in order to avoid seeing the Bell, before he got back from visiting his parents.

Mother seemed happy at my explanation, then bid me to get from my wet clothes, which I did, and Mother wrapped me in the cover from my bed, sat me before the fire, then served me a bowl of steaming hot food, for which I was grateful after my exertions of the day.

Although I had had quite a hectic day, sleep did not come easy that night. It was not the fact of the deed that was done, for that there were no regrets, but that whenever I closed my eyes I was beset by the image of the Bell, lying in the bed of the burn, and the look on his face, as he lay there. I wish now that his eyes had been closed as he lay there, for it was the thought that he was not dead and that he may emerge from his watery resting place and come seeking vengeance, that kept me awake.

My thoughts were also with Sarah, that she was much closer to the dead Bell, and what thoughts were running through her mind, and would she cope on the morrow, going to the Bells' bastle, and pretending that her dearly beloved husband had not returned. Would she react correctly when the Bell was found, and would Father agree to my wishes to go to Hexham? There were so many things that could go wrong, and Sarah's voice kept returning to me, "We will hang…"

The next morning, after a much troubled night, I awoke to Mother noisily clattering around at the fire. I rose from my bed not ready to greet the day, and staggered to the table in more laboured fashion than was my norm. Mother laid my food before me, but I had little appetite, and spent most of the time toying with the food, rather than eating. Mother came to the table after a while, and placing her hand on my shoulder, she said, "Oh, my poor man, you must have caught a chill yesterday, when you got wet." I was much relieved that my mother had come up with an excuse for my lack of appetite, for I knew that the reason lay elsewhere, but was happy to play along with the reason given.

"You better stay inside today," Mother said, but my intentions required my presence outside.

"Mother, where is Fadder?" I asked.

"He has gone to the field barn to do some repairs," she replied.

"I think I may be better with the outdoors, could I go with Fadder?" I asked.

"Only if you feel you can, but if you feel faint at any time you must promise to return here, where you must retire to your bed, 'til you recover," Mother cautioned.

I got up from the table and, having to restrain myself from my usual scurry down the ladder, went out and across the meadow to the field barn.

Father was pleased to see me, saying, "Good lad, I need help with this." He was repairing the butment to the barn, which is a ramp of stone leading up to the barn for the hay carts, which had worn away with the heavy rain there had been the previous spring. We worked there for most of the day, Mother coming across around midday to bring food and to check that I was not overdoing things after my somewhat hesitant start to the day.

I assured her that whatever had ailed me, rising from my bed, was now past, made better by working with Father. I think she returned to the bastle after eating, reassured that I was in rude health.

Working with Father all day, we had talked of many things, sometimes speaking of my time with the monks, of my return, and of my feelings of returning. I know Father was greatly pleased when I told him how wonderful it was to be home, and, in a rare moment of affection, told me that during the years I had been away, he had hoped and looked forward to the day when we would be working together, as we were today.

This was the opening I had waited for all day, and so I set about asking him if we could go to Hexham for the market, for as like him, during those years away, I had longed for the day when we could ride together, to Hexham, to visit the market, as I was only very small the last time he took me. I think that I had timed my question correctly, because Father immediately said that he needed to go to Hexham, and that this week would be a good time to go. How I had to quell my delight of achieving my goal, but quell it I did, for I needed more of my father.

"Fadder?" I said enquiringly. "When I visited Sarah yesterday, she had a desire to see you. Could we call on our way, I'm sure she would be delighted, and if it were for only a very short while when passing, I doubt that Ruben would raise any objection."

"When we return home, we will ask Mother," Father replied. My initial elation was now somewhat stifled by the anticipation of having to wait until we returned home, and the answer Mother might give.

The days were now shortening, so as the sun started to drop we set forth for the bastle, and a much-needed hot meal. I sat at the table, almost bursting with the need to bring the conversation around to going to Hexham, and thereby visit Sarah. Just as we were finishing our meal Father eventually said, "Oh Marie, Rob has said he would like to go to Hexham Market this week, what say you?"

"Oh, I am sorry, Rob, but while you were at the barn, your Uncle Thomas came calling, and he has asked me to go to the Charlton bastle, on the day of the market, for he takes up a new appointment shortly with Sir John Foster, the March Warden, and requires my assistance to ready for his departure. However, I see no reason why you two men cannot go together," Mother said apologetically.

"But Mother," I blurted out, "We might call on Sarah on our way there."

"I'm sure she will understand, and I will make it my promise to see her within the next few weeks," she replied.

Now everything was set for our day, which had worked out better than I could have ever hoped. I helped Father saddle the two horses we would use today, and while we were doing this, Uncle Thomas came for Mother, in the cart that had seats, and they rode off after bidding us a good day. I had never seen my Uncle Thomas in a cart, he had always been on a horse, and had looked very grand as he rode, and now he was preparing to join Sir John Foster, the Queen's representative for the Middle March of England, whose task, given by the Queen, was to see that order was kept in the March, and that offenders were brought to justice, and my uncle would be assisting in this duty.

We set off for our day at Hexham Market, which I hoped we would never reach, but time would tell. On our way, we passed the Dodds' bastle and called briefly, to extend our greetings, and we were received with great affection by all the family. I saw Annie, which pleased me, then we continued to Sarah's sheil. We rounded the ridge that overlooked the sheil and waited a moment to survey the scene, and all appeared still. The cattle and sheep were scattered across the fields, which meant they had been allowed to wander, and had not been rounded up in the last few days. We trotted on down towards the sheil and still there was no sign of life. I was concerned, but thought it best to hold my thoughts. Father got down from his horse, and walked toward the sheil. While drawing his sword, he called out, but there was no response. I suggested that they may be going to Hexham also, knowing quite well that no such thing were possible, and that we should continue, maybe calling at the Bells' bastle, which, I knew, was an idea neither of us were eager to pursue.

"Aye, you're maybe right, mi lad," said Father, as he mounted up and we continued on.

As we trotted towards the Bells' bastle Father suggested we ride on and see Sarah another time, which sent me into somewhat of a panic, as I did not want to show my concern, knowing what I did, but at the same time ensure my father took us to Sarah.

"No," I ventured, "I think it best to carry on and see Sarah, as she was quite insistent that she wanted to see you, Father."

"Do you know why?" Father asked.

"No, but she did not seem happy, and I thought it best not to say too much in front of Mother, as I did not want to upset her, and I didn't want to tell you, either, but you have forced me to," I replied.

A part confession I thought might swing things in my favour, without giving too much away, and still keep Father in a mood to see Sarah. It appeared to have worked, as we set off in the general direction of the Bells' bastle.

The track carried on down the valley, with the burn meandering along on its own course, the self-same burn where we had laid the dead Bell, and passing the very place, I was riding behind my father, and could not help but raise myself in the saddle, to see if there was anything in the burn. But I saw nothing.

We carried on down, the next bastle would be the Bells'. I started to feel quite tense, and I am sure that I could feel the same tension coming from Father. As we neared the farmstead, my nostrils were assaulted by the stench that emanated from the place, and getting closer, I saw a man stood by the bastle door. This was Cuthbert Bell, Heedsman of the family, a man of considerable girth, with barely a hair to his head, a rough cut beard of grey, brown and black and a deep set mouth, with not a tooth in his head. At his side was his wife, Isobel, who went by the name of Bel. Was it not bad enough to be called Bell, without being called it twice, I thought. The appearance of this delightful creature was a sight to behold, for her girth was somewhat greater than that of her husband, which was topped off with a large, round and very ruddy face. Again a deep set mouth, as her spouse, but much better endowed, in that, protruding from the lower gum, a large dark brown tooth, her only one, which stood guard, like a tall oak, to the entrance to a large cavern of a mouth. This entire sight was crowned by a mass of ginger and grey unkempt hair, like that of a haystack after a storm. The pair seemed to attract filth, like flies to a midden, and as we came to a halt before them, I shuddered as I sat in my saddle.

"Good day Cuthbert, and of course, Mistress Bell, I trust all is well with you," my father greeted.

"No, it isn't, Hafe Heed," came the reply. I had not heard this term of Hafe Heed before, but later found out that it was a term used by many for my father, since he was injured in the attack on our bastle, and it was common among the riding families to find other names for each other, and in no way were they derisive.

"What ills beset you, Cuthbert?" Father inquired.

"My eldest, Ruben, is dead, that's what besets me," came the terse reply.

"How was he killed, for there have been no raids to my knowledge?" said Father.

"It looks like an accident, walking back from here, some days back; looks as if he slipped, trying to cross the burn to free a sheep caught in a gorse bush, slipped and banged his head, landed in the burn, don't know if he died with the bang or drowned. Either way, no man should bury his son, 'specially the eldest, and a bairn on the way," said Cuthbert.

It was then that I remembered that on the other side of the burn, where we lay the Bell, there was indeed a gorse bush which did have a good covering of wool from a fleece. Fortune indeed was smiling on me.

Father then said, "Aye, Cuthbert, now you mention the bairn, what of my daughter?" At which point Sarah came to the door, with her head bowed towards the ground. Father continued, "I am greatly sorrowed by your loss, Cuthbert, Mistress Bell, and I will take my daughter back to her home, if there is no objection."

"There is," growled the Bell. "She's a Bell now and she will stay." This was said as Cuthbert Bell drew his sword and thrust it out. My father, very slowly, took his right foot from the stirrup, then brought his leg forward and over the horse's neck, slipped slowly from the saddle, while unsheathing his sword. He then lay his sword along the outstretched sword of the Bell, and with a twist, the Bell's sword was hurtling through the air. I was amazed at how he had done such a feat, and very proud of his immense skill. He then drew his sword up slowly to the throat of Bell, and with a deep guttural voice, said, "They were hand fasted and not churched, therefore she is a Milburn. Sarah, get to your brother's horse, no one will stop you, will they, Cuthbert?"

The old crone by Cuthbert's side was visibly shaken, and although Father had his back to me, I could almost smell the menace in the air, even above the stench of the farmstead. I hopped from my horse as Sarah walked from the bastle, and bent over, cupping my hands into a stirrup, levering my sister on to the saddle, where, due to her condition, she sat side saddle, and even through the filth she was forced to endure, looked every inch the lady. I then went to the other side of my nag, and stepping into the unused stirrup, heaved myself up behind my sister. Taking hold of the reins, with a hand either side of Sarah, I heeled my nag around, setting off for home. I looked around, and Father was leading his nag, in my direction, while keeping eye contact with the

Bells. I could hear old Cuthbert, as Father walked away, indignantly shouting,

"Aye you can take yur wench, but the bairn will be a Bell, do you hear me Milburn? The bairn's a Bell."

When we had cleared the farmstead, Father sheathed his sword and took to his saddle, heeling his nag to a canter, I doing likewise, until we were clear of the Bells, then fell back to a walk. No words were spoken as we journeyed on, but with Sarah being in the saddle directly in front of me, our faces were very close, and occasionally she would turn to me, our noses almost touching, and she would smile. Sometimes her eyebrows would raise as she smiled, no words being required, the look said it all; yes, we had got away with it, and we had achieved what we wanted, to be a family again.

Chapter 8

A Cloud Descends

When we arrived back at our bastle, I dismounted first, then held my hands out to assist Sarah to get down, then Father got from his nag, and turned to me and told me to tend the horses, while he saw to Sarah. There was still a degree of menace in Father's voice, therefore I bade what he said without hesitation, but I wanted to be with my sister when she went inside for the first time for an age. Mother had not yet returned from her brother's, so Father attended to Sarah's needs, and came down from the bastle using the outside steps, and asked me to leave off the horses for now and assist him. We went to the back of the bastle where there was a large wooden trough, which we carried to the front of the house, then up the outside steps. I was then instructed to fetch water from the burn, using any means I could find. I could see that though having just arrived home, Father had already got the fire rekindled and roaring heavily. I went about the farmstead, gathering whatever vessels I could find, and taking them to the top of the outside steps, though I did not know why.

After a while Father closed the upper yett and door, then emerged shortly after from the lower door, carrying a small dish holding within some glowing embers. He came outside, placing the dish on the bottom stone step. Then I saw Sarah's filthy dress dropping down the ladder from the upper floor, Father going in and gathering the garment, taking it down to the midden, along with the dish of embers. He threw the dress on to the midden, then cast the glowing embers over it, set it alight, and he stood and watched it burn.

Father then turned to me, his mood lightened, as he said, "Now, mi lad, we will let your sister get herself cleansed, and free of the stench of Bells, before Mother comes home. Come, we will bed down the horses together, have you wiped them down?"

"Yes, Fadder, I have, they will be ready to go in now," I replied.

"No, lad", he said, "When you have had your nag in filth like we have seen today, you must clean out their hooves with the small hook that always hangs over the lower door; that way you are sure that the nag's feet will not ail. The one thing I will tell you lad, is the most important thing to any person is their nag, and the most important part of a nag is its feet. If you do not look after your nag, you lose it, then you are lost. Always remember what I have told you today."

"I will, Fadder," I replied, then enquiringly, I continued, "Fadder… can I ask one thing of today? When we were at the Bells', the old fat Bell said that Sarah was a Bell, and you said that she was not, and that they were hand fasted and not churched, what does that mean?"

"Well, lad, it is like this," he started. "When two people want to come together, as a couple, they may start off by firstly tying their hands together, to show they want to be together, then for a year, they live together, and that is hand fasting, then if it works for them, then they may seek a priest to say the proper words over them in a church, then they are married properly. But until they are churched they are not properly married, so Sarah is still a Milburn."

"But why do they not just seek a priest, first, instead of all that messing around?" I asked.

"Because since Fat Harry, the old King had most of the priests killed, or they were run off, there are few left, and they travel around, and are seen rarely; sometimes more than a year will pass before a priest is seen. Therefore it is not always practical to wait, thus we use hand fasting. Now let us get back, as your mother will be returning, and Sarah should have cleansed by now."

We walked back and Sarah was sat on the outside steps, wearing a clean dress, which I discovered later Father had given her to wear, from the chest that Mother kept all her spare dresses. She was teasing her hair, which was wet. It was the first time since my arrival back from my capture to Scotland that I had seen Sarah as I had remembered her, and not with that filth which she had had to endure.

"Come, lad, said Father, "give me some help to take out the water and the trough." We both worked together, and it was not long before we had all as it was, and barely had we finished when Mother approached, in the cart, being driven by Uncle Thomas.

As the cart came closer, Mother jumped from the back, and ran, with her arms outstretched, as Sarah got down from the steps, and ran to Mother. As they came together, they embraced, with much sobbing and cries of "Mother", and "Sarah" and "Oh my darling" and sob, sob, sob, but it was very pleasing, and I noticed Father turn away, and start to busy himself with something. I think the moment was even touching for him.

Father asked Uncle Thomas to stay and eat, but he said he had much to do, and offered his apologies, but before he left, I noticed Father having a conversation with Uncle Thomas, and though I was not able to hear all that was said, I understood that it was about the events of the day, and getting Sarah back.

As Uncle Thomas departed, Father and I went inside the bastle, where Mother and Sarah were already sat, deep in conversation, Sarah telling Mother about the unfortunate demise of her beloved Ruben. She told her story with such conviction that I was almost inclined to believe her myself, and thought as she related her tale of woe, that I would not believe a word that came from my sister again. I told her so some days later, when we both laughed uncontrollably.

Mother then prepared our evening meal, and we all sat, for the first time in five years, and ate together. Not a moment was there that there was not conversation from someone. It was truly one of the best meals I have ever sat down to, and I shall always remember the joy of that night. For this moment in my life, all that had gone before, had been well worth it. That night I nestled down in my bed, with Sarah lying in hers, and Mother and Father sat beside the fire, at the other end of the room, and I was transported back in time. I did hear Mother say to Father, as I lay in my bed, "Tom, we have our babies back, this is truly a wonderful day, and one I thought would never happen. How fortunate you were bound for Hexham this day."

Had we still had hens and they were uneasy tonight, I promise, I would not venture out, not this night, for sure.

The next day we all rose early, and after all sitting around the table after rising, Father and I went out to tend the stock. As we worked through the morning, Father said, "Well, Son, we never got to Hexham yesterday after all, are you disappointed?"

"No, I am not, Fadder, for I fear we may not have come back with a better prize had we got there," I replied. Father laughed then said that we would go to Hexham the very next week, this greatly exciting me, for I knew the last time we were due to go, that I held no wish to do so.

The following week passed by uneventfully; though Father could not quite work out why I was much more excited at the prospect of going to Hexham this time than I was the last. Sarah was starting to slow down noticeably, due to her condition, and it could be seen that life was becoming very uncomfortable for her, but Mother had gained a new lease of life, and went around the place with a constant smile upon her face. It was nice to see, especially as I had some small part in our present situation.

Market Day arrived, and I would have hoped that all of our family might have been able to go to Hexham, but alas, Sarah's condition did not allow for such an outing. Therefore Father and I went, setting off very early in the morning. I had been used to very early rising for many years at the manse, far earlier than we rose at the bastle, but I had soon got into the habit of sleeping much later. Therefore this early rise did not rest well with me, but I soon let the excitement take over from the heavy eyes, and we were soon saddled and ready for our journey.

We did not call at the Dodds' when passing, as it was still too early to call, and we gave a wide sweep to the Bells' bastle, Father saying that it might anger Old Cuthbert, if he were to cast eyes on us.

It was around late morning when we arrived at Hexham, and I was quite taken by what an imposing sight it was, for I must admit that although I must have been before, I remembered none of it. We entered the town through the high gates, then went along some narrow streets, the smell of which was somewhat unpleasant. At the end of one street, the building opened out, and there was a bustling market with stalls selling all manner of goods. The first stall on the market was festooned with all manner of dead animals for meat; there were rabbits, hares, skinned sheep, pigs and sides of cattle, all ready for cutting up and selling. Underneath the stall were cages, with hens and ducks and geese; these were always sold live.

The next stall sold leather goods, from harnesses and saddles to leather clothing, like the hard-wearing breaches we were in favour of wearing. There were other stalls all along the street, selling cloth, and others selling clothes, like dresses for women, and further on still a stall that sold all manner of vegetables, some the like I had never seen. As we walked along, leading our horses, many people stopped and stared. I did not realise why at first, but it was Father's injured face that drew their attention, something I had become used to very soon after first seeing him again. I could detect people whispering about Father, but

I now realise that he looked quite sinister, therefore few would care to offend him, lest they suffer the consequences.

I wanted to stay among the market, but Father ushered me onward to beyond, to the far side of the town, where we happened upon a large smithy, where there were two people working at the forge, one younger than the other. "Come, Rob," Father said. "Come meet the best smiths in the land." The elder of the two smiths looked up from the anvil, exclaiming, "Why, Tom Milburn, as I live and breathe… you old rogue, what brings you to Hexham this fine day?"

"Good day, Walter, it is truly good to see you again, let me introduce my lad, Rob. Rob, this is Master Walter Robson, the finest smith I know," said Father jovially.

"Well, young Rob, it is indeed an honour to make your acquaintance, and let me tell you, my boy, the only way your rogue of a father can say I am the finest smith he knows is because I am the only one he does know!" replied Walter Robson, to loud laughter from all. I liked Walter, and knew our paths would cross many times in the future. The younger of the two smiths, who I was introduced to, was Walter's son, also called Walter, and I swore that day that I would limit the occasions in the future that I would shake the hand of these two, for they both possessed a grip that made me wince, when they held my hand, but nonetheless, they were truly good people.

"Well, Tom, what can be done for you? Is it shoes for the nags, or equipment for the land we may serve you?" enquired Walter.

"Neither, thank you, Walter, though it is sorry I am, but I require the services of Jacob, is he at work?" asked Father.

"Aye, Tom, go you through, your nags will be well tended where they are," replied a cordial Walter.

We left our horses at the front of the forge and walked through to the back of the building, where facing the other way, that is the outside of the back of the building, was another forge, with a small, wiry man wearing a heavy leather apron, like the two Walters, his arms bare and glistening with sweat. The two Walters were well built individuals, and it could be seen that they ate well, whereas this person had not an ounce of spare flesh about his body.

Father approached the bent over body, as he worked at his anvil, but left a distance between, before the Smith looked up and caught sight of father. On doing so, he dropped what he was doing, stepped over to Father, then embraced him in a rough jovial manner. "Tom, it has truly made my day to see you, how the devil are you, my friend?"

"I am well, Jacob, it does my heart good to see you too. Let me introduce my lad, Rob. Rob, come meet my old friend, Jacob Heron. Jacob and I rode together when we were young; as a matter of fact, we both rode on our first raid together." I stepped forward to greet Jacob Heron warily, after my encounter with the two Walters, and as before, my hand was assaulted to the point where the pain was becoming quite unbearable.

At this point the older Walter walked through from the other side of the Smithy, and stepped between Father and Jacob.

"Tom, your lad, I thought he had been killed by the Scotties years ago," he said.

"Aye, Tom," said Jacob, "the very thought I had." Father went on to tell the story of how he had happened upon me, on a raid into Scotland, and of how I had been kept in a monastery, with monks for five years, which was not quite true, but he was enjoying telling his tale so much that I did not like to correct him.

After Father had recounted his story, there was much back slapping and cheering at our exploits, then Walter returned to his station, and Father asked me to go and check that the nags were not causing a bother to anyone. I was instructed by Jacob that I must never run in a Smithy, or I might not leave in one piece. Both he and Father laughed as I walked very seriously to the front of the forge and checked the horses. All was correct, but I chose to stay with the horses, as I thought Father wanted to talk to Jacob, without my presence.

After a short while Father came walking through from the back of the forge, and we set off to walk through the town, taking in all the sights, sounds and smells of this very strange way of existence, with so many people all brought together in such a small space. I had been used to rolling fields and only a few faces, and even when I spent my time in captivity, it was rare that I was ever allowed into the town. When I was allowed that privilege, there seemed fewer people milling around than were here today, in a bustling Hexham Market.

We passed a stall where a pig was being roasted on a spit, the smell filling the air with the most mouth-watering aroma. I swear I started to drool, like some hungry dog. Father saw the hunger on my face and handed some money over to the stall holder, and we were presented with two large pieces of hot steaming meat. I could scarcely hold it, for it was so very hot, but the taste will linger on my tongue for the rest of my life. If nothing else, today had been worth it, if only for that pig meat.

We went to many stalls, Father purchasing many items for provision through the winter, resulting in both our horses being loaded with sacks of goods strapped across their backs, behind their saddles.

When we were fully loaded we set off back home, at a steady walk, due to the weight of our saddle bags; we were not able to ask more of our nags. As we were leaving the city gates we heard a voice shouting, "Thomas, Thomas Milburn, hold fast there friend."

We both looked around and it was the Dodds' family; Father, Michael, and his son, Raymond, were both on horseback, one each side of a horse drawn cart driven by mother, Mary Dodds, and seated next to her was Annie. We all greeted each other cheerily and decided we would all ride home together, which greatly pleased me, and by the look on a certain young lady's face, I was not the only one.

It transpired that they had been in Hexham all day, and had set off shortly before we had, therefore neither being aware of the other's presence, and we had spent the entire day in Hexham, never seeing each other once. The Dodds had relatives living within Hexham, and had spent time visiting them, so we came to the conclusion that this may have accounted for us not encountering each other throughout the day.

It was a very pleasant ride home and I was able to manoeuvre my nag so as to get near Annie, enabling me to pass the odd word, and she seemed content to converse with me.

We had been journeying for some time when we found ourselves nearing the bastle of the Bells, and I felt that had we been on our own, Father may have suggested we take a wide sweep of their dwelling, but as we were with company, we said nothing of what had taken place some days earlier, and just rode past. I felt quite tense as we passed, but was greatly relieved when we rode past without incident. It was dusk as we arrived back at the Dodds' bastle and they invited Father and me in to take food with them, but with the light now fading fast, we were alas unable to take advantage of their hospitality.

We bid our goodbyes, as Father and I continued our journey, and after the time spent travelling, it appeared no time at all until we were arriving home. A warm greeting awaited from Mother and Sarah, and after bedding down the nags, we sat at the table and ate, and there was much excited chatter, I being the source of that chatter. Mother cautioned that if I did not settle down, I would surely burst, and who would clean up such a mess.

This was a truly happy day; I had been to the town, seen many sights, sounds and smells, the like I had never encountered before, we had purchased many things, and had ridden with the Dodds; yes, a truly wonderful day.

After we had eaten, Father brought in the sacks of goods we had bought and we showed Mother and Sarah the things we had brought back, many of which I was not aware we had. I can only assume that I was taken up more with my surroundings than what we were buying.

My head was now a spin, with the rigours of the day starting to take their toll. Mother saw the tiredness descend upon me and bade me to my bed, and though I still had much to tell, I retired, sleep coming within an instant.

Awaking the next day, with the same excitement that took me to my bed the previous night, I rose quickly and went to the table, Mother having already prepared the morning meal. I sat down to a bowl of hot oats, trying to talk between mouthfuls, of our exploits of the previous day. My sister commented to Mother that she did not know how the monks had tolerated my presence for five years, having to endure such constant chatter. This comment was received with much laughter by the two women of the house. I gulped down the last of my meal and went out to join Father, where I stayed for the rest of the day, feeling somewhat embarrassed by my female kin, and much more comfortable in the presence of my father.

It would be some ten days after our visit to Hexham that we were all awoken as dawn broke by my sister, who was crying out in much pain. Startled, I jumped from my bed, seeing Mother already in attendance at my sister's bedside.

I was panicked by all the noise, and started to run around aimlessly. Mother, seeing my disarray, instructed me to gather myself, and run to the Charltons and say that Sarah's baby was due, and for one of the ladies of the house to come with all haste.

I set off, running for all I was worth, across the valley, in the direction of the Charltons' bastle, arriving sometime later, and being greeted by my Uncle James. Breathless, I attempted to gasp out the message I had been given.

"Rob, Rob, settle you down, boy, now take a breath and tell me slowly," said James, he and his wife being the only residents here, since the departure of Uncle Thomas, to assist Sir John Foster, the Middle March warden.

When eventually I was able to deliver my message, James greeted it with much relief, saying he thought that we had been raided by the Scotties, and that if it were only my sister giving birth, we need not panic unduly. I thought quite the opposite, that indeed it was a matter of life or death, and said so, to the laughter of James and his wife, Elizabeth. I then became quite indignant. James assured me that all would be well, and if I had only waited to think, and saddled up my nag, I would have reached the Charltons much more quickly and less out of breath. I felt the embarrassment fill my entire body, but James ruffled my hair playfully, saying, "Come along, lad, let us be off to see your sister," as we went out and harnessed a nag to the cart, and the three of us set forth for home, I considered far too slowly. I was to find out much later that the only reason I had been dispatched to the Charltons was in order to get me out of the way, so that Mother could oversee the birth of Sarah's baby.

I do not know how long it had taken me to get to the Charltons, then back again, but on arrival Sarah could still be heard, calling out, in great pain.

Elizabeth jumped from the cart as it came to a stop, and rushed inside the bastle. I rushed after, as fast as I could, only to be caught at the door, by Father, who dragged me back outside.

"No place for the likes of us men, young Rob, this is women's work; we have no skill in such matters." This was not what I wanted to hear, I wanted to be there and see what could be causing my sister such dreadful agonies. I was cursing that Bell, for placing my sister in such pain, and damned him for his existence.

After what seemed forever, eventually Elizabeth emerged from the bastle, looking much wearied, and announced that Sarah had given birth to a healthy baby boy.

James greeted the news by slapping Father on the back, and calling him Grandfather, then patting me on the back and calling me Uncle. Until James said these things, it had never occurred to me that Father would be a grandfather and I an uncle; I felt quite proud of my new status.

It was yet some time before we all entered the bastle, to see Sarah, who was lying in her bed, and in a small wooden bed, with sides – which I had seen Father making in the weeks before, but had dismissed it as a feeding trough for the young calves – was a tiny baby, with its eyes closed, asleep. I could not understand why it felt the need to sleep, when it had just come into the world. Surely Sarah, who had been in much agony, from the sound of things, should be the one who, now free of that agony, would require rest.

After all the excitement of the day, James and Elizabeth left for their home, and we tried to settle back to life once again, although nothing would ever be quite the same. At around dusk, the baby awoke, and started to cry as it opened its eyes. Sarah went to it and sat on her bed, turning her back to us all, and started to feed the infant. It seemed a long drawn out affair, with intermittent crying from the baby, and reassuring hushing sounds from Sarah.

It was not until the feeding was over that I saw the baby properly for the first time, and this was truly the bairn of a Bell; its resemblance to Ruben, with the same dark hair, was quite uncanny. I did not like this child, and would gladly relinquish my newly acquired status as uncle to be rid of it.

It was the early hours of the morning, and still dark outside, when the baby awoke the whole bastle, crying. Sarah rose from her bed, gathered up the child, and getting back into her bed, undid the front of her garment and started to feed it. I lay there, keeping still, but with my eyes partly open, watching, by the light of the fire, the baby being fed.

After the feeding, the child started to cry, and Sarah took from the child a cloth that was wrapped around its loins. The cloth was soiled and the smell was awful. She went to the fire, where there were other such pieces of cloth hanging, and bound the baby's loins again, then laid it in its bed, and as was its way, the child continued to scream for some while. Thankfully, tiredness got the better of it, and sleep ensued, after which we were all able to resume our slumbers, until dawn, when the entire procedure was gone through again.

Was this baby issue really worth all the trouble? Even the beasts bedded down in the space below were getting restless, and I warrant they would have preferred to take their chances in the field against a Scottie attack than spend another night subject to such wailings.

That day it could be seen that we were all suffering from the rigours of the night, the lack of sleep having its effect on all, but Mother said that it was early days in the baby's life, and that things would ease as time goes by. We, that is Father and I, were not so certain, if the look on his face were any measure.

The day passed all too quickly, as it had allowed Father and me time away from the screaming of the infant. After the last meal of the day, weariness took hold of me, and I was soon to bed, and was surprised to see everyone else turning in at the same time.

I knew it was the middle of the night, as yet again, the baby started its screaming. I could not help but think that this was Ruben Bell wreaking his revenge through his son.

Sarah dutifully got from her bed and lifted the baby from its bed to feed it. She got back into her bed, as the nights had started to chill quite severely, and even with the fire still on, the room was cold. She undid her garment and started to feed the baby, but she was not feeding it as I had observed before. She had always watched as the baby had started to feed, but tonight she just looked across the room towards the fire, and as she did so, she held the baby's head, and kept it held tightly to her breast. After the feeding, I noticed Sarah did not take her eyes from the fire, and was totally unaware that I was watching. She got from her bed and placed the baby back in its bed. It looked already asleep, its arm hanging limply from the cloth that bound its body, and this night it did not cry, but went straight down. Sarah returned to her bed, still staring strangely, and, getting into bed, she lay there, eyes open, just staring ahead. I thought her behaviour was possibly brought about due to her tiredness, and thought no more about it and went back to my slumbers.

The next morning, having slept the sleep of the dead, I awoke with some surprise that the baby was silent, and had been throughout the night. I looked over to Sarah's bed; she had her back to me, supposedly asleep. Looking across the room, I noticed Father, having just roused, was rubbing his face, I thought, with some discomfort, but Mother as always, was about the fire, kindling it up for the morning meal.

I got up and went over to Mother. "Ah Rob, it is so nice to have you here, in the mornings, it is this time of the day that I missed you being around the most," she said in hushed tones. I put my arm about her waist and she, her hand on my shoulder. Yes, it was nice to be home; Mother, Father, Sarah.

I turned to Mother and quietly asked if the baby had awakened through the night, as I had not heard anything. She said she had not heard anything either, and that it was unusual for a baby so young to sleep through the night.

I looked toward the far end of the room where Sarah was rising. She came across to where Mother and I were, a strange look about her face. Her eyes were open, but there was nothing there, nothing behind them. She had the eyes of Ruben Bell, as we laid him in the burn; yes, she was moving around, but she seemed dead.

Mother, seeing Sarah, cupped her hands to her mouth. "Oh no, oh my dear, heaven no," she gasped, in the deepest tones I had ever heard my mother speak. She ran over to where the baby lay, and taking it in her arms, she screamed, "Oh no, no, no!" I did not know what was happening. Father rose from his bed and went to Mother, and looked at the baby, but Sarah busied herself with the morning meal, still with that strange deathly look about her face.

Father went straight outside without eating, Mother sat on the edge of Sarah's bed, still holding the baby, and Sarah served me my meal. As I finished eating, Father returned, and stepping up the ladder, he said, "It's ready."

Mother rose from the edge of Sarah's bed, still holding the baby, tears streaming down her face. It was not until that moment that I, stupid person that I am, realised that the baby was dead. We all descended the ladder, then outside, to the wall that runs from behind the bastle outward to the crest of the hill. Father had dug a grave, next to our six brothers and sisters that had not survived, all dying before they were a year old, some born dead.

Father took the baby from Mother, and laid it in the grave, then shovelled over the soil, finishing it off by placing the grassy sods over the grave.

Mother was greatly distressed, and Father looked upset at having to bury another infant. I, strangely, was not affected by the death at all, as I did not know the child yet. Sarah was stood there, not showing any emotion, just staring blankly ahead, her eyes, cold and distant, like a cloud had descended upon her.

Chapter 9

My New Friends

The following week, since the death of the infant was difficult for everyone, Sarah was still not being herself. When she looked at you, it was if she were looking right through you, and still not seeing you. Sometimes she would be outside, and I would be working with the animals, she would look over, towards me, and smile, as she used to, but all that she did was to broaden her mouth, and maybe show her teeth, but it was so cold, her eyes were dead, and no matter what she did, it made me feel uneasy.

Two weeks after the baby's death, Father went into Hexham, alone, although I found out later that he had met with Michael Dodds, and they had rode together. I was annoyed that Father had not asked me to go, and later, when I found out that he had gone with Michael Dodds, I was annoyed at missing a chance to see Annie, but of course I could not say anything.

Father came home from Hexham; as the days were shortening now it was dark when he arrived. Excitedly, I wished to see what purchases he had made, but he would not let me see the contents of a large sack, which had been slung across his horse. What made it more intriguing was that the contents clanked whenever the bag was moved.

The following morning, after we had eaten, Father told me to go with him, as he had something for me to do, which of course I imagined was some chore, which inevitably meant getting dirty.

We descended the ladder, then opened the door, then the yett, and let out the cattle and horses, as always, then Father produced from the back of the feeding trough the sack he had brought back from Hexham. We went outside, and Father told me to sit on the outside steps, which led to the upper door. I did as instructed, and Father laid the sack on the ground, carefully placed his hand inside, then drawing it out again, produced a beautiful new shiny sword, slightly smaller than the one Father had.

"There you go, lad, meet your new friends," he announced, passing the sword to me, by the blade. "Now be warned, boy, this is not a toy, and you must listen to everything I tell you, from this day forward, for a sword wrongly used can be more perilous to the user than to anyone else. I will teach you to be a swordsman who can take anyone to task; I will teach you to ride for battle, and how to go lancing."

He then placed his hand back into the sack, this time producing a bollock knife, held in a sheath, and attached to a leather belt.

"Come, Rob," he said, and as I stepped forward, he wrapped the belt around my waist and tied it with the brass buckle. "Again, boy, this is not a toy, and used skilfully, which I will show you, they are now your best friend, and you will come to know them as such."

He then went on to tell me that it would take many years before I would be allowed to ride on a raid, and that most of my time, from this day forward, except for the chores, which had to be done, would be spent learning to become a reiver, a task I greatly relished.

Also within the sack was a steel bonnet, which was somewhat large for me, but Father said that by the time I was capable of wearing it, I would have grown into it. There were also some leather gauntlets, and a steel plate with leather straps, which was to tie on to my right forearm, but Father said I was a long way from being ready to wear this item.

He then left me to examine the items, with the strict instructions that I was to treat all of them very carefully.

I took up the sword. The hilt had a cross bar of brass, which shone so beautifully, the hand grip was covered over by a basket weave of alternate steel and brass strands, and with the gauntlet on my hand, the sword fit so snugly in my hand. The most wonderful thing about this sword was that it did not feel heavy, and I was able to handle it with ease.

I lay the sword down carefully on the steps leading to the upper bastle door, then sat on the step below, and drew out the bollock knife, which was about my waist. The handle was made of bone, and carved, so giving a slim comfortable grip, and at the hilt, the carving of the bone gave two rounded pieces, thus preventing the hand from slipping down and on to the blade. This was particularly useful when stabbing it into a body, as it allowed the knife to be pushed right in, without losing grip, or so Father said. The blade was made of shining steel, which tapered to a point, and both edges of the blade had been sharpened, this also allowing a smooth entry into flesh, and even if it caught bone on the way in, if it were kept sharp enough it would cut bone as well.

I tried the helmet on again, the inside being clad with the softest of leathers, with a draw string set within the leather to allow the size to be altered. I tightened the draw string as far as it would go, but still it did not rest well on my head. Removing the helmet and looking over it carefully, I could see it was much different from Father's; his had a peak at the front and hinged cheek plates, and a hinged neck plate. This had a brim that ran around the entire helmet, ending at both back and front, in a point, and rising upwards. On top of the crown of the helmet, another piece had been riveted on, and was raised up slightly, giving more strength, should anything be brought down on it with force.

These were the most wonderful things I had ever been given, and I would treasure them greatly.

After some time of being left to examine my new weapons, Father returned, and said that I must now take my sword, helmet and gauntlets inside the bastle, and place them under my bed, where they must be kept at all times, other than when I was practising. I asked if I could play with them for a little longer, and was greeted with such a slap across the face that it took the feet from under me, and I lay sprawled upon the ground. I lay there, holding my face, where Father had struck me, and looking up through dazed and teary eyes, I saw Father standing with his clenched fist on his hips, glowering at me. "You will never play with those weapons, they are not for play, boy, they are for learning how to stay alive. If when the next raid comes, and you were to be carried off, you might not be so fortunate to make it back again; is that what you want?" he bellowed.

"No, Fadder," I replied, sobbing. I was suddenly transported back to the manse, and Father Francis. I gathered myself up, and went and took hold of my sword and helmet, and took them inside, hurriedly, to the sounds of Father's voice, "Walk."

This was not the best of starts for a reiver, but I was hopeful that I would learn, and become a good raider, and with father as my mentor, I was sure to become one of the best raiders in the Middle March.

The following day, after the chores were complete, Father told me to go and get my sword, and he would start to teach me swordsmanship. I hurried to the bastle, with Father's voice following behind, "Walk."

I came down the ladder holding my scabbarded sword, then stepped outside and was about to strap the belt about my waist.

"No need to tie it on, Rob, not for the first week. Draw your sword, get it comfortable in your hand," he instructed, and adjusted it, so that it was held as it should be. "Now then, Rob, hold your arm out straight, with the sword held upwards, that's it, now hold it there, and do not allow your arm to drop."

I stood there for what seemed an age, holding the sword aloft, not moving, waiting for something to happen. Was I not here to learn swordplay, not just stand there like a tree in the wood. The sword was now beginning to get heavy, and I could see my arm starting to shake.

"Keep holding steady there, Rob," came Father's voice. The beads of sweat started to build on my face then started to roll down into my eyes, which stung.

"Can I rest now, Fadder?" I asked.

"No, you cannot rest, boy, you have only begun," came the reply.

Eventually, I had to drop my arm, the sword weighing that of a hundred swords; my arm, I felt sure about to drop off, the pain along my arm unbearable.

"You have far to go, Rob, very far, now return your weapon inside," said Father. I climbed the ladder inside the bastle, very disappointed that I had not got to do actual swordplay, and that if this was what swordplay was, I was not sure I wanted to continue.

The following day, after chores, Father instructed me to go fetch my sword, which I did with much less enthusiasm than I had shown the previous day. Father, seeing this, taught me a lesson I would never forget.

"Right, my boy, you may strap your sword about your person, then stand on guard," he said. This is what I wanted. I quickly buckled up, then drew my sword, and held it aloft. I had barely got the weapon raised, when Father drew his; it crashed into mine, resulting in it being knocked from my hand, sending it swirling through the air.

"That's how ready you are to handle a sword," he said. "Now go and retrieve your weapon, place it in your hand and raise it as I showed you yesterday."

I meekly gathered my sword and held it high as told, and did so for many days to come, until the sword became part of my arm, and I was able to stand, with sword held high, for as long as Father wanted.

When he was satisfied that the sword had become part of me, he then started to show me sword skills. One of the first things I was told, which quite took me aback, was that the sword was firstly a weapon of defence, not offence, and the first moves I was shown were all to stop an attack. Those moves were many and varied, and an entire year was taken up in learning how to defend myself, Father repeating himself every day,

"Defence will save your life, only attack may take it." He would spend as much as half a day raining blows down on me, and toward the latter end of the first year of my learning, those blows were coming down with great force. I often wondered, should one of these blows follow through, would he be able to pull back, before drawing blood or worse.

During that year, within the valleys that surrounded our bastle, there were three raids by the Scotties, resulting in many cattle and sheep being taken, and each time a Hot Trod ensued, and on two occasions the Hot Trod intercepted the raiding party, and were able to return the stock, and fetch back prisoners, which were held for ransom. Father informed me that a good prisoner can be worth one hundred cattle, when ransomed.

This also showed that it was better to capture Scotties than kill them. Father said he always tried not to kill if he could avoid it. That having been said, I thought that at the manse he despatched Donald and Father Francis with great skill.

I was very frustrated whenever a Hot Trod occurred or Father went on a raid, which he did some five times that raiding season, as I was never allowed to go with them. Also Mother started to give me instruction in reading and writing, saying that she did not wish me to forget what I had learnt during my capture.

Life at home continued as before, Sarah still with eyes that saw but were dead, Mother happy that we were all together again and seemingly not wishing to see that Sarah was not right, and Father ever relentless in his instruction in my knowledge of weapon handling.

I, for my part, did as much as time allowed improving my skills, and when I was not needed around the bastle, I would wander off into the woods, with my sword, and my bollock knife, and would hide and wait for the animals to come out, like deer, rabbits and birds, and see if I could sneak up on them, seeing how close I could get before they heard me. This skill improved to such a point where I once was able to get close enough to a deer to bring my sword down about its neck and take off its head. We ate well that week, but I had to be very careful when taking the beast home that I was not spotted, or my reward may have been the gallows.

My second year of instruction was taken with learning attacking moves with the sword, which were far less than defensive moves, but I had to try to use those attacking moves while Father was raining blows down on me and I was also having to use all the defensive moves I had learnt; this was not easy. I also had to endure, at least once each week, having to stand and defend myself while Father continued to attack, this carrying on until both of us would collapse, exhausted. This, I was informed, was in case I ever had to fight in a battle, as these could go on from dawn until dusk, and sometimes beyond. The message which was instilled in me for this was, the man who tires in battle and whose arms drop cannot defend himself and therefore dies.

Once being able to handle the sword, on foot, then came the handling on horseback. I thought that I had reached a good standard of swordsmanship, but when I got into the saddle and Father came at me at just a canter, I found myself unsaddled and in a crumpled mess upon the ground, feeling much embarrassed. Months were spent learning swordplay in the saddle, or should I say out of the saddle, for Father had me out of it more than in it. My body ached from all the tumbles and bruising, but one thing that I did notice was that my body had completely changed shape. My arms had doubled in size, as had my chest, and my belly had become hard, my legs had doubled their girth and become very firm. I could battle all day long, and got to the stage where I could go on beyond Father's endurance.

I now had to learn the skills of the lance, a piece of weaponry I was uncomfortable with. No matter whether I was on foot or in the saddle, this weapon and I did not work well together, Father being taken to the point of exasperation on many occasions at my lack of skill with this unwieldy thing. Eventually, as I was so very poor with the lance, Father constructed a dummy holding a shield, mounted on a pole, and as I galloped through with my lance down, if I got contact with the shield, the dummy would spin.

My poor old nag, I wore her down, and had to use Father's nag equally with mine so they could both be rested. It took the best part of another year before I became even reasonable with the lance, and I had to resign myself that the lance was never going to be my best weapon.

At the end of two long years of very hard work and learning my trade from one of the best practitioners of the art, Father declared that I might, if I were sensible, be ready to go on a raid. I had waited so long and worked so hard for this day. I was now a fully grown man, fourteen years of age and ready to take on the entire population of the Scotties who lived in the borderlands. They would not sleep easy in their beds tonight in the knowledge that Rob Milburn was about to be let loose among them.

Chapter 10

A Virgin Raid

The day began with a light frost upon the ground, and all the indications were that it would provide a clear blue sky, and another cold and frosty night; not ideal for a night of riding. It being my first outing as a rider, I was quite excited at the prospect of a clear night, thus being able to see where I was going. The experienced riders, of course, preferred an overcast night where they could move unseen in the cover of darkness. They were experienced at navigating the hazardous marsh lands of the border country, and used the dangers that lay within as a means of avoiding detection and capture, often being held up for days, in the treacherous marshes, awaiting the pursuing forces, be they Scotties or English March Wardens, either of which were in pursuit of blood.

Many a raider who had dropped his guard had ended up the victim of a Hot Trod Scottie or English Kingsman's sword, or worse still, a foot behind the neck, and held down, into a burn, and the cold waters thereof being the instrument of their death. All these stories were told to me by Father, over the years, as he prepared me for this day, and I realised now the reason for telling such tales was that I be on my guard every moment I was in the saddle.

Father and I started to saddle up at around midday, and as we were ready to ride off, after bidding Mother and Sarah farewell, Sarah still with those cold eyes, void of all emotion, Michael and Raymond

Dodds arrived, and greeted us all in their cheery way. Michael looked towards Mother, saying, "Worry not, Marie, we will fetch him home safely, he has spent enough time with the Scotties already."

Much laughter ensued as we trotted off, I with Father on one side and Michael on the other, Raymond taking up station next to his father, as we headed towards the Charlton bastle.

On arrival, Uncle James Charlton was ready along with Father's two brothers, Arthur and John, who over the past couple of years we had seen little of, but we were aware that they had both spent much time raiding over the border, along with some of the riders from the West March. These two uncles had fearsome reputations within the reiving families on both sides of the border. Father had a reputation for his skill with the sword, and it was reckoned there were none with his skill either side of the border, but Arthur and John had a ferocity that sent fear through any who came into contact with them, which was very reassuring for me on my first raid, and my first return to Scotland after my liberation, nearly three years prior.

Farther along the ride Hugh and Abel Robson caught up with us all and they told that on the way they had encountered the three Bell brothers, they being the younger brothers of Ruben, but had dissuaded them from coming any further. I knew that Ruben had three brothers, but I had not met them. There was also a sister, whom I had not met either, and harboured no desire to do so.

The topic of conversation as we rode along soon settled on the demise of the said Ruben Bell, some two years prior, the general consensus being that he must have been killed, as there did not appear sufficient evidence to support the theory that his death was an accident.

Laughingly, Hugh Robson turned to me and said, "You didn't see him off, did you lad?"

"No, Sir," I parried, "I think I was a lot too small at the time to take him on, but were it now, who knows, Sir."

"By the Lord Thomas, I like the cut of this lad of yours," said Hugh, slapping me on the back with such force, he almost unsaddled me, which brought on further laughter from all. I now felt very much part of the entire group of riders, as we trotted on at a goodly pace.

Uncle James Charlton then came and rode alongside me. "Do you know the plan for this raid, Rob?" he asked.

"No, I do not, Uncle James," I replied.

"I think, now that you are a rider, Rob, that Uncle James may be dispensed with; you are old enough to just use my name."

"Yes Un'…er, James," I said.

"Now Rob, what we are about this night, is to firstly get over the border, then continue riding north for a good while, when we should come to a large marshy area, which is difficult to navigate, we will travel through it in single file. One wrong step either side of the trail, and in an instant, horse and rider are gone." I gulped, as James continued. "Once in the centre of the marsh, there is a copse, which will afford us shelter and cover from prying eyes. We will lay up there through the daylight hours, then at dusk we will continue north, well above where we need to be. Once far enough north we will come about and drive south, sweeping all before us, and we will do so without drawing a weapon, unless we expressly have to. Rob, I want you to ride away from a sword, not to it, do I make myself understood?"

"Yes, I think you do, James," I said.

The way in which James looked at me as he was talking left no doubt how earnest his plea was, and to further intensify his intentions, he rounded off by saying, "Rob, you have only ever known me as Uncle James, and I have always treated you well, is that not so?"

"Yes it is so, James," I replied hesitantly.

"Good, then heed this, Rob, you do not do as I say on this raid and you will see a side of me that you will not like, for I will beat you to within an inch of your life if you wander from my instructions, and your father knows not to stop me," he said with a growl, spurring his horse away.

A few moments earlier I was feeling very comfortable as one of the riders; now I felt uneasy. James had never been like this to me; he was always the one who would be fun to be with, the one I always looked forward to seeing whenever we visited the Charltons or they visited us. I now saw a side of him I did not know, and was not sure I wanted to.

But soon, as I was absorbing what James had said, I found myself flanked on either side by Michael and Raymond Dodds, Michael speaking first. "Well, Rob, how is it on your first raid, do we find you nervous?" he enquired.

"I have to admit, Sir, I am somewhat," I replied.

"I am so pleased to hear you say so, Rob, for the day you do not, turn your nag homeward and ride like the devil, for you are of no worth to your fellow riders unless there is some trepidation within." Raymond then said, "Worry not, Rob, for all here will see you safely home, and I dare not enter our bastle and say to Annie that I have not brought Rob home safely."

I was very glad that it was so dark, for I felt myself blush like never before. It had been a while since last I had seen Annie Dodds, as all of my time these past two years had been taken up with preparing for this night. Though I was greatly assured that she still thought of me, I wondered was this some jest on the part of her brother. I felt it best to let the remark go unanswered lest I leave myself open to ridicule.

The order came to go single file, Michael taking up forward position of me and Raymond bringing a close rear position, so close that I could feel the warm breath of his horse upon my back.

The darkness was now subsiding slowly, and I could see either side of me standing water glistening. If I were in any doubt where I was, these leering pools dispelled that doubt. I clung on hard to the reins as we rode on, as if this would increase my safety, in this treacherous terrain.

I did not know the order we were riding in, or who was at the head, guiding the way through this marshland; I just kept my eyes pinned hard to the rear of Michael's nag, and ensured that whatever steps his nag took, that mine did likewise. Eventually I was aware of trees on either side of me, the copse I thought, very soon men were dismounting, and tying their nags to the tree. As it was very cold now, and a frost could be seen on the trees, we did not immediately unsaddle, but let the horses cool a while, then unsaddled, but kept the numnah cloth over so the nags did not lose too much heat. Standing in the cold like this without cover nags can get a cold back, which, when they are re-saddled, and the girth is tightened, causes them to keel over, and you lose your nag out there and returning home can be problematic.

After the horses were taken care of we all started to settle down for the day, my tiredness overcoming me very quickly. I had scarcely closed my eyes, or so it seemed, when my Uncle Arthur woke me. "Your turn on watch, lad," he hissed.

I awoke with a start, and quickly got to my feet and took up my sword.

"When the sun rests over yon fell top, then you can waken Hugh Robson and your Uncle John, but when you do, stand back quick, young'un, for he'll have his bollock knife to yur throat afore you can blink," he said, then lay himself down. I swear he was giggling to himself like a girl, as he lay down, the old rogue.

I took up my lookout post on the edge of the copse, overlooking the trail we had used to enter our safe haven, Michael Dodds taking up point in the direct opposite position of myself, covering the northward approach, though I did not know if it were possible to enter the copse from any other position than the one we had used.

114

The time it took for the sun to reach the fell top Uncle Arthur had indicated seemed to take ages, Michael occasionally checking on me during our watch. On the last occasion of him checking, I asked if it were time to wake the next watch, as the sun was now covered by cloud. Michael said, "Aye, wake the lazy swine from their slumbers, Rob; who is due watch?"

"Hugh Robson and Arthur," I replied.

"I'll waken Hugh, you give Arthur a nudge, but watch yourself," said Michael. He then turned away, I am sure to stifle a snigger.

I went over to where my Uncle Arthur slept, and found as I walked over, a branch, broken from one of the trees, about as long as I was tall. I took up the branch, which was quite thin, as willow is, and I set myself behind an ash tree, from where I stretched out and poked the back of Arthur, while at the same time, summoning up my best Scottish accent, said, "Are ye riddy te dee, English?" then dropped the branch, and concealed myself behind the tree.

Arthur was on his feet in a flash, sword en garde, ready to kill, as I slowly emerged from behind the tree, my sword en garde.

"I think, Uncle, it is what you had planned for me, is it not?" I said with beaming smile.

"Ye wee snotter, think ye can get the better of yer auld uncle, do yer?" he replied as he charged at me with his sword held high. I dropped my sword in fright and took to foot, with Arthur's laughter ringing in my ears. I stopped and walked back, picking up my sword as I did so. Uncle Arthur came over to me; I was greatly unnerved by his approach, but as a beaming smile lit up his face, he placed a heavy hand on my shoulder, and said, "Yur yu fadder's lad ar reet, now get yur heed down, lad," then walked off to his watch station, running his hand through his thick red beard, and shaking his head as he did so. I am sure he said something about me as he went, I heard 'Young *something*,' but I had not heard that word before, therefore I do not know what exactly he said.

My second session of sleep did not come as quickly as the first, but come it did, and again, it was as if I had just closed my eyes before I was woken by Father.

"Come, Rob, time to saddle up, the dusk is upon us. By the way, well done with Arthur, it was the first thing he greeted me with, when he roused me for my watch, he was still laughing."

I liked this reiving, the closeness of the family, and the extended family, and the feeling of their bonding as one; this truly was a side to my family that I had never felt before. I knew that all the families within the valley were close, well almost all, but the closeness of these families on the trail cannot be described; we each knew that we were dependent on each other for our lives, as we entered into the Scottish lands, where if sighted, by even a crofter, could bring down hordes of Scotties upon us. It also made me more determined to do well on this, my virgin raid.

We rode on through the night, northward for much of the time, then as I was starting to lose concentration, and just allowing my nag to carry me on, following the rest of the riders, the leading riders wheeled around and started to head south-west. Michael Dodds was on my left and Hugh Robson on my right. Hugh leaned over to me and in hushed tones, said, "Yur fadder will a' told you, but I'll just remind yur, lad, frum now on yu'll say nought 'til day breaks, we now ride silent."

"Yes, Sir," I hissed in reply. The excitement now started to grow within me, as for still some time to come we just rode, without seeing any signs of habitation or livestock.

The night was now cloaked heavily in cloud, in complete contrast to the cold clear night of yesterday. The one benefit was the temperature of this night was much warmer, and being in the saddle was much more agreeable.

How these riders could plot a trail in such darkness I could not fathom, and feared, if I were left here by myself, I should never find my way back. Suddenly, as we rounded a rise, we could see the silhouette of cattle grazing below us and over to our right, a small building, with no light coming from within; only white smoke slowly curling from a stone chimney, into the cool night sky.

Hugh Robson leaned over once again, cupping his hand to his mouth and whispered, "Stay by my side, betwixt Michael and me' where'er we go, you go also, not one hoof beyond my nag, we walk down slowly, we move the cattle without a sound, and by the time the Scotties rise from their slumbers, we will be far away." Both Michael and Hugh then drew their swords, and seeing this, I did likewise.

"Just in case," whispered Michael.

I noticed that many of the others had drawn their lances. I was much pleased that we did not; as I have mentioned, the lance was not my favoured weapon.

We rode silently down into the valley, and as we neared the cattle, we came almost to a halt, then slowly eased forward the beasts, in such a way that not one animal made the slightest sound. I looked over to my right, toward the small dwelling. Uncle John had dismounted, and was stood hard into the wall of the house, to the right of the door, his sword drawn and held high across his chest. This was explained to me later, that John had left his horse at the side of the dwelling, had crept up to the door, had checked which side of the door the catch was at, which was on the right, therefore the door would be hinged on the left. Anyone opening the door would see to the left first, and would have to step forward to see to the right, and of course, anyone stepping forward of the door would find John's sword removing their head from their shoulders. No one was going to raise the alarm tonight.

As we cleared the immediate ground in front of the house, I looked back to see John, walking away from the house, leading his nag, and not mounting until well clear, and even then, keeping his nag to a walk, so as to ensure no noise was made. We continued to ride on slowly, thus keeping the animals quiet, until we had passed over a ridge and were heading down into another valley, when we quickened the pace.

Michael and Raymond came to either side of me, Michael saying in hushed tones, though why, as there did not appear a soul around, "We three are to stay with the herd, the rest are to go over the ridge to our right; for more stock they will meet up as we go on".

I stayed in the middle, doing the main driving, Michael to my right, keeping in any beasts that cared to wander, Raymond doing likewise to my left. We pressed on at a steady trot now, just keeping a steady southerly heading, or so I hoped, and was sure if I were not, my two companions would put me right.

I watched as the other riders disappeared over the ridge, and now found myself feeling very vulnerable as we were now but three, and with the greatest respect to these fine gentlemen at my sides, the people who I thought to be the hardest fighters were no longer in sight.

Again I found out later that possibly the best fighting man on that reive was Michael Dodds; his quiet, calm and polite demeanour, his unmarked and clear complexion, like that of a gentleman, hid one of the finest fighters there is; I had undoubtedly been left in safe hands.

We continued to ride on; as time passed, and there was no sign of the rest of the riders, I became quite anxious, and rode over to say so to Michael.

"It will be fine; Rob, had there been anything untoward, even at this distance, in the quiet of the night, we would surely have heard if fighting had taken place," he assured me.

I asked Michael, "If we heard fighting would we go ride and render help?"

"No, Rob, we would continue on, with Arthur John and Thomas Milburn, not to mention the rest; they will not need the likes of us to help them, we will go onward. Now, back to your station and let us make some distance betwixt that croft back there and the border, while the Good Lord gives us such darkness."

We rode on, herding the cattle at a greater pace than we would take them to market, but it was hoped when going to market that there was no likelihood of someone about to chase you and take away your life. Having said that last year, one of the Robson family, a cousin to Hugh and Abel, who dwelt within the West March, and was on his way to market at Carlisle, had just that very thing happen, in broad daylight, and did indeed lose his life, along with several others. No one had been found to be the culprit, though there were some who it is thought to be, and their time was quickly growing nigh. I suspected that my uncles, Arthur and John, might play a major role in the retribution, and it would be far more swift than any justice handed out by any March Warden.

The night already dark, by the overcast sky, seemed to grow even darker, which made me think that dawn was not far away, when I heard a sound coming from over the hill on my right. I froze in the saddle, as I brought my nag to a halt and waited and listened. Yes, there was something, I'm sure there was something. I drew my sword and held it high, signalling first to Michael on my left, then Raymond on my right, both acknowledging me as they caught sight of me.

We stopped driving the cattle, soon all was quiet. Was I going to bloody my sword? I pondered, half with excitement, half with trepidation. The wait in the saddle, looking and listening, trying to control my breathing, peering through the darkness for the least sign of riders; were they ours, were they Scotties, would we know until they were upon us, then would it be too late? Questions upon questions rushing through my mind. Did Michael and Raymond harbour the same fears as me? This was why Father had spent so many hours working with me, showing me how to use my weapons. Would I now be able to give a good and brave account of myself?

After all that work over the past two years and more, for this very night, could I kill? Yes, I had killed before, but that was a Bell, and he had taken my sister by force. Yes, that is it, I thought, just think they are Bells, who have taken your sister, yes that is it, yes I am now ready, let them come, let me bloody my sword.

Out of my thoughts and doubts I was brought back to my surroundings. Looking to my right there were dark silhouettes slowly appearing at the tip of the ridge. My breath shortened, my buttocks tightened on the saddle, my grip of reins and sword tightened. I stood up in the stirrups, to give me a better view of what we were to face, and how many. Again the doubt; I had not thought of the prospect of having to take on more than one at a time. One moment I gained confidence, the next that confidence was dashed; my head was spinning with all these thoughts.

I continued peering through the dark for any sign of recognition. Were these cattle being driven in front of the riders? I do believe they were; if that be so it must be Father and his brothers, Uncle James, Hugh and Abel, was it? It was too dark and too far away to be sure. I held fast, but I saw Michael riding forward. Had he recognised them, or was he about to take them on? Do I stay here, do I ride forward? Then from my left I was aware of movement, I twisted around in my saddle, sword at the ready. "Easy there, Rob, it is Raymond, they are our riders, let us press forward with the herd, and merge with them at the edge of the valley," he said, still in hushed tones. I spurred my nag on, as we lifted the herd back into motion.

By the time we met up with the others, the eastern hills were starting to have some definition, which meant dawn would soon be upon us. We were still very close to the last place to be raided, therefore we now had to place as much distance between our present location and our holding place for through the day.

The first person from the raiding party I was to see was James, who came alongside, his horse sweating heavily, even in the cold night air. "Hurry them on, Rob, at the gallop if you can, we need distance and fast."

I spurred my nag hard and pressed hard into the herd, they responding, and started off at a trot, then faster, to a canter. I had never driven cattle at a pace such as this, and found it quite difficult to keep an eye on all the beasts, at speed and in the twilight of the early dawn.

We did, with great difficulty, at least on my part, seem to cover a good distance over little time, but we had to travel onward, in daylight, for some time before we were able to find cover, to secrete ourselves until nightfall. A copse appeared to our left as we pressed on, and James signalled for us to head towards it. We pressed the cattle in between the trees of the copse, which they were reluctant to do, but we kept at them, until they were all in, then we pushed forward ourselves, into the middle of the herd, and tethered our horses.

I had scarcely got from the saddle when James came to me and asked me to take first watch along with Abel Robson. I was quite pleased in a way, as due to the excitement of the wait in the valley, as the raiding party returned, plus the excitement of the hard drive to get to cover, sleep was some way off, and once my watch was over, then hopefully, I could sleep, unbroken, until nightfall.

A heavy arm came about my shoulder, with sword in hand. "Come, Rob, the old men need their slumber, come, we'll keep them safe," Abel said as we walked to our stations, laughing as we did so.

I had not had many dealings with Abel until this time, but I found him a most charming person as we talked quietly, so as not to disturb the others.

The lie of the land where we had taken refuge was such that there was but one vantage point, thus the two lookouts could stay together, keeping each other alert.

Abel was very interested in my capture and time with the brothers at Melrose, and I found myself kept fully occupied in answering his many questions. This did much to while away the time until we woke the next watch. I now had a new friend, which pleased me, as there always appeared to be people who wanted to be your foe, so another friend was always good to have.

I do not remember laying myself down to sleep, for when it came, it came instantly, and deeply, and the light of the day was almost gone before Father woke me. I suspect, had he not woken me, I would have slumbered on until the next day. The new evening offered little in comfort; it was a grey heavy clouded dusk, with low cloud and a dampening mist, which would afford our party a greater safety, but a far less comfortable ride. After mounting up, and wrapping myself in my cloak, my helmet down over my eyes, we started to urge the herd back out of the copse, which they were more reluctant to do than they were to come in, but I found, having watched some of the others, that drawing the lance, and using the point deftly placed to a beast's rump, does much to urge it upon its way.

We were soon underway and making good progress, when John peeled off from the herding party, and galloped off back in the direction we had come. I heeled my nag over to where Father was and asked what was afoot.

"He is going back to cover our backs," said Father. "Should there be a Hot Trod, John will catch sight of it early, then gallop back and warn us, so we can ready ourselves for an attack."

I had learnt so much on this adventure, more than I had ever learnt in such a short time, and I was sure I would learn much more as the time went by.

I did voice my anxiety to Father that if John were riding back, was there not a possibility that he may get caught by a pursuing Hot Trod. Father said that indeed there was such a possibility, but John would not give in lightly, and it was likely that if such a Hot Trod did catch up with him, he would likely see them all off. I'm sure Father made such a statement in jest; however, I knew of no man who would take on either willingly.

Father then rode off to herd in some beast that had wandered from the main drive. I could not help feeling that he was as anxious as myself, but we drove on, ever harder.

The weather was worsening all the while, causing the ground to become heavier. James took up station at the head of the drive, raising his hand to bring all to a standstill. I called over to Hugh, who was nearest to me, "Why do we stop?"

"The marshes ahead, they are treacherous," he called back.

I waited and watched, occasionally standing in the stirrups to better my view, though what I hoped to see I knew not. A strange thing, but when driving the herd forward, my mind was on the way ahead; however, now I was stationary, I felt nervous of what may be behind; the longer I sat there waiting, the more nervous I became.

Then, in front of me, I saw James signal back to the rest of the riders. Father came galloping over. "You wait here, Rob; we will all ride forward, taking up stations on either edge of the marshes. When we are all in position, you drive the herd on, between the riders, and hopefully we may not lose a beast."

Soon ahead of me were two lines of men on horseback, James up ahead, with his hand raised high, in signal for me to commence the drive. I drew my lance, in case any beast not be willing to go forward, and slowly I urged the cattle forward, giving the odd reluctant beast a spur with my lance. This weapon, of which I had little love, was now becoming a useful implement. By using it, I started to feel more comfortable with it than at any other time.

Slowly I drove onward, and as I passed each rider, they fell in behind me, and helped to urge on the herd. Eventually we reached firmer ground, but looking back, even before the marshes, with the ground now being so heavy, we had left a trail that even a blind man could follow. I mentioned this to Abel who was now at my side, and he rode to the head of the herd, to where James was, who then rode back to me, and looked at the well-trod trail.

"Well spotted, Rob," said James. "We will have to take the herd eastward to the edge of Kerr territory."

Once on firmer ground we herded the cattle eastward, but this also meant driving them uphill, as the lie of the land to the east took in the Teviot hills, and trying to drive already tired beasts uphill was far more difficult than I imagined; the going became increasingly slow. If there was a Trod in pursuit, they would surely be upon us this night. I was aware of a growing tension within my fellow riders, which caused me, being on my virgin raid, to become very anxious, resulting in me spending more time looking backward than forward.

With this extended journey home, it would mean spending another day and night away from home, but if we had taken a straight trail home, it would lead anyone following, straight to our doors, and we could not only lose what we had worked so hard to get, our new cattle, there were some fine beasts indeed, but also those cattle which we already owned, and maybe our lives, so there was no alternative but to endure our hardship.

I little realised how long we had been in the saddle, but the rain, although not stopped, had now eased, and the sky though still with cloud cover, did, from behind a cloud, give an indication of where the moon was; it was now well across the sky. We pressed on, ever urging these stupid Scottie beasts, who did all in their power to hinder our progress; the odd one kept trying to wander from the main drive. I became very impressed with the skills of my fellow riders in the finer arts of droving. My station continued to be at the rear, setting the pace of the drive, though I felt my efforts were not to the standard of my fellows. The cape I wore, made by my mother, from untreated sheepskin, had proved a most valuable garment; it had kept me dry and warm throughout a most disagreeable night, and would, hopefully, continue to do so throughout the day, should I be allowed to sleep. With the thought that Mother had made this garment for me, my thoughts went out to her, and Sarah. Would Sarah continue with her present state, those awful dead eyes, the cold detachedness; would Mother continue to carry on as if nothing were untoward; could I continue through life without confiding in someone, the fact that I had killed her man, that I had seen my sister kill her baby, that all of this led to her present state; is this really what life is like for everyone?

Life was never easy within the manse, getting up in the middle of the night to the sound of a bell, to say prayers, and eight further times through the day, having to watch every moment, should Father Francis appear and want to attack me, but the life was simple and did not involve the complications that I had encountered in the years since my return home.

After pressing the herd upwards for a long period, we started to descend and the going became much easier. Father rode over to me and said we would haul up in the valley. I said I thought there was still some time before dawn, but Father said that the cattle had struggled along the trail this night and would benefit from an early stop, as would we all, and that the valley bottom would afford us good cover from anyone on our trail.

Once in the valley basin, the two Robsons were sent on to the high ground either side of the valley to keep watch. I trotted over to James, and asked what was wanted of me. "Sleep, my lad, we are pleased with you this night, you have proved a worthy rider, you deserve rest," he said.

I went and found a flat rocky outcrop, laid myself down, tying the horse's lead rein loosely to my wrist, thus stopping it from wandering off but should it get spooked, as I slept, it would not drag me away. As there was nothing to tether it to this was what had to be done. The last of the night had given way to heavy cloud but no longer the rain, as I wrapped my cape about me, sleep taking over quickly.

It must have been just after midday when I was woken by Raymond. "Your watch, Rob," he said, as I wearily opened my eyes to a new day, to be greeted with a hazy winter sun. There was still the dampness in the air but at least the sun was out and it was a day without frost.

Father came over to where I still lay, propped up on one arm. "Rob, get saddled up and ready to go," he said tersely.

"To take up watch?" I enquired.

"No, lad, we are setting off now, there is no time to waste; there is a Trod afoot," he answered.

I quickly got to my feet, and looking around I spied John, now back with us. It must have been he who had brought this news. I gathered my goods and chattels and saddled up, then swung myself into the saddle, heeling my nag forward, towards the herd and my fellow riders. James came over. "Rob, you did a fine job yesterday; hold the same station, this day, but haste is of the essence, for as you know, a Trod is afoot; we must be over the border before they cast an eye upon us; we're relying on you, lad, to get us home."

I knew that I was the least important member of that band of riders, but was grateful to my uncle for his words, which if not exactly true, did much to encourage me. With James' words still rolling about my mind, I drew my lance and started to urge the cattle forward, the Robsons to my right, the Dodds to my left, James galloping forward to get to the head of the herd, my father and his two brothers staying back, on the ridge, to keep watch and hinder the progress of our pursuers, should they appear. Oh how I wanted to stay with them, a chance to bloody my sword, for had I not spent over two years readying for this, for it to be snatched from me, to go herding cattle.

I then removed such thoughts from my mind, and concentrated on the task in hand, and there may indeed be something in what James said; yes, I will be the driving force on this raid. With yet new impetus, I urged my nag even harder, and many a Scottie beast's rump felt the point of my lance that day. It was much easier to herd cattle in daylight than at night; they seemed more willing to harry along, and before very long the herd was heading at a goodly canter.

Soon the beasts' backs were steaming from their exertions as we pressed ever harder, through the heart of the Kerr lands. The Kerrs were one of the Scottie riding families, but they carried great sway with the Scottish Royal Court, and therefore we did not want to get caught within their lands, as the consequences could be severe. The irony of this is that they were not averse to taking to horse raiding, and in some cases, even against their fellow Scotties.

By mid-afternoon we had passed through the lands of the Kerrs, and were at the border, now back in England, though well to the east of our destination. Even with this wide swing from our course, we would be home before nightfall, and though my sleep had been deep, it had been short, and my warm dry bed beckoned, even this early in the day.

Now back in England, the urgency of the drive seemed less intense, and my thoughts were now with my father and his two brothers. Had they come across a Trod in pursuit of our band of riders? If so, what had become of them? Surely if there had been nothing untoward, they would have ridden back by now; where had they got to? I had to clear my mind of such thoughts; the drive may not now be so urgent, but nonetheless, it takes concentration to keep a herd together, even one of only fifty head, and I was not doing my duty as I should.

I spurred my nag on, but it did not respond as it should; as with us all, it was now feeling the exhaustion of the last few days of hard riding, and before I could think of turning in, on my arrival home, the nag would have to be cooled, then brushed, then foddered, and only when its needs are attended to may I seek rest.

As mid-afternoon approached, Raymond Dodds cried out, "Behind you!" I swiftly turned in my saddle, all thoughts of what I would do on arrival home immediately washed from my thoughts. Riders coming over the ridge to our right, too far off to distinguish who or what they might be. I reined my weary nag about to face the oncoming riders, my lance from its saddle hold, and held in readiness, my stomach tightening, my buttocks clenching on the saddle, my knees tightening into the nag's side. I did not know what my fellow riders were doing, for I kept my eyes firmly on the oncoming riders, and dared not break my gaze, but hoped that they also were in readiness for the assault.

Then a cry from behind me, "It's those Milburns!" and yes indeed, it was Father and my two uncles. I holstered my lance as they neared. Arthur was slightly ahead of the other two.

"Fancy yur chances du you, Rob? I hope you fight better thun the Scotties," he said as his two brothers came to his side, both laughing heartily.

Hugh Robson and James Charlton came forward, taking station at either side of me. "Is all quiet behind, lads?" asked James.

"My lance and sword tell their own story," replied John.

His remarks drew all our eyes to his holstered lance, which ran red from one end to the other, and both he and his nag were heavily blooded, as were both other riders. Arthur then told of how they had ridden back over our trail, found a good place to rest, and at the same time, watched over a wide area, for signs of a Hot Trod.

Father had been the one to spot some fifteen riders heading in our direction, on the line of the heavy trail we had left. The three brothers had not waited to ambush the riders, but had set off from their vantage point, with lances levelled, at full gallop, and while some distance off, had reined their nags to the left, that is the right of the pursuing party, then come in hard from that left side, which hampered the Scotties' use of their weapons. The three brothers took out three Scotties at the first onslaught, and as they unsaddled the three Scotties, dropped their lances, reined their nags hard around, and drawing their swords, came in from behind of the Scotties, taking out another three. With six riders down, before the Scotties could come to bear, they sent them into a panic, and they set flight from whence they came. I think Father and his two brothers had laughed all the way back, until they reunited with the rest of us; indeed they were still laughing long after.

Though it was good to hear such tales, I was nevertheless somewhat put out that I had not been party to this wonderful rout. My weapons would have to wait to be blooded another day.

Chapter 11

Revenge Raid

Some weeks after our return from my first raid, and as the winter was now starting to bite hard, there was now a covering of snow upon the ground, and the nights were bitterly cold. Within our small valley, there had not been any raids for some long time, though we had waited on many a night for one to happen, when the conditions were right, but none had happened, for which we were grateful.

The cattle we had brought back from our raid were well settled within our herd, we having taken ten, as had Arthur and John, as well as the Robsons and Dodds and James.

With the conditions being as they were, we had little fear of a raid, until the weather eased, but still we took in the best of the cattle and horses, if only to shield them from the harshness of the nights.

It was proving to be one of the hardest winters there had been for many years; we did not venture far in these conditions; through the day we did little but let out the cattle and try and keep them foddered with hay, which we loaded on to the sledge, which was drawn by one of the nags. Sometimes this chore was carried out in a blinding blizzard, as our stock was now even more of a lifeline than usual; Father seemed to be affected by the weather, as he was not able to get around as normal, outside. I thought that this was possibly due to him just having the one eye, and the brightness of the snow impaired his vision.

This left me to undertake most of the duties, including the slaughter of any stock, for food. Normally we would only kill one beast at a time, but I decided, as it was so cold, I would slaughter a couple of the cattle, and a couple of the sheep, and the cold weather would help preserve the meat. The reason for my decision was that it was a task I disliked with great intensity. To kill a man who wanted to kill me, or who had offended me, and I had only killed one man before, that was acceptable, or even a wild animal, that was acceptable, but to kill the stock, even though it was to eat, held no pleasure for me. Therefore in a somewhat twisted idea, I resolved to get the killing and butchering over in one session, and not have it hanging over me.

The day therefore was spent undertaking this most unpleasant of tasks, but at the end, I had managed to accumulate a goodly stock of meat, which would sustain the family for many weeks.

Mother had warmed some water for me, after the labours of the day, and I was able to rid myself of the blood and stench of the butchered beasts. I was also issued with clean clothes, after my cleaning, as the ones I had worn were heavily blooded.

Father was not best pleased at my endeavours, as he thought I was wrong to slaughter so many animals at once, but it was now done. I settled to the fact that my endeavours would serve us all for some time and that by the time we needed to slaughter more, Father would be feeling better, and would therefore undertake the task himself.

I sat to my evening meal with little stomach for food and only took it to ward off the cold of the night to come, and afterward lay upon my bed, and took a stone to the blade of my bollock knife, which had served me well throughout the day, and was in need of sharpening.

After achieving a satisfactory edge to the knife, I set it back in the belt that lay by my bed, along with my sword, should I require it quickly during the night.

The next I was aware, was the sound of voices outside the bastle, but it was still the dead of night. I looked from the arrow slits in the bastle walls, and could see riders outlined against the snow covered ground, rounding up our stock and beginning to drive them off. I rushed to the other side of the room, to where Mother and Father slept and woke Father.

"Fadder, thurs Scotties outside tekin the stock," I whispered, as if not to wake anyone else, but my whispers were of the nature that all were aware of what was taking place.

"There's nowt you can do, lad, I am still not ready to fight, and if you go out, you will surely be killed, if there are many. Go to yur bed and get rest, they will be easy to trail when we rise," said Father.

"But Fadder, how did they get here? We can scarcely move out of the valley, and they have come from over the border," I asked.

"Brave lads, Son, brave, brave lads, now to yur bed, and sleep, we have some hard days ahead," he replied.

I reluctantly went to my bed. Sarah was sat up in her bed, not outwardly alarmed, still with those cold eyes, yet I knew that although her eyes were incapable of showing feeling, she was perturbed. Just before getting into my bed, I went over to her and gently placed my hand on the side of her face, and smiled. In the light of the fire she appeared worse than she did through the day, but, as I placed my hand to her face, she took hold of my wrist and held my hand to her. This was the first sign of any feeling she had shown, since the night she held her baby tight to her breast, until all life had disappeared from it, and she placed it back in its cot. Her eyes were still cold, but she had shown some feeling, which did much to hearten me, and to give me something else to occupy my mind, when outside there were Scotties taking away all we had, and were we to fail in retrieving our stock, the harsh winter would surely consume us all.

With such thoughts dancing on my mind, sleep did not come readily. The thought that here I lay, while our very livelihood was being driven away. The thought that we were cut off due to the snow, and here were Scotties, who had travelled in what must be the most dreadful conditions, conditions that I would have to contend with on the morrow.

The day broke, and as usual Mother was the first to rise, and had everything underway for our first meal of the day, but this morning the table was laden with far more than we were used to. Mother was used to the ways of the riding families; she was well aware that we would be setting off as soon as we could, gathering together with other riding families, and setting off on a Hot Trod, and as it was less than a day since the raid, it would be a Hot Trod. The rules governing the Trod differed from Hot Trod, which was undertaken within a day of the raid, and allowed virtually whatever means was required to retrieve one's property, and let all be assured, we would employ all means, for if we failed we would die anyway, so let it be by the lance or sword, than by cold and starvation.

The Cold Trod, which was undertaken after a few days from the raid, did not allow for very much action to be taken against the perpetrators, other than to identify such persons and report them to the March Warden, and representation made at the next truce day. However, many have entered upon a Cold Trod and shed blood, and have ended upon the gallows, or found themselves looking into a burn with a foot held down behind their head.

After eating our fill with hot oats and berries dried from the autumn picking and hot spiced wine, which was something that we rarely drank, but Mother was determined that she would send us forth well provided for, we saddled our nags, which thankfully had been safely stabled in with the best cattle, in the base of the bastle, and should we return with nothing, the stock we had may just sustain us for the winter, if we were very careful and the winter was mercifully short.

Father and I kissed Mother and Sarah before leaving and headed down the valley towards the Dodds. Sarah had returned to the coldness, her fleeting show of affection now but a memory. We had not gone far when we saw the approach of many riders; there were Michael and Raymond Dodds, also the two Robsons, who had brought along another five of their kinsmen; there were also around ten Bells, old Cuthbert, his three remaining sons and eight of his kinsmen. The Bells would not be my choice of companions normally, but if there was blood to let, a Bell was a worthy companion to have, for they were all capable with lance and sword, even though Father made old Cuthbert look very stupid, the day we got Sarah back.

Father and I turned our nags and fell in with the rest of the riders, Cuthbert speaking first. "Aye, Hafe Heed, it was a bad night, they have cleared the whole valley of every living thing. If we do not get all back there will be many starve this winter."

Father nodded in agreement, then replied, "Aye, Cuthbert, we will have our revenge this day," then we all rode on with little conversation between any of the riders.

We reached the Charlton bastle, and James was already mounted, along with ten other riders, some his kinsmen and others, I found out later, were of the Fenwick family, who were large land-owners and carried sway with the March Warden, Sir John Foster, a man I had yet to meet. The Fenwicks, because of their position, were not given to riding, as we did, but much of their stock had been taken in the night. Their presence within the group would not be talked of, either during or after, and we would only speak to them using their first names, thereby not involving them in the eyes of the authorities; that is of course the March Warden.

We had not ridden far when from the left, over the valley ridge, came some dozen riders. At the head rode two familiar figures, Uncles Arthur and John with kinsmen of mine, some rarely seen and some never seen. I heard Cuthbert's voice from within our group of riders say, "There will be much blood letting this day, if this family has been roused," meaning the Milburns.

I have to admit that some of my kinsmen were gentlemen of particularly severe appearance, and was much pleased that they were with me and not against. Did the Scotties know what terrible thing they had unleashed, this body of riders who were hell bent not only on retrieving their stock, but of exacting a terrible revenge?

The progress was slow, the snow cover was heavy, and the horses had to work harder to trudge through the snow, and the sky threatened more within the next few hours. For whatever hardships we may be enduring, we had all just left warm beds, had warm meals, and were fresh in the saddle. Our adversaries were cold, tired, hungry, saddle weary, on cold weary nags, and driving reluctant beasts, cattle who were reluctant to move in snow at the best of times, let alone on a long drive. There was the added burden that, regardless of how many riders they had, the quantity of stock they had reived was so great, that any drive with that number of beasts was going to be very slow, even in good weather.

Such thoughts kept my spirits high, thinking that we would soon find our quarry, and despatch them, then return to our homes. The trail left by the reivers was so very clear that we were all able to sit back and ride, but I noticed two of our riders far out on the flanks; to my left it looked like one of the Robsons, but on the right, the rider was too far off to recognise. They were placed on the flanks to check that no Scottie riders had broken away from the main party and thus may cause a threat to our party.

As we rode on, whenever the depth of the snow allowed, we would pick up our speed to a canter, as one, it let the nags stretch their limbs and warm themselves, two, it allowed the riders to move more within the saddle, and warm them, and three, it allowed us to lessen the gap between our two parties.

Father rode over to me. "Come with me, Rob," he ordered. I pulled my nag over and rode out to follow Father, who had stopped at the side of Michael and Raymond Dodds.

As I pulled along the side of the three, Father said, "Raymond, you have rode scout before?"

"Yes, Tom," came the terse reply.

"Good, then you and Rob, as you are possibly the lightest of all our party, your horses will be swifter through the snow, I want you to ride forward and try and pick up the Scotties' position. You must not be spotted, and as soon as you see any sign, you will ride back with your news. Rob, you will listen and obey every word that Raymond says, do you hear me, lad?"

"Yes, Fadder," I said, bowing my head.

"Away wid yur then," Father ordered, as Raymond and I broke free from the rest of the riders. My excitement was so great I thought I may explode, there and then; only my second ride, and my first Hot Trod, and I was scouting.

The snow at this point was fairly thin, so we were able to gallop off; yes, this was what I was born to do, riding with my kinsmen, no, at the head of my kinsmen, Raymond and I were now responsible for this raid's success.

We were soon brought back to a walk as the snow once again thickened, and the threat of more from the skies increased. We rode onward, pushing as hard as our nags could stand, then, after some considerable time, in the middle of the trail, a fresh cow pat, still steaming, but the lie of the land did not let us see the drive ahead. We brought our nags to a halt, and sat quietly, both of us standing in our saddles to gain vision ahead.

"Raymond, was that a cow lowing?" I asked.

"I was about to ask you the same, Rob," said Raymond. "To foot," said Raymond, as we dismounted.

Raymond took out his lance from its holster and drove it into the ground, then tethered his nag to it, then I tied mine to the same pole. When the horses were secured, we both ran forward to the tip of the ridge ahead, then lay in the snow, slowly bringing our heads up to peer over the brow. The sight before us made us both gasp. Neither of us had ever seen so many cattle and sheep in one place, they seemed to cover the entire valley ahead.

We looked at each other with great surprise written upon both our faces, then we both broke out into the broadest of smiles; we had done it, we had accomplished the task set to us. Raymond put forward his hand, and I took it and we shook hands in self-congratulation, after which we scurried back to our nags, and Raymond went to retrieve his lance, which took the two of us to prise it from its frozen anchorage, we both giggling like little girls. We soon swung into the saddle and rode off, gently at first, so as not to make any noise, and as the distance grew, so did our pace, until we were at full gallop. Again I was swamped with the exhilaration of the gallop and the thoughts that this was my destiny, to ride as my ancestors had done, as far back as time.

It was not long before we met up with the rest of our party, who had made good progress since we had set off on our scouting mission. Excitedly I exclaimed that we had found them, to which I was asked by my Uncle John, "How many?"

I sat in my saddle, lost for words, as I had not taken in the numbers involved. Quickly, Raymond answered, "There must be more than fifty riders, but cattle, sheep and horses, too many to count."

James came over and said, "You said more than fifty, how many more?"

Raymond was able to tell James that he had counted fifty-two riders, but because the herd was so large, it was likely that there may be others afoot.

Again, I did not see what Raymond had, and it acted as a strong lesson for any future times I was asked to scout, for I fear, had it been down to me we would not have been in possession of the information we now had. James then turned to me and asked if I were able to confirm the information Raymond had given.

"I am not, Sir, for I have to admit, I did not take in anywhere near that amount of information, for I was too excited at having found the Scotties."

"Thank you, boy, for your honesty," said James as he pulled his horse away toward the rest of the group. I stayed where I was at, greatly embarrassed at my inability to carry out a simple task.

As I sat there, I was beckoned over to the rest of the riders by Michael. I slowly and sheepishly cantered over, and lined up beside Michael and Father. James was sat facing the other riders, and as he started to speak, the snow started to come down. The sky now had covered over with those heavy mid-grey snow clouds that told us we were in for a heavy fall. James started to speak.

"I feel, gentlemen, that our best line of attack is to come at them from the direction they least expect; therefore I propose that we ride out to the eastward side, where the ridge affords us better cover, and circle around and come in from the direction they are driving. Is there a man among you who has a better plan?" James waited a moment for a reply, of which there was none, then he reined his horse out from the party, heading eastward, and we all followed on.

The snow was now becoming very heavy, and visibility was greatly reduced. Father was at my side, and leaned over to speak. "Worry not,

Rob, you did well, you were not expected to know everything the first time out, but you will the next time. This snow will greatly help us, as they will not see us coming, and because we will come from the wrong direction, they will think it is their own people come to meet them, and help them with their ill-gotten gains. Before they realise, we will be upon them, and a fine rout will be had."

Father did much to ease my discomfort at my shortcomings, and his assessment of the conflict to come gave me strength to confront my first battle. The riding was hard, and the nags were not at their ease at having to battle against such harsh conditions, but the one consolation would be that when we got ahead of the drive and turned south to confront them, the wind would be at our backs, but in their eyes, and our nags would be more at ease and better able to cope with the needs of battle.

It took far longer to circle the drive than I had expected, but eventually we turned southward, and the order came to draw our lances, then we started to trot forward. Father leaned over again, and said, "Remember all you have learnt, pick your quarry, then do not run directly at him but to his right, which makes it harder for him to level his lance to you, then as late as you dare rein your nag hard right, into him, and go for the middle of the chest. You do not need to kill, to unsaddle will be enough."

James lifted his left arm to indicate that he had seen our quarry, and as he lowered it, he broke his horse into a canter, and we all followed, all levelling our lances as we went.

"Take the one to your left, Rob," I heard Father say. I looked to my left and I saw what Father had seen, which to be truthful, I had not until then. I spurred my nag forward, harder and harder, until we were at the gallop, keeping my knees tightly in to my nag's side, tightly gripping the reins, my heart beating faster than the sound of the horses' hooves in the snow. Usually, in the snow, horses' hooves can barely be heard, but I could hear them as loud as if we were galloping over rock. My quarry was barely an instant away, he still was unaware of me; he must have had his head down against the driving snow. He looked up as the lance, which I thought was levelled at his chest, was just about to enter his throat. The impact of hitting him ripped the lance from my hand, and the Scottie rolled back out of his saddle, falling on his back, with my lance still embedded in his neck, the blood pouring from the wound, turning the snow crimson. As I had lost my lance, I had little option but to draw my sword, which was not full size as those of the Scotties, which put me at a slight disadvantage.

A Scottie had me in his sight, and was galloping toward me, his sword drawn and being waved above his head as he approached. I could feel my eyes widen at the spectacle, and my stomach tighten. I held my nag firm and awaited the attack, and just before he was upon me I reined my nag hard to the right and out of range of his blade, and he rode through. I continued to rein hard to the right, my nag snorting its disapproval. As I brought the nag about I spurred it hard and we were at a gallop in an instant, hard after my attacker, the snow now in my eyes, but I was so centred upon him that it made little difference to me. I came in fast behind him, levelling my sword to the middle of his back, then drew back slightly, then forward, allowing the speed of my nag to bring a crushing blow to the Scottie's back. He let out a scream of pain that will live with me forever, as he slumped forward in his saddle, exposing a deep and bloody gash across his back. I rode through and beyond, and when I was sure it was safe, reined my nag around to come back at him, should he still pose a threat. The Scottie was still in the saddle, but slumped forward, and crying out in the most horrid pain. I reined out to my right and came in at him from the side so that he could not easily attack should he be feigning, and as I neared, I raised my sword and brought it down about the nape of his neck. His cries of pain stopped, as he fell from his saddle, landing face down in the snow. I never saw what my adversary looked like, a fact for which I am grateful, but his body lying in the snow with blood from two wounds staining the whiteness that surrounded him was a sight to remain with me for the rest of my life. I sat there for a few moments, unaware of what was happening about me, staring at the body, my sword lowered to my side.

I was brought back to reality by the sound of some other poor soul being despatched, and as I became aware of my surroundings, I looked and saw my sword dripping blood on to the crisp white snow, leaving a small crimson pool.

I heeled my nag off slowly as I was unaware of the situation beyond where I had been engaged in combat. The snow was still making visibility difficult, and as I walked my nag forward, I encountered body after body, in various positions, slumped in the snow, leaving their stains of crimson, the result of an English lance or sword. I eventually met up with Father, who was with John, Arthur, Michael and Raymond. All five still had their swords drawn, all showing signs of Scottish blood.

Arthur was the first to speak. "Looks like we have a new warrior in the family, Tom," he exclaimed.

"Aye, the lad's done well," replied Father. I did not take pleasure in his remark. I just felt an emptiness within. I had worked so very hard to be one of the riders, and now it all felt so worthless.

James came galloping over, and reined his nag hard in, sliding to a halt. "Is there even one left alive?" he barked out.

"I think not," replied Michael.

"Then we shall return with nothing more than was taken. I would have hoped to capture some for ransom, and make the trip worthwhile," said James. Just then the Bells came trotting over, the three younger ones heavily splattered with blood, and laughing wildly at the carnage that lay about us. I found out later that they had been going about the bodies, firstly slitting their throats, to ensure they were dead, then searching the bodies, and removing anything of worth.

At this scene I broke from the body of riders, and went back to where I had been engaged, to retrieve my lance, and as I did so I found the two bodies not as I had left them, no doubt as a result of the Bells. The lance was still embedded in the neck of the first Scottie, the Bells obviously accepting that no further mutilation was required. I slid from my nag, into the snow, and avoiding the bloodied areas, I tried to draw my lance from the body, but as I pulled, the body lifted. I very nearly took to foot, thinking he were alive, then realised that the lance was stuck in the neck. I had to place my foot upon the head, doing so with my eyes closed, and pulled hard, releasing my weapon. On doing so, I stepped back quickly, not looking upon the person who lay there. I dragged my lance through the snow in an effort to clean some of the blood from it, and after doing so holstered it on the nag, then swung into the saddle, and rode back to the main body of riders.

The snow had not abated as we started to round up the herd, some of which had scattered at the onset of the conflict. This was going to be a hard drive home, and as we were not stealing the herd, but merely retrieving it, we would not have to seek cover through daylight; we would press on without rest, for who could rest in such conditions as these. The one consolation was that I was now able to wrap myself in the sheepskin cape, which kept off the cold and dampness of the snow.

The snow was at our backs, which aided vision, but the cold was as biting as ever, and the light was starting to wane quite quickly, which made the drive much harder, and it was possible to feel the temperature dropping. With ice on top of the snow, it would be down to the sure-footedness of the nag to get us all back. Beasts like the cattle we were driving, and worse still the sheep, were not given to any degree of intelligence, but a good nag could make the difference between life and death on a night like this.

Thankfully my nag had done these journeys more often than myself, used by Father, Uncle James, and on the odd occasion Uncle John, and thus carried all the traits required of a reiver's horse. A good horse in battle, which this nag had shown this very day, and had I not had such a worthy animal, I might not have been so successful in the conflict, sure-footed in this treacherous border country, and a good herding horse, which the nag indeed was. I was indeed fortunate to be paired with such an animal, though I wondered how many more raids this wonderful creature had left, as it had travelled many miles in its long life. I would always treat it better than myself, for as long as it was mine, and hopefully we would have many years of riding ahead.

The snow was now starting to ease, and small breaks were starting to appear in the clouds, allowing the odd glimmer of moonlight through. Normally we would not be thankful of this extra light, but tonight, the light would help our journey home, and it would be a good while before the bodies of the Scotties were found, as the place of our conflict was extremely remote.

Our nags were having to work hard as the snow was up to their knees, and they were having to pick up their legs to push on through the deep snow. We kept the cattle at the front of the drive, as they flattened the snow ahead of the sheep. It would be quite easy to lose many of the sheep on a drive like this, for though they are hardy beasts, well able to withstand the harshest of conditions, on a drive like this it was very easy for their fleeces to become snowbound, thus weighing down the sheep until it was unable to continue. We were determined that we would not lose a single beast this night as we rode onward and closer to home.

I had taken up position at the rear of the drive, without being asked, as it had been my place before, and I felt capable of the duties it entailed. James and one of the Robsons had taken up the lead position. Father, I noticed, rode at the side of his brother, Arthur; I thought they may be engaged in deep conversation. Alas, I had not had much opportunity to become better acquainted with my more distant kinsmen, who apparently had acquitted themselves well on confronting the Scotties, but I would not have expected anything else from a Milburn.

The Bells rode together, in a huddle, lending little to the drive; the other Robsons and the Dodds I had not seen since setting off on the drive. I liked to be with Raymond and Michael, as they always treated me as if I were their kinsman, and I had great affection for the entire family, then Annie came to mind as I drove on; such a pretty young girl. The thought that filled my head on these long drives helped pass the time and warmed the soul, if not the body.

The thickness of the snow varied as we continued, but James and Hugh Robson, as I found out was James' companion, navigated a good course through these difficult conditions, avoiding the drifted areas, which in this light, the cattle could be in before anyone noticed.

The clouds were breaking up quite a lot now, and the moon lit up the way ahead. The scene now quite beautiful, as the entire land around covered by a deep blanket of snow was lit by the moon, giving a blue glow to the entire scene.

A rider came alongside to my left, and stretched out a hand, which I took hold of as he introduced himself. "I am your cousin, Richard, Richard Milburn; my father was called William; he was killed some five years back, in a raid on the Scotties West March. I am from near Carlisle, but was visiting our Uncle Arthur when the Scotties raided, so I am always pleased when I can seek some revenge for his death."

"I am Rob; have you sought revenge often, in the last five years?" I asked.

"Maybe too often," he replied with a laugh. "That's why I am visiting Arthur. The West March warden, Old Scrope, is after me."

"Who is Old Scrope?" I enquired.

"That's Lord Scrope; he is not a bad old soul, but he does like to have a regular hanging; it makes people think he is doing his job, which does have merit, I concede, just so long as it is not me." He laughed again.

"Did you bag many this day, Rob?" asked Richard, quite light heartedly. I think he found all the raiding to be great fun.

"Yes," I replied, "I got two."

"Well done, my cousin, I am truly proud of you, and honoured to be your kin," he replied. I did not know if he mocked me as he continued to have the broadest of smiles on his face. "Tell me, how old are you, my fine warrior?" he asked.

"Fourteen," I replied.

"Fourteen, and you bagged two… damn it man, I only got one, and my word he was a frisky one, but he died like all the rest. Fourteen!" he said incredulously. "Have you been doing this long then, Rob?" he continued.

"No, this is but my second time," I replied.

"Damn it man, how many did you bag the first time then?" he asked.

"I did not bag any, it was just like a cattle drive to market," I replied. He laughed loudly, and as we continued, I had to tell him of my capture and subsequent exile in Scotland, with the monks, and of how I was released and brought back to my home, some of which he was already aware of, which I found quite extraordinary, for him to have heard of my story.

The hours passed quickly, talking to Richard, who was such a jolly fellow, a man in his mid to late twenties, quite a handsome chap, with that bright broad smile, and a demeanour that took away the chill of the night, a kinsman and now friend.

With the help of Richard, to divert my attention away from the long drive and bitter cold, I soon found myself on familiar ground, the snow now much deeper, and the herding much more difficult, but because of the lie of the land, it all seemed to be easier, and now the day was starting to break.

When we arrived at the Charlton bastle, James, along with the Fenwicks and some of the Robsons, stayed there; the Dodds, Bells, the remainder of the Robsons, and all the Milburns rode on. We left the stock at the Charltons; the Heedsmen had sorted out along the trail about the way the stock would be allocated. The one thing we could be assured of was that it would be done fairly, for all present were honourable men; yes, in a case like this, even the Bells.

As we arrived home, the rest of our party bid a hearty farewell, Richard once again shaking my hand vigorously, and with that now familiar broad smile, bid me farewell with the words, "Goodbye, Cousin, we will meet again, God willing, and hopefully fight again side by side…" His final words tailed off, as he had reined his horse mid-sentence, and was riding off as fast as the ground would allow.

Uncle Arthur then came alongside and said, "Do not wager on that, young Rob, for I fear the gibbet will have him first." Then he rode off.

The Dodds and Bells, along with the Robsons, rode off together. The Bells had conducted themselves considerably well on the drive home, although contributing little to the drive, but had not gone out of their way to antagonise other members of the party, which was very much their way. I feared their minds may have been upon the booty they had robbed from the bodies of the fallen Scotties.

The hour was far too early for Mother and Sarah to be risen, but as always, Mother was ahead of us all, and was indeed risen with hot food ready for the returning heroes. I never quite understood how she always managed to be out of bed and ready, no matter what the occasion. I would never mention such to a living soul, for fear that she be reported for witchcraft, for this most distasteful practice was starting to raise its ugly head throughout the land.

We ate heartily, that morning, and told our tales. Mother was horrified when I told of the conflict I had been involved in, casting her arm about my neck and drawing me in, to receive a large kiss, on the forehead. I was beyond being treated like a boy now; I had been on raids, I had fought, fought as my father, and as his father had, but it was still comforting, those displays of affection.

Both Father and I slept until midday, when Mother woke us, saying, "You will not sleep tonight, now up with you both, and get from under my feet."

That was so Mother, from under her feet indeed; there was nowhere to go, the ground outside was thick with snow, and all our stock was at the Charltons.

Father remained in bed and did so for over a week, the exertion of the raid taking its toll. He had not been well before we went, and now he was very poorly. Mother and Sarah tended to him, throughout the day and night, and his discomfort at times was severe. There were times through the day when I saw him clasping his head and rolling around on his bed in great pain. On one occasion when Father was without pain, I sat at his bed and we talked. I asked of his discomfort, and he said that it was due to the injury to his head, and that it always got better eventually. He said that he had been very proud of my conduct on the raid and of the manner I had taken to the conflict. He asked of my feelings of having dispatched two souls to their maker, and I had said that after spending so much time and effort into achieving the standard to be able to fight, I did not gain great satisfaction from my efforts. This reaction greatly pleased him, and he said that when a person gets a fondness for killing, the hangman's noose often follows. I mentioned my cousin, Richard, and Father said that he was that type of person, and warned me to steer clear of him, no matter how charming a fellow he may be.

I asked Father why, if he did not like killing, had he become so very well versed in the use of weapons. He said that it was the way of life, and had always been so within the border lands, and if you were not able to handle yourself in the correct manner, then you became a victim.

Chapter 12

The Quiet Time

That winter there were no more raids by the Scotties into our valley or the next valley, for the news had spread far and wide of the awful retribution that had taken place, after the Scotties had raided our valleys.

The cattle had been split up, and we received back every single beast we had lost, a little thinner perhaps, after their exertions, but maybe fitter for it. The snow had lain heavy for many weeks, but the thaw came in good time for the lambing season.

This time of the year was one that allowed for little sleep, for if you did not want to lose ewes or lambs, then time had to be spent in sheep husbandry, and ewes found the most inconvenient times of day and night to go into lambing. By mid-April the valley was strewn with the product of our labours; those white woolly mischievous animals that bleated throughout the day and night.

This out of the way, it was time to sow whatever crops we required, then it was time for shearing the sheep, which could take days, but the rewards were great, as was the demand for the fleeces for shipping out of the country for weaving in countries across the sea.

When I was at the manse, there was always great excitement at shearing time, and the manse bought all the fleeces from miles around; Donald and one of the brothers would load up a couple of carts and transport it to the coast, where they sold it for a great profit. I could never quite understand why the people did not transport their own fleeces to the coast, but I did find out that only the monks were permitted to trade in fleeces at some ports.

Once the weather allowed, the sheep and cattle were taken to the high country for summer grazing, and it was always advisable to take the horses up to the higher ground where the grass was less lush, as a horse feeding on the new lush grass can get a malady which causes the hooves to become inflamed, which then become very hot and the leg around the hoof swells, and the nag becomes lame.

Father, although now up and around, was still not in the best of health, and it became incumbent on me to shoulder more responsibility. As a result of this, I was asked to take the stock to the high country for the summer grazing, where I built a sheil from fallen wood to make a frame, and animal skins tied to the frame to give me cover. It was not the most handsome of dwellings but it afforded some shelter, and I made myself as comfortable as possible.

Two days into my time in the high country, it would be around midday, when I saw another herd of cattle and sheep being driven over the crest of the ridge and toward my direction. As it neared I saw it was Michael and Raymond Dodds, doing the driving. On their arrival, they both got from their nags and Michael was the first to speak.

"Well, Rob, we are to rob you of your peace and solitude. Your father and I have thought it best if we graze our animals together, therefore, Raymond will stay with you and keep you company."

What wonderful news I thought, and greeted the news with much enthusiasm, but better was yet to come. Michael went on to say that Annie would be coming once a day, as the Dodds were in the habit of milking their sheep to make cheese, and she would milk the sheep and Raymond and I would milk the cows, after which Annie would return with the cart laden with milk.

This truly was going to be a good summer, as long as the Scotties stayed away, but it was rare that any raids took place during the summer months.

Michael and Raymond set about erecting a much more substantial sheil than the one I had managed to assemble, and after some time they had produced a quite spacious dwelling. There were stone walls and a doorway large enough to walk in; the wooden poles that had been the main frame of my dwelling were now the joists for the roof, and overlaid with divots dug from nearby, which now gave a substantial roof.

As early evening came Michael left, promising to call and see Mother and Father, to inform them of my good health, while Raymond and I built up our fire in order to set the cauldron, for our meal.

Later, as we ate, I asked Raymond if when we had time to spare, of which there should be ample, could we practise our swordplay, which he readily agreed, but with one provision, which surprised me greatly. If he spent time with me on swordplay, then I would have to teach him to read and write. I readily agreed, though I doubted I had the necessary knowledge to undertake such a task, but the agreement was made and our summer was now mapped out.

The following day, after tending the animals, and the afternoon was just past its height, I spotted a horse and cart coming slowly up the hillside; it was Annie. I waved excitedly to her as she advanced, and she returned my waves with the same enthusiasm. My heart skipped a beat at seeing her again. It had been some time since we last met and time had done wondrous things to her, for it had transformed this once pretty little girl into a strikingly beautiful young woman. I waited at the top of the hill until she had crested the summit and stopped, then I held a hand out, to assist her from the cart, but she just jumped down, ignoring my hand, and landed in my arms, then standing on tiptoe, gave me a kiss on the cheek. "Hello, Rob, you devil, why have you not visited me in all this time?" she said, as she gently and mockingly lightly smacked my face.

I was so taken aback by this display of affection that I just stood there, unable to reply.

"Oh, Rob, have I embarrassed you so? I am sorry, but still upset that it has been so long," she added, with a most beautiful smile that shone with more brilliance than the sun itself. My only reply was a broad smile, then gaining my composure I said, "Come and see our new sheil that your father and Raymond built."

We walked along together, and I knew that there could never be anyone else for me but this wonderful Annie Dodds.

After greeting her brother, Annie then told us both to round up all the sheep, in order that she might milk them, so we all set to work, and by the time we had finished the early evening was upon us. Before leaving, we insisted that she ate with us, and I say this with the greatest respect for my mother's cooking, but no meal had tasted so good as that, as we three sat and chatted and laughed. It came time for Annie to go; there were still a few hours of daylight as the evenings stretched out, and we bade her a fond farewell. It was as if we would not see her for an age, as I stood on the edge of the hill watching her descend in the horse and cart, now laden with the sheep's milk, for cheese making, returning her waves, as she occasionally lifted her arm and waved.

When I got back to the sheil Raymond was laughing. I could feel myself blush. "Well, brother-in-law," he said in a mocking way.

"Stop that, Raymond," I said, turning away.

"You really like my sister, don't you?" he said.

"I would be a fool not to, I have liked her since the first time I saw her at your bastle, when I first got home from Scotland, and I was on my way to see Sarah, and then we were but children," I said.

"It pleases me, Rob, for if my sister is to marry anyone, both I and my parents would wish for no one else," Raymond said.

"Marry!" I exclaimed.

"It will be," is all Raymond said. I quickly changed the subject.

As the days passed by, Annie visited every day for the milking, and this was the high point of my day; she would always either kiss my cheek on arrival or on departure, always with a beaming smile; she brought such joy to our camp.

On the long evenings after she had left and the herd was settled, we would sit and talk. I was surprised when Raymond told me that had my sister been well enough, he would have courted her, but felt she would not be able to fully respond to any approach he made. It had never occurred to me that Sarah might have had admirers; the Bell had certainly found her attractive, and I had always thought her beautiful, even now with her cold eyes, but I understood what Raymond said, for no man would approach such a woman so cold. It had also never occurred to me that she might have been the subject of discussion between people outside the family, but she obviously had, for Raymond told me how everyone thought she had gone like this because of the early demise of her husband. I told Raymond that that is indeed how it was. I was never given to lying, and hoped that I was able to give a convincing account. How could I tell anyone of how Sarah and I had taken the Bell's life, or how I had watched Sarah take the life of her newborn, and done nothing; no, things were far better left as people thought, than the truth, which was too awful to deal with, and that's why Sarah was as she is; the truth was too awful to deal with.

The weeks passed by as Raymond and I enjoyed the lazy days of summer, tending the herd, practising our swordplay and waiting for the visits of Annie, then helping her with the milking. Each evening, it had now become a habit, where I would stand and wave to Annie, as she left, and continue waving until she had disappeared from view.

There had been many high spots since my return home and indeed many lows, but this summer was turning out to be my best time.

Many nights, Raymond and I would lie in the sheil, talking, for most of the night, until sleep would take over. We would discuss our lives and how we wished them to develop, and of raising families, and of how we wanted to be the best fighters either side of the border.

It was such a night that we were talking, after an easy day, the night was warm, and the sky never really got dark, when we were both startled by the sound of galloping horses. At the height of summer, at this hour, who could it be? We both rose and each tied on his sword belt, then went out, to be confronted by about twenty riders, rounding up our herd. I drew my sword, as did Raymond; we stood back to back to defend each other in case of attack. Suddenly, a rider came galloping in, with lance down, toward Raymond. I watched as Raymond parried the lance away with his sword, the blow severing the metal tip from the wooden shaft, but the rider continued his hold of the lance, striking Raymond a hard glancing blow to the shoulder. I saw the flat wooden end of the lance take out a large lump of flesh, and blood spurt from the wound. The impact of the blow sent Raymond staggering backwards, crashing into me with such force that I was thrown back against the sheil wall. My head hit against the wall, I heard it make contact with the stone work, then blackness.

I regained my senses some time later, but how long I know not. I felt bilious, and my sight was blurred, I shook as if struck by severe cold. I looked around me. It was still semi dark. I tried to get to my feet, but found that when I did so, I just fell to the ground again, adding to the feeling of biliousness. I got to my hands and knees, and crawled about, looking for Raymond, and thankfully he was nearby. I could not see what state he was in because of the half-light, but put my hands out and felt for him. My hands first made contact with him about his waist.

I then ran my hands along his body, all the time checking for injury. As I reached the top of his body, my hands felt something wet and sticky; it must be blood, it must be, and there was lots of it.

"Raymond, Raymond!" I screamed, "Raymond, please, please don't die, please don't die, Raymond, speak to me, please, please." My senses were slowly starting to return, and I got to my feet. I had to do something for my friend, but what, what could I do. Wait, think, is he still alive? I checked, yes I think he is, yes, yes, he is, I'm sure he is still breathing, but only just. What do I do now, what would Father do? No wait, Mother, yes, Mother, she is the one, yes I remember when Father cut himself quite badly, once, and Mother used moss, and placed it on the wound, to stop the blood. The roof had been covered in moss. I reached up and grabbed a handful of moss, which after the weeks it had been on the roof was now dry. I found out later that it should have been moist, new moss. I took the moss, and kneeling down beside Raymond, I fumbled about his body until I felt the wet stickiness. I was much relieved that the light was poor, for I did not want to set my eyes on this gruesome sight. I placed the moss in the centre of what I took to be the wound, then taking my bollock knife, I went into the sheil, and took one of the skins we used as our bedding and cut it into strips, then made a wad to cover the moss, with a large piece of skin, tying down with the strips, which I bound about his body.

Once I had done as much as I was able, I sat by my friend, not knowing what to do next. If I waited here, the next person to visit would be Annie, that evening, which would be much too late. I had to do something; I had to get Raymond to someone who could properly tend his wound, and that of course had to be Mother, but how? All the horses and cattle had been taken.

I would have to carry him, but could I manage such an undertaking, and even if I could, it would surely kill my friend. Think, Rob, what to do, think, think! I think I might just have it. I resolved to make a bed out of the wooden poles we had used for the roof beams and tie the skins that were used initially for the first sheil. Although it was still dark, I set about my task, firstly making the frame, then tying the skins to the frame. By the time I had finished, the dawn was starting to break, and I could view my handiwork. It was not pretty, but I hoped that I would be able to pull my friend down the hillside and back to our bastle.

I tied a length of leather, which I had cut from one of the skins, to a pole at each side of the frame, to make a harness that would fit about my shoulders, thus allowing me to drag the frame, and along with it, my friend. After checking that the harness fit correctly, I then laid the frame beside Raymond, then as gently as I was able, lifted him on to the frame.

I was not sure, when I lifted him, whether there was any life within him, but there was little more I could do for him. Only someone with the skills of my mother could improve him now. I knew that unless I was able to get him to my home without delay, he would die.

I then harnessed myself into the frame, then set about my journey, which at first seemed quite easy, but having rounded the ridge and starting the descent, I found that it became less easy. I had hoped that dragging the frame downhill would have been easier, but alas, it did not prove to be so, and I soon found myself struggling to keep the frame steady and even, and not throwing Raymond on to the ground, as such a jolt at this stage could prove fatal. With the struggle my strength soon started to sap, and by the time I had managed to get to the bottom of the hill I felt totally drained of all my energy, but there was still a goodly distance yet to travel. I had to go on, and faster if my legs could manage. By this time the sweat was running so freely from me that all my clothes were drenched, and the day was now starting to warm considerably.

I was travelling south now, and the sun was directly in front of me, and at its height, as it relentlessly beat down upon me, draining me more, each step I took. The sun having took its toll, I collapsed out of sheer exhaustion, my breathing was now deep, and I was struggling to inflate my lungs. The breaths I was taking in were now starting to burn as they entered my throat. I had to get to my feet, I simply had to, not for me, but for my friend. Stupid fool, you stupid, stupid fool, I thought, you have not brought any water, why did you not bring some, it would now fortify you, you fool. Just a month ago you could have found water within a foot's length from anywhere you stood, but now, not a drop. Get up and stop feeling sorry for yourself; behind you is someone who will die unless you move your stupid body; move yourself, move, I heard my mind tell me. I struggled to my feet, and with renewed determination, I set off once again. I gritted my teeth, set my head and shoulders forward, then stepped onward. I was going to get there, nothing was going to stop me. If Raymond were to die then it would be better that I die also, for I could not live knowing that because I had not done my best he had died. There was now no more pain, I had gone beyond that; no pain, just a grim determination.

My thoughts were carrying me through. Why had they attacked? It is the quiet time, there are no raids in the summer, but they will pay dearly for this, if my friend dies, I will not leave a Scottie alive. Then my mind went blank, I could not think. I looked up, but could see nothing. I had been walking with my head down to avoid the glare of the sun, and though my thoughts had carried me through, and taken away the pain, they had stopped me from seeing the way ahead, and now I could not see. I had become so fatigued, so completely drained, that my mind no longer functioned, and not only that, but my eyes no longer functioned either. I did not know where I was, whether I was still travelling in the right direction, was anyone likely to find me, the worse thing of all, I had got so engrossed with my own dilemma, that I had completely forgotten about Raymond, the fact that I was dragging him, whether he was still alive, could I get him to help before he died; none of this had any relevance anymore. Then blackness.

Little was I aware, but I had in fact reached to within sight of my home, before I collapsed, and I know not how long I lay there before discovery, but discovered I was. Sarah, through those cold eyes, those eyes that did not appear to see, had seen something sticking up from the ground, and not knowing what it was had run to see, and had found us both. Alerting Father and Mother, she had started to attend to me first, and I can vaguely remember moaning, trying to say, "Not me, not me," but I doubt Sarah could hear me, or indeed understand.

My next recollection is being carried in the arms of my father, with Sarah and mother dragging the frame with Raymond on it, behind. The blackness descended once again, and I must have been in a stupor for some time. When eventually I did regain my senses, I was lying in Sarah's bed. It was now dark, and my clothes had been removed, as they had been sodden with my sweat; Sarah was wiping my body with a cold wet cloth, trying to reduce the heat from my body. My first word was "Raymond," that one word which came out in a rasping voice, burnt my throat. I heard Mother's voice reply, "He is still alive, but more dead than alive." I turned to my right and Raymond was on my bed, with Mother sat by him. His wound had been freshly dressed, and Mother was wiping his face, as he had now developed a fever. I tried to raise myself up, but did not have the strength. Sarah lay her hand on my shoulder, pressing me to the bed, while gently shaking her head.

"Father," I rasped.

"He has gone to fetch the Dodds," replied Mother. She had barely got the words from her mouth when I heard the sound of horses outside and voices. The next thing I saw was Mary Dodds ascending the ladder, followed very closely by Annie, who both went directly to where Raymond lay. Mother told them that Raymond was very weak, but he was a strong lad, and that we should hope that he recovers. I thought as I lay there, that Mother's tone did not give out great hope for my friend. I think if I had been capable, I might have felt my eyes water at such news, but my body had become so dry that crying would have been impossible. After a short time, Mary said, "What of Rob?" as everyone turned to me.

"Oh my brave Rob," said Annie, as she got up from the side of Raymond and came over to where I lay and took my hand. Sarah, although beset with those cold eyes, even managed to show some surprise at the show of affection shown by Annie.

Annie sat on the opposite side of the bed from Sarah, and still holding my hand said, "Your father has told us all about what you did to save our Raymond; we will be eternally grateful to you, Rob." I heard Mary Dodds say, "Yes, we will indeed." I remember nothing more after that, as I must have fallen asleep and did not wake up until the following day.

All the Dodds family had stayed the night, sleeping on the floor, Father having put some hay down to make their night more comfortable. I awoke quite late, to find everyone else already up and all having had their morning meal. I found myself somewhat disorientated, being still very tired and very sore, and surrounded by so many people. My mother, Mary Dodds and Annie huddled together talking feverishly by the fire; Father and Michael sat at the table, talking, but in a much quieter manner than the women. I looked to my side, and in the other bed lay Raymond, still not conscious, but looking more rested than when last I saw him.

I struggled from my bed, Annie running over and taking my arm and leading me to the table. A truly lovely girl, but she was starting to smother me, with her fussing so. Mary asked after my health, to which I replied that I felt much improved, which of course I did not, but I knew that there was likely to be a Trod mounted shortly, and I wanted to be on it. I sat and ate a light meal, far less than I was used to, then sat back, enjoying a moment of quiet calm that had descended upon our bastle.

The quiet calm was quickly broken by Annie jumping about excitedly, having spied through the small slit opening in the wall many riders advancing on our home. Father opened the upper door, and, along with Michael, they descended the outer stairs. I got up from the table and went to the door to see what must have been in excess of two hundred riders.

"I'm coming," I yelled. "Wait," but Father turned to me and said, "No, lad you are far from well enough to ride." I was about to protest, but Father gave one of those looks that you know not to question him. I stood at the top of the stairs and watched them mount, and ride off, along with many of the usual riders, the Dodds, Robsons, Bells and of course the Milburns, Arthur and John at the front along with my cousin Richard, who when seeing me at the top of the stairs, gave a gentle, almost secretive wave, but as always, accompanied by that beaming smile. I don't know what ached the most; my body from the rigours of getting down from the hillside with Raymond, or my heart, from the fact that I was not riding with my family.

The next few days passed quietly. Each day I would try and venture farther from the bastle, always accompanied by Annie. One day I was feeling a particular disquiet, having missed the ride, coupled with my weakness, and snapped at Annie, for always trying to smother me, and to let me be. Oh dear, how very stupid of me, for the poor girl was only showing concern and gratitude for bringing her brother home. She ran off, sobbing, and saying something quite inaudible through her sobs. I ran after her, and quickly catching her, took hold of her upper arm and spun her around, until she was in my arms, our faces so close together that our noses almost touched.

"I am so very sorry, my darling Annie, I do not deserve such a friend as you," I said pleadingly, then kissed her on the lips. We stood there in our embrace for a good time, her tears running down her cheeks, on to my lips, and I could taste their saltiness. As we broke our embrace, Annie kept me held close, her eyes still full of tears.

"Oh my darling Rob, I could forgive you anything," she said. She certainly knew the right thing to say, for I now felt lower than the lowest serpent that crawls on the earth.

"Come, you silly man," she said as she took my arm and led me back to the bastle.

For the rest of that day and into the night and before falling asleep, all I could think of was my dear Annie, and my nostrils were filled with the smell of her hair, and my lips tingled at the thought of touching hers. These feelings were new to me, yes, I had cared for people before, and with deep feelings, but now my life had been turned around by a mere girl, how could this be?

The riders had been away for nearly a week now, and we were all becoming quite anxious, the one consolation being that Raymond had now regained a conscious state, and was steadily improving, but far from ready to leave for his own home. This state of affairs pleased me greatly, for it meant that the Dodds stayed with us, and this gave me more time with Annie.

On the eighth day after setting forth, the riders returned, but not all, for it had been a bloody outing, the truth of which I shall never truly know, but my Uncle John had been killed in an ambush set by the Scotties. This brought a great sadness, for I had grown very fond of him. Also Hugh Robson had perished at the hands of a Scottie sword and one of the Fenwicks had also perished. The perils of raiding were always great, but to lose so many, who had become friends and fellows in arms was not an easy task to endure. This was supposed to be the quiet time, a time when no raids took place, a time when we were able to take advantage of the summer months, and gather in, ready for whatever the winter would have in store for us.

The Dodds stayed with us for the next two days, then reluctantly they departed, much to the protests of dear Annie, and leaving Raymond in the care of my mother, who had undertook the main part in his recovery, and subsequent improvement in health. Mother assured all that as soon as his health was improved to a sufficient level, we would undertake to return him home.

Chapter 13

Is This the Truth?

Two weeks after the Dodds left our bastle, Raymond, under the wonderful care of my mother, had made a remarkable improvement, and was ready to undertake the journey home, albeit in a cart, and not astride a horse. He still had limited use of his right arm, which we hoped might come with time.

The raid had taxed Father greatly, and he wished to stay at home, along with Sarah, whilst Mother and I would accompany Raymond home. It was early afternoon when we set off, after first lining the bottom of the cart with a goodly covering of straw, to enhance the comfort of our passenger.

Due to the lateness of our departure, we agreed that it would be prudent to stay with the Dodds overnight, and then return home the next day.

The journey was slow but uneventful, and it was mid-evening when we arrived, much to everyone's great joy, at the Dodds' bastle. We were greeted with much cheer, and after taking Raymond in, we all settled down to a tasty dish of pottage, Mary having added some wild herbs which made it most flavoursome.

After a very pleasant meal, we all sat around talking, the conversation flitting from subject to subject, and it was nice to hear laughter again, after all the sorrow there had been. As the evening progressed,

Annie got closer and closer, until she was holding herself tightly to my side, with her hand wrapped about my arm.

I became quite embarrassed, when I noticed Mary catch the eye of Mother, then nod knowingly, in our direction, then both women smiled to each other. I felt the rush of blood to my face, as I tried to find somewhere to look.

We bedded down on the floor, I in front of Annie's bed, much to her pleasure, and Mother in front of Raymond's, and strangely enough, a good sleep was had. The next morning I awoke to Annie, on her knees, by my side, bent over me, her long blonde hair engulfing my face.

"Come on, lazy," she said playfully. I got from the floor slowly and somewhat stiffly, and staggered to the table, as is my way, where a large dish of oats with a liberal covering of late summer fruits awaited me. I devoured the meal hungrily, then went outside to start and harness up, ready for the journey home. Having completed my preparations, Mother then joined me, and after all the farewells and embraces, we were just about to start our journey, when Raymond, who had stayed inside, came to the door.

"Thank you, Marie," he said to Mother. "I would surely not be here, if it were not for you, but may I beg one more thing from you."

"Yes, anything, Raymond," she replied.

"Can that worthless object of a son of yours come and stay with us when it is convenient?" he asked.

"Oh yes, please, Marie, please," interrupted Annie, excitedly.

"But of course he can, there is little to do at this time of year, and what there is, I'm sure Thomas can manage; he will return on the morrow, if that rests well with you, Mary," Mother said.

"Marie, Rob saved my son's life, it would be a great honour to have him stay," said Mary, to the accompaniment of Annie jumping up and down, clapping her hands.

Mother and I set upon our journey home, a journey of more embarrassment for me as Mother questioned me endlessly about Annie, and that I was but fifteen, and we must wait before we get involved, and she went on and on. What a relief it was to see our bastle come into view, in the hope that she might find other things to occupy her thoughts. Alas, at meal time, she commenced to tell Father of Annie and myself, Father taking all in with some amusement, much to Mother's annoyance.

The next day, bright and early, I saddled up and headed toward the Dodds' bastle, arriving in the afternoon, and settled in as if I had been there all my life. The Dodds were more than good friends, friends I had known since birth; they were as close as kin.

After an afternoon meal, I helped Michael with the chores until evening, when we returned inside, and ate again, Annie ensuring she was able to sit by my side.

Later that evening we all sat around the table, and I asked Michael to tell me of the raid into Scotland, and of how my uncle and the others perished. Michael was somewhat reluctant to relate what had taken place, but after much pleading by Raymond, Annie and myself, he relented. I feared Mary was somewhat less eager to hear what took place. The rest of this part of my story is related by Michael Dodds, a man I trust implicitly, and whose word is his bond; however, I fear that in relating the events of the raid into Scotland, he may have kept some of the details from us, due to the sensibilities of the ladies present.

After leaving the Milburn bastle, the riders crossed to the Charlton bastle, where James had gathered a host of other riders, some two hundred or more, so that by the time the party set off, there could well have been five hundred riders. James was busily engaged with setting out the plan for the days ahead, as Father and the rest arrived. Father got from his horse on arrival, and just stood directly in front of James, but said nothing, just looked. James quickly became aware that a much stronger presence than he was in charge, and became silent. Father, still saying nothing, took to his saddle and rode off, the rest following on.

As the party continued, the three Milburns, Father, John and Arthur, rode at the head and alongside them were Michael and his kinsmen. Behind came other Milburns and Dodds, then Charltons, James, with a somewhat sullen expression about his face, Robsons, Bells, Routledges, then Fenwicks. The Fenwicks, as I have already mentioned, were land owners and people of substance, and therefore found it better to mingle into the crowd, unseen, should there be repercussions thereafter, thus retaining their status.

The riding was hard and the border was soon reached, and straightaway the raiding started, at the very first homestead, which was put to the torch and all about put to the sword; men, women and children. The stock from the homestead was left, the intention being that it would be gathered up on the return journey.

A further three inhabitancies were torched and all killed from within, during that first day, the last not being torched until the next morning, as it offered a reasonable accommodation for the night, offering good all round vision, and food on the hoof, with good cattle and sheep ripe for slaughter.

The following day the ride made an early start, and continued north, raiding and killing, and leaving the cattle and sheep, so as not to hamper the riders' progress. As Raymond and I had been caught out, thinking it to be the quiet time, so the Scotties were making easy prey for the raiding party, offering little resistance.

For four days the raiding continued, first travelling north, then turning east, and coming across the land, but word had obviously spread, and preparations were afoot, by the Scotties, to bring a halt to these English raiders.

On the fifth day the raiders were now starting to gather up the beasts from the places that had already been attacked, and had doubled back to the homestead where they had made their first overnight camp, when from nowhere, a group of a great number of riders appeared, riding at full gallop, with lances levelled. The English quickly drew their lances and set about engaging the Scotties, at which the Scotties reined hard and turned about, the English giving full chase. The pursuit continued along the valley, until the hills on either side became much steeper and the valley floor became narrower. A point was reached in the valley where only two or three horses could go side by side. The Scotties managed to scramble through, the odd straggler being caught by the pursuing English. As the English then squeezed their way through this narrow gorge, the Scotties had appeared to vanish. The last English raider through being the signal for rocks to come tumbling down from both sides of the gorge, effectively closing the door behind them. This done, the Scotties appeared from the far side of the valley, in greater numbers than before. The English were trapped, their retreat cut off, there was but one way out, through the Scotties.

The battle commenced, firstly with the Scotties reappearing from both sides of the valley, with lances levelled and at full gallop. Father drew his sword, the rest following, but many in total amazement. Why draw a sword in a lance charge? But Father had seen the gap between the two ranks of galloping Scotties, and had headed for this gap, the others following behind. The last few of the English got caught up in the coming together of the two Scottie ranks, but amazingly, though they were all unseated from their nags, not one took any injury, and all ran to the side of the valley, taking shelter behind some high rocks. A rider unsaddled is a dead man, when one's foe is still in the saddle. With the two ranks of Scotties coming together, for a moment, some confusion reigned, and during this moment of confusion was the time when Father reined hard to the right, at the same time signalling to some of the other riders to go left, and as they all came about, the Scotties still in some disorder, the English charged, with swords. As they came into the Scottie ranks, they still holding their lances and unable to draw their swords, were easy prey for the English swordsmen, who slashed their way through to the other side, creating a swathe of dead bodies as they did so.

Having ridden through the Scottie ranks, the English turned for a second run, but by this time there were many Scottie swords drawn. The second assault was an entirely different attack, where Uncle John, being the first to engage in battle, and crossing swords with a Scottie, was taken from behind, by another Scottie, bringing his sword hard into the base of his neck, his head falling forward limply, the cut very deep, and the blood bursting out in a torrent. The moment that blade caught the back of his neck, he was dead. As the melee continued, Hugh Robson was seen to go down, but it was hard to see the circumstances. By this time, the riders who had been unsaddled early on in the conflict had now come out from their refuge and were doing a sterling job from the ground, pricking up into Scottish thighs, and under breastplates, and because the riders were so engaged with swordplay with other riders, the men on the ground were able to move around the horses, almost unnoticed, and attack at will. Usually they worked in pairs, walking through the melee, back to back, covering one another, then when a target is selected, by either, he would shout "Yan," meaning one, and would attack while the other watches his back. This was a very effective form of working in a pitched battle, which, fortunately, happened very rarely.

The battling went on for some time, and yet the English had lost but five, though many were blooded, but the Scotties, who had created the ambush, had fared badly, with as many as twenty being downed on the very first assault, and a further twenty or thirty grounded, either dead or so heavily bloodied, that they were unable to continue.

Eventually the Scotties yielded, this giving Father somewhat of a dilemma. Did he slaughter the lot, or did he allow them to live? Should he take them for ransom, should he take their nags, and leave them to walk? A strange decision was then made; one that could see all the English hang. Father decided that he would disarm all the Scotties, but allow them their liberty and their nags. This caused great consternation within the English ranks, many yelling for blood, but Father stood by his decision, inviting any man brave enough to come forward and fight for a different decision, but no one stepped forward.

The leader of the Scotties then stepped forward, and surprisingly held forward his hand, and said, "Dee a speak te the one they call Hafe Heed?" and bowed his head forward when doing so.

"I believe some do call me that," was Father's reply.

"Then I thank you fur yur mercy, but wid ask fur yur favour once more," said the Scottie.

"Ask," was the terse reply from Father.

"Can a gather all ma deed and wounded," asked the Scot.

"Aye," came another terse reply. Then the strangest thing that was ever seen on any battlefield or conflict happened; men who until just a few moments ago were intent on killing each other, started to work together in gathering up the dead and wounded. One of the English, it was thought one of the Fenwicks, was seen binding the wound of one of the Scotties.

When all were gathered up, and the wounded attended to as best as was possible, the Scotties rode off, but their leader stayed, once more putting forward his hand to Father, who took it, and as they shook hands, the Scottie was heard to say, "Yur an honourable man, Hafe Heed, al nay forget, and quite a fighter," ending his words with a smile, and Father, through his injured face, was seen to almost make a smile.

As the Scotties left, their leader, when riding away, turned and raised his hand, almost leaving as friends.

After they had gone, there was still some unrest by some at Father's decision to let the Scotties go, but there was little that could be done now, other than go against Father's word, and go after them and slay them all, which would be ever so easy, they all now being unarmed.

It was decided that where they were would be a good place to make camp for the night, and large fires were started. As the night went on and the fires became increasingly hot, the Scotties' weapons were hurled on to the flames, to render them useless.

The dead were buried beside the field of conflict, along with all their arms, their lances broken, and laid by their side, to show they died in battle. Although there was a victory to be cheerful about, there were few celebrations, for there were losses, of kin and friends, the sort of friends that every man was able to put faith in, but now gone and sadly lamented.

The next morning an early start was made, and the riding continued, gathering up the stock from the places that had been raided along the way. The ride then changed direction, and went easterly, where there were fresh places to raid, and a few small crofts were released of their property, but a much kinder raid now ensued, where the riders would leave the crofters with two things; the clothes they stood up in and their lives, that is of course if they offered no resistance. Those that did sealed their own fate.

Towards the end of that day, the ride came upon a pele tower, which was like a bastle, a very heavily built dwelling, well able to withstand an attack, but unlike the bastle, the pele tower was much higher, with three floors, unlike the bastle with two. They were very hard to penetrate, and it was often necessary to set a fire by the door, and smoke the occupants out, or if they did not come out, burn them within the tower.

As the riders approached the tower, they were met with a hail of arrows coming from within. The riders swung wide of the volley, and rode out of range, where it was decided what action to be taken. It was William Fenwick who suggested that it was far too perilous to attempt burning out, and that on the ride in, he had spotted some very large boulders, and that if there were sufficient riders with ropes, they could drag the boulders to the top of the ridge, then roll them in to the doorway, and instead of trying to get them out, seal them in. It was agreed by all that this was a sterling suggestion, and work began immediately.

It was not very long until the large stones were rolling down towards the tower, and soon started to pile up, in front of the entrance. When it was thought that there were sufficient stones in place, the riders set up camp near the tower, as if to lay siege. This, however, was not the plan. The plan was, that at the dead of night, and at this time of year, that does not last for long, the riders would steal towards the tower, and stealthily place the stones upon each other, in front of the door, effectively sealing the entrance. This was undertaken when the hour was right, and it would appear that it was carried out undetected by the occupants.

When morning broke the camp was struck, and the Scotties left to their fate, while the riders relieved them of their stock, and fine animals they were too. The ride continued yet further eastwards, raiding as they went, gathering up yet more stock, and thankfully sustaining no further losses.

On the sixth day the ride turned back to a westerly direction, driving back along the border, catching the odd dwelling and gathering up what they had, then moving on, for another day and a half, until eventually arriving back, and replenishing the stock in our valley, assuring us all of a comfortable winter ahead, with plenty of food for all.

This is the story as told to me by Michael Dodds. It may contain somewhat less detail than I had hoped to record for all time, but I must rest by the word of such an honest gentleman, but this is not the end of this part of my story.

One week later, after going to stay with the Dodds, I returned home, where I found Father had taken to his bed, the rigours of the past week taking their toll upon him. Father was by no means a weak person, but the injury to his head rendered him incapable after severe exertions, like those endured riding for a week, and doing battle along the way.

Two days after my return, we received a visit from a senior gentleman, riding a fine horse and dressed as finely as no other I had ever seen. Along with him were a number of other riders, about ten in total. As this gentleman arrived, I was working outside our bastle, and by his appearance alone, I judged it best to afford such a fine gentleman a deep bow, as Mother had brought me up to do.

"Now then, young fellow, who might you be?" came the well dictioned enquiry.

"Rob Milburn, Sir," I replied.

"Might you be the son of Thomas?" came a second enquiry.

"Yes Sir, he is within, laid up with a malady," I replied again.

"Pray, take me to him, lad," the fine gentleman said as he stepped from his horse.

We both entered the bastle, I in front, leading the way up the ladder, and as I entered, and before the fine gentleman came up, I announced, "A gentleman to see you, Fadder." The fine gentleman stepped from the ladder, and at setting foot upon the boards said, "Well, Tom, not so well I see."

"Good to see you, Sir John, it has been far too long. You have met my lad, Rob," said Father.

"Indeed, a fine lad," replied the fine gentleman.

"Rob, this is Sir John Foster, the March Warden," said Father. "And of course you have met my wife, Marie, and my daughter before," continued Father.

"Ah yes, I do believe I did, when your lad was taken, and you were freshly injured; pray, is that injury the reason for your confinement?" said Sir John.

"Aye, it lays me low more often these days, Sir John," said Father.

"And have you been laid low for long, Tom?" asked Sir John.

"Aye, these three weeks past, as Rob will vouch," said Father.

"Is that the truth, my boy?" said Sir John, lowering his voice.

"Aye Sir, it will be about that time, though it feels longer, when I am left to carry out all the chores," I said.

"You would not lie to me boy, for there are those who have hung for lying to me," said Sir John.

"I have no reason to hide the truth from you, Sir, and now even less, with a threat like that attached, but why do you enquire so, is there something amiss?" I said.

"Indeed, young Rob, there is something very amiss; a raid has taken place over the border and there has been much killing, looting and rustling. Know you of such things, boy?" said Sir John.

"I know the Scotties raided here, Sir, for was I not a victim of their raids?" I said.

"Aye lad, but you know fine well what I mean, have you been a raiding?" said Sir John, quite loudly and in a terse manner. It was evident that Sir John was in no mood for verbal follies.

"I have indeed taken part in such a raid; it was the Hot Trod in the winter snows, which I was led to believe was with your blessing. Are you telling me now that that was not the case?" I challenged, in an equally loud and terse manner. Father interceded, saying, "Now, Rob, let there be none of that, I want you to apologise to Sir John for your rudeness, he has a task to do, set by the Queen, and we must respect that".

"I do apologise, Sir, for my rudeness, it is unforgivable, but we have suffered greatly, at the hands of the Scotties, as you know, that it irks me greatly for anyone to say I am as bad as they," I said, while bowing slightly, in the direction of Sir John.

"I'll bother you no more, Thomas, I am assured that this family has nothing to do with the events of the past weeks, I will take my leave," said Sir John as he bowed in the direction of Mother.

"Sir John, you will not take your leave until you have sat at my table and taken refreshment," said Mother.

"But Mistress Milburn, to do so would be to impose too heavily on your hospitality," replied Sir John, bowing lower this time.

"A seat, Sir John," said Mother, holding the back of the chair Father usually sat in, and engaging Sir John with a fixed stare.

"How could I refuse such an invitation, Ma'am," said Sir John with a broad smile.

"Rob, go tell Sir John's men to join us," said Mother, and as I went down the ladder to invite the other riders in I could hear Sir John protesting that so many was not fair on Mother, with Mother casting aside Sir John's protests.

When all had gathered within the bastle, things were somewhat overcrowded, but Sir John's men sat upon the floor, using the walls as back rests, and Mother and Sarah set about serving everyone with a dish of the pottage and a drink of ale. As I have mentioned, we were not people who were in the habit of partaking in ale, but always kept a small supply, for such an occasion.

It was not long before the bastle was filled with busy chatter, the like of which I had never heard, but I noticed that Mother and Father engaged Sir John in conversation, which he seemed to greatly enjoy, and an occasional burst of laughter could be heard from their quarter, over the hum of the other conversations. I also noticed one or two strange looks from some of Sir John's riders, when confronted by Sarah, and those dead eyes, which if you were not used to her, seemed to penetrate your very being.

After some time, when all had eaten, and supped, Sir John rose from his seat, and declared that they must depart, then turned to Mother and said, "Mistress Milburn, I cannot begin to thank you enough for your hospitality," as he took her hand and raised it to his lips, bowing graciously as he did so.

"Sir John," began Mother, slightly curtseying "On your return, may I beg your indulgence, but would it be an imposition for you to dispense with the Mistress Milburn, and to use my name instead?"

"Ma'am, it would be a great honour so to do," said Sir John, bowing in an exaggerated manner.

"Then, Sir John, I beg that your return be soon," replied Mother.

Sir John and his band of riders then left, with myself and Mother accompanying them down the ladder and to the door, and just as he was about to take to his saddle, he stopped, then turned to Mother. "Marie," he said uncertainly, "pray do keep me informed of your husband's health, and I beseech you, should there be any need of assistance, you must send word to me, and I shall do all that is possible to ease your burden."

"Sir John, we are fortunate to have in you a true friend, I thank you for your kindness," answered Mother.

Sir John, though far from being a young man, swung himself into the saddle like that of a man half his age, then nodded in the direction of Mother, after which he looked to me and said, "Stay well, young Rob," then reined his horse around and galloped off, his men following on.

Mother and I returned inside the bastle, where Sarah sat at the table as if nothing had taken place, and Father now sat up on one arm in bed. "Well, I am truly proud of my family," he declared. "I think we all carried that off well; I am sure Sir John has gone away assured that this branch of the Milburns took no part in any raid," and he lay back down, with a stifled chortle.

Chapter 14

Love and Heartache

Two years had now passed since that terrible night when Raymond and I were attacked by a Scottie raid, and alas, I am sad to say that my dear friend's injury, although healed, had rendered his right arm greatly impaired, and he would never hold lance nor sword again.

My relationship with my dear Annie had grown ever deeper, and I carried her image within my heart and thoughts always, and we were soon to be handfast, until such time as a priest may be available, though in those days, they were becoming a very rare beast indeed. To think that I spent five years surrounded by priests, and was, if fortune had not played its hand, destined to be trained into holy orders myself. How distant such thoughts were from my life now, and my future.

Father's health had improved little those two years, and it now rested upon myself to carry out the duties required for the upkeep of our home. The visit of Sir John Foster to our home had a profound effect upon my life, for the threat of the gallows had rested uneasily with me; therefore I resisted many opportunities to go a raiding, excusing myself by the fact that Father was laid low and that I had my mother, sister and he to tend. The thought, or lack of thought, to being despatched while in combat held no fear, but the thought of dangling at the end of a rope, or lying with my head in some burn, with a

Kingsman's foot at the back of my neck, was something I endeavoured to avoid.

Mother was greatly excited at the prospect of Annie and myself being handfast, and had arranged with Mary Dodds that a celebration should take place, in the same manner as if we were being married. This was not my wish, but against Mother, Mary Dodds, and of course Annie, who was such an excitable creature at the best of times, I was but a voice in the wilderness. The celebrations were due to take place at the end of this month of June, some two weeks away.

That very day, Mother had been at the Dodds, making arrangements for the day, where I was told, there would be a calf slaughtered and roast upon a spit, for there would be many to feed, as they had summoned the whole valley to witness our union.

As early evening approached, Mother returned, and alighting from the cart, bustled into the bastle, and at the same time, shouted as I had never heard her before, "Robert, in!" I cannot ever remember Mother calling me Robert; it is not a name I am familiar with, but dutifully, I did as I was bade, and followed Mother inside, climbing the ladder to our living area. I had scarcely laid a foot upon the boards when from nowhere came a hand across my face, taking the feet from under me.

I fell to the floor in an untidy heap, with Mother standing over me, her hands now clasped to her hips.

"You vile disgusting creature!" she yelled, and for a brief moment, I was transported back to the manse, and Father Francis.

"What have I done?" I gasped, holding my forearm across my face, in case any further blows were likely.

"What have you done? What have you done? You have taken advantage of that dear sweet Annie Dodds, you do not deserve her," Mother spat.

"But what do you mean, Mother?" I asked, still in my prone and defensive position.

"She is with child, that's what I mean, how could you?" said Mother, still spitting out her words.

To the question, how could you, I was tempted to say very easily, for I remember it was some weeks back, when I had gone visiting, and we had walked out. It had been a warm late spring evening, and we had walked to the top of one of the hills near her home, to where a mountain tarn lay, surrounded by reeds, where curlews were nesting. We sat by the water's edge, with our arms about each other, and embraced. I had felt within my body, on other such occasions, that I wanted more than embraces, but had resisted such urges; however, on this evening, after resisting for longer than I care to think, I gave in, and started to undo the laces at the back of Annie's dress.

"Rob, what do you think you are doing?" asked Annie.

"Annie, my dearest little angel, I cannot hold back any more, I need you so very badly," I pleaded.

"Oh Rob, I love you so much, I think I always have," she gasped, then kissed me so very hard I felt my upper lip start to bleed. We continued to embrace, while fumbling and pulling at each other's clothes, until we were both lying upon the ground, naked. The sight of her body excited me greatly, her skin was so very soft, and the colour of milk, so pale, so soft. I felt guilty touching her with my large rough hands, but she bade me caress her, and I gently passed my hand over her firm white belly, coming up and cupping her beautiful rounded breast. Our hearts were beating, as if we had run the entire length of the valley, and we both gasped for breath, frantically kissing and caressing each other's body, then we came together, the feeling of being joined washing over me like a river in flood. As I entered her body, she gave a whimper, which alarmed me, and I asked, "Are you all right my pet?"

"Don't stop, Rob, oh please don't stop," she bleated out breathlessly. We pressed against each other, harder and harder, the sweat pouring from my brow and dropping on to her chest, making it glisten in the last embers of the spring sunshine. I felt the tension rising within me, as Annie pushed her body even harder against me, then an explosion erupted within me, causing my body to shudder as never before, and I called out, almost as if in pain, but this was no pain, but absolute pleasure. As I reached this ultimate point Annie, who had her hand about my back, curled her fingers in, digging her nails into my flesh, then drew her hands down, ripping into my skin, the pain intensifying the feelings rushing through my body; then it had passed, as we both collapsed into each other's arms, both sweating heavily, both gasping for breath, and both enjoying the last moments of such wonderful feeling that is a man and a woman joined.

I turned to Mother and said that I could not say sorry, because I was not; indeed, I learnt on that spring evening my true depth of feeling towards Annie, and that if there were any doubts in my mind about becoming handfast with her, they were erased that evening. I was delighted at the prospect of her having our child, and I felt sure she would be an excellent mother to our child, as I hoped I would be a good father.

Mother's attitude changed when I had said my piece, and she started to say, "You are only children yourselves, she is but sixteen years old, and only just." I said to Mother, "But we will be here, and there will be both you and Sarah to help, what better start could we have?" That appeared to strike the right chord with Mother, for she then started to say, "Oh yes, we will have a baby, we must start to get things ready, we will need this and we will need that." Father, who had been sat near the fire in his usual chair, turned to Mother and said, "For pity's sake, woman, there is no child for months yet, settle down; you see what you have done now, Rob?" We all looked at each other and burst into laughter; that is of course, except Sarah. Sarah was not given to laughter, but we were all used to that by now.

The weeks soon passed until the day came when the entire valley came together to celebrate our union. We all assembled at the Dodds' bastle, where everyone was dressed in their finest attire, although it would be hard for an outsider to notice, where the Bells were concerned, but, there were few occasions when anyone had anything to celebrate in these days, that it was a great delight to see so many gathered together to raise a cup.

We had been joined early that day by my Mother's two brothers, Thomas and James, along with their families, and great news was brought. Thomas, who some years before had gone to become part of Sir John Foster's staff, and had later been asked to attend the court of Queen Bess, had found much favour with Her Majesty, that she had been disposed to confer a knighthood upon him. My uncle, Sir Thomas Charlton, what a great honour, and it must be said, he did take a central role throughout the day.

When we arrived at the Dodds, many of our kinfolk were there; in fact, I do think all were there. It was delightful to see Uncle Arthur again, and that rogue, Richard, who by some great good fortune had still managed to cheat the gallows, and was still smiling continuously. We were all assembled outside the bastle, when Michael appeared at the door, with Annie on his arm, Mary and Raymond stood behind. They walked out into the centre of the crowd, where Mother pushed me forward, towards them. As we came together, Michael took the hand of Annie, and raised it up. Mother, from behind me, lifted my arm up, so that it was alongside Annie's. Michael then took from his belt a leather strap, which, without a word spoken, he proceeded to bind our hands together, and once complete, said, "Those whom I have bound, let no man step between," then stood back, to great cheers from all stood around.

Father, unusually, stepped forward and said, "Well lad, kiss the poor lass," which I dutifully did to further loud cheering. I was so proud and so full of joy. It had been many years before when I had first set eyes on my sweet Annie, and I think that very first time I saw her, I knew we would be together for all time.

The merriment soon started, and I walked through the throng of people, with Annie clinging to my arm, stopping and talking to everyone, some who I did not know, but Annie did, some that I knew and Annie didn't, and some that neither of us knew. After a while, Mary Dodds and Mother were stood before us, each with a plate of food, Mary handing me mine and Mother handing Annie hers, with Mary saying, "Come along you two, this is the first carving from the roasted calf, you are the guests of honour, now eat." Mary then looked to Mother and Mother to Mary, then Mary wrapped her arms around Mother and sobbed, "They are only children," as Mother consoled her.

There were quite a few of the people I had ridden with, asking why I had not been on a raid recently, and I always said that with Father and Annie and all the extra work I now had, that it was very difficult, but I hoped to resume soon, which of course was a lie. Now that I had a child on the way, and Annie who was now my responsibility, I felt I should devote all my time to them. The fact that Sir John Foster had awoken a fear in me of the possible consequences of being caught raiding, was in fact the main obstacle in my way. Although I loved my new partner, and wanted to do all to keep her well, I did enjoy the riding and the fighting and the friendship of my fellow riders. Nothing was quite like the family, then the extended family, then one's riding fellows, who were like a third branch of the family.

After Annie moved to our bastle, she spent most of her time helping me, to Mother's dismay, due to her condition, but Annie, quite rightly, said she would feel awkward working about the house, with already two women sharing the chores, which I thought for one so young to be a sound judgement. The other point being, I was extremely grateful for the extra help, and Annie was indeed a great help and much fun to be with. Occasionally when we were working we would sneak a kiss, if we thought no one was looking, then giggle like little girls; yes, silly but it was so lovely.

The weeks passed into months and before we were aware, the nights started to become colder, and Annie started to swell. With each day I became more nervous at what was ahead, but kept my fears to myself, as I thought Annie had enough to deal with. Due to her becoming heavy with child, she was less able to help with many of the chores, which she found frustrating and became quite short tempered at times, but we all allowed for that and tried to help her through these difficult times. I feel that had Sarah been able to be more forthcoming, and were it not for her malady, and she had been the Sarah of old, that Annie's time might have been made easier. Nonetheless, Annie was able to relate to Sarah far better than I and a bond was growing between them. I say that but with Sarah it was very difficult to tell.

There was a day when I had to go to Hexham to purchase supplies in readiness for the winter months, and had to make the journey alone. Father was still not well enough to make the journey, Mother would not allow Annie to go due to her condition, and she, Mother, did not want to go in case Annie were to start with child, and of course, there was no way of knowing what Sarah would do, should she find herself in the midst of a place like Hexham alone, should I require to venture into some establishment, where ladies do not generally frequent, and there are many places where it is not regarded as correct for ladies to enter, where men conduct business. It is a strange world where such things occur, yet we have a woman as our Queen.

I readied my horse before the sun had risen, and set upon my journey, and it was still quite early morning when I approached the Dodds' bastle, and of course called in, and was greeted very well by all, and was able to tell of how Annie was getting on, telling them of how Mother would not allow her to accompany me due to her condition, which Mary and Michael drew great solace from, knowing that we were not about to compromise her health. Alas, I had to make my visit short as I wished to return from Hexham before it got too dark, but assured everyone that I would call as I passed by on my return.

As I pressed onward, I thought of the people I had to see in Hexham, one being Jacob Heron, as I had decided that although I had not been a raiding of late, this would not be a permanent arrangement and I would require a full sized sword. My shorter one had served me well, but I needed to have a weapon befitting my size.

I reached my destination early afternoon, and got right down to my purchasing. Mother had got hold of some paper, when last visiting her brother, and had written a list of things she required, but I was told that under no circumstances should I allow anyone to see me reading the list. I had worn my morion to travel in and secreted the note within, and each time I went to purchase an item, I would remove the helmet from my head as if I were finding it uncomfortable, check the contents of the list, then make my purchase. The first purchases I made were on the direct route to the forge, where I wanted to make my main purchase.

As I approached the smithy I could see young Walter Robson at the anvil, fashioning some red hot metal, with that familiar clanging of the hammer against the hot metal and anvil underneath. I thought the strangest thing of all was that, as I neared, even over the noise of his labours, he was aware of my approach, and looked up, with a broad smile. "I recognise you, you're a Milburn, aren't you?" he ventured.

"Aye, it's Rob," I called back.

"Aye, that's right, you came with your father the last we met," he replied.

"You have a fine memory, Master Robson," I said as I placed out my hand, and he laid down his hammer and took my hand. I was ready for the vice-like grip that I had experienced those years before from both him and his father and held on tight to his hand.

"You have changed somewhat, Master Milburn, you must have held that there sword plenty for a fine grip as that," said Walter, as we both laughed.

"What of your father, I trust he is well?" I enquired.

"Alas, he passed away just over a year past," he said, then pulling me in to him by my shoulder, he spoke quietly into my ear, "Old fool had to go on one last raid, as he had done all those years before with your father; still, he died doing what he loved, raiding. He had talked endlessly of his days raiding, and after your last visit, it rekindled his passion, which he tried to resist, and did do for some time, but eventually he gave into it."

"I am so sorry to hear your bad news, Walter, I am especially troubled that it was our visit that unsettled your father, which led to his demise," I said.

"Think nought of it, Rob, the man died reliving his youth, can there be a better way?" said Walter, bringing his heavy hand down on my shoulder.

"Now then, Rob, as much as I am pleased to see you, I am sure you have not travelled all this way to renew our acquaintance, so how may I be of service?" he said.

"Well, Walter, if you have the time, I would be grateful for my nag reshod, and while I wait, I would like to see Jacob Heron if he is available," I answered.

"I thought you raiders liked your nags unshod, so you could ride silently and undetected," he said, to which I replied, "Aye, it is truly a consideration, but to be far beyond the border and your nag split its hoof, you have a long walk home, which I fear you may never reach, least not alive. I'll go shod every time I think."

"A wise choice, Rob, leave the nag and I'll attend to it. Jacob is at his anvil, away through, you remember the way," said Walter.

"Aye, thank you, Walter," I said, patting his shoulder as I passed him.

As I walked through the smithy the tapping on the anvil became louder, a different sound from that of Walter's, who engaged in the manufacture of those heavier items required in everyday use. Apart from horse shoes, there was the ever demand for door hinges, implements for tilling the land, like hoes, rakes and forks, and those items of special commission. A smith's life was a demanding one, where not a moment of the day was wasted. If there were ever a lull, nails were made by the hundred, and applied to endless uses.

Jacob's hammering on the anvil was of a more delicate nature, which was required in the fashioning of fine weaponry, and Jacob Heron was indeed a maker of fine weaponry. I rounded the corner to where Jacob laboured; he had his back to me, but stopped and without turning, said, "How may I be of service, Sir?" I thought, what have these smiths got about them, that they are able to know people are about before they have laid an eye upon them? He then turned to face me and said, "I cannot recall the face, but would recognise that three-quarter sword anywhere."

"Indeed you should, Sir," I said, extending my hand towards Jacob. "Rob Milburn," I said.

"Ah! Tom's lad, aye I remember now," he said. "Is it time for a new weapon?" he enquired.

"You read my mind, Sir," I said.

"Then I have the very thing, it must be destined for you, young Rob, for this very week I fashioned the very double of the sword you carry, but to full size, and you will hardly notice the difference in weight," Jacob said with some glee, as he went to a large wooden cabinet, which sported a large lock. From under his heavy leather apron, he produced a large key, which had been attached to his belt, and unlocking the padlock, he opened the heavy wooden door, revealing an array of the most exquisite weapons.

Reaching in, Jacob took down a sword, the exact replica of the one I wore upon my belt, but somewhat larger. He handed me the sword, which I examined closely, and yes, it was the image of mine, the same hand grip, the same basket weave hilt cover, the same brass accessories, all the same but longer. I held the sword aloft, with outstretched arm, to feel the weight and balance, and surprisingly there was little weight difference; it would not take long to get used to this. The feel of the sword gave me a longing to go raiding again, but I must not think so, not when our baby was on the way. Jacob interrupted my thoughts. "Well, Rob, will that attend your needs?" he asked.

"Aye, it will do me fine, Jacob, you are without doubt the finest armourer in the land," I complimented.

"Will you leave your old weapon in exchange?" he asked.

"I fear not, for this blade has served me well, and saw me draw first blood, I could not walk away from such a faithful old friend," I replied sentimentally.

"You may be a fighting man, Rob Milburn, but you are a romantic, like a minstrel, which is good for a man to have a heart, but mark me well, never allow your heart to cloud your judgement," said Jacob.

"They sound wise words; a fine armourer, and a fine sage; thank you, Jacob," I said. We completed our transaction, then shook hands, Jacob placing a firm hand upon my shoulder, in a gesture of friendship, and saying, "Use that blade wisely, my boy." I smiled back at him, then turned and walked through to the other side of the smithy, where Walter was busy attending my nag.

"I shall be a short while yet, Rob; if you still have business, attend it now, and on your return your horse will be ready, and we shall break bread before you return to your family."

I did as Walter suggested and completed the purchases on Mother's list, and returned to the smithy. He had finished the shoeing of my nag, and without being disrespectful, I inspected his work, and a fine job it was too. "Walter, I doubt there will be a day where your services are never needed," I said.

"Enough of your flattery, Milburn, it will not reduce your bill, now come and eat," he said laughingly. We sat and ate a meal of a flat dark bread and a cheese, which I had never tasted before, very strong, but most enjoyable, it was much different from the cheese made from sheep's milk that I was used to.

The time came when I had to take my leave of Walter, and we parted as old friends, and as I rode away, with saddlebags bulging and my new sword bound in sack cloth, away from the view of prying eyes, I left Hexham and headed home.

The journey back was uneventful, thankfully, as it is always a tense time; with saddlebags full for all to see, it can be a temptation for many to try and relieve you of your wares, which is why I always travelled with sword on belt and morion upon my head, which served as a fine protection for my head, but served to hide my list from everyone, and wearing a helmet like the morion served to give the appearance of a hardened fighting man.

I called at the Dodds on my return journey as promised, and took food with them before continuing further. Mary embraced me, before I mounted my nag, with the instruction that, as soon as Annie had issue, that I was to take to horse and gallop all the way to their bastle to bring the news. I so promised, mounted up, waved my goodbyes and went on my way.

As I arrived home darkness had descended and Annie had taken to our bed, the days now weighing heavy upon her. Mother was ready with food for me, but I had to tell her that I had tarried on my way home, at the Dodds. I could see she was disappointed that I had not waited to eat with the family, but was eager for any news that I might bring. It was nice to sit on the edge of the bed and tell Annie that I had been with her family, and through tired eyes, I could see she was pleased I had called in to see them. But at the same time, I felt that she longed to be back in the bosom of her family, as she had been before our hand fasting, and not among us Milburns, as much as I knew she loved me, and not in the condition she now found herself.

I showed Father my new sword, and taking it from me, he held it aloft, and admired the skill it had taken to make it and the beauty of the finished article. He said he was particularly impressed by the weight and balance of the weapon, saying he wished that he had such a weapon when he went raiding. He was very surprised that I had retained my old, shorter sword, but as I had told Jacob Heron, I felt an attachment to it, that made handing it back very difficult. I could see Mother was less than impressed by my purchase, and it was beyond her how anyone could find such an implement, as she termed it, a thing of beauty, something that would eventually be used to end someone's life. I found her reasoning quite extraordinary. How could she not see that my new sword was made by a true craftsman, and therefore was a joy to behold, and as for it being used to end someone's life, would he, the one whose life is to end, not strike first, if given the opportunity, and end mine, and with such a fine blade, I would smite quicker, harder, cleaner and deeper?

I had had some time away from raiding, but my new weapon rekindled a yearning to ride again, but enough of such thoughts, for my Annie was due any time now and my duties lay with her and my child.

Three days had passed since my visit to Hexham, and I had busied myself about the bastle, tending the stock, and making preparations for the winter. Father had been of a fettle, that he had been able to help a little, and on the second day back, I had even coaxed him into helping me test my new sword, an exercise we had both enjoyed enormously, though the exertions had taxed Father greatly. Mother said that I should not over tax him so, but said that I should continue to encourage him with swordplay, as, although it did tax him, it did much to help his overall wellbeing, and that he would go inside and flop down, with the broadest of grins about his face.

This in turn encouraged me, and I asked Father that now I had a full length sword, would he teach me how to remove a sword from the hand of an opponent, as he had done all those years before, with Cuthbert Bell, when we had gone to bring Sarah home? He agreed to my request, and instruction began that very day.

When Father had first got all my weapons and armour, among the many items had been a wrist guard which was a metal piece that was strapped to the arm by two leathers with buckles. I had worn this piece of armour every time I had ridden out, thinking it to be solely to protect my hand when engaged in swordplay, but Father showed me the true purpose for this article. Taking me through the procedure very slowly, he showed how you slid your blade along that of your opponent, allowing his blade to pass the hilt of your own, thus the need for the wrist armour. Once your blade had run along the other, your blade was quickly twisted under the other's hilt, and then levered upwards, by pressing downward on one's own hilt. This served to prise the handle from your opponent's hand, or if he managed to hold his grip, would cause great pain, as it twisted the wrist against the joint. I say these things as if I now am the great expert, but it took me many, many attempts before I was even reasonable at it, and it would take much time before I would dare attempt such a feat in combat.

The very night Father had showed me this wonderful swordplay, which I was sure would serve me well in years to come, Annie was taken by great pain in the middle of the night. She started by grabbing my arm as we lay upon the bed; I had been asleep at the time. "Rob," she whispered in a pained manner, "Rob, the time has come, get your mother." I jumped from my bed, and went over to Mother's bed and gently roused her, placing my forefinger to my lips, as I did so, then whispered, "Annie." Mother jumped from her bed, and went to where Annie lay. I heard her whisper to Annie, "Has it started, my dear?" Annie did not reply, merely nodded her head, while biting her bottom lip, the sweat already starting to run from her forehead, with the effort of fighting the pain. Mother then roused Sarah, who without flinching rose from her bed, and immediately started to busy herself. As I have mentioned before, Sarah was not given to speak a great deal, if at all, so when she did you tended to listen. She looked over towards me and said, "Rob, water, now." Without hesitation, I rushed away at her command, and took two wooden pails to the nearby burn, and filled them both then rushed back, so that I missed nothing. I had been away but a moment, but on my return, Annie was crying out, her screams passing through my body, and making my very bones tremble. I scrambled up the ladder, spilling most of the water I had gathered, in my effort to see why my Annie was in such torment. Sarah was now at the top of the bed, with Annie's head in her lap, and was gently wiping her brow, with a dampened cloth. I found the scene somewhat strange, for Sarah who was not able to show or express any emotion, was gently tending my Annie, with that blank expression upon her face. Mother was sat at the foot of the bed, holding Annie's hand in her left hand, while stroking the top of her hand with her right hand. I could see that Annie was being tended to as well as anyone could be, but was eager to assist in any way I could.

"Mother, what can I do?" I blurted out desperately.

"Keep out of the way," she snapped back, as if I had done something wrong. I sheepishly retreated from the room, descending the now slippery ladder, and as I took my last view of the room, I could see Father now sat up in his bed, looking less than pleased with the events taking place. Halfway down the ladder I slipped on the wet rung and fell in a crumpled heap at the bottom, under cows' hooves and animal matter. Picking myself up from the filth, I wiped the mess from my clothes, and when I felt that I had removed as much as I could, I used the nearest animal back to clean my hands on, after which I went outside. On my earlier trip outside I had not felt the cold of this December night as I did now, as a shiver passed through my body. The cold of the night was soon a distant concern, as I heard Annie cry out once again. Her cries were entering my very soul, and were starting to make me feel quite sick. I sat on the stone steps outside the bastle, for what seemed a lifetime, being continually tortured by her plaintiff cries. Eventually, the dawn started to break, which in these winter months meant it was well on in the morning, and the cries continued. My poor Annie had been racked in agony for an absolute age. I doubt there is a man alive able to withstand the agonies that Annie suffered that night. It would be almost mid-morning when the anguished cries ceased. I rushed in, scrambling up the ladder, throwing myself into the room, expectantly, glad that the agonies were over, and hoping to see my poor Annie, with that melting smile, and my baby, oh yes, my new baby. Mother was stood directly in front of me as I entered the room, her expression sombre and strained. She looked directly at me, and not saying a word, dipped her head, while at the same time shaking it, then walked away, holding her head in her hands. As she walked away, her hands came from her face and reached skywards, and she screamed out, "Why God, oh why, why, why?" She then collapsed to the floor, sobbing. Father rose from his bed, and went to Mother, kneeling down and placing his arms about her shoulders and comforting her. Sarah was kneeling by Annie, wiping the floor next to the bed. I dropped to my knees by the side of Sarah and taking her arm in my right hand I said, "The baby?" She turned to me and just shook her head, then continued her cleaning.

I do not know what gripped me but I just had to get out of there, and rushed down the ladder, and outside, where I had saddled and tethered my nag, earlier in the night, while waiting, in readiness to ride to the Dodds with the news. I mounted that nag and I rode like never before, I just had to ride like the devil, for the anger I felt now possessed me like a demon.

Had any man confronted me on that morning ride, I know I would have torn him limb from limb with my bare hands. I hated the world as I rode, and I wanted to take a life, for the life that had been taken from me. Without realising where I had ridden to I soon found myself approaching the Dodds' bastle. As I arrived, I fell from my horse, as if exhausted. Mary Dodds must have heard my approach and ran from the bastle. I picked myself from the ground, and as she looked at me, all I could see was Annie's face. I wrapped my arms about her and collapsed into uncontrollable tears, trying between sobs to tell what had happened, and how we all had lost our Annie.

Although I was among friends, friends who all shared the same sorrow, I also had to contend with the guilt. I was the one who had killed her, I was the one who had caused her to have a baby, and therefore I had killed her. Yes, I had killed her, but I did not feel remorse for what I had done, I felt anger; no, it was not anger, it was rage, and it was burning me up inside. Of course I had felt anger before, but never a rage such as this, a rage I felt sure would consume me, if I did not do something, but what? I did not know.

After some time with the Dodds, it was Raymond who said that they should all accompany me back to the Milburn bastle, in order to be there, when Annie was interred. I would have liked her to have been buried near a church, not that I had taken a lot of interest in religion since my days at the manse, but since old fat Harry had seen off most of the churches, and priests, it was not an option open to anyone, but

Annie was so innocent, just a child herself, giving birth to a child. She was an angel, and deserved the very best, but alas, not in this land.

I gave Raymond help to harness up the cart, so that he and Mary could travel in it. Raymond's impairment from his shoulder injury was a great encumbrance to him, and he struggled with the most simple of tasks. Although, before we had been attacked that summer day at the sheil, I felt I could share anything with him, I felt uncomfortable at the thought of asking him about his injury, and of how it was affecting him, so I just got on with the harnessing, trying not to make him feel a lesser person.

We all set off together, Raymond and Mary in the cart, with Michael and me riding, and not a word passed any lips on the entire journey. We arrived at my home by early afternoon, and on arrival I noticed Father at the rear of the bastle, digging a grave. As we entered the bastle, Mary and Mother fell into each other's arms and cried, which set Raymond off again, and Michael was starting as well, so I quietly left and joined Father, who was struggling with the effort of digging. I stepped forward and said to Father, "Can I do that?"

"No, it is all right lad, I will do it," Father replied.

"Give me that damned spade!" I yelled, as I snatched it from his hands, then stood square to my father, and just stared, much as Michael had described Father did with James on the day of the Trod, after Raymond and I had been attacked. Father turned his back and walked away. I had never spoken to Father like that before, I would never have dared speak to him like that, but the rage was still with me, burning ever deeper, and with greater ferocity. Would Father have reacted differently had the circumstances been different, or had I entered a new chapter in my life? I knew not, but I could not see things very clearly, and felt I must have taken on some of the traits of my sister. I started to dig, but with a fury, the sweat was pouring from my brow, on that cold December day, although I was unaware of whether it was hot or cold. Every spadeful of earth I moved from the hard ground was, in my mind, another life I was taking, for I had caused Annie's death, and in my mind others must die because of it.

Once the grave was sufficiently deep, I laid down the spade, and went inside. I do not know who had done it, but Annie's body was now wrapped in sackcloth and bound by stout cord. I wanted to see her once more, and I felt the rage reach new heights, but managed to contain myself.

I went to the bed and gathered her up in my arms. I could feel my Annie and dearly wanted to cry, but the rage would not let me, it had me in a firmer grip than that I had on Annie. I walked down the ladder, with Mary and Mother following behind, then Michael and Raymond. Father came last, and appeared to be affected more by what was taking place than the Dodds; or was it me that had affected him in this way?

As I got to the graveside I dropped to my knees, gently lowering Annie's body into the ground, and as I did so Mary and Mother sobbed uncontrollably. I looked up from the grave and saw that Michael had his arm around Raymond's shoulder and both had tears running down their faces. Father was stood behind them, and Sarah had now joined him. What was Sarah feeling, I thought, that expressionless face; what lay behind it on an occasion like this? Did she really feel nothing? Oh, how I wish I were her now, numb from all that was happening.

I started to cover the body with the soil that I had piled up at the graveside, but only got two or three spadefuls in when I just threw the spade down and walked away. I just kept on walking, where to I knew not and cared less. By now the long night was starting to descend, the darkness rapidly enveloping the land, and I was grateful for this, for I felt more able to cope, knowing no one could see me. I reached a rocky outcrop and sat myself down, and stared into the darkness. I think I was trying to seek an answer in the dark, an answer for what, I did not even know what the question was.

I sat there for an age, my mind wandering from first one thing and then another, then, my thoughts settled on that first time I had set eyes on Annie. Just a few days after my return from Scotland, on my way to see Sarah. I remember how light her hair was, with the sun reflecting off it, and those beautiful happy eyes staring back at me, and that realisation, even back then, that this was the girl I wanted to be with. All that time ago, and all that had taken place in between, to be ended so very quickly, then the rage started to consume me again. I looked about me, and through the dark I could see the frost gathering on the ground, but I felt none of it; I was hot, very hot. I regained some composure, and set about returning to the bastle, now with a blank mind. I had used up all my thoughts for that day.

On my return home everyone had settled down for the night; Mary and Michael had taken my bed, Raymond was on the floor, just across from the top of the ladder. I don't think anyone was asleep, but I crept in and laid myself down on the floor near Raymond. Strangely, sleep came easily, and when I think back, of course, I had not slept the night before. The next morning I was awoken by Mother and Mary preparing the morning meal; Sarah was next to rise. Before long we were all risen and sat at the table, but not a word was spoken. We were all still suffering from the events of yesterday. After the morning meal was eaten, I went down to check the stock in the fields, and on my return, Michael was readying the cart for their return home. I quietly assisted him, and as we finished Mary and Raymond came down the ladder, followed by Mother, Sarah, then Father. I stood back as Mary and Raymond got into the cart, and Michael mounted up.

Mary was sat with her left hand on the side of the cart to steady herself. I stepped forward and lay my hand over hers and said, "I don't know if you can ever forgive me, Mary." She looked down at me and smiled; again, all I could see was Annie looking back at me.

"Rob, you saved my son's life, nearly losing your own doing so, and my daughter loved you from the first time she saw you. All she ever wanted was to be with you, and she died loving you. There is nothing to forgive, and you are as dear to this family as any of mine. Rob, you are, and always will be, part of my family." She then placed her other hand on my head, as if to stress physically what she had said.

I lowered my head, as if to acknowledge what she had said and done, and Raymond, who had taken hold of the reins, geed on the horse and cart and Mary's hand slipped from under mine. As they drove off they all waved as if leaving from a social gathering. The Dodds were as close as kin to us, that was for sure.

Mother then stepped forward and laid a hand on my shoulder and said, "Come, Rob, it will be all right." I pulled away and said, "No, it will not be all right, it will never be all right." As I walked off into the fields, the rage once more took hold of me, and I could feel it entering my very soul. I shivered, but not with the cold; with the emotions that were enveloping my being.

I came to a rocky outcrop and sat me down and took time to ponder the events of the past days. Just a few days ago I was with a woman who I was going to spend my life with, and we were about to have a child; it was something that had taken years to develop, then, it was gone. How can such things happen, what force is it that, one minute there is love, then the next there is heartache? This thought did little to dampen the burning within me; it did exactly the opposite, it kindled the flames even more.

That which had kept me from the raiding, Sir John Foster, and the thought of the gallows, no longer figured in my thoughts. If my fate is the gallows, then so be it, but before I go, I will take as much as I can, from as many as I can, and if they wish to stand in my way, they will seal their own fate.

Chapter 15

Let the Riding Resume

I stayed out for a very long time, not wishing to go home with such a fierce rage burning in me. I wished I could cry over my Annie, but I could not. Eventually the cold of the day started to overcome me; it was this that made me realise that the day was almost past, and that the light was starting to fade. I trudged back and went inside and sat down at the table. Looking around I saw that Father, Mother and Sarah were all looking at me. I turned to my family and said I was sorry for the way I had behaved. I turned to Father and said that I would never speak to him again, in the way I had at Annie's grave. Father quite surprisingly said, "I was proud of you, my lad, for there are few who would dare speak to me like that, and you did, but should you ever feel like trying that again, I shall surely rip your head from your shoulders." As he was saying this he was walking over towards me, and as he finished the sentence, he laid his hand on my shoulder, giving it a shake, then laughed.

Mother said that she understood that I would feel anger at losing someone I loved, so young, and that I must look for ways of overcoming my feelings. I told her that I had given the matter much thought, and that I felt I needed to start riding again. This was greeted with silence, and thus determined that any more was best left unsaid.

The very next day I started to practise my swordplay, with my new blade, and started to ride and improve my lance work, but found it hard to improve beyond basic work without an opponent. Father was not well enough to be able to put sufficient time in, and I no longer had Raymond, as he would never hold a sword again, and Michael, I feared, would find my wish to partake in swordplay so soon after his daughter had died, in bad taste.

There was but one course of action. I resolved to go and stay with my Uncle Arthur, as he was still actively riding, and if not as good as Father, when at his best, still, he was a fierce fighting man. After coming to my decision to leave home, it became time to break the news to my family. I waited until the evening meal, and after we had eaten, I announced my decision by saying, "Because of what has happened with Annie, and the fact that she died in this very room, and that she is buried just outside the bastle, I feel I need to get away; therefore I intend to go and stay with Uncle Arthur, if he will have me." For a moment there was silence, then Mother said she thought it the right thing to do, and Father said that he agreed. I asked Father if he would be able to cope alone, to which he replied he could and would, and that Mother and Sarah were more than capable of keeping things going.

The next morning I saddled up, made my goodbyes and rode out; my only regret was that when I left I had embraced Sarah, and it would have been somewhat encouraging if there had been some kind of response.

By mid-afternoon I had crossed over into the next valley and was nearing the bastle of my Uncle Arthur, when I was greeted by the scene of him and my cousin, Richard, heavily engaged in swordplay, or at least I hoped it was swordplay, because with these two hot heads, they could flare up in moments.

Richard spied me first, and right in the middle of their play, Richard raised his sword in greeting, with that ever present smile on his face, just as Arthur took a wide sweep with his sword. I reined hard on my nag, out of sheer terror, as I saw the sword coming ever closer to the neck of Richard. With the sword almost within contact of his neck, Richard ducked and immediately bobbed up again, and smiling at Arthur, said, "Nearly, dear uncle, nearly, and pray, what would you have done had you made contact?"

Without any change of expression, Uncle Arthur replied, "Put you on your nag and take you to old Scrope in Carlisle." Master Scrope was the March Warden for the West March, and he had been after Richard for some time, and had threatened to hang him on sight.

"And would you ask a reward, dear uncle?" enquired Richard playfully. "A damned waste of a journey to Carlisle, without," came the terse reply; not quite what Richard was expecting; I think neither he nor me were in any doubt as to the sincerity of Arthur's reply.

"Come, Uncle, let us greet my cousin, your nephew," said Richard cheerily, hoping to change the subject. He then strode purposely over to my nag and took my hand, shaking it heartily. "It's good to see you, Rob, but are you not to be a father soon, what brings you here?" he said. I was unable to give a reply, I just shook my head and slid down from the saddle. Richard put an arm around me, and drew me close in an embrace. "Come, little cousin, let's go and take food and talk."

We all went in, and I was confronted by the most striking woman; she was tall, slim and with the most beautiful jet black shiny hair set against the whitest and smoothest skin I have ever seen. "You know your Aunt Alice, Rob," said Arthur. I just stood there stammering, lost for words. "Of course he doesn't, I was ill for the hand fasting, and we were not together before he went to Scotland. Come, Rob," she said as she put a hand out, and pulled me to her, and kissed my cheek. "My, you're a handsome lad, not like these two I have to put up with," she said laughingly.

We sat and Aunt Alice served food, and while we ate I told my story, after which Aunt Alice came behind me, wrapped both her arms around my neck and kissed me on the cheek again, saying, "We will look after you, Rob my lad, have no fear." Arthur then said, "After a couple of days with your Aunt Alice, you will never want to see another woman," as both he and Richard laughed loudly.

"I don't want to see another woman again, anyway," I blurted out, before realising what I had said, then felt myself blushing, then stammering to try and make amends.

I then heard a loud thwack! And saw Alice give Arthur a tremendous smack across his face, while at the same time and with the other hand, catch Richard across the face with a swift backhand. This was indeed a woman with spirit and little fear. I have seen Arthur take on three people at once when on raids, and Richard, as I have spoken of before, is the most savage of beasts to ride the marches, yet these two fighting men were of little consequence to this fiery woman.

That night we all bedded down, but sleep was not to be part of my night, due to the rather over exuberant coupling of Arthur and Alice. At times I thought that he was murdering her, from the loud guttural moanings coming from Alice, which could be heard far into the night. I think Arthur might have retired much sooner, but Alice could be heard loudly demanding more. I now knew how Arthur was able to engage in battle without tiring; Alice's demands of him were the secret.

I think it was almost dawn before I eventually found sleep, only to be awoken shortly after, by Alice declaring that food was ready. How did this woman do it? For the rest of the day I dragged myself about, feeling decidedly under my best. Arthur and Richard spent much of the day engaged in swordplay, involving me along with them. Suddenly, while in the midst of swordplay with Richard, he dropped his sword, just as I was about to strike a downward blow. I was only just able to prevent contact betwixt sword and shoulder, when from his belt he removed a leather strap and from a pouch about his belt he took a small smooth pebble like those found in the bottom of a burn, placing the pebble into the strap, then twisted the strap above his head, released the pebble, which struck a hare that was running across the field some distance off, which I had not seen. As the pebble made contact, the hare leapt into the air, then landed back down again, dead.

I was amazed at how Richard had done this, and eagerly asked about the leather strap. He told me it was called a sling shot, and that it had better range and was quicker to reload than these new weapons that some liked to use, called guns, where an evil smelling black powder has to be lit and there is much smoke and loud bangs.

I asked Richard to show me how to use the strap; we spent much time over the next few days, learning the art of the slingshot, until I was becoming a reasonable shot, but still very far from the proficiency of my cousin. Richard then found some well-tanned calf leather, from which he fashioned a new sling. Having completed his leather work, he called me over and in flamboyant manner, bowing deeply, he presented me with the fruits of his labour. I thanked my cousin in equally flamboyant manner, then scurried off to the burn to gather pebbles. I had a purse about my belt, which rarely saw any coin, therefore it was an ideal holder for my stones.

For the next few days I spent as much time as I was able in familiarising myself with my new weapon, and though not of the same mastery of the weapon as my cousin, nonetheless, at a larger target, the like of trees, which I chose, resembling the size of man, which I would be targeting, I became quite accurate.

It was always helpful to have a secondary form of defence or attack, as the case may be, when in a confrontational situation, as there was always the possibility of losing one's weapon in the heat of battle, which I had seen when on a raid, the result of such a catastrophe.

Towards the end of the week Arthur came to me and announced that on the morrow we were to saddle up and ride westwards then veer right before Carlisle, and head into the Scottish West March, where the pickings were rich. When the day broke, we set off mid-morning leaving the valley, with Alice's demands ringing in our ears. She had set Arthur and Richard a list of goods she required, which entailed the likes of pewter plates to eat from, as she was fed up with the wooden ones. She would prefer silver, but would settle for no less than pewter. She also wanted some fine cloth, to make herself dresses.

I never liked raiding houses; stealing cattle, and killing the odd Scottie who got in the way was part of life, but I always thought entering a house, and putting the women to the sword, a most distasteful course of action.

As we went on our way we met with others, who would accompany us on our raid. Over the past days since arriving at Arthur's, I had tried to suppress the feelings of anger that lay within me. I felt that my endeavours had been successful, but as I now rode, with an ever increasing band of raiders, the heat of rage was starting to build within me again. There was a purpose in me being there, and that was to rid myself of this feeling that had overtaken me since Annie's death, and raiding was the only answer.

We had ridden west for some time and had just got to the top of a ridge when far on the horizon I could see a church spire and beyond it what looked like a large castle. I turned to Richard. "What is that I see on the far horizon?" I enquired.

"My home, dear cousin, Carlisle, the cathedral and beyond, the dreaded Carlisle castle. Not a place you want to frequent, for once a resident within, they will wheel you out to the gallows. Enough of this, time to turn northward to ford the river."

Richard spurred his nag onwards, reining it away from me, as if he did not wish to continue our conversation. Some short time later we arrived at the banks of a wide river, the Esk, I was informed by one of our party. I had seen the River Tyne, many times, but had never been required to cross it. The River Esk was not as wide, but here I was required to cross. I entered the water with great trepidation, holding tight to the reins, while at the same time, tightening my legs about my nag's girth. The further we went, the higher the water, until I felt my nag no longer walking, but swimming, struggling under my weight and that of my arms and armour, but it bravely kept its head above the water, transporting its nervous load until I could feel it start to walk again. The level of water about me then started to drop quite rapidly as we reached the other side.

As we pulled from the muddy river bank, Richard galloped over. "Are you well, Cousin?" he enquired. Trying to muster some air of composure, I answered in a manner that the crossing had been of no consequence. His ever present smile broadened as he rode away, fully aware of the terror I had just experienced.

We rode onwards to the north-west, now entering a region known as the debatable lands. This was land neither English nor Scots, which stretched from just north of Carlisle across to a wide estuary and the sea beyond. It also spanned northwards for some distance. I was told by my uncle, who had now joined me for the first time since setting off, that few lived here, and that no one was allowed to build any permanent structure within these lands, but that the Grahams inhabited the area. They were a family who regarded themselves as neither English nor Scottish, and would fight for either if the terms or numbers were right. I was left with these words of advice, "That for any man who has no allegiance, then that man should not be trusted."

As we rode ever more northward the land became more dotted with hills and we soon saw in the distance a small settlement. "Lockerbie," called out my uncle.

"What is Lockerbie?" I asked.

"That there is Lockerbie, that small hamlet, too small to bother with, we will give it a wide berth, so that the locals do not alarm others of our presence." We then veered east for a short while, then north, then west. "Johnston country, lad," said Uncle. "Fine hard fighting men, but they are often too wrapped up with fighting another Scottie family, the Maxwells, to be bothered with the likes of us, but keep a sharp eye out lad, for if you see a Johnston, we will have a good fight on our hands before the day's out." He laughed, then rode off, leaving me with only my thoughts. This was what I wanted, a good fighting family, someone who wanted to fight, someone I could draw blood from. The anger started to rage within me, I wanted to fight. Where are these hard fighting men who would cross swords with me? I had no regard for cattle or horses, that is not why I was there; I had come to fight, for only by fighting could this anger be exorcised.

As we rode to the west of this small hamlet, I kept my eyes peeled for any who may appear from there to engage in battle, but alas, there were none. Onward we rode, and I was now saddle weary. It was only then that I realised that it had been quite some time since last I had taken part in such a venture. Sir John Foster came to my thoughts as I rode, and the stark warning he had given, but was this indeed what I wanted? Did I really want to die, because of the loss of my dear Annie? What nonsense, or was it?

Then I looked to my right and a lone horseman stood on the ridge of a hill, watching as we passed by. Without saying a word, I reined my nag hard to the right and galloped off toward the lone figure. As I neared him, he drew his sword and came to meet me at a gallop. He was coming downhill at full gallop on a fresh horse, and striking hard at me. I was luckily able to raise my sword and parry his blow, but the sheer force of his attack was such as to unsaddle me. I went crashing to the ground, the impact stunning me. I slowly got to my feet and could see him, having turned to engage again, bearing down on me at full gallop. I stood transfixed to the spot, my sword lying on the ground, out of reach. If death was really my wish, then it was nigh, but as he came closer, I rolled across the ground, gathering up my sword as I rolled, nimbly coming to my feet, as I dodged his slashing blade, then came about, bringing my sword in a wide sweeping move, catching the small of his back as he passed. The blow was accompanied by a high pitched squeal from the rider. Was this a woman, that would make such a noise? The rider galloped on, then slipped from the saddle. I ran over to where the body had landed, to ensure my quarry was despatched. I raised my sword as I rolled the body over with my foot to see that it was not a woman, but a mere boy. He could scarcely have been twelve years old, and thankfully the blow had been swift and lethal, and I did not have to strike him again.

I have despatched others in the past, but never a boy so young. The contents of my stomach rushed to my mouth. I held it tight shut, swallowing hard, returning the acrid tasting bile from whence it came.

I felt the sweat engulf my entire body, it now trickling from my brow, down my face. Was this really what I wanted, to kill? Well, I had done so, and it did not feel better, no, worse, far worse.

I sheathed my sword, and walked away from the boy, towards my nag, scarcely able to lift my feet from the ground, my head deeply bowed. I no longer wished to set eyes on the dreadful deed I had done. Reaching my nag, I swung myself into the saddle.

I rode back to where my fellow riders were, they all having watched the swift contact. I must have still been showing signs of the aftermath of my actions, for one of my fellow riders brought his nag alongside mine and sneeringly said, "What's the matter, no stomach for fighting?" Instantly, my bollock knife was out and held tightly to his throat. "Make peace with your maker, for now you die," I snarled through clenched teeth. "No one, no one, ever questions a Milburn, do you all hear?" I screamed out at the top of my voice. "Now scum, you die!" I growled, from the very pit of my being.

"No, Rob, you cannot kill a fellow rider," I heard, but not taking my eye from my intended victim, I sensed someone coming to my other side.

"Rob, dear cousin, let's not end our day like this," I heard Richard say. Already holding my victim by his collar, I heaved him over toward me, bringing his head hard down on the front of my saddle, pressing his face so hard down, it distorted his features to those of a gargoyle, while at the same time bringing the hand holding the knife across to the throat of my cousin. "Do you really think you can escape as well?" I uttered, while looking at Richard from the corner of my eyes. For the very first time since first I had met Richard, the smile was not there; just fear, total fear. I think it was observing this total transformation that brought me back to my senses, but I had to leave it as a victor and not the vanquished. "Even you, Richard, a Milburn, never question my actions, do you understand?" I continued.

"Yes, Rob, yes," replied Richard, who now was quite ashen.

I slowly drew my blade from his neck, but still keeping it ready, then lifted the now slavering head from my saddle, and still gripping his collar, held the face in front of mine for a moment, as if to emphasise my already severe threat. I then pushed him away from me in a dismissive manner, slowly returning my knife to its sheath. Having secured the blade, I casually reined my horse away, cutting in front of Richard's nag, which shied away, as if with fear that the threat was not yet over.

For the rest of that ride I was left alone by my fellow riders, and acted merely as an observer, with me my only company, and my thoughts.

I contented myself that, if my actions were not those which I would normally undertake, nonetheless, I had possibly shown to all about that I was indeed worthy of the Milburn name, and was as fierce a man as my father and uncles.

My Uncle Arthur then took up station at my side, and with a stern face he glared at me and said, "Clean up your mess boy, now," by which he meant that the body had to be disposed of, in order that no one would discover it before we were well away, and thereby raise the alarm.

I reluctantly reined my nag around and went back to where the boy lay. A large pool of blood now amassed around the ground by his back. I alighted from my nag and hesitantly neared the body. His steel bonnet lay on the ground a short distance from his head; I could see that the inside had been padded out with soft leather, in order that it would fit his young head, but apart from that, he carried no armour to protect him. The poor lad must have been sent out as a sentinel, most likely with the instruction that if he spied anything, to ride back and raise the alarm, but he wanted to be a brave rider and take on the English raider.

To the left of the ridge where the lad had been stood was a small copse of trees. This would be the perfect place to hide the body. I gathered him up in my arms and slung him over his nag, then walked him over to the copse, where, having entered, I scraped out a shallow grave with the blade of the lad's sword, then lay him in the depression, and heaped the soil over the body. I then went about, gathering fallen leaves, and scattered these over the grave. Having satisfied myself that the body was well hid, I tied the young Scottie lad's nag to the rear of my saddle, by its lead rein, and rode off to join my fellow riders. They had ridden off, and were well ahead of me; by the time I eventually caught up with them they were in the midst of raiding a substantial homestead. The building was unusually of two-storey construction, unlike the normal grounded croft, or the high three-storey pele tower, preferred by the richer peoples of the Scottish border lands.

On my arrival, I saw Arthur and Richard emerging from the door, both with swords in hand, and both swords dripping with blood.

Arthur held in his other hand a large cloth, which was wrapped around various objects, which clanged as he caught the bundle on the side of the door frame. I assumed that he had acquired the goods that Alice had sent him for. Arthur looked quite grim, but Richard was smiling as ever, as they took hold of their nags that were being held by others of our group, mounted together, then we all rode off, gathering up the cattle that were grazing around the homestead.

I did not know what had gone on inside that house, nor did I want to, but I fear that women and children may have perished within, but one thought struck me as we rode off. Where were the men? There had been the boy, who I had encountered, and now a homestead that I assumed had only women and children?

I shook the thought from my head and rode onward, to the next dwelling, which appeared deserted, but I suspected that our approach had been detected, and that the occupants had gone to ground. We did not linger, but cleared all the stock that we came across and drove ever onwards.

A further six homesteads of varying size were encountered on our ride, each yielding a good measure of stock, cattle, sheep, pigs, but few horses. At each place we relieved of stock there was not the least sign of resistance. Was this some plot by the Scotties or some greater force, to deny me the very thing I had ridden for, to cross swords with another who was worthy to do so and offer a goodly fight, that afterwards I could ride off in the knowledge that my sword had despatched a good fighting man and that in so doing, the fires within had been somewhat quenched.

At a point where the land allowed, we herded the beasts tightly together, look-outs were posted, and the rest of our band settled for the day. I had scarcely laid my head down when sleep engulfed me, but for how long I cannot tell. All that I do know is that I woke up with a start, seeing that Scottie boy's face bearing down on me, his eyes black with death, and his sword at my throat. A dream, an awful dream. I sat upright, breathing heavily, the sweat running from my brow. I looked about me. Had anyone noticed me? No, I did not think so. The relief of being awake and away from such images, I wiped the sweat from my face, then got to my feet. To attempt further sleep would be futile, I would take over watch.

I walked from the camp to the look-out post and spoke to my fellow rider, who I was not acquainted with, and had not yet had occasion to speak to. I found him a most charming fellow; he was of the Little family who lived south of Carlisle, and was the last of four brothers. The eldest had been killed when raiding deep into Dumfriesshire some five years past; the next eldest brother had lost his life in a skirmish near Carlisle with some raiding Scotties two years gone, and the third brother had lost his life to the gibbet, the result of the West March warden, Lord Scrope, just this very year. He went on to tell me that my cousin, Richard, would fare the same as his last brother to die, for he was regarded by all that knew him as one of the most dangerous men to walk the earth.

I told my new acquaintance that were it not for the fact that he was my cousin, I would no doubt fear him also. At this remark he laughed, saying, "But did you not draw your bollock knife to his throat and threaten to kill him this very day, and it is that very thing that makes all who ride here today fear you with greater dread than he."

"Enough of this," I cautioned. "Go lay your head down, we have a hard ride ahead tonight."

He went away, back to the camp, I feeling quite elated that my fellow riders should hold me with such regard. Did they really fear me, was I that formidable? If only they knew that prior to holding a knife to my cousin, I had been fighting back the bile from my stomach at the thought of killing a boy, but it was better that they did not know, and would never know, for in these times, a sense of fear was always accompanied by respect.

As that sun now settled over the rolling hills of south-west Scotland, I could see that things were starting to stir back at the camp. No one had relieved me of my lonely vigil, but that had been how I wanted it. When I saw the riders mounting up, I started to walk back to the camp, but then saw Richard riding out with my nag on its lead rein. "There you are, Cousin, your trusty steed," he said, as he handed the rein, then spurred off to help the rest gather up the herd, for the long slow ride back. Cattle and sheep were not bad to drove, and it was relatively easy to maintain a reasonable progress with such beasts, but pigs were the most difficult of animals to encourage forward, and even at their fastest, seemed incapable of gaining more than a walking pace. Therefore the night would be long and arduous.

The trail back to the border was indeed a toilsome labour, but just as the sun was breaking from its easterly slumbers, we reached the River Esk, well to the east of any inhabited area, and where the banks were closer together and the water not so deep. We started to ford the flowing waters, and my friends the pigs, of whom I had spoken so disparagingly, now showed their worth, by merrily taking to the water and making good headway. We held back the cattle and horses, and let the sheep go next; the pigs having gone, the sheep would follow, and indeed did, with riders either side of the throng, ensuring that none were lost. The cattle were then let across, then the horses, they being the better swimmers of our haul, though the pigs may dispute my assumption.

An easterly direction was then taken, thus avoiding the more inhabited areas, and as we progressed the light of the day increased, and by mid-morning I was back on land that was vaguely familiar. There was an eerie stillness about this morning, a stillness that caused me some unease. As we continued our journey we drove our herd over a ridge and I crested the ridge, allowing a wide view of the surrounding countryside. There was still some light morning mist lying in the valley bottom, but little else. As far as the eye could see, there was not a living thing within the valley.

At this point, the herd was split between the various families, and for the first time since we had set off the previous night, I was reunited with Richard and Arthur. We took our spoils, some six Highland cattle, ten sheep and one pig, and set about the final part of our journey.

I had gained through the night's journey a new lightness of heart. I was not yet free of the anger, but much less burdened, and now looked forward to seeing again the fire brand that was my Aunt Alice. We came through the first valley and crossed the second ridge into the valley that was home to Arthur, and again, it was devoid of life, as if some great fire breathing beast had entered and consumed all life from within. There had been little conversation between the three of us as we had proceeded, and I felt that the unease was upon my kinsmen, as it was upon me, none wishing to speak in case our voices confirmed our suspicions.

The rate of our progress quickened as we got closer to Arthur's bastle, until the stock we were driving were left and all three of us spurred our weary nags forward to full gallop. As we neared the bastle there was no sight of Alice; she was not at the door as I had hoped, then as we got closer, I heard Arthur yell out, "No!" in a long, mournful cry. I could not see what should prompt such a reaction, then I did. At the very mouth of the door, where I had been looking, lay Alice, her body face down in the dirt, the bodice on her upper body ripped to shreds, and her lower garments left high above her waist, revealing her beaten bare buttocks. She had been savagely ravished for there was blood between her legs and much bruising about her thighs. Arthur was out of his saddle and running to her side, clasping in his hand the spoil from the Scottie farmstead, which Alice had ordered, before we left, and on reaching her, gently took her in his arms and rolled her over. Her throat had been slit, the blood heavily crusted about her bare chest. Arthur cradled her in his arms and, as he did so, Alice's eyes opened. She raised her left hand slightly, as if to touch Arthur; there was a gurgling sound from her throat, then she was gone.

It is a strange sight to see a man as rugged and fierce as Arthur, reduced to sobbing like a child. I slid from my saddle and fell to the ground, every trace of strength having left my body. I could not look at Arthur and Alice; I did not know what Richard was doing, and cared less; I just sat there unable to cry for Alice or cry with Arthur, I just felt numb. As I sat in my crumpled state, my thoughts returned to my family, Father, Mother and Sarah. Was this how Sarah felt all the time; numb, unable to feel or react to anything? What an awful thing to be afflicted with.

I had sat there for some time when I was brought back from my numbness by Richard. "Come, Cousin," he beckoned. "We have work."

"Work," I replied in disbelief. Richard raised a finger to his lips and beckoned me again. I followed him to the rear of the bastle where he handed me a spade, as he started to dig. Without a word I accompanied my cousin in this dreadful chore.

When we had completed the digging we both returned to the front of the bastle where Arthur still sat, cradling his wife. Richard spoke quietly, saying but, "Uncle," while at the same time holding out his hand as if to help Arthur up. Arthur got to his feet unaided, then gathered Alice in his arms and carried her to where we had dug the grave, Richard having led the way. As we gathered by the grave Arthur gently lowered Alice's body into the ground, but had to let her drop the final part into the ground. Her body made an awful dull thud as it reached its final resting place, and I could almost hear Alice chiding Arthur for letting her drop in such an undignified manner. We three stood there in silence, all with our individual thoughts of that once so full of life and vigour person that was Alice. After some while stood there, Richard handed Arthur the spade, without saying a word, then Richard and I walked away, leaving Arthur to cover the grave. The two of us sat on the ground in front of the bastle, maintaining our silence, until Arthur joined us. He laid the spade against the bastle wall, and without altering his stride or looking at either of us he said, "Away home the pair of you, I want to be alone."

Richard and I just looked at each other. Richard shrugged, we both got to our feet, went to our nags, then Richard turned to me and said, "Little cousin, when you drew your knife to my throat, would you have used it?"

"There are some questions best not asked and the answers best not heard," I replied. Richard then swung himself into the saddle and spurred his nag away, waving his hand as he went and calling back, "You worry me, little cousin, you really worry me," then laughed as he disappeared over the ridge of the valley.

With Richard gone, I walked back to where Arthur was sat, and placing my arm about his shoulder I said, "I really feel your loss," then walked back to my nag, mounted and slowly rode away, in the direction of home. As I rode away, I was overcome by the loss of Alice, and tears started to roll from my eyes. It was then that I realised I had come to terms with my own loss of Annie. It was not killing that would take my anger away, but to be involved with another's loss and not just my own, to see such a loss from a little farther away than I had endured. The pain was no less, in fact it was worse, for indeed, I had known Alice but a few days, but she had made such an impression on me, with her lust for life, that my words to Arthur were not hollow, but spoken from the heart. I truly did share his loss.

Chapter 16

My New Mentor

I arrived back at our bastle by mid-afternoon, and as I dismounted Sarah came out. I knew I had not been away long but I ran over to her and wrapped my arms about her and held her tightly. I knew that I would get no response, but a short while ago, after finding Alice dead, I had felt numb, and would have given my soul for someone to embrace me, and I thought that Sarah, although unable to respond, would nonetheless appreciate my embrace. I held on to her and whispered in her ear, "Sister, I do love you," then let go and tended my horse.

Mother emerged down the ladder as I did so, and now it was her turn to embrace me, strangely saying, as I had just done to Sarah, "Rob, I do love you." I smiled back and for a moment remained silent, concentrating on my nag, then turned to her and said, "I know where I belong." Those words seemed to touch Mother very deeply, as her eyes welled up with tears and she quickly scrambled up the ladder to the living area.

After seeing to my nag I ascended the ladder and went over to the table where Father was sat, and was greeted with a "Do you fare well, lad?" as if I had just popped out for a short while. Mother laid a dish of pottage in front of me, and it was not until then that I realised how long it had been since last I ate, but I did not dispose of it in my usual manner, but toyed with the food, as I told of the events of the past few days, and of Alice's death.

Neither Mother nor Father had got really well acquainted with Alice, since she had come into Arthur's life, but nonetheless, they greeted the news badly. It took much persuading to stop them from setting forth to Arthur's, to offer what help they could render.

After I had eaten and all news had been exchanged, I asked if I may lay my head down as it had been some time since last I slept, and was grateful when I did lie down, quickly to be gathered up into a deep sleep.

It felt scarcely a moment since lying down when I was awoken by Father. "Come lad, get you up, there is someone to see you." I wearily rose from my bed and unsteadily descended the ladder, stepping out into the bright daylight, shielding my eyes as I did so, to be greeted by some hundred and fifty riders at least, headed by Sir John Foster. "Now then, lad, is that any way to conduct yourself, sleeping 'til this hour, you should be about doing the chores and taking the weight off your beautiful mother," he said as he bowed gracefully in the direction of Mother. This man was a real charmer of womankind.

"Sir, I was with a calving heifer all night, and have just laid down this hour since," I lied.

"Well lad, we have work, we head for Carter Bar for a Truce Day, and it is our wish you accompany us, what say you?"

"I am your servant, Sir," I replied.

"Indeed you are, my boy, indeed you are," came Sir John's retort.

Father came from within the bastle, leading his nag. "Your nag, lad," he said, pressing the lead rein into my hand, and engaging me with a knowing stare. I took the horse and mounted up, and it was Sarah who came out holding my lance and sword. Feeling quite embarrassed at my remiss, I coyly took the weapons from my sister, as Sir John said,

"That must have been a calving from hell last night," scarcely able to hold back his laughter.

As I rode away from my home, not wishing to look back at my family, should my fellow riders think less of me, Sir John instructed me to stay close to him. My thoughts were running wild as we went along. Why had Sir John wanted me along, was he going to hang me along the trail, had he found out about the dead Bell, or had he found out about the raids I had been on, and the people I had despatched? My nervousness grew, until Sir John engaged me in conversation. There were no searching questions, and I didn't feel as if he were trying to catch me out; it was not long until I felt well at ease with my riding companion.

This would be my first Truce Day meeting, and as we rode on I asked Sir John what was entailed in such an event. He explained the purpose of the Truce Day was to address any misdoings between the English and the Scots and to make redress for any losses incurred by either side, and if need be, punish any who may have offended. It was his task as Middle March Warden to meet with the Scottish March Warden, a Mr Carmichael, and to satisfactorily resolve all disputes.

We had been riding for some time when one of the other riders came between me and Sir John; a finely dressed gentleman, indeed more finely dressed than I had seen him last, on a raid into Scotland. It was Hugh Fenwick. He just rudely interrupted and said to Sir John in a very terse manner, "I hope we will see a proper account of the English side, and none of your shilly-shallying, Sir John. I'm sure Her Majesty will expect full measure from you."

Sir John, without turning his head from where he was going, retorted, "I'm sure if I don't, that Her Majesty will be the very first to know, Fenwick," then spurred forward his horse. I did likewise and came alongside Sir John again, leaving Fenwick to savour the fart from my horse.

"Far be it from me to talk ill of such a fine gentleman, Sir John, but there rides a man who seems to carry some animosity towards you," I said.

"Aye lad, he has designs on the Wardenship of this Middle March. Your uncle, Thomas Charlton, has told me that this Fenwick has been at the court of Queen Bess attempting to set me in a bad light. And by the way, your uncle is much favoured within court circles, I see him doing great things."

"Do you not worry that Fenwick's utterances may turn people against you, Sir John?" I asked.

"I will tell you this, lad. The reason I wished for you to accompany me on this Truce Day is that I thought you to have a keen mind, one that could be of benefit to me and the rest of the Middle March, and bless my soul, lad, that last remark proves me right; you show a keen sense of what things are about. Yes, Fenwick could sway some opinions, indeed, may have done so already, but I am blessed that the Queen holds me in some esteem, for I have, in the past, done much for her in battle, as I did for her father, King Henry. I do hope that she knows that I am true to the throne."

"Would that the Fenwick were not about to cause such bother, Sir John," I remarked.

"Aye lad, it would ease things, indeed it would. Enough of this, now, let's talk of happier things; what have you being doing since last we met, young Milburn?"

Just then could be heard a loud, harsh whinny of a horse. We reined back on our nags and pulled them around to see a horse on its side, its rider lying on the ground with his leg trapped underneath the horse. Two riders quickly dismounted and pulled the horse back to its feet. It seemed no worse for its tumble, but the rider was in great pain from his leg, and was bleeding quite badly from a cut to the side of his head.

"Damn!" exclaimed Sir John.

"Is he all right?" he called out to the dismounted riders. One called back, "He'll not ride another step this day, Sir John."

"Damn," exclaimed Sir John again. "That's my scribe. Is there a man among you who will step into his place?" There were some who could and indeed there were many who could not, but none stepped forward.

"You will be my scribe, young Milburn, indeed you will do well," he said, pointing at me. As Sir John said the words, Fenwick had ridden his horse between Sir John and myself.

"A Milburn a scribe; Sir John, you surely jest, what use would a Milburn be as a scribe? Methinks that your duties are perhaps beyond your advancing years," he said sneeringly, and looked about the gathered riders, getting the odd snigger from his audience.

"Sir John, would you require I write in English or Latin?" I enquired, knowing that if he said Latin I was undone.

"English will be fine, young Rob," answered Sir John with a broad smile. This was met with far more sniggers than before, and Fenwick reined his horse away with a look that could kill.

After the scribe had been tended to and was sent back with two other riders, Sir John came alongside me as we rode on. "Well done, young Rob, you put that Fenwick in his place, though I suspect you may have made an enemy of the bold Hugh."

"That worries me little at this stage, Sir John; what really worries me are the duties you wish me to carry out; I fear they may be beyond me," I said, with hesitation.

"Nonsense, lad, you will be well capable, you only have to keep a record of the events of the day, and I will tell you all you have to write. You can do that, can't you?" said Sir John.

"Well, yes, Sir," I said unconvincingly.

As we rode along I questioned Sir John on all aspects of the Truce Day, and I found Sir John a most informative person, and one I enjoyed listening to. He was a man of goodly age at this time, maybe in his seventies, an age few attain and even fewer are able to continue in the service of the crown, but Sir John was no ordinary man, and with each step of my horse my admiration of this man grew.

Towards the end of the day as light was starting to ebb, I saw in the distance what must have been five hundred or more riders. "Sir John," I gasped, my body tense in the saddle, as I stood up in my stirrups, and pointed forward.

"Aye lad, our welcoming committee," said Sir John, in what I regarded as a rather light hearted manner, considering what lay in front. "Settle, lad, they mean us no harm, it is a Truce Day, no weapon should or will be drawn," continued Sir John. I was less certain.

Two riders from the Scottish side rode forward of the rest, and on doing so, two gentlemen riders from our side broke rank and rode forward to meet them. I was at the edge of my saddle, my hand grasped tightly about my lance, ready to draw and charge should the need arise. As the riders neared each other, hands were raised in acknowledgement of each other, then it appeared something was passed between them. At this point they broke away from each other, and each rode back to their respective line. Our two riders came back at a steady canter, and pulled up in front Sir John, one handing him a rolled up paper, which, on receiving it, Sir John unrolled and read. "Well, gentlemen, we have written assurance of our safety until this hour on the morrow; let us ride on and enjoy our Scottish friends' hospitality."

I did not like the way things were going. I was not in the habit of enjoying Scottie hospitality, unless by that it meant taking anything of theirs I could lay my hands on.

We all rode on, and struck camp just outside a small hamlet. Once we had the horses bedded down and the fires on, we were joined by some Scottish gentlemen. One man at the front of the group extended his hand forward, calling out, "Sir John, how very good to see you again."

"Mister Carmichael, as charming a host as ever," replied Sir John. These two appeared firm friends and indeed chatted away in a most amiable manner for some time, as did the others who were in the camp. After some long time in conversation, of which I took no part, but listened intently, they broke off, the Scotties going their way and we preparing ourselves for the night.

My sleep was light, waking many times through the night to ensure we were not about to be attacked. I was much relieved when morning came and I was able to rise from my sleeping place and get my weapons about me. The rest of the camp soon burst into a hive of activity, and it was not long before we were joined by a group of Scotties. The morning had greeted us with a harsh greyness that threatened rain, so the Scotties escorted us to the small hamlet, where we were ushered into a large empty barn type building with burning torches set in wall mounts. There would be a hundred or more people already in the building, all sat or stood to one side. Now with the light of day and the burning torches I was better able to see these Scotties, and as I did so, I was much relieved I never took time out to look at these people before crossing swords with them, for they were a fearsome people.

Sir John walked forward and I stayed close by as I knew nothing of what was going on. Again, the one called Carmichael came forward with hand outstretched toward Sir John and they shook hands, the Carmichael saying, "I trust you had a good night, Sir John."

"Indeed so, Mister Carmichael, indeed so," came the reply.

"To business, Sir John, with your approval," said Carmichael. "To business, Mister Carmichael," said Sir John.

Sir John sat down, summoning me to sit by his side, as I took out the paper from the bag Sir John had given me, along with the quill, and from another bag I took out a container holding the ink. I felt very nervous as I prepared myself for the unknown, but Sir John, who must have seen my tension, gave a reassuring pat on my shoulder, and quietly said, "You'll be fine, lad; just take notes as best you can and we will sort through it later."

The first case was a Scottie, who claimed that he had lost twenty fine head of cattle and eighty sheep in a raid some four weeks before and if Mr Carmichael would offer him protection, he would gladly point out the raiders who were stood in the room. Mr Carmichael offered such an assurance to the Scottie, who then indicated five people who were in the room, of whom I knew four, as I had rode with them on a few occasions, and because of which, even though I had not been on this particular raid, I found it necessary to lower my head, in case I was identified also.

I furiously scribbled away, as the day went on, at times finding it hard to distinguish what I had written, but Sir John kept looking over to what I was doing and would give a knowing smile, accompanied by the odd, "Well done, lad."

With the first case of the day, the judgment was set by Mr Carmichael and agreed by Sir John, that the perpetrators of this offence would, before the next Truce Day, restore all cattle and sheep to their owner. Failure to do so would render the offenders liable to hanging.

As the day progressed, there was a continuous parade of claim and counter claim, of sentence and of imprisonment on each side, and as the day progressed the bartering between Sir John on behalf of the English and Mr Carmichael for the Scotties became more intense, sometimes reaching a stage where both men would be almost at blows, and their voices at screaming pitch, and I was supposed to record all the events of the day.

It was during one such encounter I recalled when Sir John first asked me to scribe for him and the Fenwick derided me, that I said to Sir John, would you require English or Latin. God forbid he had said Latin, as I scribbled at fever pitch, I could not have hoped to do so in Latin. Truth be told, I could not have done it in Latin at whatever speed.

The day seemed endless, but eventually Mr Carmichael stood and thanked all for the attendance and crossed the floor and warmly shook the hand of Sir John, both men placing their left hand on each other's shoulder as they did so.

We went back to where we were camped and as we did so the Fenwick could be heard above all other voices criticising the decisions of the day, with the greater emphasis on the penalties Sir John was able to incur against the Scotties.

As we sat down and food was prepared and after the continual tirade from the Fenwick, I turned to Sir John and said, "Sir John, how long do you intend to put up with this nonsense from the Fenwick?" to which Sir John replied, "He will go short of wind before such will affect me, for he thinks he provokes me and he does not; my silence provokes him." I was somewhat surprised at Sir John's reply, but as I sat and ate and his words went through my head I realised what great wisdom this man had.

That night after eating, sleep followed quickly, and deeply, only yielding to some heavy movement, as one of our band woke me at daybreak. It was Uncle James.

"Uncle James!" I declared with some surprise, "When did you get here?"

"I have been here all the time, but you have been so taken up with your new friend, Sir John, that I left you to it." I jumped to my feet and gave him a hug.

"I am so sorry, Uncle, I have indeed been very much engaged with the events of the past day or so," I said.

"Worry not, Rob, we will have plenty of time for talking as we ride back. Come, let's saddle up."

As we rode back that morning, I had Sir John to my right and James to my left, and the conversation never stopped, and what would have been a very long ride passed so very quickly.

As we neared our home, the light was quickly fading, and our band of riders had greatly reduced, as one by one, or should I say, family by family, they peeled off.

I, with some hesitation, turned to Sir John and asked if he would stay at our bastle until the next day, to which he replied, "I thought you were not going to ask," then burst into loud laughter, reaching across from his horse and giving me a heavy slap in the middle of my back. After his laughter had subsided, he turned to me and said that we would need the next day to re-write the report of the Truce Day. I felt a slight disappointment at that remark, thinking that I had not done the duty of a scribe as best as I should.

After saying our goodbyes to James we were soon home. I felt somewhat uncomfortable saying to Mother about Sir John staying with us, but she seemed delighted and was soon busying herself in preparation for our guest, Sarah as always blankly doing much of what was required.

Sir John, Father, and I sat at the table, and the conversation was wonderful. As food was brought and all were sat down, Sir John stood and said, "I would like to say how grateful I am for the wonderful efforts of my new scribe," as he raised his wooden goblet. I was greatly embarrassed and could feel the redness welling within my face, but looked up to see Mother swollen with pride. After food we stayed at the table talking. I say we, but it was Father and Sir John who regaled us with their tales of the many battles they had fought together, before Sir John had been appointed the March Warden.

It was late when we all went to bed, I giving over my bed to Sir John and taking up position on the floor, but nonetheless, sleeping soundly.

The next day was spent at the table with Sir John, going over the events of the Truce Day. I was amazed at the recall that Sir John had, which I was unable to match even with the scribbled notes before me. The strangest thing I found though was that when writing the final report, I was instructed to omit many of the English raids and to add to every recorded Scottish raid more than was actually taken. Sir John assured me that this was the way the Crown wished the reports to be done.

It was late into the day before we were finished, so Mother and Father insisted that Sir John stayed a second night, which he did with relish.

The following day Sir John packed up, and it was Father who suggested that I ride much of the way with Sir John, for his safety, which I willingly did.

I made the main topic of conversation as we rode, the Fenwick, and how best to address his constant niggling, but Sir John seemed dismissive of him, although he did admit that it would be better if he were not about to cause such trouble. About mid-afternoon, Sir John bade me return home as he was now close to home and for me to travel any longer would cause me to be in darkness before I reached home. He thanked me again and said he may have need of me again, should his scribe be not able to perform his duties, and I welcomed the opportunity to repeat the experience.

We shook hands as we parted, Sir John's parting words being, "Yer a grand lad, young Rob, don't let them catch you." I did not quite understand the final part to his farewell, but was glad of his regard, that I was a grand lad, the words playing in my head as I proudly rode home.

With these words in my head, my thoughts turned to the Fenwick and his constant sniping at what I regarded as one of the finest gentlemen I had encountered in my life, and certainly, my father seemed to hold him in high regard. Yes, the Fenwick must be showed the error of his ways. Was I the person to attend such a mission? Yes, I thought so.

Sir John had told me that in two days' time he would head to London to the Royal Court to hand in the record of the Truce Day. Therefore, in four days' time I would attend the business of the Fenwick. I had made good progress home and arrived back before the dusk set in. Mother came down the ladder at hearing my arrival, greeting me with a tight hug. "What is that for?" I enquired.

"Because I could not do it properly when Sir John was here, and I am so very proud of you. It will seem very ordinary to resume your chores again," said Mother. I told Mother that in four days' time I had some duties to carry out on behalf of Sir John and might be gone for two or three days. Mother enquired what were the duties that I would be carrying out, but I told her that I would not know that until I had seen someone, which Mother seemed satisfied with, and by the time I had bedded down my nag and gone up to the living area, Mother was telling Father and Sarah about the special work I was to carry out for Sir John.

Father asked me as I sat down what was the nature of the work Sir John required me to do. Just some copying of some documents, I told him. He gave me a half glance, then looked away, as if he did not believe me, and I felt my face redden, so looked down at my meal, and ate, only answering when necessary, until I could feel the redness had gone.

Mother and Father spent the rest of the night asking all the questions they had wanted to ask but did not like to when Sir John was there. I was able to keep them entertained with what had gone on at the Truce Day, for the rest of the night. I would not have been able to do that the previous night for I could barely remember any of it, but having spent the day with Sir John, rewriting what had taken place, it was now clear in my mind.

Four days later, I rose early, and prepared my nag, also packing a goodly supply of food. Mother protested at the amount I was taking, saying, "Surely they will feed you if you are working for Sir John," but I just shrugged, as I mounted up, then leaned from the saddle and gave Mother a kiss. Father had come down the ladder, unusually, to see me off, and as Mother turned to go back inside, Father stepped forward and placed a heavy hand on my thigh. "Be careful," he said knowingly, and I returned his look with a reassuring half smile.

I rode off in a jolly mood, going over in my mind, as I had done many times over the past few days, how I intended to address my task. It was as I neared the Dodds' bastle that I realised the anger had not been with me for some time, and was heartened by that fact, so it was with good heart that I was able to call on the Dodds. I was greeted, as always, with much fuss, and ushered in, sat at the table and had food forced upon me, although, if truth be known, I never have had to have food forced upon me.

How strange I found it to be asked how I was coping, by the mother of the girl I lost. I was able to inform her that I had handled it badly, and had been overcome by a great rage, and had had to go away for a short while.

Raymond, with great glee, said, "Aye, and I'll wager you were raiding when you were away," to which I raised a finger to my lips, and everyone laughed. As the laughter waned, I felt a tear at the edge of my eye. It was the laughter, which in this setting had always, in the past, had the laughter of Annie as part of it, and she was not there. Mary placed a hand on my shoulder, gripping quite tightly, and said, "Don't worry, Rob, we none of us are over it yet, and doubt we ever will be."

After such seriousness, we soon reverted back to jollier things, and it was with regret that I had to leave my dear friends, but I did so with their best wishes and the thought that they were greatly impressed with my new position working for Sir John Foster, albeit a temporary appointment.

I did not tell them where I was going, and just left it for them to assume I was going to Hexham.

I arrived at a point of dense woodland on some high ground, which overlooked the grand hall that was the home to the Fenwicks. After dismounting, and walking through the woods for some time, I eventually found a spot that afforded me good cover, good shelter and a good observation point from which to watch the comings and goings of the Fenwick brood.

I had arrived there as the light was fading, but resolved to keep my position until I was no longer able to see, then I would find my way deeper into the woods and make camp, hopefully catching something that I could cook, thereby keeping what I had brought in reserve, should I need it.

It was not long until the light gave out and so I moved to deeper cover, but was unable to find anything in the darkness to kill for food, so used some of what I had brought, then settled down for the night.

The following morning I rose before full light and before taking up the position that I had occupied the previous day, I laid snares along the route to my observation point, so that I could check them on my way back at night, gathering anything that had given itself up to me. As I reached the place I had occupied the previous day I could see that fresh fires had been lit within the house, by the heavy smoke that rose from the chimney, but nothing stirred outside. There was quite a chill in the air this morning and I was not quite sure how I was going to cope with keeping watch in this manner and cope with the cold. It was a different matter riding in the cold, with the heat of the horse and the fact you were moving; but staying still, in order not to make a sound, the cold took over.

It was mid-morning before I saw any life at the Fenwick house, when I saw the large heavily hinged and studded wooden door slowly ease open and four finely dressed gentlemen emerge, all speaking very loudly and strutting along to the stable area, which was obscured from my vision, so maybe there had been movement about the place of which I had been unaware. Because of their loud conversation, I gathered they were bound for Hexham for the day, and the Fenwick was one of them. The others I did not know and presumed they were acquaintances of Fenwick who had stayed the night.

There was little I could do this day, and was much relieved to be able to move from my position once the four had ridden off. I went back into the forest and decided I would see if I could find some food on the hoof as I familiarised myself with my surroundings. My snares had yielded nothing as yet, and at this time of the day, especially with me tramping around the forest, it was hardly unexpected. Having returned to my night position, to where my nag was also tethered, I used my sword to make a shallow scrape, where just before leaving I would place any bodily wastes left by the nag or myself, then cover them over with soil, then a good covering of fallen leaves, of which there was an abundance. I would also have to remove any signs of a fire being lit before leaving.

Having organised myself to leaving as little sign of my presence as possible, I went further into the forest and thought it a good time to practice my slingshot skills. I did not want to use the stones I had brought with me, as they were perfect for the use I had in mind, so I scavenged around on the forest floor for ammunition. Having accumulated a goodly arsenal, I started to improve my skills, and after the first few tries, I was aware that I required all the practise it was possible to gain. By late afternoon my arm was starting to ache with the amount of shots I had made, and even with this amount of practice, I could not hope to match the skill of my cousin, Richard.

With my lack of prowess with the sling I was becoming very nervous about the task I had set myself, but hoped that when it came time I might succeed.

As the light started to fade, I made my way back to the observation position, and lay there until the Fenwick returned. I seemed to wait for a very long time, thinking at times that I had missed their return, but they did eventually return, long after dark, and only two. The Fenwick was one. The other was much shorter and by his gait, much younger, but both were affected by a day of taking in much ale or wine.

Once they were safely within the house, I was then able to return to my night site, slowly feeling my way in the darkness, but tripped over something, luckily landing softly. I then realised that I had tripped over the fruits of one of my snares, a rabbit, which would feed me well this night and help keep me warm, and hopefully bring sleep quickly, with a full belly. I soon had a good fire going from wood I had gathered earlier and within no time my food was ready for eating, and good eating it was, after which I laid me down and sleep ensued.

I woke with a start the next morning; it was light, too light, I should have been up sooner. I quickly gathered up my sword and scurried to my observation position, looking down over the Fenwick house. I had scarcely got myself comfortable when the large front door opened, and the Fenwick emerged, alone. This could be it, the time I had been waiting for. I got into a crouching position, ready to move, if I had to. The Fenwick went to the back of the house, the stables I presumed, and was soon back, riding a chestnut gelding. Yes, this was it, it must be. I scurried back out of sight, then ran as fast as I could, to where my nag was tethered, mounted, and was working my way through the trees, holding my forearm across my face, to shield my eyes. I came to the edge of the wood, could not see the Fenwick, so dismounted and stooped over, ran forward, in the hope that I had not missed him. He was there, not far in front, could I get him from here, could I?

I removed my sling and quickly placed a stone from my pouch into the leather. My intention being to catch his nag a good strike on the rump, it would rear, unsaddling the Fenwick. I would rush forward and finish off what was needed. I swung the sling above my head, then let it go. Wrong, wrong, wrong, no, it was too high, it would not strike the horse. After all my practice of yesterday, I had got it wrong. I started to run for the cover of the trees, for if the stone landed near the Fenwick, he would turn, see me, then I was undone. As I scampered back to the wood, I looked towards the Fenwick, watching for where the stone would land. Everything seemed to be going so slowly, but wait, what was this? The stone caught the Fenwick behind the head, he pulled back on the reins, the horse reared, he came over the back of the horse and landed on the ground, with a clatter, as he landed with his sword underneath him. I stopped and turned, running back towards the Fenwick; he was not moving, but as I ran I was drawing my sword, should he start to get to his feet. As I came upon him I stood just above his head, sword raised, just in case. His eyes were closed, but I saw his chest rise. The fall had not killed him, what to do? I looked around, not knowing what it was I was looking for, what was there? A stone, two body lengths in front of the Fenwick, a rough stone, the size of a large fist; that would do. I ran forward, gathering up the stone, then ran back. Laying my sword at my feet, I took hold of the Fenwick by his long hair, and with my right hand, placed the stone on the ground, where his head had laid. Then, taking hold of more hair with my right hand, I lifted his head as high as I could. He groaned; I then brought his head down on to the stone as hard as I could. Immediately, blood started to seep from under his head, I saw blood emerge from the side of his mouth and down his nose. I stood there waiting to see if there was any rise and fall of his chest; there was none.

Once satisfied that I had succeeded in my mission, I gathered up my sword, sheathed it, then ran back to the edge of the forest, where my nag was waiting. Taking hold of the rein, I led the nag back under cover, retracing my steps back to my night camp. Once there, I removed all trace of my occupancy, burying both my horse's and my waste, covering it with leaves. I then went back to where I had kept my daytime vigil, to check I had left no sign of me being here. As I did, I gathered up the snares I had set, one yielding forth a fine hare, which I tied to my belt with the snare. I noticed an old branch lying under a bush, so taking hold of this, I dragged it behind me on my way back to my nag, thus removing any likely signs of footprints. When back at my nag, I looked about me for a larger fallen branch, to sweep about where I stood, then drag behind me as I rode from the forest. I eventually found what I was looking for and after sweeping around the area, I mounted up and gently rode away, with the branch in tow.

Having reached the edge of the forest, well ahead of where the Fenwick lay, I dropped the branch and rode on but at a walk, in order to leave as faint a hoof print as possible. Once on harder ground, I spurred my nag onward, to make as much space as possible between me and the fallen Fenwick. It was as I rode at full gallop that I thought of riding to my Uncle Arthur's, and spending the night there, instead of going straight home. I veered westwards, in the direction of Arthur's, which meant that I would not have to pass the Dodds' bastle, which would be better for me later should awkward questions be asked.

I arrived at Arthur's by late afternoon, after a hard ride, and was greeted with a wonderful welcome. Arthur emerged from his bastle, looking in a dreadful state, clearly underfed since last we met and looking filthy and dishevelled. "What do you want?" he growled. "I thought I told you I wanted to be alone, be off with you." Ignoring Arthur's displeasure at my arrival I dismounted and held up the hare I had caught earlier. "Supper, Uncle," I declared.

"I don't want yur damned supper, now be gone!" he snapped.

"Well, I do," I snapped back, "so get out of the way while I get this skinned and under flame." I could see Uncle was quite taken aback by my attitude and stepped back and lowered his head. This was a broken man, who needed company, even though he did not realise it.

Silently I set about preparing a meal, with hare and some rather wilted vegetables I found growing at the back of the bastle, but given a quick boil, they soon cheered up. I cut the hare in two and placed each piece on a pewter plate, which Arthur had dutifully brought back from Scotland, for Alice. I then heaped the vegetables on the side of the plate. Placing the plates on the table, my first words since entering the bastle were, "Eat."

"I told you, I don't want yur damned food," Arthur protested. I did not look up from the table, but merely removed my bollock knife from my belt and slammed it down on the table. Arthur sat, and we ate, albeit reluctantly at first, but once the succulent hare reached Arthur's palate he tucked in greedily, but not a word was spoken.

It was quite clear that Arthur had not eaten for days, or at least not properly, possibly since the last time Alice had cooked, before our departure to Scotland. Placing down his spoon on a clean plate, he looked over and nodded his approval. I reached across the table with my left hand, taking the side of his neck and shook him gently, saying, "You old rogue." He took hold of me by the wrist, pulling my hand away and said, "Yur a good lad, but yur not stopping."

I then told him what I had been doing for the past few days; he then changed his mind, and suggested I stay a couple of days, which was what I intended in the first place.

During the following two days I carefully worked on my uncle, gently persuading him to come and stay with me at my home. Uncle and Father had never been the closest of brothers, John and Arthur always being the closest, Father being somewhat on his own, the wages of being the Heedsman of the family and sometimes being called on to make decisions that did not rest easy on the rest of the family.

Arthur eventually accepted my invitation, not because he wanted to, but to stop me forever going on to him.

Chapter 17

A Flame in my Life

Arthur had spent two weeks with us, having only intended to spend a couple of days, but he and Father had been good for each other, both cheering each other up; Arthur from his loss of Alice and Father from his now constant discomfort from his injury.

My uncle was about to depart on the morrow when we had the arrival of a body of riders, Sir John at the head, summoning us to a Hot Trod. There had been some raiding Scotties, which fortunately had passed by our valley, but had carried out some raids further to the east. Uncle, Father and I eagerly saddled up, sending the other riders on to the Charltons, so we would catch up later.

During the past two weeks, Uncle and I had told Mother and Father that I had spent my entire time away from home, at Arthur's, and had just used the story of going to work for Sir John as a ruse, as I thought Mother and Father might have not wanted me to visit Arthur so soon after his loss. They had seemed to accept this story so we had left things at that.

We left the bastle, three riders together, Father in the middle, Arthur to the right and I to the left, waving back to Mother and Sarah as we galloped off. We were soon at the Charltons, James and his kinsmen all saddled as we arrived.

There had been so much that had happened in the recent past, that it seemed an age since we had last ridden together, and it felt good to be with all the family, riding and legal.

We rode hard throughout the day, the nags sweating heavily under the strain and even the riders showing the strain. The most amazing thing being that Sir John, by far the oldest there, seemed unaffected by the rigour of the gallop. I was never quite able to understand this man; how could such a person be so very strong, clever, fight like a twenty year old, and still walk the Royal courts, in the presence of the Queen, like the best of courtiers; I so admired him.

The light of the day was now disappearing fast, but we rode on, not giving any rest to the pace. We had been riding in the dark for some time when Sir John raised his hand, for us to stop. We were atop of a plateau, looking forward across a flat heath land and could see at the far edge of the plateau, men and beasts shuffling along; this was our prey. Sir John lowered his hand in a pointing gesture towards the Scotties, and although we had ridden at a gallop for the best part of the day, we set forth at full charge, lances drawn and lowered, ready to engage. This felt so good, with Father and Uncle by my side, at full gallop and Scotties in sight.

We were upon them in no time and a rout ensued; there were but twenty of them and nearly a couple of hundred of us, the result being twenty dead Scotties, not a single Englishman with even a scratch, and I did not engage a single Scottie. After the rout, we quickly moved on, taking with us the stolen English beasts, but were soon bedding down for the night. I volunteered for the first watch, for although we were on official business, the Scotties were not past having a go if they thought we might be an easy target. I had been at my watch for some time when I heard someone approach from behind. I crouched down, removing my sword in readiness. A hushed voice came, "Tis me, Rob, Sir John." I slowly stood, with sword at the ready, then lowered it as I saw it was Sir John nearing me. He continued to speak in hushed tones, "I have laid off from seeing you 'til now, Rob, as I thought it should be something we discussed apart from anyone." As he started to speak, he reached forward, taking my left hand, raising it up, then placed a weighty purse in it, enclosing my fingers around it. "Your payment for scribing, Rob, and by the way there are others who would have my wardenship, but I would prefer they stay alive." He then placed his hand upon my shoulder, then turned and walked back to the camp. As he did so, the realisation of what he said struck me and I started to shake. How could he possibly know it was me? I had taken every precaution to cover my tracks, but this wily old dog knew everything.

The next morning we woke to a bright but cold morning and before we set off, Sir John, said, "Well, my boys, would that we had some sport, what say you all, we take back a little more than we came after, as payment for our inconvenience?" Which was greeted with a loud cheer. "We will head east into Kerr country; I believe there is some fine stock to be had thereabouts," he continued, laughing.

We rode for the rest of the day, held back by having to herd a few miserable cattle. Had there been a few hundred head of prime Scottish beast at our front, I would have found the task much more to my liking. It was just starting into dusk when we arrived at a long winding valley, and on a high spot at the far side of the valley, a pele tower, at the foot of which were some cattle pens of dry stone wall construction. From our distant position, we could still see that the pens were full of beasts. "That, gentlemen, is what we have come for. Let's relieve our friends of such an encumbrance," said Sir John. This the very same Sir John Foster, who not long past, did threaten me with the gallows, if I raided the Scotties. We closed in on the pele tower at little more than a canter, keeping the noise to a minimum, and as we were upon it, Sir John turned to me and said, "Open the pens, lad." I slipped from my saddle, with sword in hand, and started to slide the wooden poles from the pen entrance, which was full of horses, who started to become uneasy at my arrival. I had just removed the bottom of the three poles, when I was aware of movement to my right side. I quickly turned and was confronted by a rugged looking man with sword held high, about to come down on me. Raising my sword to meet his, I was able to parry his blow, but the force at which it crashed down on me sent a shuddering pain up my arm. After the first blow, we both composed ourselves, ready for swordplay. It was then that I realised that my riding companions had ridden on and left me to my fate. My adversary came at me again, and it was then that I realised he held his sword in the wrong hand. I had never come across anyone who fought like this and it greatly unnerved me as I was not able to get the measure of the man. He rained blow after blow down on me; I was only able to parry what was thrown at me. He then came with his sword straight at me; I did not know how to handle this man with his ungainly stance. I thrust my sword forward in order to hold back his, and the next instant, my sword was ripped from my hand, and sent slithering across the ground. At this stage the horses were galloping all about us, in their escape from the pen. I fell to the ground and rolled over several times, in order to retrieve my sword, with horses' hooves all about me, and in my efforts to do so, was soundly struck by a galloping hoof, about my side, the blow taking the very breath from my body. I then saw my sword and reached out, taking it not by the handle because of the basket weave, but by the hilt and as I did so, scrambled to my feet. I had no more fight left in me, and was no match for this left handed aggressor; therefore I took to foot, running like a scared rabbit, with a fox at my heels. I did not even have hold of my sword in a manner whereby I could defend myself. Some short distance ahead, I thankfully saw my old nag standing there, holding fast against the other horses. I ran to it and swung myself into the saddle, spurring it onward, away from danger. My poor old nag, what a faithful old friend it was, staying by me in my moment of danger. Had it not been for it, I may have perished on the Scottie field, but now I needed speed, and although it gave me all it could, at that moment I wanted more.

As I galloped on, I was soon with my fellow riders, and playing down the events of my encounter, but as I started to help with the herding of our new acquisitions, I noticed one nag which seemed to stand out from the rest. Its head was held higher than the others, in a proud manner, its mane the colour of flames in a fire, and as I saw more of it I could see that all of its upper body was a rich flame red, with darker, almost brown legs. This was one of the famed Galloway nags, the finest horses to ride the border, and at that moment, I resolved that it would be mine, for had I not liberated these very beasts?

We rode ever onwards, picking up the odd few sheep and cattle as we went, and were soon driving a goodly selection of beasts for our trouble, encountering little resistance on our way.

After a long day in the saddle, Sir John suggested we make camp and continue tomorrow. Having brought all the beasts together, and placed lookouts, we were soon sat around a warming fire. As we started to eat, Sir John mentioned about the horses we had acquired. I said about the one I had noticed, but Sir John said he thought that might be the one that he had eyed, and had reserved it for himself, to my great disappointment.

Later that night, I was able to talk to Sir John alone, and brought up the subject of the Galloway nag. I told him I was prepared to purchase the beast, to which he laughed and said, "How, pray, could you purchase such a beast?" I took from my belt the purse that Sir John had given me, and lifting up his hand, I placed it there, curling his fingers around it, in similar fashion to the way he gave it me. "My Lord Rob, I do believe you have purchased yourself a fine Galloway mare," he said laughingly, as he placed his other hand on my shoulder, as he had done before.

The following day we struck camp early and made for home. Apart from my fine new mare, I was awarded six cattle, which I proudly drove homeward. I arrived back in late afternoon; having circled around from the east, it meant I, with Father and Arthur, and also Uncle James, returned from the south instead of the north, which would have been our normal way to return.

Once home, and readying our nags for bedding down, along with my new mare, Father took me to one side as Arthur finished off. "What in Heaven's name have you been up to, boy?" he enquired.

"Merely doing Sir John a good deed, Fadder," I replied.

"You went out and killed a Fenwick; have you taken leave of your senses?" he ventured.

"Fadder," I replied. "There's not a person in the land could accuse me of that," I said rather cockily.

"Aye, maybe so, but heed this, lad, Sir John knows what is afoot," Father said with his finger pressed on my nose. Almost in the same breath, he slapped me on the back, saying, "Get yur sell up that ladder and greet yur mother and sister."

The incident of the left handed swordsman I had encountered when on the Hot Trod played on my mind for some weeks after, and I decided that I would not allow such a thing to happen again, so started to practise swordplay with my other hand, but found it almost impossible, the weight was far too great for me to be able to fight for more than an instant.

My father caught me in the middle of practice one day and asked what in Heaven's name was I doing. I confided in him what had taken place on the Trod, and how I had been left running away from the fierce Kerr. He was alarmed that he had been unaware of my dilemma, and had he been aware, would have ridden back to my aid. I told him that I should have been capable of defending myself, without my father having to defend me. I think he realised that it was not just the fact of my defence, but of the very essence of being able to cope with whatever I came across in my life.

Father was wonderful, and suggested that I pull my old sword from under the bed, the small one I had used as a boy. Its presence had quite slipped my mind.

Having rushed in and retrieved my trusty old blade, then back out to where Father stood, I then started to engage him in swordplay, me using my left hand, and the small sword. It was much easier, but nonetheless, I felt very vulnerable, using my wrong hand. We had been practising some short while, when Arthur came from the bastle, carrying his bed roll and other personal items.

"Where do you think you are going?" barked Father.

"I have imposed long enough on you, Tom, time to get back and sort myself out. You have all been so kind, but I must go," said Arthur.

"You haven't paid for your stay yet, Arthur," said Father.

"Pay, damned well pay, I thought I was your guest, there's your damned payment," he snorted as he pulled his purse from his belt, throwing it to the ground.

"Not enough, not nearly enough, this lad needs practice in his swordplay, so that he is equally as good with both hands, which I am not able to do. Also there is that fine nag that is not yet fully broken, he will need that done, so take yur damned goods and get them back inside, then get back out here and start paying off yur debt."

Arthur did not reply, but merely turned back to the bastle, with head down, shaking it in disbelief. Father turned to me and said, "He is not ready yet, and you do need all these things doing, so he might as well occupy his mind with us while still getting well fed," then laughed loudly.

Arthur and I spent long days battling, and many a time I would have to plead for mercy, as my arm would ache from all the work.

Often in the midst of these long battles my thoughts would wander to my new Galloway nag, and my desire to ride it, it was not long before we could combine both swordplay and horse breaking. Although a very spirited beast, my new flame-haired friend had a kindness within it, which it showed to me particularly, whereas with others, it would tend to shy away.

Arthur was an exceptional horse trainer, I could see now why Father had been so keen for him to stay longer with us. Within a short period, my new nag and I were as one, I had never ridden a horse quite like it. The speed at which it could gallop was by far the fastest thing I had encountered, and its durability was beyond question; it could be ridden hard for day upon day and never be short of breath.

I counted myself fortunate to have such a beast, and now with my extra weaponry, I felt I was a force to be reckoned with.

The riding season was now coming to an end. Arthur had stayed with us over the winter period, and had helped me tremendously in both riding skill and swordsmanship, and had brought on my lance work to what was now a reasonable standard, which it had needed, but I put this advancement down more to my horse than to me.

Once, since that last Hot Trod, I had been required to scribe for Sir John, and had taken great pleasure in riding forth on my new horse, which Sir John had insisted that I name. After some time deliberating, I came forth with the name of Flame, which its colour so richly embodied.

I also engaged in some rather profitable incursions into Scotland, helping to gather up many cattle and sheep, selling them quickly and enjoying the benefits.

Due to my new weaponry, I had also gained a name for myself of 'Twa Blades', which I was greatly honoured to carry, though I do believe there were some who derided my name and mocked my two swords, but none dared face me and say it, and while none dared face me, then I should worry little of their envy.

Chapter 18

A Flower of Scotland

The last four years since Uncle Arthur had stayed with us after the death of Alice had seen little of any significance. There had been raids by myself and my fellow riders into Scotland, and the Scotties had tried to pay our kindness back, but had not been as successful as we had been. My nag, Flame, had proved a most loyal and useful animal, and friend, and had become as close to me as any of my kinsmen.

Alas, my great friend and mentor, Sir John, had retired his post, and had been succeeded by a Master Carey, a very diligent person and loyal to the Crown, but who carried little of the knowledge and authority that Sir John did.

It was noted by all that no liberties could be taken with him in place, but many of those who tried to oust Sir John had failed in their endeavours to gain the wardenship for themselves, much to our relief.

My uncle, Thomas Charlton, had been Knighted by the Queen and was now Sir Thomas Charlton. Fortunately, his brother, James had continued raiding, along with the rest of us, and we were now greatly feared by those Scotties.

Father had become less able to fulfil his chores, due to his injury, the onus of which fell on my shoulders. Sarah's malady had not eased, but she had become like a right arm to me, taking on tasks about the bastle that many men would quake at. In the early period of last summer saw Sarah shear some fifty sheep in one day, as we had worked back to back, while Mother and, to some lesser degree, Father, had rounded the beasts up and penned them, awaiting the attentions of Sarah and myself. It had become quite a talking point about our valley, and had Sarah not been quite so afflicted, we were sure there would have been a constant trail of suitors to our bastle.

It was now early autumn and the riding season was upon us. James had been rallying everyone around, for a good raid, early on in the season, in order to let the Scotties know we meant business. Arthur had arrived and stayed with us, but alas Father was no longer able to ride. I had hoped Richard might have been able to join us, but whether word had not got to him, or he was engaged in raiding in the West March, I did not know.

The morning of our departure arrived, and though only early autumn, there was a cold wind blowing, accompanied with a fine rain, which was blowing into our faces as we left. My nag was uneasy of foot, which I put down to the long lazy days of summer, which she disliked. She was a horse who liked to be ridden, and took badly to endless days of standing in a meadow. Father had suggested using her for work about the bastle, but the thought of placing Flame in the traces did not lay easily with me. Flame was a riding horse, the harder the ride the better she liked it, and when engaged in conflict, she showed how good a beast she really was. Now that she was being used for what she had been bred for, she was excited, and was eager to be on the trail.

It was late afternoon when we crossed into Scotland, and we continued northward for some time before circling westward. This was unfamiliar territory for me, even after all my years of riding. I thought I knew my way over all these lands, but was at a loss, having travelled so far north.

Having ridden westerly for some time, we then turned south and were soon upon our first encounter. We had entered a valley so richly stocked with beasts that we could scarcely believe our eyes. James called us all together and instructed us to spread out and slowly and quietly start to move the cattle forward. As we started to do this, James called myself, two of the Bells and Michael Dodds and asked us to follow him. We rode off, further west, up the side of the valley, and soon found ourselves facing the black silhouette of a foreboding pele tower. About its base were pens with fine horses secured for the night. As we approached stealthily, one of the Bells slid from his saddle and started to remove the poles which secured the pens. Suddenly there was noise, shouting and the crashing of steel all about us. The horses broke out before the Bell had got the last pole out, throwing him to the ground, but he managed to scramble in behind the wall, staying there until all the horses were out, but with all the noise frightening the horses, they had bolted in the wrong direction. I reined hard on Flame, turning back to retrieve the errant nags. As I did so, I was aware of Scotties all about, their swords glinting in the night light, for although it had rained all day and night and there was no moon, it was still possible to catch the glint of a sword. Much to my annoyance, I had to avoid the Scotties, my main task being getting back the nags.

I was soon past the nags, thanks to Flame's great speed, and was turning the running nags back in the direction I required. Once they were underway, they became much easier, but one had gone the wrong side of the pele tower, so with the main herd running on, I swung to my right, the other side of the tower, to bring in the one loose nag. This also meant that I would avoid the place I had seen all the Scotties.

By the time I had circled the tower, the nag was running back towards the rest of the herd. I came back around the tower, keeping close to the walls, in order not to be seen, or to be taken unawares. I thought I saw someone on horseback behind me, so I spurred Flame forward; she kicked ahead, gaining great speed in just a couple of strides. I rounded the corner of the tower, and felt something jolt against my nag, which shied away. I saw something fall in front of the horse, but could not quite make it out. I was about to spur Flame on harder, but noticed that what we had hit appeared to be a body lying on the ground; a woman's body. I quickly dropped from the saddle, to make sure it was a woman, lying on her side, motionless, more than likely dead. I did not want to leave the body, on the ground, to be accused of murdering a woman; no, I did not want that, so I quickly scooped the body up in my arms and heaved her over the saddle of my nag. Hardly had I got this done when I could see the glint of a sword coming towards me. Taking no chances, I quickly drew my sword, scarcely it being clear of the scabbard, and my assailant was upon me, slashing wildly at me. I stepped back, dragging my feet as I went backwards, in order to feel the ground under me, in the dark, and not trip. I went back, step after step, my assailant coming forward on to me all the time, giving no quarter, but as he did so I noticed him stumble; he reached forward with his sword hand to regain his balance, and in doing so his sword came into contact with the ground. This was the opportunity I was waiting for. I stepped forward, putting my right foot firmly down on his sword, pinning it and my assailant to the ground.

I drew my sword up slowly to his throat so that even in the dark he could be in no doubt of the situation. I then said, "Drop it," but he clung on, heaving against my weight to free his blade. Again, but this time through clenched teeth, I growled, "Drop it," which he now did. "Be away with you, Scottie," I barked, as he stood straight, turned and ran around the front of the tower and out of sight.

I ran back to my horse, the body still slumped over the saddle. I swung myself over the back of the horse, reaching forward for the reins and spurred away, keeping well to the side of where the main noise of the conflict was coming, as I was not in a position to engage, with my passenger in the way. If I were accosted, I had reckoned on dropping the body to the ground, before engaging.

I was now riding hard, with my right hand holding my sword in readiness, while at the same time pressing down on the body, so as not to lose it. If the body was not dead, then I could possibly seek a ransom, if she were worth anything, and if it was dead, I would drop it off along the trail, possibly scrape out a shallow grave in order to keep the body from discovery.

Slowly, as the night went on, and early signs of the dawn started to appear, the rest of our merry band started to catch up. Some could be heard laughingly telling the others of their encounters, and how they had seen off their adversaries. I just kept at my task, herding on the nags I had acquired, and keeping a firm hold of my other acquisition, which no one was aware of yet.

Suddenly I was aware of a stiffening of the body, then slight movement. It was alive, what to do now? I looked over to my left and could see young Israel Bell in the distance. I called over to him and asked him to take my point. As he rode over, I peeled off and rode away. He would assume I needed to relieve myself, as we often did after a good fight, and would think nothing of it. As I rode away, the movement from the body increased. When I was sufficiently away from the main throng I pulled up and dropped from my horse, then slowly drew the body from the saddle. When I tried to stand her up her legs buckled, so I held her tightly by her shoulders, then stood there for a moment. Even in this half-light I could see she was very pretty, maybe about sixteen, quite small, with a small round face that displayed rounded cheeks that had dimples on either side. Her hair was the colour of straw that had been lightened by the hot sun, with darker streaks running through it.

Suddenly her body tightened and she was aware; she turned her face to mine and in an instant was filled with rage. She broke free of my grip and started to beat against my chest with clenched fists, at the same time screaming at me, but with her Scottie accent and her fury, I was unable to understand much of what she said.

I regained my hold of her, which only intensified her rage; she started to kick and scream louder. There was little else for it; I wrapped my arms about her body and held her tightly to me. She resisted, but I just held on, until eventually she either calmed or tired. When she at last quietened, my face at the side of hers, I spoke quietly into her ear, "Fear not, little one, I will not harm you, and while you are with me, nor will anyone else."

The tension within her body lessened gradually, and when I thought it safe to do so, I slowly released my grip, then stood back, removing my morion as I did so. She just stood there staring at me; not a blink crossed her eyes, I could see tears starting to run from her eyes. She then fell to the ground, her hand to her face, quietly sobbing. I went down on my knees in front of her, reaching out and taking hold of her upper arms gently. "I am sorry for causing you distress, but when my horse knocked you down, I thought I had killed you, and could not leave your body to be discovered, so I put you on my horse and brought you with me."

"What will you do with me? Kill me or worse?" she enquired in a lovely low soft voice, broken by the odd sob.

"No, most definitely not," I protested. "I have said that no harm will come to you while you are with me, and I will fight any man who tries to lay one single finger upon you. I promise you this upon my life." She looked straight at me for a short while almost as if she were judging my words as to their honesty, then with her forehead slightly furrowed she looked straight into my eyes and said, "And what is to become of me?" I hesitated for a while, not exactly sure of my answer, then blurted out, "I have not thought beyond this moment."

"Well, you're a fine one, I would have hoped to be abducted by someone with a lot more about him than you appear to have." I was so taken aback by this sudden show of spirit, that I just looked at her, then laughed loudly. She looked at me with absolute disgust, then her face started to contort, and I could see that she was trying her best to conceal a laugh.

For anyone placed in the situation that this girl found herself in, and still have the ability to laugh, was indeed a person to be admired, and within that moment, I gained the utmost respect for her.

Placing my hand on her shoulder, still smiling, I said, "Come, let's get you on to my nag and catch up with the rest." I held Flame, while the girl mounted, then swung up behind her, then slowly rode off. This was becoming a most pleasurable experience, sat behind this spirited young lady. I broke out the sheepskin cape I always carried, wrapping it around the both of us, to keep us both warm, and the feel of this girl between my arms, as I held the reins, and the smell of her hair, as she sat in front of me, was quite a wonderful thing.

We were soon with the others, and I made it my business to seek out James and my Uncle Arthur first. Luckily, they were both riding together; as I rode up to them, they were both very surprised to see my captive.

"My," James exclaimed. "That's a fine prize you have there, she should fetch a good ransom, if that is your intention."

"The only intention I have, Uncle, is that this young lady should not have a hair of her head harmed while she is with me, and I would ask that you, Uncle James, and you, Uncle Arthur, assist me in ensuring that my wishes are adhered to," I retorted.

"Those are fine ideals that you carry, young Rob," said James, almost mockingly.

"Aye, they are indeed," interrupted Arthur, "And ones I shall ensure are indeed adhered to, Rob; that is very noble of you."

I was quite surprised by Arthur's attitude; it was not like him, but then I thought of how the fate of Alice had affected him, it must be that, that had changed him.

Having got this assurance from Arthur, and knowing that James would not go against this, I peeled off and took a position behind the herd that kept the two of us separate from the rest. As we rode, the girl turned to me and said, "So it's Rab, is it?" I could not help but smile, for it was all those years ago, on the trail, that I first heard the name Rab, by the Scottie who had taken me from my home.

"And may I ask your name, young lady?" I enquired.

"Aye, it's Fleur," she imparted.

"Fleur!" I exclaimed. "Is that a Scottie name?"

The anger returned to her voice, that same anger that she displayed when her consciousness returned.

"Let us get one thing quite plain, here and now," she started, in a very assertive manner. "Neither I nor my fellow countrymen are Scotties, we are Scots, is that clear?" she demanded. I was so taken aback, that I replied like a naughty little boy to his mother, "Yes."

She continued, "And no, it is not a Scottish name," with great emphasis on the Scottish. "It is a French name."

"Then you are French, not a Scot." I then hesitated.

"Yes," she said, with an air of exasperation. "Scot, if you try hard enough, you will get there."

She went on to explain that when she was born, her family had an old Frenchman who had been a soldier many years before, and had been brought over to Scotland by the then Scottish Queen, to help fight against the English, and when it came time for him to return to France, he preferred to stay in Scotland, and had found work with Fleur's family. Apparently when Fleur was born the Frenchman had said she was like a "petite fleur," which means a little flower. Fleur's mother had liked that so much, that she called her Fleur.

I then asked what her family name was, and was not surprised to find it was Armstrong, for there were many Armstrongs across the border, and a fierce bunch they were. I was very pleased I did not linger back where I came across Fleur.

I was quite pleased with the way we were engaging in conversation; I found her very easy to talk to, and she appeared to have relaxed in my company, so it was particularly annoying when I saw James signalling for us to round up the herd, as we were now about to make camp for the rest of the day, and await nightfall before moving further on.

Once we were content that the herd was settled, we all entered a small wooded area to take rest. This was the first time many of my companions were aware of my captive, and there was much comment passed about her. One brave fellow stepped forward, a Robson, I think, took hold of her shoulder and started to pull her away from me. He was soon acquainted with the edge of my bollock knife, as it rested hard against his throat. Blood started to slowly trickle down his neck, as I spoke through gritted teeth, "Should any among you try such a thing I hereby make this promise, they will surely die." Then, raising my voice to almost a yell, I said, "Do you all understand, well do you?" There was no definite answer, just an overall mumble, which I took as agreement. I then pushed hard against the Robson; he fell to the ground, holding his neck, then pulling his hand away to inspect the blood that was on it. Still lying there and returning his hand to his neck, he said, "And you would take sides with that Scottie witch against your fellow English rider."

"She is a Scot, not a Scottie," I retorted, "And not a witch. And any man who would disrespect a woman as you would have liked, is no fellow Englishman of mine," I hissed back.

I put my hand on the shoulder of Fleur and pulled her away from the crowd, saying as I did so, "Come along, lass."

I led Fleur over to where I had laid my bed roll and told her to unfold it and for her to use it. She turned square on to me and looked up to me; it was then that I saw for the first time the most beautiful big blue eyes staring at me. She smiled, and her eyes sparkled like the stars on a clear autumn night, as she said, "Thank you," then turned away and lay down. I was about to walk away, when she lifted herself up on one elbow and said, "You will stay by me, Rab, please."

"Aye, I'll be right here, now rest."

The poor wee thing was soon asleep, the rigours of the long night taking their toll. Once she was asleep, I allowed myself to close my eyes, but did not lie easy. I did get some sleep, but precious little, and was soon up and wandering around the camp uneasily. I would normally have taken a period of watch, but did not want to leave Fleur, as I had promised to stay close. James came over to me and said in hushed tones, "You have done well, Rob, yur Scots lass should fetch a good ransom, but meantime she will be useful to keep the Scotties off our backs. I rest assured that they will not raise a Hot Trod, lest we kill her."

"I do not know what I will do with her, Uncle, but as I have already said, I will not allow a hair of her head to be harmed," I replied.

"Once we are underway tonight, there are a few crofts hereabouts. Once we have taken their stock, leave word that you have the girl, just in case the Scotties think she is dead and raise a Hot Trod. You can also tell them to pass word of the ransom you demand," said James.

"I shall," I replied, and James walked away, as I remained stood there, waiting for the night to descend in order that we resume our journey. Never before had I wanted to return home so much, as I did this day.

Eventually nightfall came. I was the first into the saddle, with Fleur sat in front. One or two of my fellow riders were laughing as we set forth, I heard one comment to the effect, "Oh that I were so closely guarded as I sleep. I should surely sleep the soundest in the land," to which there was loud laughter. It did indeed cause me to smile as I rode off and started to lift the herd from its grazing, so accompanied by the rest of our band.

Considering the size of the herd, we made very good progress and were soon upon a lonely croft high on the Scottish hills. My fellow riders engaged themselves with rounding up all the sheep that were around the croft, whereas I along with Fleur rode over to the croft and kicked at the door from my seat on the horse. After giving a kick I shouted, "Come out and no harm will befall you." We waited a while, then slowly the door was opened, but not fully. I could not see who or what was stood there, but I said, "I want you to pass a message for me. Do you know a Will Armstrong?"

"Aye, a ken Will Armstrong, wit business dee ye have wee hem?" came the reply.

"Tell him his daughter passed this way and she is well. She shall be returned at the next Truce Day, do you understand?" I said.

"Aye, a ken wit ye say, yev Will's wee lassie an' yer te tak her back the next Truce Day," came the voice from behind the door.

I started to ride away when Fleur turned to me and said, "Can ye no let me be, here, the crofter will take care of me and get me home."

"I fear that if I did such a thing, some of my fellow riders would turn back and kill the crofter and all that is within, then set about you, doing unspeakable things," I replied.

"Aye, I can believe it of you English," she snapped.

"No, that is what you Scotties did to my aunt," I snapped back.

She remained silent for a short while, then turned to face me, our noses almost touching as she smiled gently and said, "Sorry."

We rode onwards with few words passing between us, then she turned to face me again. I could see, although now quite dark, that she had a broad smile about her face.

"Tell me," she started, "Why is it that you carry two swords? I have never seen such a thing." Then, mockingly, she continued, "Is it that you are not very good, therefore you need two?"

"Do you know," I said laughingly, "I think you might be right," to which we both laughed out loud.

I did like this girl, for although she could say things that were made to insult or deride, there was something about her tone which endeared her to me.

We had now reached the border after an extremely hard ride, made worse by the discomfort of riding behind the saddle instead of on it, but the night had passed quickly with having a companion.

The dawn was breaking and although I had wrapped both myself and Fleur in the sheepskin, she was feeling the cold of the morning. Therefore I asked James if I might break free of the drive and ride on home. James, never one to miss an opportunity to make a gain, said, "Yes of course you may, my boy, but you can take no part in the spoils of our raid." I was not about to start and argue with him, and did not even acknowledge him, merely reined my nag away and rode off. Fleur, I think, was quite astounded by my reaction, for as we rode off she turned and said, "Why would you not wait and get your equal share of what you have stolen from my family and others of my countrymen?"

I felt there was a bitterness in her remark, but did not give it credence by direct reply. I just said, "You need warmth and food, I can live without a few cattle." She turned to me, her nose almost touching mine; again, she knew what she was doing. She smiled, and in that soft husky voice, belying her age, said, "Thank you." She knew she need say no more.

It was early afternoon when we arrived back at the bastle, and since leaving James and the rest of our group, I had spent the time preparing Fleur for my family, not that there was any dreadful secret, but to inform her of Sarah's malady, and of the injuries to Father's face.

I did not use the opportunity to say that his injuries were caused by her countrymen, but left it for her to reason that for herself. As we arrived back, Mother and Sarah came out of the bastle to meet me. Mother was quite shocked to see what I had brought back from my journey. With her hand raised to her mouth, she said in a surprised manner, "Who is this you have with you?"

I slipped from the back of the horse, removed my morion, then held out my hands to help Fleur down, while at the same time explaining what had happened.

As I did so, Mother stepped forward, placing her arm around Fleur's shoulder, pulling her in, while at the same time striking wildly at my head with the flat of her hand, accompanying each contact her hand made with my head with a word, in the manner of, slap, "How," slap, "Could," slap, "You," slap, "Be," slap, "So," slap, "Stupid," then turning to Fleur and holding her in tightly to herself, she said, "You poor girl, come let us get you warmed, and some food. That idiot son of mine has not laid a hand on you, has he?" Then pausing slightly, she resumed, "Or any of the oafs he rides with?" Fleur was amused by my mother's reaction to her arrival and the manner of her chastisement to me. As she looked around at me from the security of my mother's arm, she was stifling laughter as she said, "No, he has been a gentleman."

Mother then bustled her into the bastle, Sarah dutifully following on, while I attended to Flame's needs, giving her a good wiping down, before getting her water, then ensuring the manger was full of fodder. As she was sweating heavily after the exertion of carrying two, I stabled her in the bottom of the bastle for the night, before ascending the ladder.

Fleur was sat at the table, eating from a wooden bowl, while Mother and Sarah were busying themselves beside my bed. Father was sat beside the fire; he looked up as I entered, and passed a smile towards me, or what I knew passed as a smile for my father, as if to say, well done son. I smiled back, in acknowledgement, then looked towards Mother.

"You can sleep on the floor while we have a guest, you better get your bed roll from your saddle," she said bluntly.

I turned and went back down the ladder to get my bed roll, then swiftly returned, and asked if there was any food for me, to which Mother replied, "Get it yourself." I sheepishly went to the fire, gathering up a bowl as I did so, and started to spoon out the pottage from the heavy vessel on the fire. As I sat down, Fleur looked up at me, still very amused at the manner Mother was treating me. Mother then came over to the table and said to Fleur, "Your bed is ready, my pet, you may go to it as soon as you have eaten, you must be so very tired from your journey," then reached over the table and gave me a hefty slap to the top of my head. "Do you realise, oaf, the distress that this poor girl's mother will be in, not knowing what has happened to her little girl, you stupid boy, you really are quite stupid, Rob." Fleur could not contain herself any longer and laughed out loudly. Mother was quite surprised at her reaction, and when I started to laugh, she turned to Father for support, but he too had found the whole situation and Mother's attitude amusing; we all laughed, except Sarah that is.

Once everything had calmed down, I explained to Mother and Father that I did not intend to seek a ransom, and had left word, to get back to Fleur's family, that she was safe and would be returned at the next Truce Day. At this, Mother seemed more relaxed. I then went on to explain all that had taken place, and how I came to meet Fleur. Fleur, however, was struggling to stay awake, I was quite surprised to see Sarah put her arm around Fleur's shoulder, lift her from the table and walk her over to my bed, then lay her down. She was asleep instantly, and I thought her to be the most beautiful sight, lying there at peace, her face almost smiling as she slept.

My gaze was broken by Mother saying, "She is so pretty," then at the same time as landing another hard flat hand to my head, "Look after her," she continued, but in harsher tones. After a somewhat uncomfortable night spent on the floor, I awoke early to start the day's chores. Fleur was still asleep and Sarah, seeing me rise, immediately got up and came with me to attend the cattle. When we returned inside, sometime later, Mother and Fleur were busy getting the morning meal ready. We all sat at the table and ate, that is except Father, who was now in the habit of lingering in his bed, and taking the first food of the day lying there. For the rest of the day I busied myself about the bastle and was content to know that Fleur had settled into life with us with apparently little distress.

After our evening meal, it had become my habit to lock away as much stock as was possible in case of raids, then walk around the remaining beasts to see they were all in good health. On that first day of Fleur being with us, she asked if she may accompany me, which I was glad to accept, without sounding too eager, and she proved to be an exceptionally gifted young person around the stock. After penning the best of the stock, we walked around the remainder as the light started to disappear. With Fleur being unsure of the lie of the land she chose to link my arm as we walked, which I enjoyed. I found with this person a great pleasure in her close proximity, as I had when we had ridden from Scotland. On our evening strolls we would talk at length. She asked me of my early childhood, and I was able to tell her of my abduction and transportation to Scotland, and of my years with the monks, of Brother Matthias, Daniel and Donald. Fleur seemed to take a great deal of interest in this period of my life, particularly in the Scots who took me, with a great interest in the person who actually took me, as if she might have come across the very person.

I am sure that being told of my early life did much to soften any animosity towards me, for my part in her abduction from her home. I found that as the days and weeks passed by, I looked forward to the end of each day, for our time together, though it was always in my mind that the time drew ever nearer for her to go home.

It was the third week after returning from Scotland when my Uncle James Charlton arrived at our bastle. He had come especially to see me, though made a lot of fuss about seeing Mother. As he went to leave, and I assisted in readying his nag, he seized the opportunity to say his piece. "Rob, what have you done about the Scottie girl?" he enquired.

"Nothing, why, what should I do?" I answered.

"Well, Rob, it would be far simpler if she was ransomed," he said.

"No," I sternly replied. "I'll not have anything to do with that."

"Then, Rob, you should go and see Master Carey and tell him that you found her unconscious on the ground, when you were in Scotland, that you foolishly brought her home, and that you wish to return her under the safety of a Truce Day. Not that he will believe a word of it, and may have you hanged there and then, but perhaps, I say perhaps, he may just let you away with your folly."

"Thank you, Uncle James, I will think over what you have said, and act accordingly," I replied.

As James rode off, his words rested heavily upon me, and I spent the rest of the evening and most of the night mulling over what to do. Fleur was the one person out of all of this that would be affected the least at whatever happened; she would eventually be returned to Scotland, whereas if Master Carey should deem it, and have me hanged or incarcerated, Mother, Father and Sarah would be the ones who would suffer, with no one able to attend the needs of the bastle.

The next morning when I awoke, I informed every one of my decision to go that very day and inform Master Carey of Fleur and my wish that she be returned on the next Truce Day. Father was not best pleased at what I had planned, and even Mother expressed caution, but I was adamant. I went to saddle up and Fleur said that she wished to come with me. I said that that would not be possible, that I needed to go alone. She said, "Rob Milburn, you obstinate English fool, if you do not ready me a horse, I shall walk or even run behind you, but I am coming." I just brushed past her, ignoring her protestation, at which she stamped her foot, then blew out breath from pursed lips in exasperation.

After saddling up, I swung into the saddle, then slowly trotted off. After a short while I looked around to see if anyone had come out to watch me go, and saw Fleur, with her dress held above her ankles, trying her best to follow on behind, her light shoes offering little in the way of grip on the damp ground, but with a determined look upon her pretty face. I turned Flame, and rode back. "Get you back, you silly girl," I said.

"I will not, and if you think that you can be stubborn, Rob Milburn, you know nothing of stubbornness 'til you have come across an Armstrong."

Even with such gander about her, as she looked up at me with that pretty face, I could not help but feel my own unfairness towards her.

"Come along then, young Scottie," I said as I reached out for her, and hauled her aloft, on to the back of Flame, behind me. "Do I not get the saddle now that you know me, Rob Milburn?" she said.

"No, I was up first and it's my nag," I said, to which she gave me a good hard punch to the side of the body, then after a short while placed her arms about me to steady her ride. It was at this point that I realised what a fool I had been to refuse her in the first place; this was indeed most pleasurable.

It was mid-afternoon when we reached the residence of Master Carey, and after riding to the rear of his fine house, to the stable, I spoke to one of the grooms, attending a chestnut mare. "Excuse me, Sir, but I wish to speak to Master Carey," I enquired.

"Would you? Well maybe he would not wish to see the likes of you," came back the reply.

I slipped from the saddle, while unsheathing my sword, so that as my feet made contact with the ground, I took one step forward, while bringing my sword up to the groom's chin.

"Wrong answer," I said. The groom looked greatly startled; I am sure he knew he had overstepped with me, and indeed he had. Just then a head popped up from behind a stable door; I recognised it as Master Carey. Not wishing to be put off by his appearance, I held my stance. "A particularly rude person, Master Carey, do you have need of such, or should I rid you of him right now?" I said.

"Well, young Sir, indeed he does sometimes lapse into rudeness; alas, good grooms are hard to come by, therefore I would be grateful if you could spare him," said Master Carey. I slowly lowered my sword from the groom's chin, turned and bowed lightly in the direction of Master Carey, who then drew open the stable door and stepped out into the yard. "I would be glad to see that placed back in its scabbard, before I step forward," said Carey.

"I do beg your pardon, Sir," I said as I put the sword away. "I see you take no chances with life, young Sir; two swords," he said.

"Aye, 'tis a long story of which I shall not bore you," I said.

"You wish to see me?" said Carey, as he stepped forward, placing a friendly hand upon my shoulder, guiding me away from the stables, when I heard the clearing of a throat, and looked around to see Fleur still perched on the back of my nag.

"Excuse me, Master Carey," I said, as I stepped back and raised my arms to help Fleur from her seat. Once done I walked back to where Master Carey stood, then introduced myself, then Fleur. Master Carey was most intrigued by Fleur's name, but I said I would need to explain my business before I could explain about her name.

"Go ahead, young man," said Carey.

"Sir, I was in Scotland on a matter of business, when I came upon this young lady, who had been rendered unconscious. Because of certain circumstances, I placed her on my horse and rode away, not thinking to take her anywhere on my way back, should whoever I took her to think the worse of me, and cause me to be harmed. I would therefore be most grateful if, when next you attend a Truce Day, I could come along under the safety of that day, and return her to her family."

"Well, young Sir, that is a fine tale you bring me, and you felt the need to fetch the young lady along with your fanciful tale, that I might believe you better," he said.

"Oh no, Sir, 'twas not my idea, but she insisted in accompanying me today," I hastily retorted.

"Well, I am pleased she did, for there is little enough of beauty in this world, so any opportunity of feasting my eyes, I am grateful for," he said. He then turned square to me and said, "Sir John Foster did tell me of a Rob Milburn, whom he had used as a temporary scribe on occasions, would that be yourself?"

"Yes, Sir, I was so honoured," I replied.

"He spoke highly of you, said there may be a scrap of goodness in you for all your breeding, but if you would have me believe such a story, then you insult me, Sir," he said, at which I felt my body tense and I did surely think that I had been extremely foolish in coming here this day. His mouth then broadened into a smile as he replaced his hand upon my shoulder, then said, "I do not know what you have heard of me, young Milburn, but I can assure you, I am fair. You have been foolish in your *business* in Scotland, and if this incident halts any further *business* in Scotland," each time placing great emphasis on the word business, "then maybe it has not all been in vain, and I may also have need of a scribe sometime, and as good grooms, they are hard to come by," he said.

"Now, come, take food before your journey home," he said, placing a hand on both our shoulders and guiding us towards the house.

"No, Sir, I could not impose, we must be off, and take no more of your time," I said.

"I ask you in for purely selfish reasons; as I have said, there is little enough beauty in this world. Allow my eyes the pleasure of Miss Armstrong for a few moments longer. As for you, young Milburn, had you been on your own, you would starve," he said then burst out into loud laughter, Fleur finding it equally amusing.

We all went inside the grand house, the entrance hall panelled from wall to ceiling in oak panels. Master Carey then directed us to a room on the left of the hall, and as we entered, it opened out into a large panelled room, with a long dark table with fine chairs running along either side. Looking down the table one's eyes were drawn to the large leaded window, in the top quarter of each window. The leading was in coloured glass, which shone down into the room, giving strange patterns on the polished wooden floor.

"Sit, sit, the pair of you," invited Master Carey; as we did, a serving girl entered the room, carrying a large wooden tray, placed upon which were pewter plates with cold meats and three pewter goblets. As she entered, a male attendant entered, carrying a ewer filled with wine. The girl placed the plates before us, then the goblets. That done she then started to place the cold meats on our plates, Fleur first, then me then Master Carey. As she finished with each of us the male attendant would step behind each of us in turn, and fill our goblets with a rich ruby coloured wine, the flavour of which I had never encountered before, but hoped to again. The meats were beef and lamb, and were cooked to be the tenderest of meats I had ever eaten.

"Now then, Master Milburn, I know rather more of you than you can possibly realise. Sir John Foster, as I have already stated, has informed me of your role as a scribe, but has also told me that you and your family, your kinsmen, the Charltons and the rest of your ilk, and he often being no better himself, therefore I must assume, being somewhat sparse with the whole truth, tells me that you are very much a leading light within the reiving community. I, Sir, am here to rid this country of your like, so I want you to take from here a stern message to all your reiving friends. I know who you are, I am not of the ilk of Sir John, and there will be many who will be departing this life, very soon, and at the end of a rope."

The wine and the meats suddenly started to sour in my mouth, I felt my stomach churning and had to swallow hard to stop myself from vomiting the entire lot back. I could see Fleur was not enjoying the experience either. After noticing her discomfort I rose from the table and said, "Master Carey, Sir, I feel we may have imposed upon your hospitality long enough. I thank you on behalf of us both for the fine food and wine, and ask that we may be excused, in order to resume our journey home."

"Indeed you may, and Miss Armstrong, you are more than welcome to remain, until the next Truce Day, when I will assure your safe return to your family," replied Carey.

"That is an extremely generous offer, Sir, but it is with regret I must turn it down. Mistress Milburn has been so welcoming that to shorten my stay with her I fear may insult, and it would grieve me to do such a thing," said Fleur, subduing her Scottish accent as she spoke.

"As you will, young Miss, for often an Armstrong is no better than a Milburn," replied Carey, with sarcasm.

I could see the fire well up in the eyes of Fleur so hastily I ran around the table and took her by the arm and started to guide her from the room, and was able to feel more than a modicum of resistance from her as we went.

At the door, I turned to Carey and thanked him once again for his hospitality, and said I looked forward to our trip to Scotland. "Mark me well, young Milburn, the days of murdering and stealing are numbered. I shall see that your captive is returned without bloodshed, but I do it for me, not you or your Scottie woman," he said in a threatening manner.

"Thank you, Sir," I said while lowering my head slightly, then remarked, "It's Scottish Sir, Scottish," then walked around the house towards the stables, to collect my nag.

Once clear of the grounds of the house, I felt Fleur's arms tighten about me. "Rob, he frightens me," she said quietly into my ear.

"He does me," I replied, then continued, "But such never live long."

"Now, promise me this right now; you will not kill him, promise, he is far too dangerous a man for that, now promise me," Fleur said, her voice getting louder and more shrill as she spoke. How could this girl, as pretty as she was, how could she know what was going on in my head? Due to my hesitation in answering, with her taking me quite by surprise, she then took hold tightly of either side of my jack, then shook me, whilst yelling at me, "Promise!"

"Yes, yes, I so promise, but," I was broken off from saying any more.

"There can be no buts," she said whilst giving me another stern shake.

"Yes, I promise," I said exasperatedly.

We rode on, but little was said, my thoughts deeply engaged in the words of Master Carey, these thoughts only broken by the occasional sensation of Fleur's arms about my body.

It was dark as we arrived back at the bastle, much to everyone's relief, both Mother and Father questioning us both, before we had even got sat down. Father said that we should be particularly careful from now on, and limit our raids to Hot Trods, where we might have the law on our side. Fleur sat there, then said, "I cannot believe you are talking in this manner, in front of me." Father then quite surprised us all when he said, "Sorry my dear, but I regard you as one of my family, I have got quite used to you with us."

Fleur beamed at this remark, got up from the table, turned, then walked to the bed, but it was plain to see by her walk that she was quite proud of her new status within our family.

Chapter 19

A Friendship Rekindled

As the weeks passed by, Fleur and I continued to deepen our friendship, but I found that I started to pull away as I knew the day grew ever nearer for her to return to her family, and I would never see her again.

Indeed, the day was upon us very suddenly, and on the morning, I got up soon and readied the nags, and had scarce got food into our bellies, when Carey and his riders passed our bastle. Sir John would have stopped and passed a kindly word before continuing; not Carey, he just rode on. Before mounting up, Fleur went over to Father, who had come to see us off, put her arms about his neck and embraced him, then Fleur and Mother embraced, with much sobbing. "I shall miss you so very much, my child," said Mother. Fleur, I could just make out, as she nestled into Mother's neck, said, "I shall miss you also, thank you so much for being so kind, you shall all remain in my thoughts and prayers."

"Come, Fleur, we must make haste to catch the others," I said, but was struggling with the emotion of the situation, and turned away, as if distracted by something.

As we rode off, I would have normally turned to wave goodbye, but this day I kept my eyes to the front, not even looking at Fleur, until I saw the mass of riders ahead and was now sufficiently composed. "We can steady now and give the nags a rest," I said.

"Rab, you are strange today, distant, what is the matter?" asked Fleur. I pulled up, then turned Flame in the direction we had come. She stopped her nag, turning, then coming alongside.

"What is it, Rab?" she said, leaning out of the saddle and taking my arm. I looked at her through eyes that were now blurred; I could not speak, I turned back around, then trotted on, Fleur following.

I had made a stupid mistake, I had allowed myself to have feelings for this Scots lass, and I knew as I rode onward that she must go back to her family, and I would see her no more. So why punish myself, why hold out wild hopes of something that would never be, why even talk to her? Tonight she will be with her family, and I will be that English reiver who stole her away. Surely if it were not a Truce Day, her family, or any other Scot, would hang me on sight for taking the girl.

The riding was hard, we had much ground to cover before nightfall; Fleur followed behind all the way. Did she not want to speak to me now; had I upset her; did it matter? Then my mind went back to those evenings spent walking with her, her arm entwined with mine, our conversations, the many subjects we had covered. There was a time when it seemed that it would never end, but now the end was in sight. Stop, stop now, torturing yourself, is this not painful enough?

For the entire ride, I had stayed back from the rest of the riders. I did not know who was with us; were there any kinsmen? Was Michael Dodds with us? I had not seen Raymond for such a long time, it had seemed inappropriate to visit and take Fleur, although there was no reason not to.

The light was fading and on the horizon was a dim outline of Carter Bar. My heart sank. We were soon met by a number of Scots riders; I could not see who they were, as we remained at the rear of the English riders. For the first time for some time, I looked around at Fleur; she looked away. Did she not want to see me now, or did she feel as me? I thought not.

Our riders set camp outside Carter Bar, and as they did so, after tethering Flame, and placing my finger to my mouth, to tell Fleur to be silent, we slipped from camp, and into the town. I said to Fleur that she should ask the whereabouts of her father, she merely nodding agreement.

As we came into the town there were Scotsmen stood outside of a large building. Fleur approached two men who were stood slightly apart from the rest. "Have ye seen Wull Armstrang aboot?" she enquired.

"Aye lassie, wah asks?" came the reply.

"His daughter," said Fleur.

"Wait ye here, lassie," said the Scot, and walked up to the building, then entered. I could hear the Scot shout, "Wull Armstrang, yuv a visitor." Fleur took me by the arm and led me away from where we stood, so that her father would not see us immediately he came out. Then she said quietly, "Better he does not see you, Rab."

"But I must see him," I said.

Before another word could be said, her father was there. Fleur rushed to his arms, then in the poor light given off from the buildings I could see her father's face. Oh my goodness, it could be; even after nearly fifteen years, I would recognise that face anywhere, it was so deeply engraved in my mind. Will Armstrong, of course, why had I not realised before? Will Armstrong, as if I would ever forget.

"Is this the heathen that took yer?" he growled.

"Father, he has been a gentleman, he has not laid a finger on me, and has treated me with respect," pleaded Fleur.

As Fleur spoke, I went down on one knee, slowly drawing my sword, and laying it across my left forearm. Will, quite roughly, pushed Fleur behind him, saying, "Away, see Tam, he's by the door, he'll tak ye home? Fleur dutifully obeyed her father, and walked along the dark street, the last I would see of her. The pain within my chest was like a sword entering it.

Will then approached me and said, "I could quite happily kill yer where yer are, were it not the Truce."

"Now you know what my family went through when you did it to me," I said.

"What is that you say? I did it to you, what nonsense, who are you?" said Will, with some anger about his tone.

"Rob Milburn; you took me to Melrose fifteen years ago and left me there," I said.

"By the Gods! Rab, wee Rab, a cannae believe it, my wee boy, put yur sword awa', and stand before me." I stood, while carefully replacing my sword.

"My, my, I did'nae think I wid ever set ma eyes on ye again! Come lad, I still hate ye for the anguish yev caused, but it's na worse than I've done myself." Having gained what I thought was a good manner within Will, I stood back and went down on one knee again.

"Sir, I have treated your daughter with the respect that you showed to me in similar circumstances, and over the weeks I have grown fond of her, very fond. Sir, I would ask her hand in marriage," I said, with as much respect in my voice as I could muster.

"Nonsense, utter nonsense, never, never, never. Aye lad, we may have crossed before, and aye, ye may have not harmed ma wee lassie, but an Englishman marry a Scot, and worse still, ma daughter, yer mad, boy, mad. Get ye away from me now, away, ye hear, before I forget the Truce, for I will tell ye boy, I would gladly swing on the end of a rope for ye, right now, be gone, be gone, now," he scowled.

I think he would have carried out his threat, had I stayed there much longer, so I thought it best to scurry away. I could not return to the camp, so kept to the dark and edged my way through the town, towards the outskirts. The narrow road opened up and on one side was a river, quite swollen after some heavy rain in recent days, and on the other side, dark silhouettes of buildings. After a short way, I came across a livery stable. The door was ajar, so I slipped inside. I could see very little, which suited me. I entered warily, dragging my feet along the ground in order not to trip over anything, then I felt the softness of hay against my legs. I stepped over the edge of the hay, then slowly lowered myself down and sat there in the dark. It was not long until my eyes started to burn, with the tears running freely down my face.

What was it with this Will Armstrong? I had only met him twice in my life and each time he caused me great anguish, both resulting in tears. When I lost my dear Annie, I mourned her passing, I loved her, yes I most certainly loved her, but I did not feel the pain that I felt now. I had never felt the pain that I did now, but I did love Annie, I did. I now felt guilt that I never felt this pain at her passing, when she, my dearest Annie, was trying to provide me with a child.

Who was this Armstrong girl, a Scot, the daughter of my enemy, the one who took me from my home, my family, the one who brutally attacked my father, maiming him and causing my mother and sister so much grief, this girl of only sixteen years, how could she capture me so? But how it hurt! If this was love, I wanted none of it. Ride you home tomorrow, Rob Milburn, I thought, and have no more to do with these Scots, for they bring you nought but grief.

I sat there for what seemed an age, and now having resolved to return home and forget everything, my grief seemed to wane somewhat, so once I had composed myself, I gathered myself up and hauled myself to my feet, taking a good wide sweep of my sleeve across my eyes, to remove the last remnants of this episode.

As carefully as I entered, I endeavoured to make my exit, and by this time, the moon had played a part in making my exit somewhat easier, as long beams of blue light were finding their way into the stable, through the partly opened door. Having reached the door, I pulled it slightly more open, and after being in the dense darkness of the building, now found myself screwing my eyes at the glare of a full harvest moon.

I left the stable and walked down the road, not really knowing where I was going, and caring less, but kept myself to the side of the road where the buildings were, not on the side where the river could be heard rushing by, and in full glow of the moonlight. I had not gone far when I was aware of voices ahead, English voices, but nonetheless, I proceeded with caution. I now kept hard into the buildings to give myself as much cover as I could. Still not knowing what lay ahead, I drew my large sword, so as to be prepared, should anything untoward befall me. The voices got louder, but still, they were in hushed tones. Then I saw who they were; Bells.

I knew that if Bells were out, together, there would be trouble afoot. I could see them stood at the entrance to a small courtyard, all stood side by side; they all had their swords drawn. The nearest me was young Israel, in the middle was the eldest, since Ruben died, Elijah, and at the far end was Elias.

I could not quite see who they were talking to, so carefully stepped out, one pace into the road, in order to see. It was Will Armstrong; they had Will cornered in the courtyard, and they were about to dispatch him, Elijah's words putting that beyond all doubt. "Who would miss a Scottie, another one gone would be a blessing," he said mockingly. I quickly stepped back into the shadow of the building, and as quietly as was able, drew out my second sword. Once I had them both held comfortably in my hands, I edged nearer, to within striking distance, waited momentarily, then with my right hand, lifted the large sword high, and with a sweeping action, brought it hard into the back of the neck of Elijah, while at the same time, bringing the sword in my left hand up, into the fleshiest part of Israel's side, driving it ever upwards. As I did so I could feel the blade cutting into bone.

I had hoped that the surprise of my attack would so startle Elias that it would give Will time to strike, and indeed he did; taking one long stride forward, he lunged straight forward, taking his blade direct into the chest of Elias.

With the force of the sweeping blow, Elijah was the first to fall, followed very swiftly by Israel, who fell across his brother. Finally Elias fell, apart from the others, the only one to utter a sound, before his demise.

Will did not know who his saviour was, until I stepped into the middle of the courtyard entrance. As I would have expected, as I did so, Will raised his sword, until he knew who was there, then I felt he could scarce believe his eyes, when he saw me stood there.

"Rab," he exclaimed. "Rab, you would kill Englishmen to save me, why?"

"They are not Englishmen, they are Bells, I saw off their eldest brother, I might as well have the rest of the family, and do us all a good deed this fine night," I replied.

As I looked down at the result of my efforts, I could clearly see a deep dark gash in the back of the neck of Elijah; indeed, I may just have missed totally removing his head, whereas Israel looked to be asleep as he lay there, but for the black shining pool that was welling from his left side, the scene made worse by the light of the moon making the blood look black.

I was quickly brought to my senses by Will. "Rab, regardless of the circumstances, we will hang for this, killing three Englishmen on a Truce Day, we are done for."

"They have to find the bodies first, Will, and behind me is the answer to our problem," I remarked.

"Wit du ye mean?" said Will incredulously.

"The river, Will, it is high and flowing with some force. If we remove their belts and any other weighty objects from their person, then put them in the river, they will be far off before discovered, and we will be farther off, with nothing to link us to their demise," I explained.

"Rab, have you done this sort of thing before, for you show an uncanny ability to resolve such a problem?" said Will.

"Come, Will, help me get them ready for their journey to oblivion," I said, ignoring what Will had just said.

We quickly undid the belts of our victims and removed the plated jacks they wore about their upper bodies, then carefully, one by one, and watching all about, we stealthily carried the bodies to the other side of the road, hurling the bodies, so that they landed in mid-stream, where they were less likely to get snagged on any branches.

It was not until the third body was attended to that a word passed between us, and it was Will that spoke first. "Rab, I owe you my life, they would surely have seen me in the river had you not happened by."

"Merely paying back an old debt, Will," I said, with a smile.

"An auld debt, wit ever dee you mean?" said Will.

"When you took me to Melrose all those years ago, I seem to remember, because I was a Milburn, and therefore not worth a ransom, you were told to kill me, but you chose to leave me at the manse. Debt paid in full I think," I said.

"You would be very generous to say so, Rab, but had I not took you in the first place, the situation would not have arisen. No, Rab, I owe you, but doubt I could find a way to repay such an act," said Will graciously.

"Oh yes, there is, Will," I said.

Will appeared to ignore my answer and said, "Rab, we need to be away from here with haste, and when I say away, I mean away from this place, and as far as we can before anything comes to light."

"Aye, yur right, Will, but where?" I enquired.

"Away, get yur nag, and meet me at the far edge of town; there is a large building there, on the west side, I shall be waiting there for you," he said.

"You had better find somewhere to hide the weapons and belts, Will," I said.

"I'll tak them wi' me, Rab, they may come in to see off some English," he said, laughing.

I carefully walked back the way I had come, watching that there was no one around who could later identify me. I was soon back at the encampment, and as I entered, I was greeted by Mathew Robson, who was on watch, for, though it was a Truce Day, there was always the chance of some untoward practice; therefore guards were always placed.

"Rob, where have you been? Carey has been asking for you all night, but I should think he will be sleeping now. Hopefully he wakes in better mood than when last I saw him," said Mathew.

Hardly had the words passed his lips than Carey was there, striding across the encampment. "And where, may I ask, have you been, Milburn?" he hissed.

"Taking the girl back to her family," I said quite tersely.

"What?" Carey boomed. "How dare you, how dare you; I was to return the girl, not an object like you, get out of my sight, get out!" he stormed.

His reaction could not have been better, as it gave me the ideal excuse to gather my nag and break camp. I told Mathew that I would ride home, as Father had not been in the best of health, and I did not wish to stay away too long. Mathew bid me God's speed, and that riding alone to be extra careful, then just as I was about to pull away, he said, "Have you seen the three Bell brothers on your travels?"

"No, I haven't, Mathew, when did they slip away?" I answered.

"No one is quite sure," said Mathew.

"Aye, well they'll be up to no good, you can rest assured of that. I will see you when you return, hopefully, Mathew," I said, then pulled away and slowly rode off, heading westward and circling the silhouetted buildings. As I broke free of the buildings, I looked about me, for any sign of Will.

"I could have killed ye a hundred times, ye wee blind Englishman," I heard from behind me, in hushed tones. I looked around and saw Will emerging from the darkness.

"Come, Rab, we have a goodly ride ahead," said Will, as he spurred his nag ahead.

"Where are we going, Will?" I asked.

"Jist ride and 'ald yur blether," Will responded. I was not sure what he had said, but I think he wished me to ride swiftly without speaking, so I obliged. As we rode west, the sky remained dark, but I turned to check that we were not followed, and could see the outline of the hills we had left, stood out against a sky of uncertain colour.

By mid-morning, with a hazy sun at our backs, the landscape started to become quite familiar; then I saw it, the pele tower, that very pele tower from where I had taken Fleur. What foolishness; I had let myself be fooled by this cunning Scot; he had led me away from my kinsmen and friends, and here would kill me out of sight of everyone, or would at least ransom me. But had he learned when last he captured me? A Milburn is not worth a lot.

As we reached the tower, my heart now racing, not knowing what fate there was in store for me, Will got from his horse and tied it to a hook in the wall of the tower.

"Come Rab, tie yur nag by mine, they will be fine, there should'nae be any English about this soon," he said, laughing loudly.

We entered through an iron yett, then a heavy wooden door, much as the bastle. There were signs that cattle had been held here, but instead of going up a ladder, we went up a strange curved stone staircase to the next level, which opened out into a large room, with a very large fireplace, which one could have almost walked into. Just in front of the fire was a long wooden table, with benches along either side, a high backed chair at the end closest to the stairs, and at the other end was a large high backed chair, but with arm rests.

At the far end of the room stood a slim pretty woman, who I assumed was Will's wife and Fleur's mother. When she saw us she walked forward to greet us. "Wull, yur soon home, what has happened, have those English been causing bother again, and who have ye brought?" she said.

"This is Rab who I have brought, Mary," he said.

"Rab," she said hesitantly. "Rab who?"

"Rab Milburn," said Will.

Mary took two steps forward, raising her hand, I thought to greet me, then thwack! She brought the full force of her hand across my face. The power she was able to deliver was such that I found myself tumbling over the long table, dropping on to one of the wooden benches, then rolling into the fire, which was alight and extremely hot. As I tried to regain my feet, before I got roasted to death, I could see at the far side of the room, where another curving staircase was, someone descending from the next floor. It was Fleur, and my heart leapt at the sight of her.

"Oh, Rab!" she called out as she ran from the last stairs to where I was trying to regain some form of dignity. As she reached me she pulled her arms about my waist and gently placed her head against my chest. "Rab, I never thought I would see you again, what has happened?" she said.

"Get away from that murdering English filth!" Mary Armstrong screamed.

"Now, Mary, we will sit down and talk, this is no murdering Englishman; well, yes he is, but he saved my life last night, and he killed three Englishmen to do so," said Will. At this point I interrupted saying, "Just two," holding up two fingers. "Will saw the third off."

"Oh my goodness!" exclaimed Fleur, but Mary seemed less impressed, just sitting there scowling. Will went on to tell the full story of the night's events, then he told of how he had taken me from my home all those years before, and left me with the monks. "This is the wee lad that ye took to Father Francis," Mary said.

"Aye, the same," said Will.

After a brief moment Mary came back with, "I don't care who he is, I want this Englishman oot o' my hoose," she said very forcefully. I got up from the bench I was sat at, and nodded my head towards the Armstrongs as if to go.

"Sit you down, Rab," said Will, in a manner that made doing other than requested not an option. I returned to the bench.

Will continued, "There is more to my story, Mary. I believe young Rab, when he says he treated Fleur properly, which Fleur has confirmed. I believe him to be an honourable young man, well, for an Englishman, and also having spoken to Fleur at Carters Bar, when she was returned, Rab, yur faither, is he the one they call Hafe Heed?"

"Yes, Sir, I believe that is his name," I replied.

"Mary, can you recall many years ago, when I had been caught up in a battle with some English in Closed Glen, and after the fighting, one Englishman stood against the rest, to allow us to take away our dead and bury them? Aye, well that was Rab's faither, Hafe Heed."

"And yur point, Wull Armstrong?" said Mary, quite tersely.

"Mary, Rab has asked to marry Fleur," said Will. Fleur jumped up from the bench she sat at, her face beaming with delight. I was quite taken aback by what Will said, as I was not expecting that at all. I could scarcely keep the smile from my face, until Mary screamed out, so loud the whole of Scotland would hear, "Never, I will never allow my wee girl to marry an Englishman, never, never, never!"

"Mary," Will continued. "In the very short time I have been reacquainted with Rab, there's no a Scots lad that I know could make the measure of him, and I will not plead for him, but I only want the best for ma wee Fleur, as I know you do, and Rab is maybe not the best, but I know of none better."

"No, no, no, I will not have ma wee girl marry an Englishman, you know that I will only have Fleur marry a Catholic, and there's no' an Englishman left of the old religion, so ye can forget any such notion," said Mary.

"Excuse me, Mistress Armstrong," I interrupted hesitantly. "I was baptised into the Catholic Church and was beginning my early studies to become a monk, under Father Francis and Brother Matthias at Melrose."

A silence descended on the room, and for a short moment no one seemed to know what to say. Then Fleur spoke, "But Mother, I love him," then made to join me on the fire side of the table. I smiled and gently shook my head, for her to stay by her parents. Being the bright intelligent girl I knew she was, she understood and resumed her seat.

"How many brave Scotsmen have you slaughtered?" Mary asked, while fixing a harsh stare upon me. I was stunned to the core by her question, and took a few moments to compose myself, then responded, "I don't know the answer to that, but would imagine it to be somewhat less than half the Englishmen that your husband has slain." The words were hardly past my lips, when I wished I could take them back, for I was sure to anger both Mary and Will.

Just then, there was movement on the stairs, and a body emerged from the lower floor.

"Ah, come yerself in, Tam," said Will, and a squarely built figure came into the room. I had the strange feeling that I knew the fellow, so thought it best not to look directly at it, but he immediately came to me, and said, "I think we've met, young man, the last time you were here, we crossed swords." I then realised that yes, this was indeed the fellow I had fought with.

"Maybe it is time for us to resume where we left off," he continued. I was shocked into silence, with this Tam and Will and everyone else here, I was dead. Tam then laughed, placed out his hand and said, "Yer no' a bad fighter for an Englishman, but more important lad, you fight with honour." I took hold of Tam's hand and we shook as friends, then he sat on the bench by my side. It was almost reassuring to have someone sat by me, even someone I had crossed swords with.

Mary then spoke very quietly. "Listen to me, all of you, you seem to have decided for me, but hear this, my daughter will only be married by a Catholic priest, and if you can find one now, with all these Calvinists about, ridding this land of the only true religion, then yes, you may marry. But mark this, Will Armstrong, if a hair of my wee girl's head is ever harmed while with this Englishman, so help me, I will run you through with your own sword."

"A priest then, Rab; all you have to do is come up with a priest, here in Scotland," said Will, quite smugly. Mary also sat back with a certain satisfaction about her person. I sat up, with a bright expression upon my face. "Brother Matthias, I think; we will have to go to Melrose, I have longed to see my old friend again."

Fleur could not contain herself any longer and jumped from her seat, ran around the table and wrapped her arms about my neck. This was the first sign of affection that either of us had shown towards each other; our only time of contact before had been on the ride home from Scotland, when we first met, and in the evenings back at the bastle as we walked through the fields.

Although it appeared that all was now settled, and we decided that on the morrow we would ride to Melrose, to see if Brother Matthias was still there, and able to marry us, there was a definite atmosphere within the tower for the rest of the day. After the evening meal, Fleur mentioned that when in England we had walked out of an evening, and would there be any objection to us doing so now. Both Mary and Will nodded their agreement, so we busily made our escape. Once outside, Fleur's excitement rose to the surface and she chatted as if there would be no tomorrow. I had to try and calm her down, by taking hold of both of her arms, holding them tight to her side, much as I had done when first we met. I quietly explain why I had asked for her hand in marriage, because I could not get thoughts of her from my mind, and life seemed quite pointless without her. I also explained that we would always have her mother's wishes to respect, and that she was against us being together, and we must show her that it was the right thing to do. Fleur calmed somewhat, then said, "But it is the right thing to do, Rab, I love you. Yes, I was happy to see my father and mother again, but I wanted to be back with you. How I looked forward to our walks each evening, where we could talk, and sometimes we talked nonsense, but it didn't matter, we were together. But you are right, I will give more thought to Mother's feelings."

The next day, we all rose early, the horses were readied, and Tam would also ride with us. As we set off I found myself flanked by Fleur to one side and Mary to the other. I took the opportunity to talk to Mary, and started to tell her all about that fateful night when Will and his merry band fell upon the bastle, and of how he carried me away. Of being taken to the manse, and my first encounter with Father Francis, of Daniel, Donald and of course Brother Matthias. I told her of the daily routine, getting up in the middle of the night, of the prayers and the masses, which we had to attend from behind a wooden screen, and of the relentless persecution I endured at the hands of Father Francis. I set upon my tale only to engage Mary in conversation, but I soon became aware of a softening of attitude from her, by the way she asked about my family, especially as to the welfare of my father. I did not think to say less of Father's injuries, than they were, and I fear that I may at some stage have overstated, for we had to stop riding, as I feared Mary might swoon from the saddle. I quickly dropped from my horse, running around to the left side of her nag, and helped her down, gently. I held her for a moment, as Will wheeled his nag around.

Mary quickly regained her composure, lifting her arms to hold my forearms. "Rab, I never thought I would say this; you will never ever be good enough for my daughter, but you are quite a nice boy, for an Englishman." I looked up to where Fleur sat in her saddle, her face beaming far brighter than the sun.

It was early evening when we reached Melrose, my first sight of it. The towering ruin that was Melrose Abbey set my heart pounding. Did it really feel like coming home? I do not know, my feelings were quite mixed, but nonetheless, there was an excitement about being here. We were soon in the town, and once there, although it had been many years since last I trod these streets, I went directly to the manse. Once outside I dismounted, as did Tam and Will, the ladies remaining in the saddle. The heavy iron yett had gone, just the old oak studded door remained. I stood before the door with a mixture of excitement and trepidation. Who was at the other side? Would they know me? Had our journey been in vain? Would I never marry Fleur? I took a deep breath, then knocked, then waited, but no one came. I knocked again, but this time louder and longer, and waited again. After another wait, from behind the door could be heard the large bolt being pulled back, then slowly the door opened, but only enough to allow the occupant to show an eye at the small opening. "Who knocks there?" came the slightly muffled voice.

"I wish to speak to Brother Matthias," I said.

"There is no Brother Matthias here, who is it?" came the voice, but clearer this time, and with the clearness, a slight recognition of who it was.

"Brother Matthias, it is I, Rob, Rob Milburn, don't you recognise me? It's Rob." The door did not move, nor the occupant behind it.

"I know no Rob Milburn, away with you," he said as the door started to close. I quickly placed my foot in the gap.

"Brother Matthias, it is Isaac, Isaac who you used to teach; I worked with Daniel, please, Brother Matthias," I pleaded. The door opened, and there stood Brother Matthias, but no longer in the habit of a monk, and no longer the tonsure haircut that came with the habit.

He stood back, then beckoned us inside, hastening us in. Tam was the last one in; as he entered, Brother Matthias quickly closed the door behind him.

"Isaac, Isaac my boy, I would scarce have recognised you, you have changed so much, you are a man now, and a fighting man by your style. I would have preferred that those weapons had not been brought to my home," he said.

"I am sorry, Brother Matthias, but—" I said as Brother Matthias interrupted, "I am no longer Brother Matthias, just Matthias; I am now a teacher for the townsfolk of Melrose. They now have their own Protestant Priest; I am no longer allowed to conduct masses or any sacraments. There are no Catholic priests any more, not here." He said it with a certain regret in his voice.

"Sorry Bro', sorry Matthias, let me introduce my companions," I said as I placed a hand on the arm of Will. "This is Will Armstrong, the same Will Armstrong who first brought me here." Both men gently bowed toward each other in acknowledgement. Then I indicated with my hand, Mary. "This is Mary Armstrong, wife of Will, and stood behind Mary is Tam, then here," I said, as I put an arm about Fleur's shoulder, "this is Fleur, the daughter of Will and Mary, whom I wish to marry, but her mother has insisted that she will not allow her daughter to marry without a Catholic service." For a short moment there was silence, and in that short moment, it dawned on me that Mary

Armstrong had known exactly what she was saying, when she said she would not allow Fleur to marry without a Catholic priest. Yes, she was a shrewd woman.

"Come, we will talk and you must take food with me," said Matthias, as he guided us through the dark corridor to the kitchen. The old wooden table that Daniel sat at for most of the day was still there. I almost expected to see him still sat there, and the wooden benches that stood at each side of the table had not changed. As a matter of fact, when I got fully into the kitchen, everything was as I left it.

The silence was broken by Matthias. "We lost Daniel a short time after you had gone; he missed you so very much. Father Francis was buried within the grounds of the Abbey, and Donald was buried in the field where he tended the flock. We thought that that would be his wish. Daniel said that he would like to lie with Donald, where he could keep watch over the manse and the Abbey. After the death of Father Francis, it was the wish of the other Brothers that, although I was the most junior, they would prefer me to become the Father. I made contact with the Bishop of Glasgow and he ordained me to full priesthood."

"So you are a priest, Bro', Matthias, are you still a priest?" I asked.

"Well, yes, I suppose I am," he replied hesitantly, "but the Calvinists will not allow any Catholic services to take place; they would burn us all at the stake should they ever find out." His tone now carried a deal of fear.

"But Father Matthias, how could they ever find out, there is the Chapel upstairs, could we not use that?" I said excitedly.

Mary interrupted, "Father, would the Chapel not have to be consecrated before a marriage could take place there?"

"Yes indeed, Mistress Armstrong, you are very right, and it is indeed consecrated, it was so blessed by the Bishop, after the Abbey had been despoiled, in order that we may, as Brothers of our Order, continue our devotions."

After another short silence Matthias spoke, "Isaac, yes, Isaac, I will, I will; we will have a service; it will be a full mass, and if it is God's will, I will burn at the stake, but I will conduct one final mass."

Fleur, who had remained silent since entering the manse, clapped her hands with joy. I then looked to Mary, who showed much less joy than that of her daughter.

Father Matthias spoke again. "But before anyone goes any further, you will remove all weapons now, and they must remain here in the kitchen until you leave tomorrow."

"Tomorrow!" exclaimed Will. "We would have hoped to be away home within the time it takes to marry the young ones."

"Alas, dear friend, if all were equal, indeed it should be so, but before a single one of you could set a foot within the Chapel, which, as Isaac will attest, only the monks could enter, when he lived with us, I will require you all to take confession, and do full penance, so that the soul is washed of all sin." I looked to Mary again, and she now took on the look of glee that her daughter had previously adopted.

Matthias then left us in the kitchen, and as he left, Fleur asked, "Why are you called Isaac, when your name is Rab?" A shuffling of feet could be heard, and Matthias was back with us. "Because he was the promised child; your mother will tell you about the promised child, Father Francis confided in me, how Isaac came to be with us."

I could feel the discomfort felt by Mary at the comment made by Father Matthias, but what could possibly cause such in a person, when all that was asked was, why had I been called Isaac? There were a few moments of silence, then Fleur said, "Mother, whatever does Father Matthias mean? You know about Isaac, err, or Rab?"

A longer silence ensued, then Mary, in an exasperated manner, said, "Yes, yes, all right, it was me." Then a short silence descended, when Fleur said, "What do you mean it was you?"

Mary continued, "When Father Francis was here, before being butchered by the English, I would come here as often as possible, so that I could give my confession to him. It was the only place left, after the Abbey had been razed to the ground and the Calvinists had overrun the land. Father Francis was a stern man but fair." I could feel my eyebrows lifting at this comment, in some disbelief. Mary carried on, "He knew what your father did, as did many around, and still do, and he told me after one of my confessions that within the manse was an old man who did all the cooking and cleaning and gathering of food from the town, and that he kept what was left of the monks together and sustained, that without him he doubted how long the monks could continue. He explained how this old man was becoming frail with age and that they needed a young boy, who could be trained to carry out the duties of this old man, before he died. Father Francis explained that if he could get a young boy, he would know no other life and would be content with the life within a Cistercian community. I told your father of this when I got home, and asked him to get a boy, when next he rode into England. Father Francis said that if we could succeed in accomplishing his wish, both your father's and my sins would be absolved, regardless of whatever we may have done."

Fleur interrupted and said in total disbelief, "And you went and captured Rab, then brought him back here? Then you have the affront to criticise Rab?! You are far worse!"

"No, it did not happen like that," said Will. "I told your mother I would have no part in such a venture, but when I did next raid into England and Rab presented himself to me, bravely fending me off with his wee wooden sword, and I carried him away, it was not to fetch him here, but as the raid continued, the rest of the riders wanted him dead;

as he was of no value, it came to me that the manse was the best and safest place for him. And Rab, you can now see, that you were never likely to be killed, not with me there."

"And you think that that makes amends for what you did?" said Fleur.

"Fleur," I interrupted, "Do you love me?"

"Yes, of course I do, what has that got to do with anything?" she replied.

"Everything," I answered. "Everything I am and everything you know of me has been fashioned by what has taken place throughout my life. And this is a major part of that life. Yes, I was taken away from my family, as a little boy, and yes I was subjected to a harsh life with the Brothers, but I learnt so much more here than I could ever have hoped for at home; I came to know one of the most wonderful people it is possible to meet, Father Matthias, and in a roundabout sort of way, I came to know you, and we are here, here to get married, and Father Matthias is to carry out our marriage. Fleur, I cannot hold any of this against either your mother or father."

Mary took a step forward. I could see that her eyes were moist around the edges. She looked up at me and with a slight smile, turned to Will and said, "Yes, Will, you were right, he is a good man."

We were interrupted by the reappearance of Father Matthias, but now attired in the habit of a Cistercian monk. "I will take you one at a time for your confession. Who wishes to come first?" he said. Mary was the first to go, and followed Father Matthias to where the confessions were taken, with a spring in her step. The rest of us remained at the kitchen table, where I was able to keep them all entertained by my reminiscences of my time in this building.

I chose to go last, and before giving my confession, I asked Father Mathias about the other Brothers. He told me that two had chosen to become Protestant Priests, and the others had chosen to leave the service of God. Matthias remained to continue the one duty he loved; teaching, which he said had arisen from first teaching me, and the joy he got from seeing me blossom. As I thought that we were renewing our friendship so well, I thought that the penance I would be given after my confession would be not too heavy; alas, how wrong I was. I could tell from the tone adopted by Father Matthias that he was far from impressed by my life since last he saw me. The result was that I gained little sleep that night as most of it was spent on my knees, on the cold hard stone floor, saying prayer after prayer. Father Matthias being the diligent person I knew him to be, continually came by through the night to ensure I was not missing a single 'Hail Mary' or 'Our Father', that he had given me to say.

The next morning I was put to work in the kitchen by Father Matthias, it being his opinion that I was best qualified to do such duties while the women could ready themselves. Apparently, Matthias had a widow come in from the town to run the manse, but she took one day off each week to look after an ageing mother, and as luck would have it, today was her day off.

I did not quibble at being set to work in these familiar surroundings; my only wish was that Daniel were there with me, and that Donald would walk through the back door at around mid-morning, as he always did.

It was not very long until we were all asked to go upstairs to the chapel, the two ladies already there. I led the way, and for the first time, found myself actually inside the chapel, the wooden screen having been pulled away from the side door, allowing full access. Stood at the top end of the chapel were Mary and Fleur, Fleur having a garland of flowers about her head, like a crown. She looked every inch a princess, her face beaming with absolute joy. Father Matthias was stood in front of them, facing them from a high step. As we walked in, Will walked to my right, Tam to my left. I thought that by the way they had took their positions, that after putting them through the harsh penances we had had to endure, they did not want me to escape.

I was fortunate that, although I had forgotten much of the Latin I had been taught, I was able to understand much of what was said. The full nuptial mass seemed to take an age, but I could see that both Mary and Matthias took the greatest of pleasure from the service.

After the lengthy service we all retired to the kitchen where I served the oatmeal breakfast I had prepared earlier. It was some time into the meal before Mary turned to Father Matthias and said, "Father, you are quite fortunate with who looks after your needs; this oatmeal is quite the best I have ever eaten."

With a beaming smile, Father Matthias proudly proclaimed, "Your son-in-law." Mary was quite taken aback. "You prepared this?" she said.

I did not answer, but smiled in her direction and nodded. A long silence ensued, then Fleur interrupted the silence with the ill-chosen words, "I suppose you should all refer to me as Mistress Milburn from henceforth."

I could feel the cold enter the room, a chill that entered the bones, as I scrambled to my feet, and quickly started to gather the wooden bowls we had all eaten from.

"No, no, you are the groom, you should be by your wife; I shall attend the cleaning of the bowls," said Mary.

Turning and smiling at Mary, I said, "Shall we do them together?"

We stood together cleaning all that had been used, then Mary said, "I can scarce believe that an Englishman would ever bring me to see a Catholic Priest, have me take confession, then have me attend a full mass."

I turned to her and smiled again, knowing that she, for all her reservations about me, had thoroughly enjoyed the whole experience. "It has been lovely," was all I said. Her face became radiant, even though she tried to look away, so that I could not see her pleasure.

Once all had been stacked away, Mary and I went back to the table and sat with the others. Will spoke first, and suggested we all ride to the border, for safety, and it would allow plenty of time to conduct our goodbyes. Mary agreed, and I could see that Fleur was quite pleased to be spending a little more time with her mother and father. Tam had already gone out to ready the horses, and as we rose to go, Father Matthias returned to the kitchen, dressed in normal attire. "Well, my friends, it looks as though I shall not be having your company for much longer. May I say what a pleasure it has been to have you all as my guests, and I truly thank you all for allowing me the chance of being the priest that I always wanted to be. As for you, Isaac, or should I say Rob Milburn, now that you have a fine Scottish bride, you will not be staying away for as long in the future. I want to see you both regularly. And I am sure that Mistress Armstrong is wishing to ask, and I shall say yes, I will baptise the children, but pray, do have caution, for one single word in the wrong quarter, and I will surely burn." Mary beamed at the thought of her grandchildren being baptised into the Catholic Church, as I feel did Fleur, but she nonetheless blushed heavily at the suggestion.

We all readied ourselves. The last thing Will and I did was to replace our weapons about our waists. Father Matthias mentioned the two swords on my belt, but I told him that it was a long story, and that if I were to relate it now, I should not get past the door for another two days with the penance that he would hand out. Everyone laughed loudly, and as we all went up the long dark passage to the door, I walked with Matthias. "You have brought such joy to me, returning as you have. I have often wondered if we here have been in your thoughts, since leaving," he said.

"Yes, Father, you have indeed, many, many times, and I thank you so very much for doing this thing for me. I would not have wished for anyone else to carry out my marriage service," I replied. When we got to the door, Matthias and I embraced, and as I pulled away, there was a tear in his eye. I swallowed deeply, then placed my arm about Fleur, and led her to her nag, helping her into the saddle. I raised myself into the saddle, bid farewell once again, then reined Flame away from the manse.

Chapter 20

The Mist Rises

As we left the town, I turned to see that ever-familiar profile of Melrose, and was reminded of the last time I left, on the back of my father's nag. That time I was excited at being free, and full of thoughts of being reunited with my family. This time, although accompanied with the most beautiful woman in the land, who was now my wife, and the thoughts of our future together, my heart was slightly tinged with sorrow. Was this what I regarded as my real home or that bastle, set in a valley in Northumberland? I was confused. I turned back and as I did so, Fleur was looking directly at me, her beauty washing away any melancholy thoughts.

The silence was broken by the voice of Mary, who was now at my side. "Now then, young Rab, I have wished to ask this question since first I saw you. What in Heaven's name is the idea of carrying two swords; can you not fight with just one, or do you English need two to take on a Scotsman?"

I explained how I first came to use two swords, out of being made a fool by a Kerr.

"A Kerr!" she exclaimed, mockingly. "A Kerr; if it only takes one of those to make you a fool, you would stand no chance against an Armstrong."

We all laughed, which set the day off well, but I could not help but return her slight. "Aye, yull be right, Mary, but I'll take my chance against any male Armstrong ye want to put in front of me, but the female, no, I think I will run first," which was greeted with much laughter, even from Will and Tam. Then I said, "Just one thing, Mary; had it not been for my two swords I may now have been talking to the widow Armstrong, so I will always be grateful to my two blades."

"Aye, ye may be right there, Rab, and I'll be always grateful to ye."

We both smiled and I now really warmed to her, and hoped that her daughter had inherited all that her mother was.

We trotted along, the morning chill giving away grudgingly to the afternoon sun, which struggled to make any impact on the warmth of the day. But there was much jolly banter between us all, and I knew that I was as much a part of this family as any Armstrong, and felt proud to be so, almost as much as being a Milburn.

As the sun crossed in front of us as we headed south, and it reached its highest point of the day, we reached the border. Will raised his hand for us all to stop. "This is as far as we go, we must leave ye to yer new life, let us make our goodbyes." Much embracing followed, Mary and Fleur both in floods of tears, Will sitting proud in his saddle, trying to look as if none of this was having any effect, but the welling up within his eyes told a different story. Mary brought her horse to my side, reached over with her right arm, taking hold of me behind my neck, and pulling me almost from my saddle, said, "Now you hear me now, you look after ma wee lassie. Aye, I may not dislike ye as much as I first did, but that does not say that I won't rip yer arms and legs from yer body if a hair of her head is ever harmed." Then she stood up in her stirrups, leaned over and kissed me on the cheek.

I had been coping with the emotive situation up until this point, but Mary had broken me down, my vision was starting to blur. I turned from Mary and reached over to Fleur, taking her hand, as we rode away from the Armstrongs. We rode for some time, before turning and facing each other, then I said, "Fleur, I make you this promise; I will always try to make you happy, and help ease the pain of taking you from your family."

"I know ye will, Rab; I would not be here if I thought different," she said.

The sun was just dipping over the hills to our right as we entered the valley, and the level of excitement welled up within my body. My family would be astounded when I arrived back with Fleur. "Are you excited, Rab?" said Fleur, her face beaming, making up for the waning light of the sun.

"Aye, I am," I replied.

"I cannot wait to see your mother and the rest of your family," she gushed.

"Aye, *your* family," I said.

"Oh my goodness," she exclaimed, bringing her hand up to her chest, as if to catch her breath.

As we neared the bastle, Mother emerged from within, and almost shied away, not recognising us, as there were two, then she realised who it was and her hand went to her mouth in disbelief. "Rob!" she exclaimed, then a rather elongated "Fleur! What are you doing here?"

I jumped from my horse without saying a word, ran around to help Fleur from hers, and as her feet touched the ground, I turned to Mother and said, "Mistress Milburn, may I introduce Mistress Milburn," pointing my hand to Fleur and bowing.

"What folly do you say, Boy?" Mother said.

"It is true, we were married this very day at Melrose," said Fleur.

Mother rushed forward, embracing Fleur, with a grip that almost drew the very breath from her body. "Oh my darling child, I am so happy to have you back, you have been gone such a short time but I have missed you so very much," said Mother. She then reached out, I thought to embrace me, but I received a hefty swipe at the back of the neck. She then ushered Fleur into the bastle, while I was left to tend the nags. I knew nothing of the reception Fleur got from within the bastle, and was somewhat disappointed not to have been there, as I had imagined, standing there, with my arm about Fleur, announcing my return as a married man, as I had ridden back from Melrose.

Eventually, after bedding down the nags for the night, I ascended the ladder to the living area, where the entire family, including Fleur, were sat at the table.

"Come, Rob, get seated, then I may serve the food," said Mother. I sat beside Fleur; as I did, she linked my arm, and when Mother turned from the fire, a broad smile fell upon her face.

"Now then, Rob," said Father. "Fleur has told us all as much as she knows of how you managed to end up wedded to this beautiful girl. What can you add?"

The food came to the table, which instead of being the usual pottage, was indeed freshly slaughtered mutton, with a mixture of vegetables, which I thought was wonderful. Then I thought, they did not know I was due back, so they must have planned to eat so well in my absence, or would they? Nonetheless, I was pleased that such a spread was there to greet our return. My thoughts were interrupted by Father. "Well lad, come along, tell all."

I started my tale from the moment we left the bastle to return, to Scotland, of my first encounter with Will, after all these years, of my request of marriage to Fleur, of the rejection, then I swore everyone to silence, even turning to Sarah and saying, "I know you do not reply, and I know your eyes see only what they want to, but you must never ever repeat a single word I now say." I then went on to tell of the slaying of the three Bells, and the disposal of the bodies in the river. Mother sat there as if in a witch's spell; Father I could see was quite impressed at the thought of three Bells being dispatched in one swoop; even Fleur, who had heard most of the tale before, gasped at various points of my story. When I included the part about Mary's devastating punch, Mother interrupted and said that without meeting her, she already liked Fleur's mother immensely, which was greeted with much laughter; alas, not by Sarah.

Before my tale was complete, Fleur's head fell upon my shoulder, so we stopped and went to our beds, I holding Fleur up by her waist as I escorted her to our bed. I laid her down and within an instant, she was sound asleep. I lay at her side, and was soon asleep myself.

I can scarce remember sleeping as sound as I did, and did not wake until the morning was fully lit. Mother would normally have had me out of bed at the rising of the sun, but because it was the night of our wedding, she let us lie on, and she said that she thought we looked far too lovely, lying side by side, to disturb us.

When I did rise, Mother placed a large bowl of steaming oats before me, doing so with a broad smile about her face. I could not understand what I could possibly have done to merit such a welcome to the day. After I had feverishly devoured the steaming oats, Fleur rose from her slumbers with a start, jumping from the bed, with reddened face, apologising to all and sundry for her laziness. Mother reassured her that no one was in the least bit bothered, and summoned her to the table to eat. As Fleur neared the table, she passed me, and while doing so, struck out at my side, blaming me for her extended slumber. I found the entire scene quite amusing, so leaned forward and kissed her on the cheek, then made my escape. As I descended the ladder to where the animals were housed, I was taken aback that there were none to be seen, so rushed out to see if there were any in the fields, only to be greeted by my sister, who had taken care of everything. I fear that had Sarah been of full wit, her look at me would have been the same as it was this morning, for although with dead eyes, she seemed capable of staring right through you. A chill ran through my body, and I physically shuddered, then stepped forward and kissed her on the cheek, her skin as cold as her eyes.

I quickly got about my daily chores, with thoughts of Fleur dancing about my head. What an adventure it had all been, and how lucky I was to have such a prize as Fleur. The day soon passed, and I was soon at the table again for the evening meal. How pleasant it was as we all sat there, talking, Mother and Father still wanting to know more about Fleur, and she only too willing to tell her story, but she had a wonderful talent for relating her stories in such a way that each word was so riveting.

Mother and Sarah had just cleared away the dishes from the table. Fleur was mid-way between her reply to one of Mother's many questions, when there was a hammering at the door. I rushed to the arrow-slit in the bastle wall, to see if we were under attack. Fleur ran to my side, clinging to my arm. "What is it, Rab?" she gasped. "I can't see a thing out there, there certainly does not appear to be a raid," I replied, as I squinted, and moved from side to side, to try and see as much as was possible outside. Then I heard a voice shouting, but could scarce hear what was being said. I pressed my ear to the slit, while signalling all within to stay silent. After a moment I thought I heard the voice say, "Arthur," but the rest was taken away by the wind.

I turned to Father, who was still sat at the table. "I think it may be Uncle Arthur."

"What, this late hour, I would doubt it very much, unless it is of the greatest urgency," said Father.

"You had best gather your sword, Father, for if it is not him, we have a fight on our hands," I replied.

"No, Rab, don't go, please," pleaded Fleur.

"It is all right, my sweet flower, two Milburns side by side, there'll be many dead bodies, but none ours," I said reassuringly, and choosing my words carefully so as not to mention that we may be facing Scots, a problem I had never encountered before. I could also see Father was holding his tongue, lest anything untoward should spring forth.

I went to the top of the ladder, slowly easing myself down, with large sword in hand, and second sword about my waist, Father but two steps behind, silently descending, and listening. The banging on the door continued, the shouting likewise, but now the voice was clearer. "Let me in, it's Arthur, I have urgent news," I could now make out. Even so, I unbolted the door carefully, only opening it slightly, keeping my foot hard against it, while holding my sword high, should anyone try to rush the door. Father was stood tight in behind me, giving extra support should we be under attack.

As I peered out, I saw the outline of a man, and as my eyes quickly accustomed to the dark, I could make out that it was indeed Arthur, with what could only be described as a pained expression upon his face.

"Quick, man, let me in," said Arthur, in exasperation. I slowly opened the door, then the yett and as I did so, Father took some steps backwards, but still with sword aloft. Arthur stumbled in through the door, falling into my arms.

"Tom, Rob, it's Richard. Scrope has got him, he is being held in Carlisle Castle," blurted out Arthur, very much out of breath. He then broke free from me, and as I went to close the yett and the door, I peered out and could see Arthur's nag, foaming under its bridle and saddle; it had been ridden hard. I stepped out, taking hold of its rein, and led it in. Father and Arthur went up the ladder, I stayed and tended Arthur's nag. When I had finished, I went up the ladder and saw everyone gathered around the table, Arthur in mid-story.

I did not want to interrupt, but I dearly wanted the whole story. When I sat down, Arthur was at the stage where he said, "The day after the morrow, he is to be taken from the Castle to the Hilltop, which is in Carlisle, where the gallows are, and hanged."

As I sat at the table, I asked, "What has he done to deserve such a thing?"

Arthur gave a dry humourless laugh and said, "What hasn't he done? Murder, rape, pillaging, cattle thieving… No, Rob, we may all have done some of these things at one time or other, but Richard went beyond what is acceptable, even in these lawless times."

"Well, who captured him?" I said.

"I was telling your father and mother; it was the new warden at Carlisle, young Scrope; his father was a harsh but fair warden, but this one, he just wants to make a name for himself, and he is intent on hanging his way to fame. There are many who have been hanged already, who have done much less than Richard."

"We must try and get him free," I said.

"Nonsense, utter nonsense," said Arthur. "There will be guards all over the Castle, plus he will be held far beneath the Castle; no one has ever, since it was built, entered Carlisle Castle by force, and that includes armies, not just the Milburns. Get such folly from your thoughts. Richard's fate is written in stone and nothing can change that."

We all sat for some moments, in complete silence, then I said, "We must be with him, for his final day."

"It's a perilous venture I fear, best not, my lad," said Arthur.

"Aye, he's right, Rob," said Father.

"But no one knows me in Carlisle. No, I must see him before the hanging, and I want to see this Scrope, and get the measure of the man," I insisted.

"Then I shall come too," said Fleur.

"You will not," I answered.

"I will, Rab Milburn, my duty is with my husband, and there's no' a man nor woman who will stop me," asserted Fleur.

"My, I will tell you, Rob," interceded Arthur, "I have sat here since your mother introduced me to your new bride, and marvelled at her beauty, but now I see there is much, much more to this fine Scottish lass. You have chosen well, what say you Tom?"

"Aye, you're right, Arthur, we have disagreed on most things throughout our lives, it's good that we now can agree on something," said Father, which caused some laughter, and Fleur some blushes. I was filled with pride that this young lady of Scottish birth, who I had brought into our house, was now being greeted with so much approval.

The next morning I readied the nags for our ride to Carlisle. We ate our usual meal of boiled oats, then set forth, with heart in mouth, or at least I did; I did not like to ask Fleur of her feelings, but if they were of trepidation, she covered them well. This woman never ceased to amaze me. Were all Scottish women like this, for if they were, then thank Heavens it was the men that I had fought.

We rode hard, for Arthur did not know when the hanging would be. Again, another fine trait of my new bride, for she was a fine horse-woman. We made good progress and were at the outskirts of the city by mid-morning.

Arthur suggested that we split up, as he was known in Carlisle, and should he be taken by Scrope's men, then Fleur and I would be able to make our escape unchallenged.

Before parting, Arthur told Fleur and myself where to go, and suggested that I hide my second sword, as it would make me stand out. Fleur said she would place it under her saddle, then drape her cape over it, which worked very well, and did not seem to cause the nag any discomfort. We rode over to the north of the city, coming in from the side of the River Eden, then riding up towards the castle, which stood forth as a dark foreboding, red sandstone edifice, the mere sight of which sent chills down my back. Fleur must have been overcome by the same feeling, as she reined her nag closer to mine. As we neared the main entrance, which on this day was well manned with guards stood with tall pikestaffs, we turned to our left, riding alongside the Cathedral, as Arthur had instructed.

There was much to-ing and fro-ing along the street, so we both dismounted. I noticed Fleur arrange her cape over the saddle, so as to hide the sword.

As we walked slowly along, a fellow asked, "Have you travelled far to see the hangings?" Without even thinking, I placed my finger to my lips, then said, "The debatable lands," then winked at him, to which he returned a broad smile of black teeth. I knew that there were indeed some lands to the north and west of Carlisle, which went by such a name, and were often frequented by people of questionable character, but who would offer no threat to today's affairs.

There were some stalls along the side of the road, selling all manner of things, from small wooden dolls hanging from small roughly hewed gibbets to hot foods. We purchased some meat from one such stall and stood there eating, when suddenly we were aware of something happening along the road towards the Castle. I strained to see what was taking place, and was just able to see a rider leaving the castle entrance, and as he rode forward, I could see he was followed by guards with tall pikestaffs, and there could be heard the slow beating of a drum. There then started a cheering from the crowd that lined the route, but Fleur and I remained silent. What did we have to cheer for, for although she was a Scot by birth, she was now a Milburn, and it was one of her kin who was bound for the gallows?

The procession neared us, and as it did so, we could see that the person on horseback was finely clothed with a hat festooned with fine feathers, and he rode with one hand on the reins, the other perched upon his thigh, his head held high, and an arrogant smirk about his face. This must be the Scrope, and to my eyes, he did not cut such a fine figure as he no doubt thought. Behind his horse walked the drummer, beating a slow rhythm upon his instrument, then the two lines of uniformed guards, and inside these two lines walked a mixed assortment of humanity, all heavily shackled. I peered hard through the lines of guards to see Richard, but it was difficult. All that were there, and I counted seven, were in such a filthy condition. Then, with disbelieving eyes, I saw a shadow of what had been my cousin; dirty, dishevelled, with head down, sunken eyes, bruising about his face, back arched, no sign of the once ever present smile; he was a broken man. I pulled my head back behind Flame, in order that no one could see, then shouted, "Richard!" As I pulled my head from behind my nag, I saw Richard's head slowly raise, then he looked about him, seemingly in a daze, his eyes blackened as if by lack of sleep. He seemed to have trouble seeing, as he peered into the crowd, then he caught sight of me, and within an instant, his broad smile reappeared, but it did not sit well within that sunken, grey and black pallor, which his confinement had placed upon him.

Fleur and I started to walk slowly through the crowds, keeping in line with Richard. He was quick to realise that Fleur was with me, and his smile broadened even wider, as he gestured lightly with his head, in the direction of my new wife, and I gestured similarly back. He then shook his head in mock disbelief, and I actually think he started to laugh lightly, I think with pleasure at my happiness. As we walked on, Richard looked to me again. This time the smile was not there, as he gestured with his head, in a backward motion, as if telling me to discontinue walking in line with him, should anyone notice, and implicate us with him. He could not have been more explicit, had he shouted out the words. I stopped, and Fleur held her nag back also, as we stood, not quite knowing what to do next, then as the procession was all but past, we continued to follow.

By this time we were starting to walk slightly downhill, the road still lined with crowds of people, some cheering, some jeering, but all making such a noise. Luckily the nags were not taken aback by this tumult, and walked steadily along, by our sides. At the bottom of the long incline, the road started to rise slightly, then I could see the procession, carrying Richard along, swung to the right, then climb a steep bank, and as I neared this, I could see a line of gallows. On seeing this, I felt Fleur grasp hold of my arm tightly. "No, Rab, no, no, this is horrible, I don't want to see," she said pleadingly.

"Then don't, my wee pet, keep your head down behind your nag, but I must stay to be with my cousin, he must not die alone," I replied.

As I shielded Fleur from the gruesome scene before us, I looked across the thronging crowd, and over to my far left, I glimpsed Arthur. It was just a glimpse, as he no sooner was there than he was swallowed up by the crowd.

The procession, once all having scaled the high bank, stopped, then the guards herded the prisoners to the side of the gallows. Not that any of those in shackles could ever hope to escape such a heavily guarded place; the guards stood two to each prisoner, placing the point of their pikestaffs to the neck of each, as if to heighten the menace.

There was one more prisoner than there was gallows, and I could not, at that point, see how the hangings would take place. The Scrope, still mounted and like a strutting peacock, took centre point, and as he did, the crowd quietened.

"Master Hangman, you may start to place the nooses," he ordered, then continuing he said, "Guards, keep that one 'til the last, it would be a shame for him to miss out on the day's entertainment."

I could see he was pointing at Richard, with his riding whip. This was truly an evil man, that would prolong a man's torture at having to watch six others hanging, before his own.

When all six of those to be hanged had the nooses placed about their necks, Scrope signalled with his stick, by first raising it, then lowering it swiftly, and as he did, the hangman heaved the first victim from the ground, pulling hard as he did so. Another man stepped forward and helped him secure the rope, as the victim thrashed about at the end of the noose. While all this was taking place, it was greeted by unbearably loud cheering from the crowd.

The hangings continued, one after another, the crowd becoming louder at each hanging. Fleur continued to hide her head from what was taking place, and after the third hanging, I felt a hard pull on my arm, and when I looked, Fleur was bent over, being violently sick.

After the sixth victim had ceased to dance at the end of the rope, Scrope was heard to order, "Cut the first one down, Master Hangman." The hangman quickly ran back to the first gibbet and started to undo the rope. The body dropped with force to the ground, the limbs folding in positions that they would never do had life still existed. When the rope was removed, two guards came forward, and dragged the body away, one to each leg.

"Now our prize, Master Hangman, and put the rope on tight, we would hate it to slip and dispatch Master Milburn before we have had our pleasure." The hangman did as he was bade, and I could see the discomfort upon poor Richard's face, but he turned to the Scrope, with a broad smile, which incensed Scrope to such a pitch, he turned the deepest colour of red. At the very sight of this Richard laughed, then turning once more to Scrope, the laugh stopped. He then spat on the ground, right in front of Scrope.

"Hang him, hang him, damn you, but pull lightly on that rope, Hangman, for I will have my pleasure this day." The crowd started to jeer, and I could see fists raised from within the crowd, and at this the guards took up defensive stances with their pikestaffs. While all this was taking place my cousin was swinging his legs about frantically, trying to bring an end to his anguish, but it took for what seemed an age. Fleur by this time was sobbing quite heavily, with her head buried hard into the neck of her nag. Eventually Richard's writhing ceased; he was now hopefully at peace. I looked up at the gallows for one last look at my cousin. It was not him, his face was a colour I had never seen on any dead body, his tongue was protruding from his mouth, and both it and his lips had a strange blue hue. I winced as my eyes fell upon the scene, then turned away, placing my arm about the shoulders of Fleur.

We walked away from the crowd, some still baying for more, and turned into a narrow street, overshadowed on either side by buildings. I say buildings, but these were hovels, the stench was overpowering, but luckily most of the hovel dwellers were within the crowd we had just left. I did not know where I was taking us, I just wanted to be away from that crowd, away from those gallows and away from that arrogant Scrope.

I could see the far end of this street, where it opened up, and my heart was lightened, to be away from this lane of poverty, but just then three dirty disgusting creatures emerged from a hovel to our left, two armed with knives, one with a wooden cudgel. The centre excuse for humanity growled something at us, and as he did so, I drew my sword, but unknown to me, Fleur had drawn the sword she had secreted under her saddle earlier, and unseen by our would-be attackers. Even though I was stood with sword in hand, they did not appear threatened. I assumed they thought that they outnumbered me, three to one, and therefore everything was in their favour. What they did not reckon for was what happened next. Fleur suddenly raised her sword, then screamed in a voice the whole of Carlisle would hear, "Let's get them!" as she rushed forward, screaming like some wounded animal. I was merely dragged along by her onrush. The hovel dwellers turned, and rushed in from whence they came. I, having got in front of Fleur by this stage, stood in the doorway peering in, the stench far greater than that of outside. Within an instant Fleur was at my back, still with sword aloft, screaming, "Let's get in and kill them all!"

I pushed back against Fleur, causing her to step back, but kept my eyes on the doorway, should any of our attackers fancy appearing from within, for I wondered how long anyone could withstand such a stench for very long. I kept on walking backwards, Fleur still pressed hard into my back, and as we got back to our nags, I said, "Mount," and gave Fleur a heave into the saddle, then swung into mine. We galloped the short distance to the end of the street, then into open country, where we continued to gallop, both still with our swords in hand. Once well clear of Carlisle, I reined in on Flame, Fleur doing likewise when she saw what I was doing.

As we stopped, Fleur turned to me, somewhat out of breath from the gallop and said, "Oh, Rab, you must teach me how to use one of these things," as she held up the sword, with a roguish smile on her face.

I sat there, totally aghast, looking for the words, but they would not come. I could feel my mouth moving, but was not able to utter a squeak, then we both burst out laughing. It turned into hysterical laughter, not necessarily from what had just taken place, but more from the entire and awful events we had both witnessed this day.

I sheathed my sword, then reached over to Fleur, and took hold of the sword she held and secured it about my person, then we rode off, towards home, hardly speaking a word between us all the way back, but for much of the time, for both our comfort, we held hands as we rode.

It was dark as we arrived back. I stayed and tended the nags, and I told Fleur to go up the ladder and get warmed, as the evening had brought with it a goodly frost. When Fleur had alighted the ladder, I could hear her sobbing loudly, and the sound of Mother comforting her. As I tended the nags, all I could see was Richard's face at the end of that rope, his tongue, that blueness about his face, and those protruding eyes. Had I not seen for myself the rope go about his neck, I would not have known it was Richard.

That night, Fleur and I held each other, throughout the night, of which neither of us slept a great deal.

The image of Richard stayed with me for many weeks thereafter, and my hope was that Fleur was able to rid her thoughts of that day better than I.

I did not want to talk to her about it, as I thought, if she had been able to overcome such thoughts and images, I did not wish to remind her of them.

Many weeks after these events, I was replenishing the wood store, having spent the morning gathering fallen trees from the nearby woods. As I busied myself chopping my harvest into manageable pieces, Mother came to talk to me. I had been expecting Fleur, as it was her habit of coming to talk whenever I was working just outside the bastle.

"Rob, I have a matter which I need to talk to you with some urgency," she said, with a stern expression on her face.

"What have I done?" I asked.

"It is not what you have done, Rob, it is what you have not," she continued.

"I don't understand, Mother," I said, now quite bewildered by the conversation.

"Rob, you have been married to Fleur for some time now and she is starting to doubt you love her," Mother continued.

"But I do love her, Mother, I love her dearly. Sometimes I feel guilty of my love, because of Annie. I did love her, but I sometimes feel not as much as Fleur, and it makes me feel as if I am dishonouring her memory," I answered.

"So is that why you have not come to her?" replied Mother.

"No, it is not," I replied.

"Then why, Rob, you have the most beautiful girl, who we all love dearly; you have taken her away from her family and all she knows, brought her to a new land amongst people she has never known, who speak differently... can you imagine how difficult that must be for her?" said Mother.

"Yes, Mother, I know exactly how difficult that must be for her," I said with some emphasis.

"Then if you know, Rob, you must understand how she needs to know you love her, or you could lose her, for there is no real marriage, Rob, unless you join with her," said Mother, quite sternly.

"What, and kill her as I did Annie?" I snapped back.

Mother stepped forward, taking me into her arms. "Rob, oh my dear sweet boy, how you must have hurt, and maybe you still do, but what happened to Annie is not going to happen to Fleur. It was unfortunate, Annie dying as she did, but lots of women have children every day; just look around at all the families we know, and of all the children that are born to them. Rob, you must think of what you are doing, that poor little girl in there loves you dearly, she needs you to be strong, she needs you to look up to and respect, and if you do not respect her, then the marriage is ended. Rob, please," she said.

As Mother broke free her embrace, she kissed me on the cheek, then stepped back, turned, and walked back into the bastle. She had just entered the doorway when she turned and looked around at me and said, "Please, Rob," then disappeared inside.

I sat down on one of the logs I was cutting, my mind whirling around like the slingshot above my head just before the stone is released. I had seen me ride all day and all night, and fought against strong hard men, until I could barely stand, but never had I felt so utterly drained of strength as I did then. Had I really caused my little Fleur such heartache, that she had spoken to my mother about her feelings towards me? I loved her dearly, but was so afraid that I may harm her. When I first realised my feelings towards her, I did not think of all that was involved in being with someone, and now, how could I make it up to her, without mentioning Annie, or she may think that I loved Annie more than her, or that I still did love Annie. Then I had to be honest with myself. Yes, I did still love Annie, and I always would, but Annie was no longer with me and as I have said, I feared that I may not have loved Annie as much as I should, or as I loved Fleur.

I did not help matters that day, for I spent the rest of it deeply within my own thoughts. Fleur did not come down to see me, as was her way, and at the meal time, we ate silently. Although I was sat in the midst of all the people who loved me most, I felt so lonely. If I felt lonely, oh my poor Fleur, how must she feel, among strangers? What could I do?

After we had eaten, I asked Fleur to come with me for a walk in the twilight. At first she seemed a little reluctant, but Mother encouraged her to join me, and told Fleur that she and Sarah would finish what needed doing. We descended the ladder and walked outside, and although quite early, the sky was displaying a full bright moon, with spangled stars adding to the spectacle. As we got outside, I wrapped my arms around Fleur, lifting her off her feet, and kissing her.

"Fleur, please don't ever doubt my love for you, I could not possibly have found anyone, anywhere, to compare with you, but I have demons from my past that I must fight, and until I can conquer them, I ask for your patience," I pleaded.

"Rab, ma wee lovely man, I now know of these demons, and together we can fight them. Your mother reminds me so very much of my own, that sometimes I think they are one and the same. She has explained everything, but Rab, you must let me in to your thoughts, for only then can we fight as one," said Fleur wisely, far more wisely than a young woman of her years.

"So we fight together, as we did in Carlisle, against the hovel dwellers. Fleur, I have not mentioned it before, but I was so proud of you that day, when you ran at that filth, with sword held high; I would have been feared if you had come at me like that, let alone those creatures," I said, then we both started to laugh, falling into each other's arms.

"Rab, we are good together, and we always will be," purred Fleur, as I held her to me.

Some weeks later, it now being the downside of winter and the days warming and lengthening slightly, I suggested to Fleur that we take two horses and ride up into the high country, so that I could see how long it would be before we could place the sheep up there for the summer grazing. Mother prepared some food of salted meat and bread she had baked, which we placed into the saddle bags on Flame, and we rode away, mid-morning.

The sun was high as we set off, and the early spring warmth came through. The ground gave off a smell of freshness that only comes with the early spring sun, and Flame walked with head and tail held high, as if she were of royal blood, and maybe she was. Fleur beamed, as she sat straight in the saddle, she also giving the air of royal birth, but rare would it be for such beauty to grace the palaces of this land.

After a slow, steady climb, we eventually reached the top of the high grounds, those same grounds where Raymond and I had spent that summer, where Annie would come and visit, and I first realised my feelings for her. With these thoughts in my head, I felt uncomfortable being here with Fleur. Was I right to bring her here, was it fair on Fleur; was it fair on Annie's memory?

I was brought out of my thoughts by Fleur as she exclaimed, "Rab," as she heeled her nag forward. I quickly spurred Flame onward, to keep beside Fleur, not knowing why she galloped on. We were approaching a beautifully calm mountain tarn, which reflected the surrounding lands in its dark blue depths. "Can you swim, Rab?" said Fleur, excitedly.

"Aye, but not well," I replied.

"Oh come on, Rab, let's away in, it looks beautiful," she said, almost cooing.

"But it will be freezing," I protested.

"Away with you, you wee girl, get yerself in and stop yer weeping," she said as she slipped from her nag, "Get me out of this," as she pointed to the laces at the back of her dress. I dropped from my saddle and walked over to Fleur, and started to undo the laces at her back. I had scarcely undone the knot, when she pulled at the shoulders of her dress, and it fell to the ground, revealing her beautiful milky form, which glistened in the afternoon sun.

Her attire at her ankles, she broke free, like a wild animal released from a cage, and hurtled towards the dark cold water of the mountain tarn, then flung herself forward, breaking the calm surface with a heavy splash. As her head bobbed above the water, she started to swim with all the ease of a fish, her legs kicking out and her arms smoothly pulling through the water. After a few strokes she turned and waved at me. "Come, Rab, it is so lovely." I started to divest myself of my clothes, and as I removed my jack, my skin could instantly feel the sun fall upon it, with the cooling mountain breeze playing across my body, undoing the warming of this early spring sun. I then removed my boots, then my leather hose, rendering myself naked. I hesitantly stumbled forward, very aware of my nakedness, and feeling very vulnerable, in front of the gaze of my wife. As I placed my right foot into the water the coldness of it almost pained my body. Fleur was out in the water, with only her head showing, her shoulders being distorted by the rippling water, the rest of her held secret by the darkness of the depths. By the time I had waded out to just below my waist, the pains running through my body were almost unbearable, then I just threw myself forward into the dark water, the shock of it taking the very breath from my body. My mind flashed back to the first day at the manse, when Father Francis had me placed in that barrel of freezing water. Brother Matthias told me some time after, that the Cistercian monks were not given to bathing of any description, and this therefore was the ultimate punishment. My mind was quickly brought back to the present day, as I reached Fleur and she placed her arms around my neck. I so wanted to feel her body next to mine, but the cold of the water and of our bodies denied me.

The early discomfort gave way to a tingling that became quite pleasurable, as we both frolicked in the water. But then the cold started to affect us both, so we made our way to the edge. As we left the water, I went over to Flame, who was enjoying the mountain grass. I pulled the heavy sheepskin that I always carried to protect me from the elements, then walked back to Fleur, who was stood, the cold of the water causing her to shiver uncontrollably. I wrapped the sheepskin over her shoulders, my arms wrapping about her neck as I did so, as we both sat down, huddled together for warmth. We soon started to feel the benefit of the sheepskin, as I could feel the warmth from her body against mine, and she started to shiver less. "Oh, Rab, that was wonderful. Rab, kiss me."

With my arm already about her neck, I pulled her to me, my other hand inside the sheepskin. As we started to kiss, I raised this hand, and soon could feel the firmness of her breast under my hand. As she felt my rough hand about her, I could feel her shudder. I broke off. "Did I hurt you?" I asked.

"Oh no, Rab, no, kiss me," she gasped. I now wanted her like I had never wanted anything in my life. I gently pushed her to the ground, as we continued kissing, my hands now feverishly about her body, wanting to discover all there was, our breaths shortening as we both so desperately wanted each other. We became one, holding each other tightly, our kissing becoming a fight between our mouths as our senses heightened. Then Fleur gave out a scream of absolute pleasure, as I felt my body reach a place I had not been before, at least not like this. We soon collapsed into each other's arms, breathless, but so very, very happy.

After a short while I asked Fleur if she was hungry. "Rab, if I did not have to ride it home, I could eat my nag, where it stands." We both laughed as I slid from the sheepskin, tiptoeing over to Flame to retrieve the food bag. We huddled together with our naked bodies touching and eagerly ate our bread and meat. We did not often have bread freshly baked, so this was a rare treat, and after our exertions both in the water and out, rarely had anything tasted so wonderful.

After eating we sat a while, occasionally kissing, our hands searching each other's bodies as we did so. We neither of us wanted the moment to end, but on the far fells I could see some dark clouds starting to appear, so told Fleur we must get ready and go. I helped Fleur into her dress, tying up the laces at the back for her, then readied myself, my attire never warming my body as much as it did now. Once fully clothed and my sword about my waist, I no longer felt the vulnerability, as I did when first unclothed. I helped Fleur back into the saddle, slipped into mine, then trotted away from our mountain idyll. We talked excitedly as we rode home, I do not know why, or of what we talked, but life just appeared so good. As we arrived back, Mother was already taking the cattle into the bastle, and as she saw us she stopped and watched as we neared. Fleur was the first to get from the saddle, and I saw Mother run to her, and place her arms about her neck, kissing her on the cheek, then still with her arm about Fleur's shoulder, take her inside. I heard Mother say to her, "Oh my darling, I am so happy for you."

I sat for a moment, astride of Flame. I was totally amazed; how did she know what had took place? Fleur had not said anything. What powers did this woman, who I knew as my mother, have that she could tell such a thing, or was this just something that women can do, that men are not privy to? I dropped down from the saddle and took care of the nags, before ascending the ladder and sitting down for my meal. Every time I caught Fleur's eye, she would give a winsome smile, then coyly look away. After we had fed, Mother came around the side of the table where I sat and playfully messed my hair, then carried on picking up the dishes.

As the early spring gave way to summer and the days became longer and warmer, it became clear that Fleur was with child, a situation I was uncomfortable with, but she was quite unperturbed by the situation, and continued to do all that she had done before. I had not thought it practical to inform Fleur's family myself, but had asked James, my uncle, to seek out either Will Armstrong or some of his kin, when next there was a Truce Day, which he had undertook, and according to James, Will had been greatly pleased with the news.

The summer had not been kind to our valley and had rained for much of the time, making getting in the winter fodder very difficult, and the ground had yielded much less than we needed. We would have to travel across the border over the autumn and winter months, with carts, and hope that the Scots had had a better harvest.

The first early frosts had settled on the ground when Fleur started with child. I was cast from the bastle when the pains started. I sat outside, my stomach turning with the anxiety; in fact I did retch, bringing back the contents of my stomach. I was not given to such weakness of body, and the vile acrid aftertaste within my mouth cast my mind back to when Will had taken me, all those years ago, and slung me over his horse, which had resulted in me losing the contents of my stomach then; the taste was the same.

I was grateful for that brief moment's release from the reality of what was taking place. The even greater worry was that, unlike before, with Annie, I could not hear anything sat out here, as I was. I seemed to be outside forever, the day not being particularly cold, but the anxiety and the lack of movement caused the cold to start attacking my body. Did I hear someone shout my name? I jumped up, ran into the bastle, and looked up the ladder, to where Mother stood. "Well, you silly lad, do you not wish to see your wife and son?" she gushed.

I scrabbled up the ladder, slipping in my rush to get up. When reaching the top, I tripped, stumbling forward, like some drunken fool, then I turned to face the bed, where Fleur lay, her hair wet and face shining with sweat, but smiling through tired eyes, and across her chest, a bundle, which I took to be my son. I stepped to the bed, peering into the top of the bundle, to see this little pink, squashed face, with dark, almost black hair, and the tiniest of mouths. But he was mine, and he was beautiful. I always thought that the love I had for my Fleur could not be surpassed, but at that moment, the feelings I had for her reached new heights. I leaned forward and kissed her on the forehead, then gasped, through misty eyes, "Are you all right, my darling, I have been sick with worry?" Before she could answer, Mother interrupted, saying, "Well, this poor girl has not been having such an easy time in here, you nincompoop," taking the opportunity to give me a slap at the back of the head, then smiling, she said, "This young lady of yours, Rob Milburn, is the bravest person I think I have ever seen in my life. Not a murmur came from her, all the while through the birth, and your son is as strong as a full grown man. You should be proud of them both."

I just kept looking at Fleur, then the baby. I was in complete wonderment, and not knowing what next to say, but I could feel myself smiling, unable to stop, or wanting to.

Fleur yawned, tired from her efforts, and Mother, seeing this, walked over and took the baby from her, saying, "You have a sleep, we will look after your son, worry not child," then turned and handed the baby to Sarah, who had been stood at the foot of the bed all the while. I started to stand up. I did not want Sarah to hold the baby. I knew what had taken place the last time she held a child. I loved my sister dearly, but did not want her to hold my son.

I stood there, not knowing what to do. How could Mother have been so stupid? Sarah gathered up the baby in her arms, then stooping her head forward over the baby, she smiled. Oh my goodness, Sarah smiled. Then she said, "You are the most beautiful one ever, my lovely boy." She spoke, she actually spoke. My eyes were glued to her. I still wanted to snatch my baby back, then I saw a miracle take place before my very eyes. May I be struck down if I do not tell the truth, I saw the mist lift from her eyes, I did, I honestly did. Sarah was whole again, she was smiling, she was talking, she was, most importantly, feeling again.

I stood beside the bed, looking at Sarah, then looking over towards Mother, but she was looking away from me. I did not want to shout out, but I wanted her to look at me, so that I may signal to her and let her know what had taken place. I wanted to embrace Sarah, because I had my sister back, but I could not; I was half-standing, half-sitting, my mouth was moving, but nothing came from within. Please, someone, please look at me. Fleur had fallen asleep, I wanted to tell the world, but fate played its hand.

"Mother, Fleur is asleep, do you want me to lay the child down, or may I keep hold of him?" Sarah said.

"You sit by Fleur and watch both her and the child," replied Mother, as if nothing had changed.

I left the bedside and almost ran over to Mother, taking her by the arm and turning her around. "Mother, can you not see what has happened? Sarah!" I exclaimed.

"Yes, my dear boy, she is back, I now have my family back, plus Fleur and your baby; I could not be happier. I am sure your father will be pleased also," Mother replied.

Father, throughout all that had taken place that day, had slept all the while, which was his way now. There was little of the day that he was aware of, and as each day passed, more and more was taken up in sleep. Mother had said that she was much relieved that Father was like this, as when he slept, he was without pain. In all the years since Father had been struck by that axe, I have never come across another man who carried an axe.

Such a weapon was not common among borderers, either Scots or English, so it had always been a disappointment that I never encountered the fellow, especially when I looked at Father, stricken, and now confined to his bed. I had often thought, as I lay in my bed, or on those lonely cold nights riding back after a visit to Scotland, how I would deal with such a fellow, if perchance our paths should cross. If it was meant to be, then I shall have my day.

Later that day, Fleur, having had a restful sleep, woke to see Sarah by her side, holding the baby, and smiling. The sight took her quite by surprise. She quickly sat up as Sarah handed her the baby. "He is beautiful, and we are now the best of friends. My dear, love him always, he is a treasure to behold," said Sarah.

Fleur, unlike the rest of us within the bastle, spoke out, "Sarah you are speaking, you are well," with more than a little surprise.

"Yes, my dear, and able to help you even more than before, especially with the baby, and that oaf of a brother of mine," said Sarah, quite matter of factly. I stood up, went over to the other side of the bed, turned Sarah around and said, "Come here, you," and embraced her, as I had wished to do for all those years. I could feel her wrapping her arms about me and holding me, as I wanted, then she pulled away, mockingly striking me, and saying, "Get away you great oaf," then turned and beamed at Fleur, then walked away and started to help Mother.

I sat back down, beside the bed, and reached over to hold Fleur's hand. "Thank you," was all I could say.

"It appears we have two births, or one birth and one rebirth," whispered Fleur. I nodded in agreement, then she asked me to tell all that had taken place, which I gladly undertook, as we sat with heads together, whispering.

Chapter 21

Family Loyalties

Alas, after a lifetime of battles, my father lost his last, that of life, and succumbed to the inevitable in the night, just eight weeks after my son was born. I am much pleased that we chose to name my son Thomas William, after both his brave grandfathers. Both Fleur and I had hoped to travel to Scotland as soon as the weather permitted, to let Fleur's mother and father see their grandchild, and perhaps call and see Father Matthias, to accept the child into the church, which would greatly please Fleur's mother. Such ideas must now wait, for there was the burial of a family Heedsman, and there was much to be attended to.

My Uncle James arrived in the morning, and went to send out riders to all our kin, both Milburn and Charlton. The news travelled faster than I could imagine, as my Uncle Arthur arrived by mid-afternoon, having been told of his brother's demise. He was very helpful and offered all manner of assistance, then as we sat down to take food, which none of us had a wish for, Arthur stunned me, and I think Fleur, by telling me that the next Heedsman of the Milburns was me. I protested at the suggestion, saying, "But surely, Uncle, you are the eldest left in the family, the honour should fall to you." Uncle Arthur replied, "No, Rob, it was your father's wish and mine that you should take over from him, and by the way, I am not the eldest, there are others, others who will crawl from under their stones, when they

316

hear Thomas has died. Rob, there is every possibility that the day we bury your father, there will be others of our own who will join him. Make sure it is not you. I will stand beside you throughout."

At such a statement I was taken aback. Was it not bad enough that my father had scarcely breathed his last, that I find I have unknown kin, and kin who possess that worst trait of man, or it appeared so, from what I was told?

By the end of the day it was decided that we would hold the burial the day after the morrow, giving all that want to be there time to travel. I asked Arthur to stay for at least the burial, and longer, if need be, and he agreed, but first he lay one stipulation down.

"Rob, as Heedsman, you must no longer call me uncle, nor any other member of this family by other than their name; that will include any Charlton. Is that not so, Marie?" he said as he looked to Mother.

"Yes, Son, it is so. You have always showed respect to your kin, but now it is their turn to respect you. When your father first became Heedsman he had much discourse to attend to, and this caused some of our kin to leave the immediate family. They are the ones that Arthur refers to, as coming from beneath their stones."

I had only just had my first child; I had only just got my sister back; for the first time, I thought my family to be whole again, and now I found that I had more problems than I feared I could handle.

In all the goings on of the day, Arthur never once acknowledged Sarah. He had Fleur and my son, but Sarah he had left alone, so that when she came up behind him, placing her arm about his neck, leaning over and saying, "Come, Uncle Arthur, you must eat, you must have ridden hard to get here so quickly," Arthur was so taken aback that he flinched away in surprise, falling from his seat and landing in a crumpled mess upon the floor. This was greeted with much laughter from us all, and Arthur, still sprawled, stammered, "Bb…but she spoke, ss… she held me!" Sarah laughingly replied, "Yes, she did!"

Father was lying in the bed, a time of great sorrow, and we were but a length away from him, laughing uncontrollably. I think Father joined us in our mirth. It was from this point we were able to take food, in the knowledge that Father would not wish us to be overly saddened by his end; indeed, as Fleur pointed out, he had suffered greatly in the short time she had known him.

The next day the family started to gather. Some I had not seen before, but was assured there were yet more to come. By the end of the day the bastle was surrounded by more Milburns than I ever thought possible, and yet there were more still to come. I had never seen such a gathering, although Father had said he could put seventy Milburns in the saddle, if needs be.

Mother told me to expect as many, if not more, Charltons, who would now be camped at their family bastle, with Uncle James, and as the day dawned for the burial of my father, there were indeed as many as one thousand riders in attendance. A truly extraordinary sight to behold, and one that holds testament to a fine border fighter and Heedsman.

Father had been wrapped in cloths of various weave for his interment and we were steadily lowering his body, from the bastle, by the outside steps, which were rarely used, when I saw a finely dressed gentleman riding up the valley, nearing the bastle, along with several other riders. One, from what I could see, was a priest.

As the riders arrived, that familiar voice rang out, "Now then, Rob, sad times, sad times, I could not miss the funeral of my friend, Tom. Have you a priest, Rob?" he ended; it was Sir John Foster. How many March Wardens would attend the burial of a Heedsman; a Milburn? There is but one, Sir John.

"I don't have a priest, Sir John," I answered.

"Thought you might have a struggle in that direction, brought one along just in case, we'll see him off right, ah lad," said Sir John cheerfully. He had scarce got the words out as Mother, Fleur and Sarah emerged from within. Sir John took off his fine feathered hat and bowed deeply in the saddle, waving his hat in a broad arcing movement. "Marie, my heartfelt regards for you in your grief; you know what regard I had for Tom, nothing would keep me from today."

Mother lightly curtsied, saying, "Thank you, Sir John, your presence is always welcome, Tom would be proud you are here."

"And who have we here?" said Sir John, as he spied Fleur, who was stood at the top of the stairs, holding our son. "This is my wife, Fleur, and my son, Tom," I proudly said.

"Enchanté, Madam," said Sir John, bowing once more.

"Thank you, Sir," said Fleur, "but I'm no' French, I'm Scots," at which there were gasps from the massed Milburns and Charltons.

"My Lord young Rob, you never cease to amaze me! A Scots lass, and a dashed fine one too, if you will pardon me, Ma'am," he said, looking towards Fleur and bowing yet again.

"Enough of this, Tom awaits," said Sir John, as we placed my father in the back of the cart. It had been our intention to carry out the burial at the side of the bastle, but Sir John turning up with a priest meant we would travel to the church at Gilsland.

Mother and Fleur, along with our son, would travel by cart; Mother driving, I, along with Sarah, rode behind, followed by Sir John, Uncle Arthur and Uncle James. I could hear certain members of the Milburns voicing their disquiet at a Charlton riding in front of Milburns. I feared they diced with death, talking ill of Uncle James, and in this case, I would disgrace myself, by standing side by side with James.

James pushed his nag forward, between Sarah and me, and turned to me as we rode and said, "I fear there may be blood this day, and I wager I shall be the one causing the blood-letting, for as you know,

Rob, I hold your father in the highest regard, as I do you, now that you are Heedsman, but if I have to dispatch a Milburn this day, then I shall."

"Uncle James, me, Heedsman, you jest," I said incredulously.

"I do not, and where do you stand, if there is blood to be let?" said James.

"By those who would stand by me, James, of that there is no question," I replied.

"A worthy Heedsman, Rob, worthy. Aye, I may be old but my hearing is as sharp as ever, and my sword hand as strong," I heard Sir John utter from behind, in low hushed tones. I thought I was going to bury my father; now, it would appear, that I was going into battle against my own kinsmen. It would have been a grand day but for Mother, Fleur and Sarah there.

We soon arrived at Gilsland, and it would appear the local people had been forewarned, for around the little church was gathered a rich assembly. Although these people were well used to goodly numbers of riders passing by, be they English, Scots or Queensmen, I could tell that they were much impressed by the number that now rode in. A fair distance before the church I pulled up, and dismounted, all the other riders doing likewise, Mother and Fleur carrying on in the cart, until they reached the gate of the church. The priest trotted forward, looking much relieved of being free of our company, and reaching Mother and Fleur, got from his horse, in an ungainly fashion, leaving the nag to wander off, and held his hands up to assist first Mother, then Fleur, from the cart. Once we were all dismounted, one man given the task of horse minder, we all walked forward, and reaching the cart, James and Arthur asked me and Sarah to stand aside, as they leaned into the cart and drew the body out. Then each taking a side, they carried Father to his final resting place. A grave was already dug. I turned and asked, "Who arranged this?" to be met by a beaming smile from Sir John.

The interment went well and some good words were said over his grave. It would appear that the good priest had been well coached in the life of my father, for he spoke of things to which I did not have knowledge. I did not have to think who was responsible for that; Sir John's seal was firmly stamped upon it.

As we all withdrew from the grounds of the church I saw Arthur guiding Fleur and Mother away from the rest of us. This I took to mean that trouble was about to befall the day. Sarah, who had stayed by my side throughout, had noticed what was afoot, and discreetly reached across me and took the bollock knife from my belt, then slipped her hand back inside her cape, concealing it from all eyes. I was not happy that she was there, but she looked up at me and gave a knowing smile. I could not say anything, or it would alert all those who would cause trouble and place Sarah in danger.

Halfway between the church and the horses, a group of people rounded from the right, fronted by a large unkempt creature, with sword in hand. "Greetings Robert," he said. "I am your Uncle Joseph. I think maybe you have little knowledge of me, that was your Father's doing, but now I am Heedsman, we shall get to know each other, after you have paid homage to me."

"Dearest Uncle Joseph, alas we are not better acquainted, and it would appear we never shall be," I replied, while taking a step back, drawing both swords. Sarah stepped back and away from my side, then I caught her, out the corner of my eye, sidle over to the side of the oncoming group. As she got alongside of the group one of the men started to draw his sword.

Sarah, in a flash, had the bollock knife to his throat, and I heard her say, "That would be a mistake." The would-be swordsman laughed, that a woman should hold a knife to his throat, and continued to draw his sword. It was a mistake, for she sliced the knife hard into his neck; the blood spurted forth, and he was beset with the greatest look of both surprise and shock, then fell to his knees. His head dropped forward, and the blood poured. Sarah stepped back, the bollock knife held out threateningly. Joseph's attention was diverted for an instant, at what was taking place at his side, which gave me the opportunity to slip my sword under his, taking his blade under my hilt, then heaving up, wrenching the weapon from his hand, and sending it hurtling through the air. Stepping forward with the smaller sword in my left hand, I thrust it hard into a fleshy stomach, twisting it ever so slightly, thus giving maximum killing effect, then withdrew the blade as swiftly as it entered.

Joseph fell forward, his head landing at my feet, but my lunge had not been as effective as I had hoped, for Joseph squirmed as he lay face down on the ground. A well placed foot on top of the head would shorten his agonies, and while doing so, I raised the blooded sword, and called out, "Who would doubt me as Heedsman now?" to which there was no reply. I spoke again. "I never thought I would ever have to raise my sword to a kinsman of mine, and may I never do so again. Milburns, I pledge you my loyalty, for which I ask but one thing; your loyalty to me. If there is any among you who cannot pledge me this, on this solemn day, then stand forward."

Not a soul moved, then one of the assembled raised his sword, saying, "I so pledge," which was followed by a chorus of the same. After the enthusiastic cheering subsided, I asked, "Who is close kin to these two?" pointing to the two bodies that were on the ground, Sarah's victim still in a kneeling position.

"They are mine," spoke a young lad.

"What are they to you, lad?" I asked.

"Father and brother," came his short answer. I placed both my swords in their scabbards, then stepped forward, taking hold of the lad with one arm about his neck and pulled him to me, and while embracing him, spoke into his ear, "I share your grief; today we have both lost our fathers."

"There is little loss, Sir, for they both would beat me, when fancy took. I am better rid of them both, and when you next ride, I would be greatly honoured to be at your side. I have a mother and sister at home who will need looking after; therefore, any plunder from the Scotties would be of great benefit," said the lad. I was thankful that Fleur was out of earshot, for such talk created much discomfort.

"Your name, lad?" I enquired.

"Daniel, Daniel Milburn, Sir," said the lad.

"Well, Daniel, I had a dear friend many years past by the name of Daniel; let us hope that you prove as loyal," I said.

"I shall, Sir," said Daniel, with great enthusiasm.

"The name is Rob, not Sir," I said with a smile, as I patted him on the shoulder, then turned, taking hold of Sarah's arm, and led her away from the throng.

"Sarah, what were you thinking, taking on that oaf? I have only just got you back, then to lose you so soon does not bear thinking about," I said angrily.

"Rob Milburn, why is it whenever we are together we always end up killing someone?" she said mockingly, then started to stifle a laugh. I also started to laugh at the entire ridiculousness of the day.

We then walked back to join the rest of the people who were still stood around. The lad, Daniel, along with others that had travelled with him, had removed his father and brother. Mother and Fleur had been in conversation with Sir John and the priest, and had seen little of what had taken place, so that when we reached them, Mother enquired, "Has there been any trouble?" to which I replied, "Merely a small disagreement, but all is well."

As Mother and Fleur got up into the cart, I was aware of someone stood behind me, and turned. It was Michael, Mary and Raymond

Dodds. Michael spoke first. "Rob, we are sorry for your loss." I did not speak, but wrapped my arms about him and embraced him, then Mary, and finally Raymond.

Mary then spoke. "I believe you have a wife and child, Rob, we are so very happy for you, it has been an age since we last saw you," she said.

I felt myself redden as I stumbled for words. "Aye, I have been caught up in so very much, time has passed so quickly," which seemed so inadequate an answer for ignoring people who had meant so much for so long, but after what happened to Annie, then meeting and marrying Fleur, I felt embarrassed in front of the Dodds. I now knew that they were true friends, whose friendship went beyond whatever life may place ahead of us all.

"Please, come with me as I introduce my wife and son," I said, as I guided them to the front of the cart, where Mother and the Dodds firstly renewed their acquaintance, then I introduced Fleur and Thomas. As I did so, Fleur handed Thomas to Mother, jumped down, then taking Mary's hand did a small curtsey, then likewise to Michael and Raymond. She then turned to Mother and stretched her arms out for Thomas, then let the Dodds see our child. I could see that Mary and Michael were much impressed with Fleur, which did much to ease my discomfort.

There was much chatter between us as we all readied for the journey home, the Dodds being much surprised at the change in Sarah. I took it that as they did not mention Sarah's quite decisive part in the little trouble we had encountered, they also had not seen what took place.

When we parted later, with happy smiles and much waving from all, it being more like a wedding than a funeral, Arthur rode up along with Sir John. "My, my, Rob, to say that was impressive would do you a grave injustice," said Arthur. "What was that, Uncle?" I said coyly.

"What was that, what was that?" The second time of saying Arthur stressed the point. "You and that sister of yours, strike me here if you both did not put the fear of damnation in the whole family. Damn it, lad, I would not take issue with either you or the lass, for fear of not seeing tomorrow." Then he laughed loudly.

Sir John, hearing Arthur's tale and not knowing what took place, was eager to learn more and Arthur was more than keen to tell all, while Sarah and I trotted along quietly, passing the odd silly glance to each other, like two naughty children.

A little further on we parted company with Sir John, but before he left, he asked if I had yet scribed for Carey. I told him that I had not, and that we had met, but were not on the best of terms. Sir John said he would have a word with Carey on my behalf. I said that it did not bother me greatly that I had not, as I regarded Carey as a nincompoop. Sir John said that I had the measure of the man, but times were changing, and that it would benefit me greatly, in time to come. I did not know what Sir John meant, but waved him off with grateful thanks.

When we arrived home, Arthur helped me tend the horses, as the women went up to prepare a meal. After we had seen to the nags and brought in most of the stock, we too went up, to find Sarah in some distress. Mother had spotted some blood on her sleeve, which we had not, and had questioned her about it. Sarah had not wanted to say anything without me there, so had endured Mother's continuous questioning. Rather than I telling what took place, I asked Arthur to do so on my behalf, which he was only too pleased to do.

Mother was appalled, and I think Fleur was quite taken aback also, not so much at me, though dispatching family members is not the way things should be done, but Sarah, a woman, slicing men's throats, that being the sentiments of Mother, but I think I worsened things when I said how efficiently Sarah had wielded the bollock knife.

The weather had been quite settled for some days now, so we resolved to travel to see Fleur's family, and although such a journey was perilous, Mother was quite pleased that we were going. As we set off, Mother, still dwelling on the events of weeks past, said, "Well, at least if you two are not together," indicating Sarah, "there might not be any trouble." I turned to Mother and said, "Aye, but I ride safe in the knowledge that you will be well looked after," to which Mother placed an arm about Sarah's waist and pulled her close, placing her head next to Sarah's. I shall never forget the sight of those two women smiling broadly as we rode off. How long I had yearned to see that.

The progress was slow, as we kept the horses to a walk, because Fleur was carrying the baby, which occasionally I would take to ease the strain on her arms. Fleur said that if we could make the border, it was just a short ride until we could get shelter for the night, as she knew people who had a croft, who would give us food and somewhere to sleep. We did eventually make the croft, and as we pulled our nags up outside, Fleur handed me the baby, then she slid down from the saddle, and stepped to the door, knocking on the rough wooden structure tentatively. The door slowly opened, but only a short way open. A quietly spoken Scottish voice enquired, "Aye?"

Fleur answered, "Mister Davison, it's Fleur Armstrong, can we come in?" The door slowly opened wider and a small willowy fellow stepped forward, crowned with a mop of red unkempt hair. "Who is with you, child?" he further enquired.

"My husband and son, Mister Davison," Fleur replied.

"Well, come yur sell in, lassie, come in indeed. I didnae ken yur were wed, and a son ye say, well, well, yur were but a wee thing the last time a saw ye, it does na seem like it was a' that lang."

Fleur turned to me and took the baby, then I got from my nag, tying both steeds to a single post that was stood in the ground, then stepped inside the small dwelling.

"Come ye in, young man, and let's a' get a look at the wee lassie's husband," said Davison. I stepped forward into the light of the fire, then stretched out my hand in greeting.

"Mister Davison, I am pleased to make your acquaintance, I am Rob," I said.

"English, my God, he's English; wit is the meaning o' this lassie? you would bring English inta ma hoose, an' you an Armstrong. Wit are ye thinking, lassie, wit in Heaven's name are ye thinking?" said Davison incredulously.

"Mister Davison, he is a good man; he saved my life, and both Mother and Father are happy at our union. We are riding back to see them, that they may see their first grandchild, but our progress has been slow, due to young Thomas. We can only ride at walking pace. If it offends you to have my husband in your house, we will ride on, through the dark," said Fleur, in such a manner that I thought maybe Davison had spoken out of turn to a better, and she was reasserting her superiority over him. It seemed to have the desired effect. Davison lowered his head, saying, "No lassie, al no' have it said that a turned away an Armstrong, especially Will's lassie, and her wee'un." I assumed that by his omission of my name, he did not include me.

As Davison finished speaking, a small, generously built, woman stepped from the gloom, into the light. "Come, child, step to the fire, an' let me see yer wee'un." Fleur walked forward towards the fire and the woman stepped to meet her, placing her arms forward to take Thomas. "Oh he's a fine wee man, an' ye call him Thomas; aye, well it's nay very Scots, but it's a fine name a' the same," the woman cooed, if somewhat derisively.

I turned to Davison. "Sir, is there anywhere more secure to tether our nags for the night?" I asked.

"Well the' should be fine just there, for if there were any English raiders oot tonight, 'am sure yid know aboot it," he said.

"Please, Mister Davison," said Fleur. The woman holding Thomas turned to Davison, saying, "Aye, get yur sell' oot and help tether the nags and dinnae be sa rude to our guests."

As we stepped outside the night sky had taken over, and we both peered into the darkness, accustoming our eyes to the lack of light. The nags seemed strangely uneasy as we led them to the rear of the small croft, to where there was a high stone wall compound, already inhabited by some cattle and sheep. We got the nags into the compound, and I immediately started to unsaddle Flame, Davison taking care of Fleur's nag, with not a word passing our lips as we went about our chores. I started to feel some unease, as had the horses. I could not gather what caused this discomfort; was it passed on by the nags, or was I just being silly? I then became aware of noise, what was that noise? Yes, I did believe it was of riders, but was not totally sure. I stopped what I was doing, and went over to where Davison was, gently taking hold of his shoulder, and as he turned, I raised my finger to my lips, signalling him to stay quiet, which I quickly realised was quite foolish, as not a word had been exchanged since coming outside.

I drew both my swords, and exited the compound. I thought Davison was behind me, closing the compound off, but I was more intent on what was in front of me. Keeping myself crouched over I quickly rounded the side of the croft, stopping at the corner to peer around. There was a horse by the front of the building, and I could see the silhouette of a man at the door, with sword drawn. I started to creep forward, to take him by surprise, but as I did so, I saw two other riders approaching. I darted back into cover. My heart was now racing. I wanted to get to this man before he got to the women and my child, but if I broke cover now, the others would surely have the better of me. I must wait and take the two who approached. I heard a scream from within. I stepped forward, then waited; I must wait, I wanted to kill, I had never wanted to kill like I did now; I wanted that creature who was causing my Fleur such anguish.

The two riders were now there; one a short distance behind the other. One dropped from his horse, and as he did so, still crouched, I sidled along the side of the croft, and as he came from behind his horse, drawing his sword, I lifted my small sword that was in my left hand and skilfully pushed it deep into his gut. Whether because of the surprise or my good swordsmanship, he made no sound, just fell to the floor, without a sound. As he dropped, a voice behind me said, "I'll hev the other, you get the women." I briefly stood at the door, to assess what was taking place. The swordsman was stood with his back to me, his arm about Fleur's neck, his sword held forward at the chest of the Davison woman. I slipped into the room, then ensuring no harm came to Fleur, I knelt down, while at the same time making a sweeping blow with the sword in my right hand, chopping through his leg, at the knee. He immediately released his grip of Fleur, and fell to the ground, screaming with the sheer pain of losing a limb. As he fell, I was immediately aware of someone behind me. I turned quickly, with both swords at the ready. Stood in the door was a rider, with sword held high, about to bring it down on me. Then the sword dropped as he, like his fellow rider, yelled out. I saw two wooden prongs start to protrude through his jack. As he fell to his knees, I saw Davison holding the handle of the pitchfork, which he had thrust into the rider's back. His screaming was short lived, as the fork did a clean job of dispatching this would-be raider. The other, with the chopped off leg, however, continued to make the most awful noises. I turned to the women and asked, "Is everyone safe and without injury?" to which the Davison woman replied, "Aye, thank God, and thanks to you." Fleur then turned and said, "Rab, will ye stop that creature making all that noise." I stood over him and brought my sword up to his throat. Through his extreme pain, he realised the inevitability of the situation, and the terror took over from the pain. He stopped his moaning and tensed his body, lifting his head from the ground. He said, "You're English," incredulously.

"Aye, is not life strange?" I answered, then slowly pressed home the blade, then all was silent.

Davison then stepped into the room, his arms outstretched, taking hold of me, embracing me, jumping up and down shouting, "We've seen them off, Maggie, we've seen them off." He suddenly broke loose of me, taking a step back, I think realising he was embracing an Englishman. He then looked straight at me and said, "They were English, were they not?" to which I replied nothing more than "Aye." Davison then said, "And you would kill an Englishman to save us?" to which I replied again, "Aye."

"Ach! Yur a fine man, an' am proud to ken you," he said, stretching out his hand and taking mine. I then answered by saying, "And I am proud to know you, for anyone who can handle a pitchfork like that is deserving of honour," to which we all laughed heartily, I think more with relief than the humour of what was said. As is the nature of babies, Thomas slept soundly throughout the entire incident, and at no time was he in danger, as the raider did not see him lying asleep in the corner of the room. Before anything else was done, I suggested to Davison that he get the raiders' nags out of sight and unsaddled, and that he hide all the horses' tack, while I dragged the bodies around to the back of the croft, where Davison said he would bury them at first light.

Thereafter, the atmosphere within the Davison croft lightened considerably, and we were soon sat down together, enjoying a meal, and all talking easily to each other. I did not wish to ponder on the three raiders, but it did occur to me that they may not be alone. Yes, there were occasions when the odd two or three riders might stray over the border and pick on a nice easy target, just for a night's fun, but equally, they may have been part of a much larger group, who may soon start to miss their fellows, and start to search for them. I slept little that night, but thankfully, Fleur and the baby slept well, readying them well for the ride ahead.

The next morning, we were fed a huge bowl of steaming oats, which was laced with honey and whisky. This, Fleur told me, was a great honour, bestowed on few, and that I must thank our hosts for the honour, which I readily did. As I stepped outside, I was greeted by the morning chill in my face, but my body was immune from such, after such a warming meal. Davison accompanied me, and as I set about harnessing the nags, he occupied himself with the digging of a large grave for our night visitors.

As I led the nags from the compound, Davison stood up from his labours and asked, "Dee ye ken any o' them, Rab?" I looked at the three bodies lying side by side, their pallor now somewhat grey. "No, not from my neck of the woods," I replied, when in actual fact, one, that is the one whose leg I cut from under him, was known to me and went by the name of Routledge, and had ridden with me on more than one occasion. I must have been so taken up with the fight that when I ran him through, to bring an end to his screaming, I had not recognised him, but I now know why he looked so surprised when he saw me and said, "You're English."

We were soon ready to commence our journey, and Davison broke from his digging to come and stand by his wife, as we rode off. Again the ride was slow, and we met few on our way. When we did meet anyone, I would signal that I was unable to speak, and left all the talking to Fleur, which had been her suggestion in the first place. Alas, all those years past, when I had left the manse, when Father had rescued me, and he told me to learn to speak with an English accent, and here I was now, too English to speak to the Scots.

It was early evening when we arrived, and were greeted with much enthusiasm and tears, at least from Mary Armstrong. I have never known a woman coo as much as she did at the baby. Will was very gracious and seemed genuinely pleased to see me. Fleur had fed the baby as we rode along, quite soon before we first took sight of the pele tower, so he was now deep in sleep, I think much to the dismay of his doting grandmother, who wanted Thomas to see his Scottish grandmother.

When we all sat down to eat, I first of all told Will and Mary of my father's death, for which they both offered their sympathies, then Will asked, "And who will be the new Heedsman then?" to which Fleur enthusiastically interrupted, "Rab, aye, 'am an English Heedsman's wife," which was greeted with more than a little dismay. I then brought up the subject of Thomas being baptised into the church and suggested we go to Melrose when convenient and ask Father Matthias if he would carry out the service. Mary jumped up from the table, came around to me, and from the back, wrapped her arms around my neck with such strength that I scarce knew if it was with glee, or she wanted to kill me, but when she leaned over and kissed me on the cheek I was greatly relieved.

"Rab, even though a' let ma Fleur marry ye, a' still had ma reservations, you being English an' all. Well, yur an Armstrong, am glad to say."

After the meal we all sat back, and talked generally, but Fleur told of the events of the previous night, to which even Will was surprised at what had taken place and the fact that I had dispatched two Englishmen, and been complicit in the dispatch of a third.

Will now spoke. "From what you tell me, I feel I am right in including you in what I am about to say. Some two weeks ago there was a Truce Day in the West March, and as the day ended there were some Scots on the north bank of the Esk River and some English on the south bank. There were the usual banter and insults passed over the water, but then the English passed near a ford, and galloped across, taking one of the Scots, ma cousin Will, that is Will of Kinmont. He was taken to Carlisle Castle, where he is still held. In four days' time, we head for Langholm Races, where all the Border family chiefs are to meet and plan a way to get ma cousin free. Rab, I wid like you te come along, for a think yur a worthy son-in-law, and could be of use. Wid you come wi me?"

I did not know what to say. To take on some English who would kill me posed little clash of conscience, but to willingly be involved in a Scottish raid on an English castle, and a castle that had stood the very worst of sieges, did not rest easy, but this was my family, be it Scots or English, and above all else, family came before anything.

"Aye, I will, and be honoured to do so," I said, but was still not sure where my loyalties correctly lay. I would never and will never say that marrying Fleur was wrong, for never had anything been so right; however, I could not have envisaged the problems that such a union could cause.

The following day, at Mary's behest, we set off for Melrose. Will had organised a cart for the women and child, in the hope that we would make better progress; hopefully a day there, a stay overnight, and return the following day, and indeed, Will had worked out the travel arrangements very well. We arrived in Melrose by late afternoon, leaving the horse and cart at a stable quite near, and walking to the manse. Will and I kept hold of our nags, as both being riders, we neither wished to be far from our mounts.

Father Matthias greeted us all as long lost relatives, and this time we were introduced to his housekeeper, a kindly looking woman, in her thirties, but one who had endured much in her life, giving her a look of someone older.

She was introduced as Agnes Muirhead, by our host, and Mary insisted in helping Agnes in preparing the meal, but before they went to the kitchen Father Matthias asked Agnes to go on ahead as he had something very important to discuss with his visitors. I did not know what the others were expecting, but I was intrigued.

When Agnes had left us, and Father Matthias had checked she had gone, he raised his finger to his lips, then said quietly, "You must not mention the reason for your last visit, while you are here, I beg you all," he said with clasped hands. We all agreed to abide by his request, but Mary then said, "But Father, we had hoped you might receive our grandchild into the church".

"Later, my dear child, much later," said Father Matthias, again with raised finger.

A fine meal was placed in front of us, after a short time; Agnes was indeed a fine housekeeper to be able to produce such a fine repast so quickly, even with Mary's help. As we started to eat, I asked Agnes if she would join us, but she refused, quite embarrassed that she had been asked, so I then insisted she sit down and join our conversation, while we ate. I could see Father Matthias was uncomfortable at having his housekeeper detained, but I wished to have her not asking questions later about who we were or what we were doing there. I asked Agnes if she knew who I was, to which she replied she did not. I said, "And has Matthias not spoken of me, of when I was a boy I was brought here, and brought up by the Brothers, and of how he taught me my lessons?"

"Ah, you are Isaac," she said with a large smile.

"Ah, he has spoken of me, then," I said.

"Oh aye, often, very often, I think that they were happy times for you both," she said. She then stood up and started to clear away some of the dishes, but Mary stood up also and insisted that Agnes go home and leave her to finish off. Father Matthias stood and said very much the same to Agnes, so she reluctantly gathered her things and left. I went to the door with Matthias, and as she went out into the cold evening air, I said, "I hope we see you before we depart in the morning".

"I hope so too, Master Isaac," she said with a broad smile.

Father Matthias quickly closed the door, and as he drew the large bolt across, he turned with eyes of fire. "Are you mad, Isaac, are you completely mad? Have you come here to have me burnt at the stake?"

"Father Matthias, I would sooner have Agnes as a friend, or at least someone who likes me, then perhaps she may not feel the need to ask awkward questions. The very last thing any of us here wishes is to have you harmed, my dear old friend," I said as I placed a friendly arm about his shoulder, as we walked down the dark corridor to the kitchen.

As we entered, Mary turned quickly from her chores. "Are we free to talk now, Father?" she said excitedly.

"Yes, my child, but first I have business to attend to," he replied as he turned and left the kitchen. I could never remember being in the kitchen so late before, apart from when we had come to be married, but it did not occur to me then, that when the Brothers were here, we would all be in bed well before now.

Matthias suddenly appeared at the kitchen door, attired in the habit of a monk, and whereas before he carried himself in a meeker fashion, he now stood tall, with almost an arrogant air. "I will receive you one by one at the foot of the stairs for your confession, then you will go to the top of the stairs to carry out your contrition beside your bed. When you have all satisfactorily carried out your penance, and you are all clean of sin, then we may go into the chapel and receive this poor unfortunate child into the church." I saw Fleur with eyes aflame at the good Father's remark as to the poor unfortunate child. My immediate thought was that Father Matthias was possibly in danger of incurring the wrath of my dear wife, not a thing I would wish to incur, for God had not put anyone sweeter on this land, but she was capable of bringing down a fierce tongue on any who would affront her.

After our last confessional, this seemed much easier, as it had not been long since last we did this and I had not killed many since last time, and all had been those who would have killed me, so it seemed unnecessary to mention them.

We were all soon in the chapel, where Father Matthias gathered us all around a small table, in the centre of which was a small wooden bowl, half filled with water. Matthias asked to take hold of Thomas, whereupon Fleur handed him over, and Matthias started to speak in Latin. It was at this point that I realised my command of this old tongue was becoming misty.

Will and Mary would be Godparents as well as Grandparents, a position Mary greatly relished, from the glow that came from her face in the dim candlelight. The service was soon over and we all retired to the dormitory, where sleep overtook us all in a short time.

Thomas slept through the night for the first time, allowing both Fleur and me our first full night's sleep for what seemed an age. However, she did wake up with a start, jumping from her bed and checking on Thomas, as she thought that some ill had befallen him through the night, but thankfully all was well. We all rose together from our beds and went downstairs. As we entered the kitchen, I heard knocking at the door, so turned and walked back to answer it, and was met by Agnes. "Master Isaac," she exclaimed, "I thought you might have made your departure."

"Come in, dear lady," I said, with a slight bow, my gesture somewhat embarrassing Agnes, as she skipped by me. As she walked in front of me toward the kitchen, I said, "We all enjoyed your offering for our meal last night; we thought we would wait 'til you sent us off with a fine first meal of the day, if you do not mind."

"Oh, Master Isaac," Agnes cooed.

After we had all eaten, I went to ready the nags, and was soon back, by which time all were ready, and after hearty goodbyes all around, we were on our way back.

Four days had passed since arriving back from Melrose, when Will and I set forth for Langholm. Tam had appeared just before we set off, and Will charged him with the safety of the women and child. I think he would sooner have accompanied Will and me, but he knew he was better placed at the pele tower.

Having set off, we arrived at Langholm by late morning, and made our way directly to the field where the races were to take place. On our arrival I was greatly taken aback by the numbers of people there were, for it seemed there was scarce enough room for any racing, with the milling hordes. We tethered our nags to a rope stretched along some posts placed in the ground. Once secured, we walked off into the throng, nearly everyone acknowledging Will as we walked. "Ah, there's Scott of Buccleuch, come Rab," said Will.

"Will, it's good to see ye, and pray who have ye brought wi ye?" said Buccleuch.

"Ma son-in-law, Rab, meet the Keeper of Liddesdale, Scott of Buccleuch."

"Good day, Sir," I said, mustering my best manners and bowing gently.

"Will, he's English, I had heard yur lassie had wedded, an' there were rumours that he was English, but a' didnae believe it. Wit were yer thinking on, to bring the lad wi' yer?" said Buccleuch.

"Sir, I am a Milburn first, then an Armstrong, then an Englishman, and I'll have no part of anyone abusing a Truce Day, be he Scot or English, and when have I ever been in league with a March Warden, especially that popinjay Scrope? Sir, it was he who hanged my cousin, and I watched as he took the greatest of pleasures in seeing him dance at the end of a rope. I have more reason to see that Scrope humiliated than any man on this field," I said in a most forceful manner.

"Will, I think we'll mak a Scot of him yet," said Buccleuch, with a smile upon his face.

Buccleuch then took Will by the arm and started to walk away, I following meekly behind, as he explained to Will what had already been planned, which was to have two men placed within Carlisle Castle, who, when the time was right, would ensure that the postern gate at the south side of the Castle would be opened, and the Scottish riders would circle the Castle around the back, from the north, burst into the Castle and extricate Will of Kinmont. A simple plan, which did not take any work to understand, but Will asked, "And who will be put in the Castle? Will they not be discovered, being Scots?"

"It has already been asked, Will. We have two Grahams who will be inside; they are often in Carlisle, from the Debatable Lands, they will go unnoticed," said Buccleuch.

"And who can trust a Graham? They don't know whether they are Scot or English, and will turn whichever way the wind blows," I said quietly, from behind. They both turned around, Buccleuch glaring at me. "You seem to know something about the Grahams, and pray what would you suggest?" he snapped in a far less Scottish voice than he had used earlier.

"That I go without anyone ever knowing, to Carlisle Castle, and ensure the Grahams do as they are bid, and attend to them, should they not," I answered.

"And you would do that, unsung, and for a Scottish Armstrong, possibly putting your own life at risk? I think not, there must be something you want out of all this," said Buccleuch, almost dismissively.

"Have you never heard of family loyalties? I care not whether the Armstrong is English, Scottish, or anything else; my wife is an Armstrong, and as I have already said to you, firstly I am a Milburn, secondly an Armstrong. Which side of a line no one can see matters nought," I answered forcefully, disregarding the high esteem that Buccleuch was held in. I think that the way in which I spoke took him and Will aback, as there was silence for a while, then Buccleuch spoke. "I'll give you one thing, Milburn, you have passion; bless my soul, Sir, you have passion, and I do believe that we can trust you. And may God go with you, Sir." He then took hold of both my shoulders, gripped hard, then turned and walked away.

Will turned to me, with a look of almost wonderment. "Rab, a' dinnae ken how you did it, but there's scarce a man alive that can talk to Buccleuch like a' just seen there, and walk away unscathed." Then he turned and walked after Buccleuch.

I thought it best to stay back and let them continue their planning; the less I knew the better. I walked aimlessly among the throng, deep in my own thoughts, when I espied a sight I had long waited for; a man with greying hair and almost white beard, carrying an axe about his belt. Time may have discoloured his hair, but the grizzled features were so deeply etched within my mind; this was the man that had almost killed my father all those years past. Now I cared not for Will of Kinmont's plight, or that I was kin to a Scottish family, or that I was amidst a heaving mass of Scots; this man would die this day, or I would die trying to kill him, it mattered not.

I put my head down and started to head in his direction, my hand firmly about my bollock knife. It would be harsh but swift, I would sink the blade deep into his gut, not bothering to retrieve my blade, just walk on through. I started to quicken my pace. He was almost in striking distance. I tightened my grip upon the knife, as I drew the blade from my belt, then, what happened, I was being forced away. There was pressure on my shoulder and the collar of my garment tightened. Will was pushing against my shoulder, his other hand at the back of my neck, pulling. "No, Rab, no, not here, yull no' get out of the field in one piece, they'll tear ye limb fra limb."

"But, but…" was all I could say, as Will said, "Aye a' ken fine what yer about."

"But, Will," I said.

"Aye, Rab, a' saw him too, and I know that ye recognised him, but Rab, that took place years and years ago, and I ken the man, he rode with me many times, and I'll tell ye this, Rab, he came back once to find his wife and three wee'uns all slaughtered by some English raiders. Rab, he has paid dearly, and each morning when he wakes, he continues to pay. Rab, ye cannae hurt him more than he already hurts," pleaded Will.

I could not answer. Yes, I had heard what he said, but I was too enraged to do anything; I only wanted to kill that man, what took place thereafter was of no consequence, so I just walked away, towards where the horses were tethered, and sought out Flame. I stood there trying to calm myself, but unable to get the thought out of my head that the man who caused my father so much suffering was here, after all these years, and I could do nothing about it.

I was startled from my deep thoughts by a voice at my side, complimenting what a fine beast Flame was. "Aye, it's been a goodly nag," I said casually.

"Yer English," said the man, who I had not immediately noticed, but as I did, I was aware of him drawing his sword. Quickly, I drew mine. The Scot just stood there, uncertain of what to do, which gave me time to slide my blade beneath his, wrenching it from his grip. The sword whirled into the air, and as it came down, I was able to snatch it at the top of the blade, where there is no edge. Once ahold of the sword, I turned it hilt first, and held it out to my assailant.

"Did you not see me talking to Buccleuch, just a short distance from here, but a moment past? And you would draw a sword against me? Why do you want to die?" I said. The Scot stood there rigid with fear, and unable to answer. "Well, man. Take back your sword, I mean you no harm," I said, still holding out his sword. He hesitantly stepped forward, stretching out a trembling hand, and as he took hold, he hastily stepped back. At that moment, I was aware of someone nearing from my right.

"There ye are, Rab, have ye been entertaining the local people?" he said laughingly, placing a heavy hand on my shoulder, then turning me away from my assailant, then continuing, "We'll a' too be away the now, Rab, we've a lang ride."

As we mounted and reined our nags away, I raised a hand, in a friendly gesture to my would-be assailant, and surprisingly, still with sword held by hilt, he raised his hand slightly, while at the same time, giving the slightest of bows. Once clear of the field, I realised that we had travelled all this way, and I had not seen a single race, but Will rounded on me, "And wit were you doing, crossing swords with that man, can a no leave ye fur one moment, without yer wanting to kill someone? Rab, a thought yur were a nice lad, one a could trust te look after ma daughter, but yer just bloodthirsty, yer always wanting to kill someone."

"Just one moment, Will Armstrong," I interrupted forcefully. "The man at the race field came up to me and spoke first, and when I answered he shouted, 'Yer English,' or some such thing, then drew his sword. I could have had his head off in one swipe, but no, I disarmed him, then handed him his sword back. And now it is my fault. My fault! You Scots cannot see beyond your own noses. Here I am, putting my life down to save one of your cousins, and all you want to do is find fault." I still had much more I wanted to say, but Will interrupted me. "All right, all right, Rab, am sorry, goodness me, you English do go on, yer worse than a lassie." We both looked at each other, then burst out laughing. Once the mirth had subsided, Will told me all he had been told.

One week from today, they would mount a raid on Carlisle Castle. What I did not know was that at the race field were families who had been sworn enemies for generations; there were Maxwells and Johnsons, who had fought for longer than anyone could remember, there were two Kerr families who also had fought against each other for years, and many more, once sworn enemies, but now brought together, because of this. Scrope, an Englishman, or at least one of his lackeys, had succeeded in bringing families together that no Scot had managed. A mass of families would ride against Carlisle, the Grahams would see to the posten gate at the Castle, and I would ensure the Grahams were true, and watch their back. A goodly raid from the sound of things, it mattered not that it was against an English Castle.

We reached the Armstrong pele tower at early evening, where Mary and Fleur waited eagerly, with a fine repast, which we eagerly devoured, before Will told of what was to take place. Fleur, although staying silent, was not best pleased that I was getting involved with a matter I could well do without. She may be silent, but the look she gave me left me in little doubt.

The following day we took our leave of the Armstrongs. Fleur was still shedding a tear some way down the trail as we slowly made our way. We had decided to avail ourselves of the Davison hospitality that night, and reached them by late afternoon. The greeting we received put beyond doubt any misgivings we may have had about not being welcome, or outstaying our welcome. As we sat at the table, talking and eating, I thought how strange things had become, that here I was, sat with friends, enjoying their company, having spent days with my family, and they were all Scots.

A good night's sleep was had by all, even Thomas, who had now quite become accustomed to slumbering throughout the night. A full stomach of hot oats and a friendly farewell saw us back on the trail again, and reaching the bastle by late afternoon. Mother and Sarah were of good sorts, but it was so very strange not to have Father there.

The day arrived for my journey to Carlisle. The previous days had been plagued by three women all continually besetting me with either pleas not to get involved, or that they wanted to come along; certainly Fleur and Sarah separately approached me, with a request to accompany me, both displaying a wish to let blood, should the occasion arise. I feared both my wife and sister showed certain traits one should not expect from a woman.

Along the way, as my journey took me near the Dodds, I decided that I should call upon them, and tell them that I was bound for Hexham, and ask if there was any small item that I might bring back for them. I felt quite bad about using my dear friends in this way, but if questions were asked later as to my whereabouts, the Dodds could vouch for me being almost at the other side of the country. Should the Dodds ask for some small purchase, then I would easily be able to obtain whatever from Carlisle as Hexham.

As I approached the Dodds' bastle, Mary was outside, washing garments, as she was once before, many years before, and in my mind, I could see Annie, her bright golden locks glistening in the sunlight. It was seeing this that made me realise, that when I fell in love with Fleur, and then felt disloyal to Annie, questioning whether I truly loved her before she died; yes, I truly did love Annie, and always would, as I would always love Fleur, and in being so, am not disloyal to either.

As I neared Mary, she ran forward. "Rob, how lovely of you to call, are you here for the day? And where is your lovely wife and child?" I dropped from the horse and Mary embraced me, and as she did so she said, "Rob, whenever I see you, you bring a little of Annie with you." At that moment Michael and Raymond appeared from within the bastle, both coming over to greet me. We stood and chatted a while,

I told them what I had intended to say, then continued on my way, turning west to Carlisle, well out of sight of the Dodds' bastle. I then set to and galloped hard towards the city, arriving well ahead of the time I expected to get there. On my last visit, I had noticed a livery on the east side of the city, and asked to stable my nag there. I told the livery man that I had ridden gently from south of Penrith, and that my nag may be ailing, as it should not be sweating so. He told me he would attend Flame, give it a good rub down and see how the beast fared. I thanked him for his kindness, then walked into the city.

I had chosen to wear a long garment over my usual attire, so that my sword and bollock knife did not stand out, and also decided that I had no need of both my swords, so set out with but the one. Nearly all about had a sword about their person; most were purely decoration, and not of sturdy construction, with basket weave hilt, as mine, and few had a bollock knife, which is preferred by those of the riding families. The long outer garment had the added feature of a hood, which I should use as I neared the Castle.

When eventually I did reach the Castle, I noticed a certain amount of to-ing and fro-ing from the large imposing red stone structure. I did not know if this was normal or not, as I was not familiar with how the Castle was run. It was this thought that made me ponder on my wisdom at setting forth upon such a venture. Would my ignorance be the undoing of me? I then noticed a cart, heavily laden with straw, turn off the main thoroughfare and head towards the Castle entrance. It was a steady incline towards the Castle gate, and almost immediately, the horse at the head of the cart started to struggle at the strain. Quickly, I pulled over my hood, wrapped my outer garment about me, and ran up behind the cart, leaning heavily into it, pushing, giving the poor old nag extra purchase in its efforts. The wagoner was unaware of my presence at the rear of his cart. By the time we reached the entrance, with the extra warmth of the outer garment, coupled with wearing the hood, I was sweating heavier than Flame, after the hard gallop to Carlisle. The guards took little notice of me, as I still leaned heavily into the back of the cart when we passed through the Castle entrance. Once through, I took the opportunity to look about me; who was afoot and what they were about. There was the odd guard walking idly about, one with a long pikestaff. I looked up to the top of the Castle, and there I saw a number of guards, all with pikestaffs, walking back and forth, looking more alert than those on the ground. I quickly slipped to my right, where I could take up position under a stone stairwell which led to the battlements, looking all about, and trying to get the measure of this strange place. I realised after a short time that fate had played me a good hand. A guard walked close by, then ascended the stairs, and I went unnoticed. I continued to search the entire area from my vantage point for this small gate Will had told me about, the posten gate, and to see if I could discover the Grahams. I did not know who they were; would I know them if I saw them? I had not given sufficient thought as to what I was to do after Will and Buccleuch had entered; my mind was starting to wander, with thoughts of what a fool I was. It had seemed a fine gesture, to put myself forward for such an undertaking, within the safety of Langholm Races, but now, what foolishness.

What do I see, yes, that surely that is he, Will of Kinmont, for he resembled his cousin greatly, walking across the courtyard, a guard at either side. I watched intently. When they reached the side of the Castle where I was secreted, they entered a door, then disappeared. As I have mentioned, I was lacking in knowledge of this Castle, but even in ignorance, I knew that that entrance was not that of the dungeons. Surely they were not keeping Will of Kinmont in quarters above ground? I continued to scan the courtyard, my heart pumping wildly within my chest, having spotted who I was sure was the target of our endeavours. Then the cart, which had served me so well in effecting my entry to the Castle, and had continued to the far side of the Castle, started to move away as to leave. As it did so, it exposed the very thing I had been searching for; the gate, and two fellows loitering within its reaches, one either side. Surely they were our Grahams. I was greatly relieved to see them, and they looked as if they were intent on staying true to their cause.

I continued to stay secreted beneath the stairwell, observing the movement within the Castle courtyard, and this went on for a while. Surely the Scottish riders had forded the river by now; surely they were within striking distance of the Castle; but the guards had spotted nothing, for surely they would call out, from their lofty vantage point? My attention was now drawn to the posten gate. The Grahams, if indeed they were the Grahams, appeared to be moving with more purpose. They turned and faced the gate, their backs to me. They seemed to be putting great effort into what they were doing, then just in front of me, and appearing from nowhere, came a guard, who must have come down from the ramparts. He spotted the Grahams at their task, and raised his pikestaff, as if to challenge the Grahams, although some way from them. He stepped forward, and although I could not see his face, I was sure he was about to call out. I quickly broke cover, and while doing so, took firm hold of my bollock knife, removing it from my belt, and stepping forward, wrapped my left arm around the guard's neck, placing my hand over his mouth and nose. He struggled. I brought my bollock knife up and drew it deep across his throat. His struggles deepened, then stopped. I was left holding the entire weight of the guard, for life had left his now limp body. I did not have time to look to see if I had been noticed, but quickly ran backwards, still holding my victim, dragging him back under the stairwell that had served me so well until now. I placed the body down, then walked quickly towards the posten gate, when suddenly it crashed open and the Scottish riders pushed through, swords drawn, Buccleuch at their head, rushing into the courtyard. I saw Will, and he looked towards me. I gestured to him, drawing my finger across my throat, then nodded in the direction of the stairwell. Will looked beyond me, and continued to rush in. I waited at the side of the gate, until all the raiders were in, all the time wondering whether Will had seen what I signed, did he understand, and what he would do. My head was starting to fill with all manner of stupid questions, then they were all in. By the time the last raider was in, the first in were at the far side of the courtyard; they appeared to know exactly where to go. I then exited through the gate, not quite sure where I was going, but as I left there were many other riders in the saddle, waiting outside. The Grahams were in front of me. They turned to the right, along the line of riders, then they seemed to disappear. I looked at the assembled riders, one raised his sword in acknowledgement, I nodded back. I did not understand how he knew me, but then noticed that the end of the sleeves of the outer garment I wore were covered in blood. I ran down the bank, away from the Castle. I could see trees and bushes ahead. I made for them, and found myself on the banks of the River Caldew. I removed my outer garment, and hid it in the deep thicket that skirted the river. I then turned to see if I could make out what was happening around the Castle, but there appeared little difference from when I left. But wait, the horses outside waiting appeared to me agitated; something must be unsettling them, then suddenly from the small gate, appeared men, rushing, two by two, as that was all the gate would allow. As each exited, they peeled off in different directions around the waiting horses, then I saw, after about the first six out; yes, I was sure that was Will of Kinmont, or at least, the fellow I saw inside the Castle, who bore an uncanny resemblance to the Will Armstrong I knew. I waited further, still hiding within the thicket. Where was Will? Come, Will, please come. Then more were disgorged by the dark suppressive structure, then, at last, Will, carrying something, something covered by a cloth. Was it a body? I think so. He ran to his nag, and as he reached it, he handed the bundle to another rider, who was with him as they left the Castle. He mounted, then the bundle was handed back to him. Oh Will, I thought, please make it my victim, for I should not know 'til next I saw him, and I knew not when that might be. If Will had removed the poor fellow, yes, they may be a guard short at the end of the day, but it was not unusual for any soldier to suddenly decide to change sides; it happens all the time, indeed, he may very well have been the one to open the gate. Suddenly the horses turned, almost all together, and galloped away. They were gone in an instant, and all was now calm, but there did not appear to have been any fighting. The riders were in and out without challenge, it was almost unbelievable. Carlisle Castle had stood for as far back as anyone could remember, and never once in all that time had anyone ever managed to breach it, even by the most dreadful sieges. But today, a band of Scottish riders had not only breached it, but took away one of its most prized possessions, one Will Armstrong of Kinmont, and it looked as though not one was challenged. How I wished I could see that imbecile, Scrope; he would not be swaggering as he did when he hanged my cousin, Richard. I truly felt justice had been done this day.

I stayed within the thicket at the edge of the river, and worked my way along, getting as far into the city as I could. I did not wish to be seen within the city, so decided to stay the night where I was. I had no stomach for food and a river full of water should I require drink. The sun had now set, but there was still some warmth in the air. It would not be too uncomfortable to spend the night here, and on the morrow, I would be away. Strangely, sleep came quite quickly, but it was still very dark when I awoke from my slumbers. The cold of the night was now being felt; therefore I got myself up, and started to stumble through the bushes, but I was falling and stumbling as I went. I worked my way away from the river, to where there was less growth, only grass. I could feel that I must have caught my face on a branch, as

I wiped my face with the back of my hand and there was a dark smear across it, which must be blood. I struggled up the bank away from the river. I was now well within the town. There was little sign of life in the streets at this early time, so I walked out, looking for some cover, until daybreak. Slowly, I sidled through the streets and alleys until I found a shed, or was it a stable; there were a couple of nags inside. I stood at the door a moment, allowing the nags to be aware of my presence, before entering, otherwise I was likely to alarm the poor beasts, thus bringing unwelcome attention. I slipped in through the door and found a pile of hay, which provided much needed warmth and comfort. I lay myself down, and was soon engulfed by sleep yet again.

Hearing voices outside, I jumped up; it was daylight. I pressed my back into the stable wall, trying to peer out. The voices disappeared. I edged to the door; the alley was clear. I slipped out of the door, then walked casually along, towards the wider street beyond. Once in the street, I found just the odd person stirring. I looked around, trying to assess where I was, and how to find the livery where I left Flame. I continued to walk, hopefully in the right direction. I looked up, and I could see the towering roof of the cathedral, which gave me the bearing I required, and was soon heading for the livery.

I arrived to find the friendly fellow I had left Flame with the previous day.

"Good day, Sir, and how is my nag this fine morning? I hope the fever has passed," I enquired.

"Aye, Sir, 'twas the first thing I checked on, on my arrival this morning, and your horse fares better than you, Sir," came back the reply.

As I neared him, he continued to speak. "Looks like you have been in the wars, young man," he said. Remembering the scratch that I sustained in the thicket, I replied, with a broad smile, "Aye, her husband came back unexpectedly, he wasn't due back 'til tomorrow."

The livery man laughed. "You rascal, I hope you have learnt your lesson, young Sir."

Still maintaining my broad smile, I replied, "I have indeed, Sir; never assume that a man who is getting on in years, and who has a young wife, is no good at handling a sword," to which my new-found friend launched into loud laughter.

"I'll tell you what, young Sir; you have given me such a fine start to my day, I've a mind not to charge you," he said, between laughing.

"And I, Sir, if you have tended my horse so well, and rid her of her malady, have a mind to give you double," I replied, and did not think it terribly funny; however, the liveryman laughed even louder. Once settled, he led me to where Flame was stabled, and I had rarely seen the animal look so well, and commented so.

"Aye, I rubbed her down well, after you left, then cooled her slowly with cold damp cloths, and when I had her cool, rubbed her dry, then brushed her. That is a fine beast you have there, it must have cost a fine purse," he said.

"Aye, it did not come cheap," I replied.

After more cheery banter, we parted company, I paying him much more than he asked, for all his hard work on my behalf. As I left, I promised that I would take the journey back to Penrith slowly, so as not to bring about the sweats again, the livery man replying that that would indeed be wise. I urged Flame on slowly, and we walked along the road down through the long main street, that would take me past the place where I had watched Richard hanged, a scene I did not relish seeing again. Not far beyond this point the buildings stopped and the open country stretched before me, and the stench lay behind. Once out of sight of Carlisle, I turned hard to the east, and spurred Flame on, into a gallop, as we headed home. As we galloped, I could feel every sinew within Flame's body, enjoying every stride she took. Rarely had there been an animal with such a love of life, and a thrill at taking the ground at a full gallop. It was a thrill to be upon such a beast.

We arrived back home by mid-afternoon, it having been very early when I had set off. We were greeted by both Fleur and Sarah, both being greatly excited and relieved at our return. On reaching the bastle, I jumped from Flame and embraced Fleur, Sarah taking hold of Flame, and leading her inside. Fleur and I followed on behind, and as we got inside, Sarah started to take the saddle off, and said she would wipe her down and feed her, while Fleur and I went up. I leaned forward and kissed Sarah on the forehead, which was repaid with a smile. How nice it was, after all these years, to return home, to such a greeting and get a response. Yes, this day I was a happy man.

Chapter 22

The Promise

S even years had now passed since I rode home after the freeing of Will Armstrong of Kinmont, and alas, all was not well. Shortly after my return, Mother gathered us all together, and announced that she would return to the Charlton bastle, to live with her brother and his family, leaving us young ones, as she termed it, to get on with our lives. Fleur and Sarah were inseparable; never have I known two people so close, and I am pleased to announce that we now had a younger sister for Thomas, who, by Fleur's own lips, was called Annie, in honour of the Annie I lost, before meeting Fleur. Was there ever a woman as generous of heart as my Fleur? I doubted it.

My wife and sister, in quieter moments, will spend time together in swordplay. Soon after my return from Carlisle, both Sarah and Fleur had me go to Hexham, and secure another small sword, so they could both be similarly equipped. I had to admit, having watched them over the past couple of years, they were really very proficient in their swordplay, and would present formidable opposition to any would-be attacker.

The Scottish king, James, over these past years had persecuted the border families, in the hope of currying favour with the English crown, and as a result, many families had either been hanged from the nearest tree, put to the sword, or rounded up like cattle, marched to the coast, and placed on a vessel bound for Ireland. Fleur's mother and father, Mary and Will, suffered the third fate, and were deported, to an unknown life in Ireland. This, naturally, caused great distress within our family, and we were now seeing an upsurge in activity from Master Carey. That very month, news had reached us that a family of Bells, I believed it to be the family of old Cuthbert's brother, nine in total, were taken from their home and every one hanged. No legal process took part in this incident, just pure mass murder, and all in the name of the crown. Even for a Bell, this was unjust. Yes, I could slay nine Bells in a day, but that would be more acceptable, as we had been feuding with that family for generations, and even they would prefer it were me than the Crown.

Old Queen Bess departed this life, and the Scottish King crossed the border, taking over the English throne. It appeared that he may be wishing to carry on as he did in Scotland, and persecute the English border families. What this pipsqueak Scot failed to remember was that it was both he and the English throne that delighted in the raiding that took place across the border; indeed, they both encouraged it, but now it did not suit our newly pious monarch, so he will have it swept away.

I received a letter from my cousin, Margaret, who lived at Grebe Hall, in Underbarrow, a small village near Kendal, in the heart of wool country. Margaret married well, into a good farming family, who were very successful, but alas, her husband died, and she feared she may no longer be able to continue. Her husband had engaged the services of an entire family, as both farm and house servants, and it now appeared that they were trying to assume the right of ownership of the farm. She wrote to me as Heedsman, asking what steps would it be possible for me to take in this instance. This I felt may be our salvation, from the imminent threat that surrounded us all. After spending much of the day considering our situation, and the dilemma Margaret found herself in, I spoke to Fleur and Sarah of the contents of the letter, and said that I felt we should leave this area, and travel to Margaret, at Underbarrow, relieve her of the scourge that she was beset with, and that we should help her run the farm, and at the same time put some distance between us and the border. As Fleur's family were no longer a consideration, she willingly agreed, mainly for the safety of our children. Sarah, on the other hand, agreed, but only because she thought there might be the possibility of a good fight when we got there. I did wonder about my sister; did all those years of blankness take their toll on her, making her so bloodthirsty? Or did I never really know her, and it was she who would have made a better reiver than I?

The next day we all rode out to the Charlton bastle, imparting our news to Mother and James. There were many tears at the news with, strangely, Sarah finding the idea that we may never see Mother again almost unbearable to take. I have just mentioned how bloodthirsty she had become, but now she showed the tenderness of the sweetest of people.

James told me to leave everything as it was, as he had a servant who had served him well, and he would place him at our bastle, to run it as it was, and take a tithe from whatever was made. James had always been of a nature never to miss an opportunity to make money. He was also of the opinion that with his brother having been Sir Thomas Charlton, for many years, and who was always thought highly of, within palace circles, he should not succumb to any of Master Carey's ill intent.

Three days after receiving cousin Margaret's communiqué, we were all set to commence our journey to an unknown land and an unknown life. The cart was packed with a few belongings, and both children sat down on the back. Fleur took the reins of the cart, while Sarah and I rode either side. Both Sarah and Fleur insisted that they carried their swords upon their person, both concealed under their capes. I thought we presented a fine raiding party, but we set off and travelled south, not north. We made an early start, and by mid-morning we approached the Dodds' bastle, and took time to say our farewells.

There were tears in the eyes of Mary, Raymond and even Michael, and as we rode on, I found myself having to look away from our small party, and was aware that I was swallowing a lot, in order to keep my composure.

The enormity of what we were doing started to dawn on me. For hundreds of years my family had struggled in this area, fighting Scots, from east to west, both on our own behalf, and sometimes at the request of the Crown. Yes, we had fought for the Crown; indeed, whenever the Crown thought they could get away with it, and needed the best fighting men, they always rallied border families together, and very often, persuading us to fight with fat purses; then when the battle was won, conveniently forgetting to pay.

By mid-afternoon, we had made steady progress, the land becoming more hilly than we were used to. As we rode on I was aware of riders over to the east, and told Sarah and Fleur to ignore them and continue our journey. The riders approached, and I thought better of my first instruction, and told everyone to stop, my hand firmly gripped to the hilt of my sword. As they neared, and I could make out who they were, I could see that Master Carey headed the throng.

"Master Carey," I said cheerily, holding up my hand in greeting, the fact being that my flesh crawled in his presence. "Have you come to escort my family, as we journey to Penrith?" I continued.

"And what business have you there, Milburn?" the Carey barked.

"A cousin, Sir, who has troubles, of which she has charged me to rid her. The troubles of being a Heedsman, Sir," I answered.

I noticed Sarah had drawn her cape over her front, and could tell from the way her arm crossed her body that she was holding her sword. This caused me to worry somewhat, for I feared that should a word be spoken out of turn then she would start slashing.

"And how long are we to be without your illustrious company?" Carey said mockingly.

"Hopefully, but a couple of days, Sir," I said, maintaining my cheery demeanour.

"Aye, and there'll be blood as a result of your visit, no doubt," growled Carey.

"May we take our leave, Sir, we still have a while to travel," I said.

"Aye, but we have business when you return," said Carey.

We pulled away, my body tense, for I did not trust Carey in the least, and was it not the measure of the man, that he never acknowledged either Sarah or Fleur. Sir John Foster would more likely have ignored me, in favour of them both, but he was a gentleman. I also noticed that the band he had surrounded himself with appeared an unsavoury rabble. The thought of leaving the valley I had known all my life, and was my home, that home that I dreamed of on those long nights in Melrose, no longer seemed so bad.

We reached Penrith by early evening, but rode wide of the town, carrying on the road, then made a slight turn to the left, taking a lesser road. It had been unfortunate that Carey had happened upon our little party, as I would have preferred that no one was aware of our journey, and certainly did not want people along the way able to give information of our direction of travel. I was not sure if this lesser road would take us where we wished to go, but put my trust in my sense of direction. I started to look for a suitable place to stay for the night, and we soon found ourselves on the edge of a large lake, the size of which none of us had ever seen. The surrounding land was heavily wooded, which made the perfect cover for the night, fresh clean sweet water, and good cover. Fleur and the children would sleep in the back of the cart, Sarah and I under it, each taking turns to stand watch. I was aware that we were not raiding, but the precaution of standing watch is an effort never wasted. Even if nothing is ever seen, at least it allows the others present to sleep soundly. We made do with cold food, of previously cooked meat, and fruit; the meal when waking would be the same. I did not want to start a fire, alerting all around of our presence.

The night passed without incident, and we started our journey as soon as we had the horse and cart harnessed, and the two other horses saddled, taking nourishment as we rode. We travelled along the side of the lake for some time, passing through a small hamlet at the far end, then the road started to rise steeply. I feared I may have judged the road badly, as the ascent was long and tiring, for us and the beasts. Apart from Annie, who was too small, we all spent time behind the cart, pushing for all our worth, helping the poor nag. We reached a part of the steep rise which levelled for a short while, and Sarah suggested she change the horses over, putting hers in the cart traces, and resting the horse which had had to do the most work. Once the change was done, the ascent became less laboured, for us all, and we were soon at the top of the hill. The view was the like of which none of us had ever seen. We just stood there, viewing the land ahead, through the eyes of a soaring eagle. Once having caught our breath, and taking in water, we set off again, the descent no less severe, and after a short distance, I brought us all to a stop, and decided to tie both loose horses to the back of the cart, and use them to take some of the strain of the cart pushing against Sarah's horse, which had to take the weight. By mid-afternoon we were at the bottom, which I found quite frustrating, as I had hoped to be at Margaret's by late afternoon, which was no longer possible.

As we continued, we soon found ourselves on the shores of another lake, even larger than the first. Again this was shrouded in a dense wooded ground, so we decided that we should settle here for the night. It was early to stop for the day, but both we and the nags would benefit from resting now, not over taxing ourselves.

As we sat by the lake, still not lighting a fire, I saw, coming along the road, from where we had just come, horses and men, one after the other, the men all walking alongside the nags, and as they neared, I could see that the nags were all heavily laden, some with barrels roped to either side, others with bundles of all shapes and sizes, covered in canvas.

On seeing them near, I stood to watch their approach, my body tense, my mouth dry; I did not know what to expect. If I had been with James, Arthur and Father, along with all the rest of the riders, I would not have been so tense, but when it was Fleur, Sarah and the children, what might have been fear was now dread.

The first fellow in the procession lifted his hand in greeting, but did not speak, merely continued on his way, and as the rest of the horses and men filed by, some acknowledged my presence, whilst others preferred to either keep their heads down, or look straight ahead, ignoring anything that was not directly in front of them. They were all soon past and the quiet returned. A similar night as at the other lake ensued, and we were all ready for another day's journeying very early.

Before we had walked the full length of this vast lake, the road turned away from the water's edge, and started in a more easterly direction. By mid-morning I had no idea where I was, but good fortune took a hand, and as we rode slowly on, a young lad was by the road, shepherding a small flock of sheep. Making sure my sword was well covered, for country folk in these parts were not given to being armed as they went about their business, I called to him. "I seek Underbarrow, I would be grateful for directions, young Sir."

"Not far, just past the church on your right, a short way past, turn right, down the hill," he answered, then turned away to tend his sheep, quite obviously not wishing to engage in further conversation.

We followed our young friend's directions, and soon found ourselves among the odd cottage on either side of the road, and, looking ahead, a more substantial building of stone, that looked like a fine house, with barns and other out buildings, all of stone; this must surely be Grebe Hall.

The main house was built by the roadside, but at a higher level than the road, and as we neared I could see that we were able to turn into the farmyard, behind the house. We had scarce got into the yard when a fellow of middle age, slightly stooped over, with a slight humpback, his face gnarled and contorted into a severe snarl, came into the yard. "And what business do you have here?" he barked out.

"I have business with your mistress, if this is Glebe Hall," I said, still staying in the saddle. The fact that I made him look up to me placed our sour friend at a disadvantage.

"I am in charge here, now be gone, there is nothing for you here," he continued to bark, while at the same time drawing a sword from his belt, one of those finer blades that townsfolk tend to carry, but of little use for fighting all day, against the like of a good Reiver's sword.

This was the signal I had been waiting for, and slid from the saddle, while drawing my sword, which our sour friend had failed to notice before. I raised my sword, to engage, then slowly lowered it, to his mid chest. My intention was to make him lift his sword, then I would have it from his hand in an instant. As I did so, I was aware of a younger fellow stepping from one of the out buildings, clutching an old rusty sword. He began running towards me, in a threatening manner. I then became aware of Sarah, stood by my side, and as the younger of the two was almost upon us, she drew her sword. The young lad came to a halt, I still with my sword to the elder one's chest, maintaining eye contact. The younger one scowled, then gave a mocking laugh. "Ah! A woman with a sword," as he lifted his sword, then I heard a clatter, as the sword fell to the ground. I could not believe how Sarah had done this, until I looked down for an instant, and saw a hand, still attached to the hilt, then the younger one fell to his knees, screaming in pain. Sarah continued her attack by raising her sword to the back of her victim's neck, as if to behead him, as the older one screamed out, "No, no, not my lad!"

The next moment, his sword was being hurled through the air, making a noisy crash as it fell to the ground.

We were next distracted by a wailing witch, scurrying from within the house, brandishing a meat cleaver, which was dripping with blood. The next thing I saw was Fleur, who had already made sure the children were well down in the back of the cart, jump from the cart, as the witch ran by the horse, and was immediately behind her, fetching her sword up and bringing it around the front of the witch's throat.

"Drop the knife, now!" Fleur screamed, with such force, I almost dropped my sword. The old witch stopped in her tracks, the cleaver falling to the ground, and she falling to her knees. At first, I thought Fleur must have dispatched her, but then the witch continued her wailing, for her injured son.

I then lowered my sword, and stepping forward, I took the wretched creature that stood before me by the throat, pulling and twisting his clothes, thus choking him, and when he started to gasp for breath and his eyes bulged and his lips started to turn blue, I brought his stinking face up in front of mine, and I spat out these words, "Get your filthy brood and get out of here now, and I assure you and any of this filth I see before me, that should I be unfortunate to set my eyes on any of you, from this day forward, I will kill you on the spot, do you hear me, wretch?"

The wretch fell to his knees, gripping his throat, and still gasping, but he failed to move as quickly as I would have liked, so I gave him a hefty kick in the side. He took a sharp intake of breath, and the colour soon returned to his blued lips, as he scurried to his feet. I then, while still keeping my eyes on my victim, said, "Sarah, bind the lad's arm, then they can be gone." Sarah, with a look of absolute displeasure, sidled towards me, handing me her sword, then went to the cart, and fumbled within its contents, pulling from it something that appeared like an undergarment, and ripped from it a long narrow strip. I moved over towards the lad as Sarah returned, and placed my sword at the back of his neck.

"One wrong move, lad; that is all it will take to meet your maker," I said quietly, but menacingly. Fleur still had the old witch held back from her offspring, still with the sword tight to her neck. As I surveyed the scene, I thought, there can scarce be a man alive who is so well served by two such wonderful women. Sarah knelt down in front of the lad and started to bind his bloody stub, which caused him to yell out in agony, the old witch accompanying him in her wailings.

The wretch then said, "I have things in the house," to which I replied, in a loud voice, "No, you do not, you have nothing. Stand still or die, wretch," to which the wretch stood, hardly daring to breathe. Sarah was soon over in her binding and stood up, and as she did so I shouted, "Out!" and took a swipe with the flat of the blade to the wretch. He screamed like a pig, for he must have thought I had hit him with the edge of the weapon. "Out!" I yelled again, as I walked behind them out of the yard and down the lane a while, until I was sure they were well on their way.

When I returned, all were inside, so I knocked at the door. Thomas and Annie came running in answer, both taking a hand and pulled me inside, excitedly.

"Come, Fadder," gasped Thomas, "Come meet Aunt Margaret, she's lovely." As I was dragged into the kitchen, the three ladies were sat at the table, all laughing at Thomas' remark, and Margaret got from the table, and walked to me, embraced me and kissed me on the cheek. "Robert, I am so very grateful to you for seeing off those dreadful people. I have just been thanking Sarah and Fleur before you returned."

"Aye, Margaret, and I doubt I could have seen them off without these two grand lasses," I said, beaming a large smile to Fleur and Sarah.

We were soon sat down and enjoying a good meal, thanks to the old witch we had sent on her way. She might well have been a witch, but she was more than a reasonable cook. We stayed at the table long after the food was gone, exchanging stories. Although Margaret was kin, we had not met before, although she did say that she had visited when I was an infant, and had taken to Mother, forming a close relationship with her in the short time they had together. I think Margaret had been well educated and appeared to want to further herself socially, and had married Humphrey Jeffries, a middle aged widower, who was a very successful sheep farmer, and as such, was an official at the local cattle market and a close associate of the Kendal town council. Such a position allowed Margaret to socialise with the local officials and their wives.

By late afternoon, I had wearied of all this conversation, so begged my leave, and that of Thomas, and we went out and walked the fields, checking the stock as we went. I found it quite unusual, as we walked; all the fields were enclosed, a fashion that was quite taking grip of the country. Back at the bastle, we had never sought to enclose the pastures, only that land close to the bastle, to keep raiders from stealing the stock, but here, the fields were all enclosed by high dry stone walls, which in the winter would certainly afford good shelter for the sheep, especially for those odd early lambs that come along, well before the winter is over. Thomas walked along with me, extremely excited at our new home, and the thought of looking after all these sheep, the numbers I could scarce count. I could see we would be well occupied with such a flock, and all the other work to keep this fine farm running.

After a good walk around, we returned to the farm house, and I said to Margaret where we had been. She then told me that there were lots more sheep on the higher ground, equally as many as we had already seen. I think she stunned me into silence, but she brought me out of my shock by taking me around the house, of which I could see she was immensely proud. Humphrey had not long completed the construction of Grebe Hall before he was taken. The downstairs rooms were all large and well lit, all with large windows giving a light airy feel to each room, and apart from the kitchen, which had a whitewash upon the walls, most of the other rooms had fine oak panels. Each room was furnished with well-made furniture, furniture of some fine quality. Upstairs there were four bedrooms; Margaret's, then one which was for Fleur and me, containing a large oak bed, with turned posts at each corner, all heavily carved, and an ornately embroidered cover over the bed. I had never slept in such a fine bed in all my life. At the foot of the bed was a large panelled chest. Margaret opened it to show bedding and night attire, which was for Fleur and me. We had always been of a habit of sleeping clothed, as should there be a raid, we could be up and ready to fight. There were also candles in the chest, which served to keep a stock to light the room, and while in the chest, served to keep away the moths.

The children's room contained two smaller individual beds, equally well made and finished, and Sarah was almost beside herself at the prospect of having a room to herself, and such a beautiful room too. All the rooms had their own window, giving light that none of us were used to, and we would wake to such wonderful views along the valley.

Once into the way of running the farm, life was hard but pleasurable, more for Fleur and the children, knowing they were safe and being brought up in such pleasant surroundings. Sarah, although quite content, I felt at times yearned for the old life, and I had little doubt that had we stayed at the bastle, she would have demanded that she come on the raids, and I would not have dared argue. That said, she and Thomas proved most worthy assistants in the running of the farm, while Margaret and Fleur kept more to the household chores, Fleur coming out to help in the fields when time and weather permitted.

Margaret would only set forth from the house on Sundays, when we were all expected to attend church. Mary Armstrong would be so very pleased, although the church was of the English faith, so she would have had reservations, nonetheless. Margaret would also expect Sarah to take her to Kendal, in the small carriage, when she had some social event. She would sooner have had a proper coachman drive her, or me, but had to settle for Sarah. Margaret could be quite forthright at times, and voiced this very opinion, at one evening mealtime. Sarah had just taken a goodly spoonful of soup as Margaret spoke, resulting in poor Thomas, who sat opposite Sarah, being sprayed with the contents of her mouth, but even he laughed loudly, after the initial shock.

Epilogue

We have now spent six years at Grebe Hall, and have come to be regarded as one of the community. My neighbours gather around, at times of need, such as when it is shearing, or dipping. I had never dipped sheep prior to my arrival here, but the local farmers built a weir across the nearby burn, or beck as they call it locally, and a walkway above it reaching to the centre. We walk the sheep along the walkway, one by one, then let them drop into the deepest water. They initially sink to the bottom, getting a good soaking, and much of any infestation is washed from the fleece and down the river. Dipped sheep are by far healthier than those not. We are very fortunate that we are able to make a good living here, and have become quite wealthy in a short time. This wealth has raised our status, and I have now become an official of the Kendal market, grading all the beasts, before they are sold. Fleur was extremely proud when I was appointed to this position, but I suspect that Margaret, through her well connected friends, might have had some part in this.

It is now late autumn, the days are shortening, and I have just come inside after a busy day looking to the feet of some of the sheep, making sure they are all well before the winter sets in. I had scarce sat down when Thomas burst through the door. "Fadder, Fadder, come quick, Flame is laying down, and she is sweating and gasping, she's not well, hurry," he said trying to catch his breath. I ran from the house, down the yard, out on to the road and across the field where the horses were kept. Flame was indeed as Thomas had described.

"Hurry, lad, get one of the other nags, and take it back to the farm and hitch up the sledge, bring a couple of ropes from the barn," I instructed Thomas. I looked around, and I had never seen that lad of mine move so quickly. He soon had one of the horses, was on its back, and galloped off, back to the farm. I knelt by Flame. "What's the matter, my old friend?" I said, as I knelt at her side, stroking her neck. Thomas was soon back, along with the entire household, which would help in getting Flame on the sledge. We wrapped a rope around her body, just behind her front legs, and another rope just in front of her back legs, and all taking up a rope, tried to heave Flame from the ground, but we could not move her at all.

"Thomas, unhitch the nag from the sledge and tie the ropes to the traces," I suggested. Thomas soon had the ropes tied in place, and he urged his nag forward, resulting in Flame starting to move. There was some at the front, and some at the back, and as Flame was dragged nearer to the sledge, we all lifted, and eased Flame on to the sledge. As soon as it was safely on, Thomas quickly unhitched the rope, and hitched his nag back into the sledge, and we were heading for the farm. Once there, we took it to the barn, it being the building with the largest doors, allowing us to pass through with the sledge. It was far easier to get Flame off the sledge, than on, and we placed the poor beast on to a soft bed of hay. I said I would stay with Flame, and asked for a bucket of water and cloth, and I would keep wiping her down through the night, to try and reduce the fever. When the water arrived, I asked everyone to leave, and I soon found myself alone with Flame. Throughout the night I kept wiping Flame's body, with the cold wet cloth, then I would sit by her head, and talk of the times we had ridden together.

Surprisingly the morning came quite quickly, and the early morning light was starting to come through the partly opened door. I got up and went and opened the barn door wider, in order to better see how Flame had come through the night. I went back and sat down by her head and started to stroke her neck again. Flame lifted her head, turning to look at me, and I swear, that if it were possible, that horse almost smiled, then her head lowered slowly, and she was gone.

With tear filled eyes, I spoke aloud, "I promise you, my brave Galloway lass, that we will again ride on the edge, betwixt the two lands, neither English nor Scots, but forever, Borderers."

The End

With deep gratitude to Brother Matthias,
for giving me the skills to record my story.